Chronicles of Osmaron V

Fertilates

He took his old battered Elepet car to the fifty-seventh street. Those cars worked mainly on electricity but could also run on expensive petrol or ethanol in an emergency. There were LPD cars, but they were too expensive and completely out of reach of the pockets of most people, including Mallory.

He parked his car in the lower section of the multistory park and stuck a handy 'DISABLED' label on the rear window. He was on his way to one of the tallest blocks in the vicinity.

'I have an appointment with Professor Okeke!' he said to the female doorperson.

'You are?... just one moment please... mister Mallory?' she said, glancing at his identification.

'Yes, that's me... always at your service!' he replied in jest with a broad grin.

The Chronicles of Galaxy Osmaron series

First Edition

Chronicles of Galaxy Osmaron

FERTILATES

Earth has been contaminated - Almost every human will
die.

By

Adrian Graye

Nutralian Publishing
http://nutralianpublishing.com

*nutralia*n
An imprint of Nutralian Publishing
5 Brayford Square, London E1 0SG
http://nutralianpublishing.com

This paperback edition 2009
B00005555

First published in Great Britain by
Amazon KDP 2024

ISBN 978-1-0687902-4-9

Printed and bound in Great Britain by Amazon KDP.

A CIP catalogue record for this title
is available from the British Library.

To those involved in ecology and the preservation of life

&

TO ALL THOSE WHO BELIEVE IN UNIVERSAL EXIS-TENCE AND APPRECIATE THE LOWLIEST OF ALL LIFE; FOR LIKE BABES, THEY ARE THE BEGINNING.

TABLE OF CONTENTS

The Anachromagnon - The book of final light

The wisdom of these words, herein, shall be like a sharp sword whose thrust will sever the hearts of all idolaters and fornicators. Including those who worship in the name of pleasure and wealth at the expense of suffering. For they are the real corruptors and predators of worlds.
Let these words hitherto shine through every corridor of darkness to show all superior intelligence throughout the Cosmos the way towards their Final Goal.

By Siend Seno at The Plains of Herron

THE PAINFUL RACE OF LIFE

On every living thing a little rain must fall,
And every drop will help, even the smallest tree grow tall.
For even in the darkest night,
The stars above will still shine bright,
And if we stay until the morn,
A glowing sunrise may adorn.

So trust in God, but do your best,
And with strong endeavour you'll win the test.
For life's a race only few attain,
So even if you fail, try and try again.
Because the entire point of life,
Is within the Eternal Race we strive.

Victor Roche

Prologue

Under strange circumstances, Plato, one of the Andromedan visitors, meets the President of the USA and arrange to have dinner at his country residence.

During dinner the President is shown a replay of the destruction of Plato's people on a planet call Caefon in Galaxy Andromeda three thousand years ago. The alien monsters called Javols were made of metallic nano-bots. They are difficult to kill and prey on all biological life, and are presently on their way to our galaxy and Earth.

During the intervening period we are to find ways to fight and resist them, if we are not to go the same way as the Andromedans. Jerry, the President of the USA, realises the grave problems ahead. He knows he cannot tell his public, so decides to go on a special interstellar trip on board the aliens' ship to visit local worlds. It is important for him to find and observe other life within his home galaxy before serious decisions can be taken.

Having made arrangement for a duplicate actor to take his place in the White House while on sick leave, Jerry and his wife Sharon, have gone on their first interstellar picnic. This trip should last about one week, during which time they will visit many stellar systems. On their return they form the new Solarian Empire with Sarah at its head. With the help of advanced robots they build their new city on planet Eden. Two great inter-galactic ships called Venusa and Martia are subsequently constructed for the federation. Their purpose is to discover new civilizations and link them with the new galactic Federation for mutual survival.

During the previous three decades human life on Earth had improved and increased significantly by the introduction of Lumak's new Class 5 technologies (from its previous Class 1). Even so, technology was one thing and the will to survive quite another. Many people simply ignored the warnings of Global Warming and its detrimental consequences on planetary life.

Lumak's microid robots had built many environmental domes

to protect animals facing extinction from mankind. The wealthier countries were constructing high walls to protect their coastal cities from the rising waters of the seas and oceans. Despite those measures, global temperatures were still rising and that was not all.

Earth's human population was still growing, although not as fast as in previous years. In the year 2064 CE it had exceeded 12 billion. As the seas and oceans spread, so did large areas of remaining fertile lands become flooded. Because of the extreme temperatures crops failed, while many in Africa and South America were starving. Most of Africa had become the Greater Sahara. Forests and crop fires were numerous. The natural order with its trade winds, monsoons and other previously dependable weather patterns had changed or their effects diminished.

Hurricanes and tornadoes increased in magnitude and frequency, placing greater financial strain on people and governments. All those problems were as a direct result of human population growth and mankind's irresponsible attitude toward conservation and planetary life in general.

To save mankind Sarah and others decided to contaminate Earth with the Terminal Disease. That disease only affected humanity and would prevent almost everyone from having children. The contagious disease were expected to remain until Earth's populations reduce to below 500 million. That process would take close to 100 years.

Despite its ubiquitous presence throughout the planet, no symptoms would ever be detected or felt by the infected and humans could live out their normal lives, although without children. This situation leads to much unrest on Earth so Mallory is chosen to save the day.

CHAPTER 1

Dr. Hal Seaton's salvation

In the wake of their move to Eden, it was necessary for Lumak to take some of Earth's better people with him. Those would include his highly qualified and most enthusiastic. Having scanned through many files several selections were made. It so happened that Hal was one of the few selected. He was too much of a genius in Bio-engineering to be left behind on Earth. Those special workers would be further interviewed by Lumak and shown the movie of Javols invasion of Caefon. Once again Lumak (Professor Jeffery Longhurst) brought all his scientist in one place.

While they were sat comfortably Lumak showed them the film of death and destruction. It was all about Lord Meron's people on their world called Caefon several thousand years before. Then Lumak explained future plans to them.

'So you see why we have to plan in the long term. We have another 200 years at the most before the arrival of their first swarms,' Lumak said.

'Can't we bargain with them?' Hal inquired.

'No! They will not! Will you bargain with a hungry lion in the wild. They see us only as food. Anyway, why bargain when they have it all. They are much more clever and can anticipate your actions. Believe me when I tell you, they will not listen!'

'Then I suppose we have a fight on our hands!'

Although Hal did not fully believed Lumak's words, he realized aliens were here. They were most likely the escapees from that world. That was most likely where all this new technology came from. He saw it all as a great opportunity to save Earth from it's reckless humans, without nano-bots. And he was right along about those deadly nano-bots, now they were on their way to destroy his galaxy and Earth. There was now a bigger fish to fry.

'So bad old Powell was right all along about those aliens. And they were responsible for creating those nano-bot creatures called Javols. Serves them right for losing all their world and galaxy for such stupidity. Now they are over here and brought those bastard Javols with them. Now we are all in dire straights. Those nano-bots will be the death of us all!' Hal was not a happy man.

'Lennox wants you!' Helen, one of Lennox secretary said while delivering a few security computer disks.

'I am on my way!' He shouted back.

'Hal! Please enter!'

'Sounds urgent!'

'I have some meetings today. Something very important has come up!' Lennox replied.

'Really! Not about me, I hope?'

'No! Boss is satisfied with your work, and latest creations. If anything, he wants to broaden your horizons. Personally, I would not miss those chances for all the tea in China!'

'What chances?'

'He wants to know if you would like to do research for him elsewhere!'

'Elsewhere?'

'It's going to be on another planet. The one where most endangered species from Earth are being bred. He wants someone like you to take control. When things are right they can be brought back to repopulate the Earth. There is a small town with humans from Earth. Most of the people there are young scientists. You should find it a new challenge!'

'What other choices do I have?'

'None! Our whole program here is being wound up. A large dome will soon be built over the Microid Complex, which is also being disbanded. The Boss is moving from Earth on a permanent basis!'

'So all aliens are moving out and no more nano-bots. I suppose you are not one of them?'

'No! But we are friendly aliens to them. It's a small universe and to some people insects and reptiles are aliens. To me they are just beautiful life-forms trying to survive in a dynamic, although sometimes very hostile and cruel universe.'

'I see where you are coming from. Personally, I like good aliens and don't mind helping them. What I can't stand are microids, parasites and planetary viruses!' Hal replied.

'There is another world called Eden. It's the most beautiful world in our galaxy. It's where all the very advanced brass live. If you play your cards right, you can become one of them with your own beautiful palace and fief the size of France. However, you must be committed to the cause.'

'You mean being a productive part of the organization to save our galaxy. I am already bought!' Hal replied.

'By the way, smart Dr Hal, no one ever dies on Eden. Also, I have been told there is a healing power on Eden. It comes from the pollen of giant flowers. On that world people become like gods. Also, they have machines that can regrow a complete human body and insert the original with little loss of memory. There are also brain implants that can expand your brain more than ten times and give you about five doctors in different chosen fields, with knowledge of advanced technologies. What do you think of that?'

'I like it all! Thanks for giving me these rear bits of info, but the Boss has already updated me on that topic. I suppose my tongue should be tied from now?'

'Yep! Completely zipped!'

'No one of these idiots will believe me, anyway! How do I travel to these places?'

'One more thing, Mr Clever Clogs! We travel by interstellar portals!'

'Portals? Like in the movies?'

'Do you know anything about Quantum Physics?'

'A little!'

'Well, you must know scientists on Earth have been transmitting atoms for years in laboratories. They have taken it a stage further. I was told they have portals that can take us to other galaxies in less than a second!'

'Wow! That bloody advanced?'

'What do you mean, that bloody advanced? There are some

things so bloody incredible that I can't even tell you! All things you see here on Earth are small fry by comparison! For real adventure, Earth is no place to be. Soon, people will be dying here like flies!'

'Due to my good work, I hope!' Hal replied and gave a sarcastic smile.

'Well, I told you much of what I know. Portals are being installed as I speak. Our Boss wants you in the organization. Once portals are fitted, you can commute to Earth on a daily basis. So travel is no problem!'

'In that case, I am in!'

'Nice one! I shall tell the Boss today that you are ready to leave so that arrangements can be made. Don't worry about salary. Everyone in the organization are multi-millionaires compared to people on Earth. And by the way this envelope is for you. It's your travel papers,' Lennox said.

Hal opened the envelope to find a strange looking metallic card with a sheet of instructions.

Hal left Lennox's office that day partly convinced. However, he was more concerned about saving his planet, Earth, than most other considerations. Nevertheless, if he could commute from distant worlds and collect information via his Group Of Thirteen, he could help when the time was right. He was still not convinced that the Terminal Disease, with it's slow progress, would stop mankind destroying his planet.

CHAPTER 2

Malik and Bailor visits Eden

Two days before the multiple wedding, two great ships from Polok and Lodor visited Eden. Malik was the first to arrive in his own Polokan Class one flagship. She was like Venusa's ship and proudly displayed the large crest of Polok with a smaller Lodorian crest just beneath the federation's insignia. It was called Invincible in their newly adopted Sunolingua language. He must have taken along most of his people, so the ship was full to bursting.

Following behind his star-ship were forty-eight large Class 1 battleships of similar construction. They were scheduled for delivery to Solaria for the federation's navy. Those were the first ships to be used jointly by the federation and constructed in the new docks on planet Safon. He also brought along many presents for Sarah and the others.

His ship was given precise landing instructions and when it docked, he and his family transposed to the main reception area of Sarah's beautiful golden palace.

Sarah was elegantly dressed in another of her cream suits with federation insignia boldly displayed on her lapel. Just behind her were the councillors. They were dressed in grey federation uniforms. The Ancients wore their braided white gowns that glittered in gold.

Malik soon appeared with his wife, Mira. His two military sons followed enthusiastically behind. They walked towards Sarah to be introduced. She elegantly took his hand and shook it.

'It gives me the greatest pleasure to receive you and your family, and may your stay on our world be a most pleasant one,' Sarah said, majestically in sunolingua.

Malik felt ecstatic, almost not believing his eyes; for standing just next to Sarah was the Shadite, Lumak, who had saved his father's life in a remote stellar system on a previous occasion and they both wore similar insignias on lapels. That was over one century ago. The Shadite really resembled him, even though he appeared to be much younger and darker than Malik himself and he wondered whether the other people on Eden also had the gift of eternal life.

He took the Shadite's hand firmly in his and shook it several times nodding and smiling, but contained his enthusiasm and emotions for a more appropriate time. Sarah then shook his wife Mira's hand and then the two young men, taking them along to be introduced to other members of the grand council. Many of whom they had already met during the great war. That was the nature of protocol, and formalities had to be observed in public places.

The public affair was soon over and they retired into the main lounge to talk more freely. Malik and his wife was amazed by the beauty and design of Eden, which included such incredible levels of technologies. No ships or cars could be seen anywhere. With the exception of Eden's busy city centre, portals were used throughout the planet to transport its inhabitants and materials from place to place. Therefore there was little need for roads or skyways, thus retaining the planet in its original and most natural state. It was thought that Eden would be a model to follow by all within the galaxy in future years. Sarah always had her way in pressing forward those decisions and everyone appreciated the unique vision of that great woman.

Later that day, Bailor, Stradon and Volt arrived in their flagship and all the formalities had to be repeated, but this time including Malik and his family, to add even more surprise to the proceedings. They brought along numerous presents and technological gadgets for Sarah and her councillors.

Bailor, despite his race's attitudes, enjoyed formalities and protocol, having recently introduced such methods to Lodor his home adopted world, but this new world was so different. Here was the topmost part of the pinnacle in such things. He was totally absorbed and amazed by it all. He felt in awe at its even grander significance in the greater scheme of things. Also, the atmosphere of Eden was saturated with certain pollen which had an effect on all its visitors and made them feel unique and all powerful. However it had a greater effect on Bailor and his kind.

He stood up in front of Sarah and stretched out his synthetic arm which she firmly took in hers. Then she spoke to him.

'Lord Bailor, we shall always be indebted to you and your people for your beautiful designs and trust we shall all work together on many such projects in the future for the common good of all,' she said.

He gently bowed, without uttering a word.

Then she met Stradon and Volt.

They were all to remain her personal guests at the palace for a period of two weeks.

Later she brought all the councillors together for one of her general announcements.

'Fellow councillors, I have decided to add Malik and Bailor's names to our list of senior councillors. Further, from this day on let Malik be known as Lord Malik and Bailor as Lord Bailor while among us. I have also decided to give them both their own fiefs on this world, where they may build their own palaces and embassies. Those in favour say yes!' she said and they all agreed with no abstentions.

'Then the decision is carried!' she said.

For the rest of that day she took her visitors around, showing them the great palace and other facilities and museums, then they went to Eden City with all its venues and mass transportation systems, including LPD street taxis which were only allowed within the city.

They were waved by the locals everywhere. The people wanted them to visit their shops and other facilities, so they went in to talk to many of the shop keepers and managers who always bowed to Sarah and the popular young ones when they entered.

The young on Eden were very much like on Earth and experimented with many types of music, art and entertainment. Although semi-isolated, they were given the freedom to follow many of Earth's cultures and traditions. The only banned items were the more violent videos and movies from Earth. Anyway they were more interested in real creative outlets. They could only have proved themselves that way.

The psychologist realized the dangers in desensitized populations that could lead to greed and violence as on Earth. Therefore the society was precisely controlled by Macrons. Those were super intelligent computers that understood the human condition. Nevertheless the many police androids were relentlessly pursuing any anti-social behaviour and penalties were high.

CHAPTER 3

Malik and Bailor on Earth

Sarah planned to visit Earth the following day. It was meant to take the form of a shopping adventure, but was intended to give the visitors from Polok and Lodor a taste of Earth-life in some of its better spots. Although security was necessary, there was much of it on Earth in the form of Solarian Banking. Therefore they used a portal to the country manor in North Dakota. From there they could take the Andromedan ship to one of the main Solarian Banks in New York. That one was built like an embassy. During transposition the ship was virtually invisible, so they could never be detected by Earth's radar systems.

They also intended to take the couples for their final dress fitting at one of the wedding specialists in New York. Sarah also needed to shop for clothes and other essentials for her guests and the wedding. Therefore they had a very busy day ahead.

Jerry had a few close acting friends within the city who knew of his travelling disguises, while others were associated with White House security. Come what may, he thought he and his friends were going to have an exciting time together.

Any other unwanted events like meeting members of the local press, which was highly unlikely, would be passed on to others and his lookalikes. Anyway, his disguise, although not perfect, was quite acceptable in a city seldom frequented by the president. Furthermore he had no plans to visit Washington DC and intended to keep well away from the White House and its politics while his important friends were on Earth.

He was astonished how quickly Malik, Bailor and the others had taken to English, even with a slight American accent and marvelled at the wonders of that type of translation technology through implants. Nevertheless if one could learn a language in two years, why not in two minutes or even two seconds. It depended mostly on technology and they had lots of it. That type of complexity was well beyond the more basic translation belts that he had used on previous occasions while on Polok II. He realised that Malik could have been using a more advanced form of Brain Implant. Perhaps another one of those clever inventions of the Lodorians?

He thought of Sarah's latest idea of humanising all diplomats by re-vectorization and wondered whether Bailor and the other Lodorians would take kindly to the idea. Sarah tended to be always so correct in those matters, but tried to take them too far too quickly. Anyway, she always got her way in the end, either by feminine charm, diplomacy or friendly persuasion.

'No one could ever say no to her and she always tended to be correct in hindsight. That woman had incredible foresight,' Jerry thought aloud.

She was the proverbial perfect leader and knew her true powers and capabilities, not to mention the weaknesses of others. Yet, she had no complexes or compulsions and would quite easily be enjoying her meal while discussing matters of life and death. He was now provisionally her personal councillor, with powers to sit at important meetings and freely discuss matters of state with other councillors.

In time, he would become a fully fledged member, after he had retired from his office as President of the United States. Until then, he would remain her advisor on important Earthly political matters and maintain a low profile with Solarians in the eyes of his political contemporaries.

Sarah had prepared everything for the day's outing. Meron and Lumak was left in charge during her absence. Everyone was happy and excited on the eve of the great occasion, and also looking forward to their shopping adventure in one of the busiest cities on the planet. Currently, New York's human population was almost twice that of planet Eden at over 22 million.

All Solarian businesses and banks were functioning efficiently on Earth. That organization had become the wealthiest on the planet and expanded throughout the globe to assist in the recruitment of young people of merit and potential within their employment. Those few chosen would be eventually promoted beyond Earth if they desired adventure, and many did. Therefore large amounts of funding were always made available to those efforts and its employees, wherever and whenever necessary. That same organization would handle all security matters regarding Sarah's visit.

Ben was presently in charge of all her charitable operations on Earth and assisted the poorer countries in building schools and hospitals. He had even donated many of the more advanced microid robots, who could be programmed as doctors, to those hospitals.

Ben was also in charge of their dome building projects. Those massive environmental domes were used to isolate certain endangered species from mankind. They also isolated certain eco-systems from the ever changing world outside.

Two large armour-plated LPD limousines were supplied by Solarian Banking for their excursions within New York City, with twelve security officers in two separate cars following front and rear.

Having special diplomatic immunity, they proudly carried the insignia and flag of Solaria, and were able to park anywhere, despite the traffic and vehicular congestion.

The armed guards were a powerful deterrent to all would-be pickpockets and robbers who were numerous at that time. But so also were the many armed local security guards within the better shopping precincts.

With the Solarian Banking crest boldly displayed on the side of their vehicles, they were afforded much respect and attention.

Malik and Bailor wanted to feel the cultural atmosphere of the city and purchase some of its more unique items, so Jerry arranged a time and place to meet and after their arrival, took the two visitors away via his own waiting limousine to several of his favourite haunts. The first one was a gambling casino and the other a gentleman's club that utilized topless dancers for entertainment. During the proceedings Bailor's android collapsed on the flow due to excessive alcoholic indulgence.

Bailor was not used to the relatively high levels of alcohol in his small body. Neither was he used to the excitement, but after a short time he couldn't get enough once having tasted a sample.

When he collapsed, the solid android mass hit the flow with such a massive thud that many of the people were surprised any human could be so heavy. However his android body was well made, and appeared to be precisely human. Jerry, Ben and Malik, who were slightly inebriated themselves, assisted the heavy android to his feet and left for another of his wild spots.

'Are you ok!' Jerry shouted, while dusting him down a little.

'Better than I've ever been in my long existence! This is what I call real undiluted fun!' Bailor replied as he staggered back on his feet.

Despite the high crime rate and other ills, people appeared to have adapted well to the higher populations and appeared to be reasonably happy despite the noise, pollution and unsightly amounts of litter on many of its major streets and highways. Luckily for its inhabitants, the motor car and other pollution driven automobiles were rarely used. They would have aggravated the situation by adding more contaminants to its already polluted environment. At that time Electric Cars had not fully taken over. That was because the electrical power grid were limited in its supply. After a change of law, Many taxi drivers had been given LPD concessions and would repay a small part of their weekly earnings over several years. Therefore they simply removed car engines and fitted LPDs for a cleaner environment.

They were not yet aware of the anti birth bacteria later to be known as the Terminal Disease and would not have realised its detrimental effects for several more years to come. By then it would have been much too late for anyone to have found a lasting cure or administer any type of permanent remedy. Only Professor Bengizara Khan(Ben) Sarah's father and his assistants knew how to thoroughly cleanse the infected from its lasting effects and the process could only be carried out in complete isolation within a special medical unit on Satellite Eta. However, all such cleansing was an in-built function of all portals leading to Eden.

Initially it only affected the still fertile part of the human population. Susceptible humans were considered between puberty and about forty five years in age.

The relatively small numbers of teenagers who were already contaminated could always be cleansed, providing they stayed away from Earth during their fertile years.

Jerry thought,

'How regrettably this problem could not have been solved in some other, even more humane way. If only Earth's humans would give a little thought for their planet and the universe instead of only towards their own species selfish needs. Why were they such a selfish and self-indulgent lot? Thank goodness many good people will survive the aftermath to form a more beautiful and better society, and the survivors will be a random mix from all races.'

The first place Sarah and her company visited was one of the main stores for specialist clothes.

The wedding dresses and other essential articles of clothing had been ordered several weeks before. Now it was just the matter of trying them on and making any necessary alterations.

'Madam Sarah! What a pleasant surprise!' Anna the shop manager greeted.

'Anna, please meet my adopted girls. I decided to take them along today for the usual checks. I hope I am not too imposing,' she said.

'No Mam! This time couldn't be better and I have selected a complete range of other products to show you,' Anna said and took them to the rear of the shop.

While the ladies waited for fitting, Sarah took the others, including Jon and his male companions with her to complete her lengthy shopping list. Their suits had been tailored earlier.

As they arrived back at the bank a police car soon arrived and two policemen accompanied Jerry, Ben and Bailor into the foyer. None of those men could stand on their feet to save their lives.

'These men belong to you, I suppose?' the police asked.

'No, I've never seen them before in my life!' Jon replied in jest.

'Sorry officer, they are with us. Can I do anything for you guys? I know, I shall donate some money to your station.'

'You will?'

'Which precinct is it?' Sarah asked.

'7th Mam,' he replied.

Then Sarah calmly wrote a cheque for 1 million dollars to "7th Precinct" and they couldn't believe their eyes. Then they realized they were speaking to the president of Solarian Banking.

After finishing their day's adventure in the city of New York, they took The Ship from the main Solarian Banking branch in the city to Sarah's country residence. The three men were soon revived from their drunkenness. Sarah didn't say a word on the subject.

They had an exciting dinner at Sarah's house, also with Ben and some of his officers. When the celebrations were over, they took a portal back to Eden to begin wedding preparations.

CHAPTER 4

Weddings

On the great day of the wedding the bridegrooms and guests were the first to arrive at the temple, to be followed several minutes later by the brides. On prepared tracks, they rode from Sarah's palace in several white old antique Rolls-Royce cars. Two were the original petrol types donated to the museum. They were borrowed and revitalized for the special occasion. It was another of Sarah's ideas. The wedding could in many ways be considered eastern, with the exception of the Ancient's temple and Meron's ancient ceremony, as portrayed by the religious Senots.

Having considered the many religious alternatives, Jon and the others voted for that type of ceremony. The best Sarah could do was respect their wishes. Even so, they could not prevent her from introducing the additional Christian and Moslem trimmings before and after the ceremony.

Nevertheless Sarah had also adopted the Senots religion. She had read their holy bibles and realized their religious beliefs was based on the love of all living creatures. Therefore she had adopted those altruistic principles for Eden's society.

Lumak, being Shadite, never followed traditional religious beliefs and always followed his own one that was embedded in the Greater Purpose. Neither did he blindly follow any religious customs for the sake of others. He knew the real supreme being of our universe but thought such religious traditions helped to bind communities and in so doing brought people closer together, which was always a good thing. Anyway, the young always enjoyed change and intrigue in their lives and such freedom did no one any harm.

Meron made them stand in front of the altar while he went through the ceremonial formalities. Finally, the men placed a ring on their respective bride's finger and kissed the relevant partner to seal the covenant. During those precious moments the smiles of happiness on their faces could never be repeated.

While they walked out of the temple the many photographers were busy taking stills and videos. It was another of Sarah's ideas for their photographic albums. Those memories would be precious to their families and friends in future.

The celebration drove through Eden City which was already in a joyous mood. That day had been nominated a national holiday. The young councillors were well respected by all, not only because of their involvement and sacrifices in saving them from the Javols on Caefon, but also because of their incredible adventures and achievements. Jon and his other young five companions were roll models and the heroes of the planet. Their faces were displayed on many billboards and in many of the people's homes.

Most of the population lined the main southern highway through the city, waving flags and shouting their greetings, while they waved back on their way to Venusa and Martia's ships. The Andromedan Ship would join the celebrations from there and take them back to their palaces for more celebrations before finally returning to Sarah's palace for the final reception.

Every important person within the Solarian Empire, including Ben, were present at the grand reception being held in the main palace hall. Many had arrived the day before, with the exception of Lord Vektron, Lord Patron and the Grand Lord, who were late arrivals. Those three could always observe events from afar if they so chose.

When Grand Lord Gerra arrived, he was accompanied by the three Plorans, Lord Vektron, Lord Patron and Lord Faemon. Those were accompanied by several Octans from the Planet Orban. Then there were the resurrected Ancients, Lord Seno, King Melor, King Micol, Lady Sefran, Lord Hale, Siit, the Shadite and others. They had arrived in a large black ship and their procession followed two very large, but beautiful bipedal bee-like creatures. They were beautiful Semonites from Lumak's home world, about five and a half feet tall. They were pushing what appeared to be a large glittering golden trunk with long handles on golden wheels. At that time the heavy trunk floated in the air and required little assistance for its continued motion. When the Grand Lord entered the great hall they immediately stopped dancing. Then he summoned the Solarian councillors forward to accept their special gifts.

The women were each given a beautiful golden headband with a large jewel inserted at the front. It included other gems around the self adjusting band. The men and women, including the young six and their real biological parents, Malik, Bailor, Stradon and Volt were each given a large priceless symbolic sword in its most beautiful jewelled scabbard. The blades glowed with sharp brilliance as if they had some type of strange energy that could make them cut through anything. The audience were stunned by their beauty and brilliance. Those items made them invulnerable against Javols. The swords could cut through Javols like a knife through butter and prevent them from reforming.

Finally, he withdrew a beautiful jewelled crown from the trunk with a large crimson stone seated within its foremost parts and went forward to place the heavy item on Sarah's head, but before he did he spoke to them:

'These unique symbols will in future represent the higher levels of power within Osmaron and are presented to you on this auspicious day, to show my sincere appreciation for your tremendous efforts and unselfish deeds, accomplished in the pursuance of a greater order within Osmaron and elsewhere.

'May we continually strive for truth and perfection in all things? But of all, love is the most important, for it conquers the hearts and minds of us all.'

The two large bees remained with the trunk which was also a present to Sarah. She wondered for a moment from whence they came, but Lord Gerra continued:

'The Empire of Solaria and its Federation is here to stay and will remain to rule this galaxy and others. Sarah has my full backing and blessings, to be hereby nominated queen and

*empress of Solaria, and may she always retain her love of nature
and responsibilities to her people and the Greater Purpose.'*

He placed the headband on her head and the whole object
shown a radiant blue for a while, slowly diminishing in brilliance
into an apparent dormant mode. They filled their glasses to cheer
Sarah, the future empire and their newly weds.

After the end of the reception celebrations, the newly weds said
their thanks and farewell. Then they left for their respective
palaces, accompanied by their surrogate parents.

They were now lords and ladies in their own right, but they felt
like kings and queens, realising their task had only just begun and
this present period of happiness was just the calm before the
storm.

They also realised that Lord Vektron was correct in his speech
to them over a year ago, when he mentioned that they would one
day become children of the sword. But even now, they were still
not sure of its true meaning and significance.

The revived ancient, Lord Seno, their greatest profit, wondered
at beautiful Caefon and realized they had taken a leaf out of his
book. He also realized that most of the people on Eden were
Senots and followed his ancient teachings. That was before Sarah
and others realized who he really was. Then he was revered
among them. They soon took his measurements for a large
monument to be built in one of the main squares.

'Our Grand Lord is truly noble in his actions, in giving eternal
life to our important ancestors like Lord Seno, King Melor, King
Micol, Lady Sefran and others of the Andromedan Ancients.
They had been through so much troubles in their past. Now they
should be able to relax for a change,' Sarah said and Lumak
agreed. However the Ancient Patriarchs would have none of it.
They had a job to do in their part of the galaxy before the arrival
of the first Javols. Nevertheless with the addition of new interstellar portals between both worlds, they could always visit each
other from time to time.

CHAPTER 5

Javols are back on Caefon

'Ak! Na! Na! Na! Na! Nat co neh la hein na grat clots!' the agitated Javols' commander exclaimed. He was about seven feet tall, dressed in an outfit which was a cross between an Egyptian god and another yet unknown by any human world. That Javol resembled a large eagle without wings, but with muscular arms and legs. His broad beak was yellow and legs bird-like. All his limbs were adorned with many rings and bangles. His screeches and other utterances when translated meant: 'Where in this universe are those pathetic humans! I was looking forward to a great bloody feast!'

Since he had travelled for many days towards that system he was banking on reward and was fuming with rage, knowing that he would miss his quotas and be ridiculed and demoted by his superiors for not completing his harvest.

'Kant, to where have they gone!' he barked to his second in command.

'Boss, our probes did report a large human population on this world, so they must have departed to another world or escaped our galaxy altogether through the abomination,' he replied.

They called the large spiral vertex made by the Plorans an abomination. That was because they couldn't use it themselves for travelling to Osmaron, and it would destroy them if they got too close to its emanating fields.

'If they travelled to another world we shall find them. If they have gone to a local galaxy they will warn the others. Then we shall prepare our forward fleet. In any event, we shall find them and when we do they will dearly pay. No one in this universe can ever defeat us! No one!' he barked in his strange language.

Caefon and all of the Ancients' Federation Worlds within Precinct Seven of Andromeda had been evacuated several months before the Javols arrival. That time corresponded on Earth to

2045 CE (AD 2045).

When the Javols arrived in that area they found, to their utmost disappointment, all planets to be completely deserted. That was despite the fact that their forward spies had surveyed the area several months before and found thriving civilizations rich in resources and ready for harvesting.

Their commander couldn't contain his rage and disappointment in such a food loss and immediately demoted those few forward scouts to menial positions among their ranks.

'To where would so many humans have gone?' He thought.

After an extensive and thorough search through all the systems, their MasterMind concluded something serious was amiss and informed all Javols throughout the galaxy to be prepared for some type of invasion from advanced civilizations outside Andromeda. Their MasterMind also assumed they had escaped through the Spiral Vertex or Abomination as they called it and gave orders to have that area of space annihilated. Very soon after, the vertex was neutralized with lots of meteors. Anyway it had fulfilled its purpose.

The Javols had since become very resourceful and decided to use those fertile worlds for farming. Caefon was selected as their main command base within that sector of Andromeda, but they continued to inquire further into the disappearance of its recent population.

'Kant, we have all been demoted and grounded by our superiors to this ridiculous outpost. I am expected to use this world as a forward base for training and farming. Therefore, you will remain my second in command. Any questions?' Testa said. Kant was not pleased with the outcome, but had to agree with his superior to avoid the alternative of the plasma pit.

'Ne! Nat! Ne!' (Meaning "I have little choice") Kant replied and saluted.

Unknown to their MasterMind, they were also being better prepared for the arrival of the first maulars from Osmaron. Those massive ships that left Osmaron three thousand years earlier were just arriving in the vicinity of those outer systems.

Despite an extensive probing of Caefon and its local systems, the Javols found no advanced life. The underworld of Lower Cantor had not been detected. That was the final phase of their crusade and having taking over the whole of Andromeda they now saw themselves as masters of that galaxy and celebrated that fact with fervour.

CHAPTER 6

A major discrepancy

ANDROMEDA... Earth time 2045 CE

The swarms of Nano-bot Javols had destroyed almost every civilization within the galaxy of Andromeda. They met little opposition during their outward trust from the galactic centre. Their orders were to destroy or enslave all advanced species that posed the slightest threat, so they did as ordered by their Master-Mind.

What they did not consume immediately were frozen and stored on cold uninhabited moons for later use. Their progress was relentless and their quantities too numerous and powerful to challenge.

Although composed mainly of heavy metals, they also needed biological tissue rich in certain chemicals and metals for their own metabolism. Plants and their offerings were not suitable for that purpose, only those life-forms with blood and minerals pumping through their bodies.

After having ravaged most of the galaxy in the intervening 3000 years, several of their scouts had arrived within the Andromedan Precinct Seven, once the seat of the greatest galactic empire when ruled by the Ancients.

All the planet's original near human Ancients had been destroyed 3000 years before. The more recent human inhabitants knew nothing about the Javols nor of their rapacious nature.

With the help of the most advanced Osmaronites, the Ancients had set a complex survival plan in operation that would be enacted over the next few millennia.

When the Javols returned 3000 years later to harvest the remnants, several scouts were sent in advance of their main assault troops. They had reported many systems rich and ready for harvesting, but on arrival their rich and live crops of humans had vanished. Somehow they had been warned of the Javols impending visit to decimate their populations.

All the Javols could observe were the remains and ruins of a once thriving civilization. Cities and industries had wilfully been laid waste by their original occupants. They searched the local planets but could find no remaining life in all the local systems.

The several hundred thousand bird people on Coln had also vanished and so did more than ten million on Caefon. Then there was the report of the explosion of a small ship close to the inter-spacial vertex, also within the perimeter of those systems. That enormous explosion had destroyed more than two hundred thousand Javols, including one of their massive carrier ships. Somehow, things did not add up.

They searched the system again but could find no trails or evidence of a mass exodus. There had been no reports from their many waves of assault troops now on their way to the local galaxies.

As always, one of the Javols' leaders, Lupher, was not pleased with the data received and called his brother, Dracma, to confer.

'I found a major discrepancy in our harvest records returned from sector fifteen of precinct seven. The population there have simply vanished!' Lupher exclaimed in bewilderment.

'Or they were eaten by one of our more unscrupulous commanders and his underlings. Check staff records to see if their numbers tally. If they have trebled their numbers that can only mean they have eaten a surplus,' Dracma replied, unconcerned.

'That has been done. I have been assured that it is not the case. I don't know how or why, but those primal civilizations have left our galaxy.' Lupher appeared quite concerned. If such behaviour could be attributed to such a demonic being.

'Perhaps it's just an error in the data you received. It could also be due to renegade units or perhaps, that area has already been harvested and the records not updated. Our commanders can sometimes be negligent in their duties and responsibilities, to say the least. Remind them of our plasma pits!' Dracma was ripping apart a female's leg. He swallowed the chunks of meat whole, followed by a crimson glass of her chilled blood.

'Now, that really hit the spot!' he burped loud and hard.

'Where are my slave girls. I need entertaining!' In walked a row of Timit women for entertainment and sacrifice. But Lupher continued his discussion.

'That can't be. The systems in question had been scanned by five of our best scouts. Furthermore, most of their cities and towns have been left in ruin. They set timed explosives before their timely departure to a place or places unknown.'

'And you think they have escaped to one of the local galaxies?' Dracma was now a little more concerned.

'What else is there to believe. A thorough search had uncovered not the slightest fragment of evidence that there had been an exodus to any outside system. Yet they are nowhere to be found,' Lupher replied.

'All you can do, Brother, is give instructions to our intergalactic voyagers and wait.'

'What if they have discovered some new means of travel that can take them to the local galaxies in months instead of centuries. How would our voyagers detect such fast moving craft and if they did, we are able to do very little about their passage before they warned the other galaxies?'

'You worry too much. No primal with such basic technologies could have left our galaxy by such means without detection.' Dracma was currently munching on a large bone trying to get to the rich marrow, then he slurped it all in and swallowed.

'You remember the abomination. It was not a natural phenomena. We have found large parts of a device used to create it. I'm sure such a wormhole could be used to transport ships to another galaxy,' Lupher replied.

'Yes, but the device was destroyed well before they disappeared. If that is what really happened.'

'Frankly, Brother, I am concerned, and there is the matter of a super-fast ship that exploded in the vicinity of the worlds in question near the abomination. That happened just after our scouts entered their system. I am sure both events are connected. I think there is a greater mind at work here.' Lupher suddenly grabbed a large raw leg from the table and quickly absorbed the meat from it. To be followed by a large mug of cool dark blood.

'Nice vintage! It tastes much better when we starve and dehydrate our Timit Women.'

'Pity we have to sacrifice so many, but we have to break eggs for the proverbial omelette.' Dracma said, but Lupher continued.

'I realise I can be too scrutinising in this matter, but I sense trouble.'

'If, as I perceive, our troops have already eaten the evidence and the primals have left for another galaxy, we should make our own preparations to do likewise. Our home galaxy, Triangulum, should be reward enough for our long stay in this virtual prison and on this desolate place among these microid idiots,' Dracma replied.

'I keep telling you, we cannot leave this place right now! We require the higher orders at the galactic centre to sustain our elemental structures and can only get such energies close to the nucleus of a galaxy. Preferably, within the vicinity of a black hole like this one. We may travel only if we can store and shield the higher and more volatile fifth order energies,' Lupher replied.

'In that case you must get your MasterMind on the task of finding the escapees. Because if they get to their destination, I am sure others will follow and we might never leave this place, ever!' Dracma shouted somewhat enraged.

He signalled to one of the smallest Timit women and she came forward. He carefully tore her head off with a single turn of his hand and lifted her greenish body so the spray of her blood was focussed on his mouth. When the spray had died down as her heart stopped, he continued sucking at her neck until he drained almost every drop. The other Timit women began to shout.

Gracious Lord! Gracious lord! Gracious lord!.... Please send us to paradise!' Then Lupher did likewise. This time he hugged the body and put much more effort into his meal.

'Brother, we now have these idiot Javols under our control through our MasterMind, which I have created. A task I thought would be impossible, knowing their pathetic dispositions. Now we can use them to conquer the universe for us. Let them eat all remaining primal life throughout the universe if they so wish. We can always have our fair share of sport with the remaining Timit slaves. In the mean time, I can focus my attention on new technologies, including a new intergalactic drive. One that will take us both to Triangulum in safety.' They were both blooded by their ravenous feast. All surpluses being devoured by scavenger bugs they carried around on their person. All Javols were contaminated with those pests.

'But Brother, if that happened and every intelligent species got eaten, there would be few pleasures left for us in an almost empty universe, filled with ignorant Timits and disgusting Javols. Then there would be no one to assist us with more advanced technologies. No one to learn and copy from,' Lupher replied, perplexed by his brother's words.

Since the release of both Hexolyte demons from their eternal confinements in their containment tanks by the Javols, they had ruled over them. That accidental encounter was in one of the Patriarch's prison caves in Andromeda.

It was more than two billion years ago when they were trapped and contained and if not for the Javols' visit to that moon and their overwhelming curiosity, they would still have been contained within that prison. Dracma and Lupher, previous leaders of the Hexolytes, had subsequently taken control of the Javols through MasterMind, which was a large computer they designed for that purpose. Using their MasterMind those two clever demonic Hexolytes had deceived the Javols into thinking they were of their own kind.

Because of their manner of escape they were partly Javol in form. Elementals like Hexolytes could only possess other life-forms if not contained within their own shielded tubular metallic body. However those specially designed bodies were not available in Andromeda and perhaps not within the present universe. A universe that had evolved and drastically changed since the Hexolytes existed in number more than two billion years ago.

Since that time the universe had grown much older. The rear higher dimensional elemental energies needed for their sustenance were presently well below their normal levels of survival.

At this time they could only survive close to the nucleus of galaxies where the stellar densities and such energies were somewhat higher.

Nevertheless, while using the bodies of Javols that they possessed, they could survive for much longer periods without that type of elemental energy.

Their only real chance of a freer long-term survival was to visit one of their ancient caves in galaxy Triangulum and find a suit of encasement. One that would prevent the continual leakage of their elemental energies. However after two billion years the chance of finding such a suit was highly unlikely.

In the mean time the Javols would continue their unimpeded conquest of Andromeda and within a few centuries reach the local galaxies, including Osmaron (our Milky Way) and Triangulum. On their arrival, decimating and laying waste beautiful planets like Earth and Eden in the process. Nevertheless despite that looming spectre of death and destruction, with the arrival of Lumak the Shadite on Earth and the Ancients on Eden, the chance of their conquest had been inexorably diminished.

The Grand Lord of our part of the universe had put certain plans in motion to secure the survival of all primal life and that plan was being followed by the Plorans and several of his servants called Shadites. Even so, Earth had to undergo a transformation in technology, population and government before she could partake in the final battle against the Javols. That transformation had begun several decades before, with Lumak as the intrepid Professor Jeffery Longhurst. Now it would be Mallory's turn and then the Son of Destiny.

CHAPTER 7

The President in New York

Planet ... Pleron (Earth)

Time ... 2051 CE, September 11

It was a beautiful autumn day in New York. President Gerald Fraser's visit was going to be well received. It was Jerry's second term in office and although involved in the more serious problems of the time, he enjoyed the occasional pomp and ceremony. This rare visit was marked by large crowds all along the route as he approached the 9/11 monument. His unquestionable fame was a testimony to one of the greatest presidents the USA had ever known.

'Mallory, you better take point! Keep your eyes peeled and stick close to the boss! Get close when he opens the door! You know the routine!' his chief Bruno Kerry Redford barked on the communicator. They never got on. Mallory never liked his new security boss. He simply didn't relish the idea of taking orders from a jumped up kid 20 years his junior. One who had got the job because of his well known father. Even worse did he like the idea of calling him, sir. But that was protocol and of all things, he had to follow rules and give respect wherever and whenever due, particularly in public.

'Yes, Boss, don't worry!' Then Mallory turned off the mobile.

'Darn jumped up kid. I've must have done it more than a dozen times before you were born!' Mallory snapped, always giving a little more than he got.

'Just the right day for it!' Jerry murmured before getting out of the limousine.

'I am to hold your hand, Sir!' Mallory said and Jerry smiled.

'We can't keep meeting like this, Mal. My wife might complain,' he replied and Mallory returned his smile.

Having placed the Tribute Wreath just below the head of the 9/11 monument Jerry slowly walked pass the firemen and other servicemen. They stood at attention wearing their best, in rank and file, while he approached to inspect and personally commend them for all their sacrifices in the line of duty.

Mallory had joined the security services directly out of the army. After that time he had met Jerry, his president, during an emergency at his country residence. Even now he still didn't know what that emergency was about, with all his most senior security people visiting as if there was going to be no tomorrow. At another time he was on a special mission to rescue the famous Lord Meron from kidnappers. Then he arrested one of the senior senators who was involved in stolen documents. Not to mention that windbag Powell. That guy was always such a slippery fish. No one could hold him in jail for long.

That Lord Meron was the one who invented the incredible LPD Drives that could take ships across space to other worlds. What a clever Britisher he was. It was soon after that time that the president made Mallory an offer he couldn't refuse. Then Mallory and his best lieutenants were chosen by the president as his own personal undercover agents in covert operations.

'Mallory, I need new blood in my secret service detail. Why don't you come and work for me. I can recommend you to Redford. He is a good friend and usually takes my advise. It's just a formality. All you do is fill a few forms and visit the security chief for an interview. While in the field you will only be answerable to me and no one else. Redford takes his orders from me and will do as I say,' Jerry said.

'I would love to, Mister President!' Mallory replied, thinking it a step in the right direction

That was several years ago. Since then his team had been disbanded and placed on hold with his guys transferred to security duties about the White House. It was all to do with funding. There were too many cutbacks in Washington and elsewhere these days. Soon after those changes Redford retired.

Presently Mallory was guarding the president and enjoyed the character of the job. Always visiting so many places and constantly receiving the affections of many waving hands. He was just a small wheel in the cog but felt like the president himself, even when the excitement of the crowds were not directed towards him. Nevertheless he loved his president and would do virtually anything for him in the line of duty.

'Mallory, I got a call from the FBI. They think there is presently an active cell in this area of New York with aims on our president, but it's not official.'

'They think?'

'Yes! But we should take this one as real! Those bastards infiltrate everywhere, you know, even the Pentagon. No where is sacred these days! So keep your eyes peeled and your ears to the ground! If they are going to make a hit, it's going to be from the crowd!' Bruno barked.

'Got it!'

Mallory was suddenly concerned for the safety of his president and immediately contacted Carl Marsden. He was following on the other side of the motorcade. Carl was one of his most trusted lieutenants.

'Carl, we might have a little problem. I have just been told of some pests in the area. Mind you, nothing official. So I want us both to protect our VIP at his most vulnerable. I don't think it's a suicide bomber or sniper. The route has been too well checked for that. Most likely it's going to be a loner posing as a normal bystander with a handgun. So stick close to me and be ready!' Mallory said. In seconds Carl was close to the car.

'Mister President, we might have some enemies in the neighbourhood. You might be at some risks. This warning is not official. Just remain on your guard and be ready to hit the deck at the first sign of trouble,' he said via his communicator.

'My job is always one of risks, but all the same I have to follow protocol... if it's not official. So you will have to be my eyes and ears, and cover my back as best you can,' Jerry replied.

'Roseanne, check the local crowd for any suspicious looking arseholes and get a few of the other guys to mingle. I sense trouble, and you take care!' Mallory stressed. Roseanne was soon on her way with three security men. She used to be another of his operatives in days gone bye.

After laying the wreath and visiting the troops Jerry greeted the mayor, captain of police and other seniors, before taking his place at the rostrum. He was flanked by security, including Mallory, who was always in the lead. Then he stood at the rostrum to utter a few encouraging words to his people and local reporters.

'Mister Mayor, Chief Fire Officer, beloved friends and people of New York. This marks an important anniversary in all our busy lives. Despite these planned attacks from the hands of our mutual enemies, we have much greater challenges ahead. You in this city face many problems in our future, most of which due to climate change from global warming. Therefore we should make it our duty to reduce waste and pollution as best we can to halt the resultant problems and unnatural disasters. As always, we must be vigilant and prepared to pull our limited resources together to fight for our mutual survival.

'As our largest city you have lived well within your annual footprint quotas. Further, the level of crime has significant reduced since the last cleanup. Therefore, with those great accomplishments in mind, I've decided to assist in the extension of New York's perimeter city wall by another 20 kilometres. This will assist in holding back the rising waters of the Atlantic for another 20 years or so. Sadly, since the latest problems in Antarctica those waters will continue rising for several more decades at a faster rate...' he said and the crowd cheered.

As he reached the end of his speech the first shot rang out, hitting the microphone stand, narrowly missing the president. Mallory, being closest jumped towards Jerry pulling him to the ground. Two more shots rang out before the shooter was brought down, cuffed and swiftly taken away.

The crowds were shocked and disturbed. They began to disperse while the president was guided back into his armoured limousine. That area was now too sensitive. Many of his security thought of worse case scenarios, including suicide bombers, and there could be more of the assassins stalking the route.

During the initial assault Mallory took a bullet between his ribs and was numbed from the waist down. He was soon taken away by ambulance.

'Mal! Mal! How are you doing?' the female voice appeared distant. He turned his head around to observe Roseanne sitting close to him on the bed.

'Hi! I feel fine above my waist, but nothing lower down. Doctor reckons it's to do with local swelling. Pressure on the spine or some such due to inflamation,' he replied.

'Will it be alright in time?'

'I think it's going to take a while. Anyway, how is the boss these days?'

'He is ok, but a little pissed you are not around. No one worthwhile to fire his mouth at. He seems to think you are the most dependable officer on the force. I insisted on taking time off to see you and he agreed. I think he cares more than he lets on.'

'Wow! That's a new one on me! Must be a father figure syndrome!' Mallory forced a smile.

'By the way, Jerry sends his best wishes. I never saw a president so nervous since your accident. Security about the White House must have tripled since.'

'And Carl?' he asked.

'He seems ok and sends his best regards, but I think he's been on the grog since. It's really affected him in a bad way. I am going to have a serious chat with him when I get back,' she said.

Mallory remained in hospital for several more weeks. Although the wound did not directly damage his spinal cord, its repercussions were serious and he could no more carry on with his chosen career.

CHAPTER 8

Population explosion

Despite the recent near miss from an assassin's bullet, President Gerald Fraser was quite pleased with himself for having accomplished so much during his previous session in office. During that time he had revitalised most of the waning industries in North America and made positive the country's lagging economy with the assistance of Doctor Jeffery Longhurst. That was all due to the introduction of LPDs, Microids, and a lasting cure for most diseases, including cancer.

Despite all those benefits, the changes had excluded more stringent methods to combat global warming and ocean spread. Although costing billions of dollars, a few of the most important coastal cities were presently contained within thick rings of reinforced concrete. They now included powerful water gates with sealed exit tunnels for vehicular transport and pumps running day and night. It was hoped those walls would hold off the rising waters of the oceans for at least another 20 years. Even so, most of the low lying cities like New Orleans would be lost forever as landmasses shrank.

There was also the longevity serum which could extend life indefinitely. That one was always a well kept secret from the general public. The present global human population was much too high to have contemplated such life improvements, leading to more dire consequences. If anything, a humane way was to be found to cull billions before the real problems of global starvation, presently on the horizon, presented itself. Thank goodness that process of population culling had already begun with the Terminal Disease.

There was also the more practical rejuvenation serum that could increase age by about twenty years. But here again, those devices, as Professor Longhurst called them, worked contrary to population reduction, so those would never be used on Earth in the foreseeable future.

In view of the present uncontrollable human population

explosion, it was ill advised to introduce anything that would further aid the problem. Subsequently those special treatments were only administered to a chosen few within Solarian Banking and directors of a few chosen charitable organizations. Those included the sincere devoted few that had been selected by Professor Khan (Ben), Sarah's father, to assist in his Terminal antidote distribution programs. They would receive all such incentives freely.

An astute Jerry thought over those matters carefully, but could do very little to stem the flow of major disasters he could see appearing over the horizon. To him the recent collision of meteor Little Solo in Antarctica had signalled the start of a countdown to Earth's demise, and that was without the evil and rapacious Javols, presently on their way.

During recent elections and despite a slump in certain world markets, the President had retained sixty-five percent of the vote, with modest campaigning. He now considered his re-election a positive vote of confidence in his ability. For once in many years he was content and happy in his successes. He was probably the only president in the history of his nation that would enter office a second term with not a single smear or blemish on his office. That was recommendation enough for his hard work and effective decisions in the line of duty. It was regrettable he had to say goodbye to all that power and wealth, not to mention his great friends on the stage and elsewhere. Anyway, he was leaving a reasonably successful economy behind and in good hands, or so Jerry thought.

His only son, Donald, now in his early twenties, had been made captain in the air force so Jerry was looking forward to seeing him within the week. It was probably the last time they would see each other.

Presently the only thing that worried him was the ever increasing population of his country. The average couple still wanted an average of about two children. That was despite the fact that wealthier, middle-classed people lived a lot longer due to advanced technologies and medicine.

With all those advancing technologies and more efficient

farming methods, the so-called third world wasn't getting any richer. Even with the continuing aid programs. Childbirth in those countries were more than double those of the developed ones and that was with extensive birth control propaganda. The poorer they became the more children they procured. There was very little the developed countries could do short of taking them over and enforcing their own will upon them. Anyway their considered it their human right, whatever that meant. Nevertheless the death rate in those countries was significantly higher due to wars and disease. Many deaths occurred at childbirth although never high enough to negate growth.

The Amazon rain forest had virtually disappeared with the loss of numerous species, flora and fauna alike. The seed of a small desert had already been planted and had begun to grow in that critical part of the planet. It gradually expanded towards the northern regions away from the more fertile areas. It was partly due to mining but mostly because of deforestation by slash and burn. The slash-and-burn methods left much devastation in their wake and further polluted the atmosphere by adding high levels of carbon dioxide in the form of smoke. Not to mention deaths due to landslides and flooding.. Because of that single factor the weather pattern in North America had significantly changed for the worst, giving rise to more frequent and stronger hurricanes and vicious tornadoes on the southern and eastern seaboards.

'It was a good thing Sarah had built several dome habitats in South America for the most endangered species or they would have disappeared by now,' he thought.

Those changes had significantly altered the character of El Niño toward more unpredictable weather. That factor alone was reason enough to invade certain countries in South America. Nevertheless scientific information was one thing and justifiable legal proof quite another. No one could be certain that other so-called sympathetic nations would not enter the fight on the side of the would-be disadvantaged adversary, leading to lengthy conflicts.

The resulting situation could have quickly escalated into global conflict, each country blaming its neighbours for the indirect abuse of natural forests and eco-systems. All such irresponsible neglect had doubtlessly led to the present unstable global weather patterns. As a consequence, many had incurred substantial financial losses in most areas of their economies. All factors had to be carefully evaluated and considered in light of the global survival equation.

President Gerald Fraser considered those topics in retrospect; for he would be out of it soon enough. If anything, his main failure in office was in not getting the poorer countries to take the matter of conservation and population growth more seriously. He soon came to the conclusion that it was not in the nature of humankind to think of anyone or anything other than itself, its families and its belongings. They were always highly suspicious of strangers and changes, and preferred to stay with the bad to which they were accustomed, rather than change for the better and different. That tendency was very much like an addicted cigarette smoker.

Gerald Fraser seriously considered his own safety and political future.

Since his periods in office only once had an assassination attempt been made on his life and it was by foreign extremist. Luckily, Mallory Colman stood in the way of that bullet. Pity he resigned from the security services soon after. He was a good man and always dedicated to his job.

Then there were the nasty nano-bot aliens called Javols that had destroyed all major life within the galaxy of Andromeda. They had devoured everything to virtual extinction, humans included. The Milky-Way or Osmaron, as they called our galaxy, would go the very same way if we were not prepared when they arrived in just under two centuries from now. In any event, that survival program under Professor Longhurst was much more important than saving Earth's self-indulgent humans.

One day soon he and his wife would leave the world on which he was born and had spent virtually all his life. Leave its golf courses, horses, restaurants... dangers, and abrasive people and pantomime friends behind for another. One called Eden. One that was a most perfect paradise in every sense of the word. Where no one ever grew old, died or felt dissatisfied with anything. One where everyone respected each other and all non-creative activities were accomplished by intelligent robots and androids.

'Sir, the items have been packed and loaded for your space trip,' Carol, his despatch manager advised.

'Carol, please add about a dozen boxes of toothpaste tubes, mouthwash, several crates of malt whisky, vodka and tonic, and whatever items you think we might need on our extended trip. I'm sure the captain and crew will overlook most of these items!' Jerry replied.

'Yes, Mister President!' she saluted and left.

'I'm not sure when they will have these products on Eden, so better safe than sorry. My dog and cat can follow after my planned demise. Yes, Jeffery can collect them for me later,' he murmured to himself.

How could he tell his son Donald, daughters and friends of his plans?... How could they believe such a bizarre tale about life on distant worlds? How could they accept a more advanced race of humans that escaped from the distant galaxy called Andromeda with a technology to make the trip to Earth in hours instead of millions of years?

Then there were the interstellar portals that could transpose several people instantly to almost any planet within Osmaron, our galaxy. Not to mention star-ships the size of a city, that could contain hundreds of thousands of passengers in comfort and travel across the galaxy in minutes.

His departure would be arranged as an accident in deep space on board good old Cleopatra, his favourite shuttle. After that deception she could be buried deep within the Martian surface somewhere close to the Solarian domes. That area on Mars was private property and always guarded by sentinel robots.

President Gerald Fraser reflected over those thoughts while rummaging through his desk draws for something.

'Ah, there you are!' he exclaimed as he retrieved the golden pen from a rear corner of the second draw.

'So sad about Sarah's little boy. I always warned them about the present lapse of security around the manor. Since they left for Eden, security had become almost non-existent. I only wish I could have helped in some little way. Nevertheless, I mentioned the name of good dependable Mallory to them. If anyone can find the little kid it will be Mallory.

'Ahhhhh! my pen... You were my first birthday present from Sarah and Jeffery.' He smiled while clipping it to his inner coat pocket. Then he went to lunch with two of his most important senators, his wife and colleagues.

He was already grooming his replacement, presently his vice president. At thirty-eight, Nicholas Wilson was one of the youngest senators from California, with many of his own original ideas on global problems, but his main concern were in present crime statistics.

It seemed to him, there were more criminals than good respectable people walking the streets at that time. Despite the present strict laws on firearms and other types of violent crime, their numbers were still rising.

Nicholas was at the top of his president's list and they had lots in common. Jerry also felt at ease with Nicholas, who was never self assured and as pompous as most of the others. He was a fighter like himself, stood for what was genuinely right and usually gave clear and unmistakable reasons for his course of action, including the negative aspects should things go wrong. Then he could retrace his steps with the option of damage limitation.

Jerry also knew of the Terminal Disease, even before it was dropped on Earth from the giant ships. They would simply transpose into Earth's atmosphere and out in seconds, even before they could be detected by radar. The large canisters of bacteria had by then exploded several miles above the surface. The disease would soon be spread by the prevailing winds and air currents globally. Most of it would be carried that way until touched by humans.

For optimum results the main canisters would be exploded over China. Due to his global wanderings man was a much better and quicker carrier than any other. A few years after that first contact most passenger airlines would be contaminated. Then the disease would spread far and wide. The contamination process had been precisely calculated, so that some countries would be infected before others in a logical chain of events.

Since having agreed the process, or method of culling humanity, he knew he could have done nothing about it after its timely initiation. Its sole purpose was to reduce Earth's population from over 10 billion to under 500 million. The latter figure was considered to be the optimum sustainable human population, given the reduced rain forests, resources and loss in surface areas by desertification and spreading oceans and seas. Anyway, who gave humankind the right to destroy a complete world like Earth with all its varied and beautiful life. They were equally important to the natural order. Earth humans had no rights to take and abuse lands and resources in that selfish way.

But for the few vanes of coal remaining, fossil fuels had been reduced to virtually zero. Most of the rain forests had been transformed to wasteland and deserts. In the process many important natural habitats had disappeared along with their innocent occupants.

After a reasonable recovery period, the planet could be rebuilt and given a clean bill of health, but that would take the better part of 200 years with the most advanced methods. Well, that was Joel Meron's theory, but it was doubtful whether things would work out exactly to plan. Earth's humans were also involved in the final conflict and the process could take well over two centuries to right itself. Much could happen in that time, including our first visit from the evil Javols.

Those Andromedan Ancients were so damn clever and precise in their undertakings. They seemed to win battles after their death, having planned for every eventuality over a period of several thousand years. With such incredible minds virtually anything was possible.

Then there were the ancient Patriarchs like Lord Vektron, who were billions of years old. Perhaps they were the oldest living entities in the galaxy. To Lord Vektron a thousand years was like a blink of an eye and even eyes were irrelevant to such a being.

Nevertheless Earth and its people were completely ignorant of their existence.

Finally there was the Empress, Sarah, who had gained incredible intuitive powers, in seeing and planning a near perfect future for her glorious Solarian Empire.

Thank goodness all those good people represented the Greater Purpose for the cosmic greater-good. What if they were interstellar predators like the Hexolytes and Drondytes, corrupting and devouring whole planetary populations within a century or so, before consuming the world and its remaining inhabitants with highly radioactive nuclear devices.

President Gerald Fraser continued to ponder those incredible thoughts, but knew he could never mention them to even his closest friends in Cabinet. He would have been considered a mad man with loopy ideas. After that revelation no one would ever have believed in his wild utterances again. Neither could he ever have betrayed Doctor Longhurst and his Andromedan friends.

'Darling, don't forget we dine today with Nicholas and Jane!' his wife Sharon reminded.

'I was just collecting some memorabilia and contemplating my past as president of this great nation of ours,' he replied.

'I know what you mean. And it all begun when that strange Andromedan ship landed near our country house. From that moment life had never been the same,' she said.

'For me it began when I came in contact with the Shadite Plato on my way to feeding the pigs,' he said and embraced her for a while.

'Darling, do you think we will be happy on Eden?' she asked.

'I think we will become the happiest people in the whole universe. Let's hope we shall see our children again before they become to old.'

'Then they can be rejuvenated if they want,' she replied and jerry accepted her comforting words.

CHAPTER 9

Goodbye Earth

Place.... North Dakota, N. America

Lumak, known to all as Doctor Jeffery Longhurst, called his people together at their manor in North Dakota.

'Family and Friends, the time has come for us to move our Microid production and other operations from Earth to the new Solarian worlds within Osmaron. Our homes on planet Eden have been completed. Therefore our work here, on Earth, is finally at an end. Hopefully, we shall return one day, after the human population has been significantly reduced by the Terminal Disease. Then this once beautiful world can be reformed and brought back to normality. By that time, however, its continental coastlines would have altered significantly by climatic change and other detrimental factors. By the measures taken, its reduced human population should have a better chance of survival.

'Henceforth, we are to discontinue all Microid and bio-organ production on this world. However, both our country homes here on Earth will remain for our organizations and infrequent visits. From this moment, Solarian Banking will remain our only contact with humanity on this world. The construction program for the large domes and other isolated living environments will continue. Those closed environmental structures will also be required to protect endangered species along with the few selected members of humanity from future turmoil. More sealed environments will be required for those few remaining fertile human families in different parts of the globe. Many are currently under construction.

During the future unrest, it is predicted that many will take advantage and ravage this world, so we must be prepared for all such eventualities. For that purpose giant sentinel robots will be installed to guard those sealed environments.

'Our first major construction project in this area will be the

Sol-Newtown dome, so named by my wife, Sarah. It will have a capacity of fifty thousand human occupants and their families, including servicing androids and robots. That environmentally sealed structure will be the largest of its kind in North America. It has been specifically designed to isolate fertile families from the terminal disease and shall be built over the LPD development area. It will contain its own energy, water supply and hydroponic farms. Within such structures the antidote can be distributed via the water supply. Those not wishing to be isolated in such domes may receive the antidote on a daily basis through other methods of delivery.

'My father-in-law, Siend Bengizara Khan (Ben), is to take over all operations here on Earth forthwith. Therefore he has been given all necessary information and samples of the antidote for mass-production purposes. Those operations can be completed by robots in our absence.

'Jeremy and Jean-Claude have been fully briefed. Therefore our new plants in Turkey are ready to commence production over there for those communities. They will serve Europe, Asia, India, China and their local islands, with trained teams under Karen Emil, Marion and others. Doctor Emil will play his part in the antidotes distribution locally. Jean-Claude is in charge of all those operations in that part of the planet.

'Even as I speak, the local microid factory is being dismantled and converted for producing the antidote and will commence full production within six months. All antidote stocks will be stored for several decades in frozen underground bunkers deep within the main domes. They are to be sited well beneath each of the domes for security reasons, until the appropriate time. Also, from this moment our strict security at the manor and elsewhere will be disbanded. That means our Macrons, Daisy and Clair will be reprogrammed and used within the local dome Sol-Newtown after its completion.'

As he continued sadness filled their eyes. Some realized they would not be back to visit friends for almost 100 years. During that time most would have died of old age. Further, after 100 years not much of Earth would be recognizable to them. Yet, Lumak continued his long speech.

'Marion, her husband Simon, Madeline and her family, are to take control of the domestic side of our affairs here on Earth and on Eden. This includes our country homes, estates and animals both here and in Turkey. They can use the newly installed portals between this building and those in different countries. This feature will save them the complications of passports and other travel inconveniences.

'The shuttle has been suitably modified so I have set our departure date to coincide with Jerry's vacation. I know it's a difficult step to take, but making a clean breast is necessary in light of those future changes.

'Any questions?' Lumak said, in a most precise and authoritative manner.

'When can we return here again?' Sarah asked, a little saddened by the permanency of their impending change of residence.

'We may return whenever we wish, providing we use disguises, remain hidden or restrict ourselves to the manor and local ranch. Preferable within the security fence and main gate. However, disguise is not a problem.

'We can remain on Earth permanently after having lived several decades away while Earth's population drops below the one billion level. By that time I'm sure we shall not be recognized and even if we were, they would not consider us to be the same people, not having aged a single day over the intervening decades. Nevertheless, the complete process of population reduction will take close to a century. By that time most of our old friends would have been long gone from this life, with the exception of our own people, of course.

'The steps we have taken are for the good of everyone in the long term. We are Solarians and galactic in our endeavours for the greater good of all. Anyway, we cannot make the proverbial omelette without breaking a few eggs,' Lumak said, sadly. Then they dispersed to prepare for their departure.

'She is so beautiful. It's a pity she is soon to come to the end of her days,' Jerry said. Lumak glanced around to observe Jerry checking Cleopatra's under carriage. The whiter than white shuttle craft was parked in the field just in front of the second house and had a beautifully curved and streamlined construction for all types of flight.

'She is our best shuttle yet. Anyway she will be buried in a shallow grave on a sterilized world. So she can always be resurrected when the time is right,' Lumak replied. Jerry glanced at the ship in sadness as if it was the real death of a close friend.

CHAPTER 10

Lost in space

Planet Pleron... *Just over 3000 years since the Ancients' extinction. That planet is situated within the Solarian Arm of the Osmaron Galaxy and is known to its human inhabitants as Earth.*

Planet Eden... *Although within a local system, its existence is unknown to Earth. That most perfect and beautiful world is now the seat of power for the new Solarian Empire.*

Galaxy Milky-Way... *Known to the past Andromedan Ancients as Osmaron.*

Earth time... *Late summer, 2058 CE.*

A large hole had been dug by robots close to the Solarian Banking domes on Mars. Its purpose, to conceal the supposed lost space-shuttle. Its crew had successfully evaded Earth's long-range detectors and arrived safely within one of the Martian domes. Lumak had devised a special cloaking device for that purpose.

Its passengers entered the basement of one of the great surface domes and were immediately transposed through an interstellar portal to the Planet Eden by their technological magic.

Their group, included: Lumak (Professor Jeffery Longhurst); Sarah, his wife; President Gerald Fraser of the USA and his wife, Sharon; Meron and his other Andromedans, Professor Harry Lennox and some other important colleagues and scientists. After their escape the supposed lost shuttle was lowered into the pit by robots and covered with Martian soil.

Their plan was to use another disposable robot controlled craft to transmit a false distress signal the moment they had arrived safely on Eden. Then they would activate that robot ship which pretended to be their original shuttle craft with the same identity while moving uncontrolled into deep space. That transformation was to mislead the Martian scanners into thinking it was the same vessel in distress. Eventually it would disintegrate leaving debris over a wide volume of space. At that time Solarian Banking had many small ships in the vicinity of Mars prospecting for minerals. They would collect debris from the area of the catastrophe, but no bodies.

It was the voice of President Gerald Fraser that repeated the distress signal.

'This is an urgent SOS distress call. I am the president of the United States of America.... We need immediate assistance....

'An explosion has occurred in the trash compressor unit. It destroyed a large part of the rear section of our ship.... Life support and oxygen is still functional but will only last for twelve hours. We are cut off from the other areas of the ship, including food supply and space suits. We are unable to control the ship, presently on route to somewhere outside our solar system and are driven into deep space by the remaining LPD pods. They are no longer under the captain's control. He thinks the control lines have been severed....

'I am afraid there is little hope for us.... Please hurry!' the president said and the transmission and carrier wave went dead as if disconnected.

The bad news was received by one of the Martian listening posts. They immediately relayed the information to the Pentagon. The Vice President immediately called NASA in order to mount a rescue mission for his president and crew. It was then decided to launch four fast shuttles from Mars to the area concerned.

After three days of an extensive effort they gave up the search and were called back to Earth for debriefing.

Known to virtually everyone on Earth, the President's shuttle had exploded in deep space without any trace of its passengers. Its occupants had most likely died of suffocation before the shuttle's destruction. Therefore the shuttle's crew including their president were to be presumed lost in space, never to be seen on

Earth again.

Soon after the supposed accident in space, a new president was inaugurated in Jerry's place and another memorial erected in Washington DC for a once great President by the name of Gerald Fraser. He was loved by all and had remained in office for just over two complete terms. During his time major changes had overtaken his country, making it the richest on the planet. He had also walled many coastal regions and cities from the rising oceans.

Donald Fraser and sisters mourned their parents passing. Within a few months everything was back to normal.

'I am going to miss all my friends and family. I just hope Donald and the girls can cope in our absence,' Sharon said tearfully, wiping her eyes and blowing her nose. For a while she considered the faith of her children on the troubled world left behind in turmoil and hoped they would be together in the not too distant future.

'Don't worry! My father will pay regular visits and assist them when they need help. Madeline is now one of us, so she can assist when my father is not around,' Sarah said, while consoling her.

'Do you think I am ever going to see my children again?'

'Without doubt, you and Jerry will definitely see your children again,' Lumak, now Doctor Jeffery Longhurst added and she smiled while wiping her tearful eyes. Sharon always had faith in Lumak's words, for in her eyes he was a super genius and could make virtually anything happen.

'Now we are home, People. So let's begin our new everlasting lives on this paradise world with vigour. Let's pray that one day in the not too distant future Earth will join with us as one,' Lumak said and they nodded in approval, realizing they had much to accomplish before the Javols arrival.

CHAPTER 11

On planet Eden

Earth time... Winter, AD 2059

A LOST CHILD

Sarah had returned to Earth briefly incognito to deliver her second son. For some strange reason Lumak insisted that she bore him in their manor on Earth. The healthy boy-child was delivered without problem and received all her motherly attention over the intervening weeks. One day, however, the child was placed in the caring hands of one of her nursing helpers. At that time Sarah had left the house briefly for a walk near the Little River to collect her thoughts. When she returned the helper lay unconscious on the floor and the child was gone. The gang involved had left their calling card that indicated they were professionals. Lumak would not trust anyone so decided to handle the matter himself.

Sarah was distraught by the incident. It took her several weeks to recover from the initial shock of her stolen baby. Nevertheless she was advised by her husband Lumak to return to the tranquil-lity of planet Eden while they arranged a thorough search. That investigation was subsequently placed in the hands of a compe-tent police inspector with a good track record.

Despite the many searches by the police and private investiga-tors, no positive leads were forthcoming. They soon came to the conclusion that the child had been taken to a foreign country by criminals. Despite her painful regrets and anxieties, Sarah always lived in the hope that her beloved child would one day be found. At that time paedo-kidnapping was pandemic. Even so, how could they have circumvented the manor's security without observation. Nevertheless since the removal of the security macron and constantly probing eyes of Clair, their intelligent security computer system was quite basic. There were many unanswered questions, with little forensics to guide the few overworked police detectives.

While on Eden, Princess Bawaki and her other companions consoled Sarah as best they could and always remained close at hand. Sarah was quite strong and resilient. She eventually recovered from the trauma of that terrible day and assumed the child was still alive but cared for by another loving mother somewhere on the planet.

The pressures of her new empire combined with the paradise environment of the new world Eden, with its own enchanting effects, helped her to ignore matters beyond her control. She soon left the search of the child in the capable hands of her father, Ben. At that time Lumak was away on another important mission for the Grand Lord.

Presently Sarah and her Solarians were busy with Lodorians and Polokans installing interstellar portals throughout the Solarian worlds, their own and Mars. Mars was subsequently chosen to be the master terminal for all such interstellar portals, being within Earth's system. That was one of the stipulations made by Grand Lord Gerra, Supreme Lord of our part of the seventh universe.

LIFE ON EDEN

Eden had slowly become the most natural paradise world aided by interstellar man. Its settlers were instilled with an unswerving respect for its own indigenous life. Its indigenous species consisted of small fairy-like creatures and other colourful giant insects that lived on nectar. There were no natural predators on land so those creatures feared no one. Nevertheless its oceans and seas were a different matter, with the most savage and ferocious aquatic life imaginable.

Lord Joel Meron and the other Andromedan Ancients were made responsible for all life within Osmaron. They had built many environmental domes on that world in which all endangered non-indigenous life could be kept in isolation. Those were free to exist normally and roam within their pseudo habitats while assisted by every type of invisible technology, aided by trained wardens and androids.

There were several Earth-type environments where many of the now extinct-on-Earth life-forms were specially cared for and encouraged to reproduce. Such animals included Lions, Tigers, Apes, Elephants, Rhinos, Hippos, to name but a few. Genes and sperm were stored in vast libraries for the future resurrection of certain endangered species. With current knowledge it was possible to create virtually any life by simply describing shape, size, muscle, skin, bone structure and other important parameters. Then the Gene Sequencer could virtualize the creature to be observed in its Virtual World. If required they could grow the new prototype life-form to specification.

Here, Virtual Animals could be tested and experimented upon in a Virtual Space until they functioned precisely as required. Finally to be created and introduced into a real-world environment. Such were their levels of technology.

They lived in a society where almost any concept could be visualized and made real. When it came to living creatures they made absolutely sure that the life-form existed within their Virtual World without pain and long term problems before subjecting it to real world conditions.

Several of the habitat domes were linked by long pathways. Animals freely ventured between each confinement, making their existence varied and more natural than could be done within a large wild-life park on earth.

The Andromedan animals that were revived from frozen embryos and genes were kept on a secured island several hundred miles away from the others, Those slowly matured into independent species.

Their main continent of Arcadia was separated into many protectorate states. Each state in turn subdivided into fiefs. Each fief being run by a Councillor or Lord Protector, with responsibilities toward all life within the environment of his or her domain. Those places contained the most beautiful golden temples and citadels. Since gold was plentiful within the Federation, it was used extensively in such buildings and palaces as would be any other inexpensive metal. Their religion was based on the Ancients' Senots.

The two largest islands, Nim and Mond were used mainly for isolating the more carnivorous types from their main continent. Even if they escaped, they could not swim the dangerous waters swarming with every type of ferocious predator.

Each palace was isolated from its surroundings, thus preventing family pets like dogs and cats, that were not indigenous to Eden, to roam freely, multiply and disrupt the natural order. In any event, there were always strict rules regarding procreation. All such creatures were neutered and electronically tagged, unless required for reproduction.

Endangered species were constantly received by Eden. Which meant quarantine stations were always bursting at their seams. They now contained a varied assortment of poor bedraggled creatures that were collected by the Federation ships while on their exploratory missions. However, many were from the continents of Earth and captured by Solarian Banking. During that period of change the team of planetologist were constantly on the move with the Federation ships, locating new worlds for the purpose of classification.

THE TERMINAL DISEASE

Professor Harry Lennox was now in charge of that particular operation under Doctor Jeffery Longhurst (Lumak). Dr. Hal Seaton was presently directly responsible for the quarantine stations. Hal had become utterly disgusted with Earth's peoples callous and selfish attitude towards their own world, its varied life and ecosystems. Presently the problem had accelerated as the human population increased in leaps and bounds. Earth's present population count was over 10 billion and still rising. Therefore it would take many years before the Terminal Virus had taken full effect.

'*Thank goodness!*' he thought, '*that pathetic populations of irresponsible mankind will soon begin to slow and then plummet to just five hundred million due to the effects of my cleverly designed pandemic disease. Otherwise most of my once beautiful world and its more lowly occupants would be lost forever... within 100 years. Mankind had always survived and would live that catastrophe down in time. A million thanks to Professor Jeffery Longhurst and his capable scientists for devising such a uniquely engineered bacteria with virus, albeit with my enthusiastic assistance in putting it together. One that would prevent humans from having more sad, deformed and unhappy children. Without the slightest knowledge of their irreversible infection. Sadly, once infected it could not be removed.*

'The human population of Earth would eventually realise the problem but were not able to devise a permanent cure in time. The Terminal Disease was a bio-engineered viral-bacterium that bred far too quickly and could not be removed without permanently damaging the patient in the process. Being so contagious it would eventually contaminate every square centimetre of Earth's surface including its oceans and deserts.

'Then the disease would be transmitted by every handshake, kiss, touch, drink, breath and could remain dormant for decades until aroused or brought in contact with any unsuspecting host.

'In just two weeks it could completely replace the natural bacteria of its host, to eventually contaminate reproductive organs. During this time it would never reveal its presence, simply because it exhibited no visible symptoms or external patterns of behaviour, either by sight, smell or discomfort and it only targeted mankind.

'What a fantastic device for population control and such an incredible feat of micro-biological engineering. I did well. The extermination of macro pests by micro ones on a global scale. That was even without their knowledge, and yet, the infected will live out their normal lifespan ... but sadly, without any offspring. Nevertheless, I wish the job could be done a lot sooner!' Dr Hal Seaton sneered for a while, proud with himself for his clever handiwork. After all, he was the main bio-engineer on that particular project and barring professor Harry Lennox's input, was the only one involved in its more clandestine development.

Hal was an earth human, born and bred in Los Angeles,

California. Yet, over the years he had become so disgusted with his human kind that he would have given anything, with the exception of his own life, to save Earth from its reckless humans.

As a most promising micro-biologist and considered a genius, he was recruited by Professor Harry Lennox, but had received all his training under Professor Jeffery Longhurst in the good old days. During that time he had found his true vocation in life.

Since he left Earth he had modified his features by adding small horns to his forehead with the occasional changes in skin colouration. Those changes made him look less human. Nevertheless, with the technology at his disposal he could do almost anything genetically. He was now an Edenian with the most advanced Brain Implants and freedom to travel to Earth when needed. He was also a member of the Group of Thirteen. That group was based in New York.

'Now, I have gained incredible status as a professor of Bio-synthesis. Currently in my heaven of Eden, more than twenty light years from Earth and practising what I preach.

'Despite my utter dislike for my fellow apelike man and woman on Earth and their inabilities, I care deeply for my home world and its other life. I have never suffered fools gladly and after all, they were responsible for destroying my once beautiful home world. For that most deplorable deed they will never be forgiven. Never by me. Never! Never! And they must pay! And pay dearly for the near loss of my world.

'Now, my colleagues and I have a complete galaxy to choose from, with all the time in the universe to fulfil our plans. Not an insignificant world like Earth, awash with irrelevant untruths, masked in the form of religions and other ignorant and primitive notions.

'What utter illogical time wasters and barbarians they are. Earth shall be ours eventually, after certain threats have been removed from its surface well within the allotted time,' he thought and sneered again.

Dr. Hal Seaton was not the only one that had become utterly disgusted with Earth's humans. Jerry and many others had tried to spread the word about over-population but could not get anywhere. It appeared to them that Earth's humans saw it their destined duty and human rights, as they called it, to thus destroy everything on the planet including themselves. It was a type of mass suicide programmed by nature deeply within their genes and psyche.

CHAPTER 12

A new career

Captain Mallory Colman was one of the best investigators in the business. Being militarily trained he reflected that aspect in his methodology.

He was in his mid forties when he left the Security Services. At that time his only son Andy was almost a teenager. He had little choice but to resign his job at the White House after the assassination attempt on President Gerald Fraser's life. On that faithful day he was next to the president and took one of the sniper's bullets in the back.

Although minor spinal damage had occurred, most of it was repaired, leaving him an almost normal person, although with somewhat reduced responses in his left leg with the occasional back pain. That problem only showed itself after sitting for long periods. Even so, the psychological trauma of that incident had taken its toll, leaving him unsuitable for the stresses of the important task of protecting his president. He could never have lived with himself if anything untoward happened to Jerry (the President) under similar circumstances again, with a somewhat slower response due to his inabilities.

It had taken him several weeks in hospital and another six convalescing. At that time he was convinced by many experts of a career change. Something of a less stressful nature for the rest of his natural life. Despite the professional advice, Security was all he knew and what he was trained to do.

After his physical and psychological recovery from that traumatic experience, his old friend Ernie White accepted him as partner. Mallory soon became a private investigator in their security business called Shark Investigations.

Although finding the business name quite uninviting, to say the least, he could not find it in his heart to mention those misgivings to Ernie, so he soldiered on with the firm. That was until Ernie was shot dead by an unknown assailant. After that unfortunate tragedy he gave Ernie's wife what he considered a fair price for Ernie's share of the business and immediately changed the name to Alpha-Omega Securities. That way he was also close to the top of the adds and yellow pages. The only problem was, he ended up getting work none of his competitors would take, including snooping and lost pets.

After their divorce his wife Cathy had custody of their son, Andy, along with the house. She had since remarried and was apparently happy with her new doctor husband and way of life. They had remained in Washington DC, while he moved to New York. Now he could only see his son during those rear visits to DC.

On occasion he would visit Jerry's remaining family to check they were all right. They had moved to DC since their parent's disappearance in space all those years ago. Since then, the past President's son, Donald, and young Andy had become good friends.

Just over five years in business and he had tackled numerous cases, from digging for divorce evidence to finding stolen and kidnapped kids. During that short period he had acquired a good reputation for the latter, particularly among the leading newspapers. With a few contacts in the right places many important jobs got passed his way in the hope of getting a good result and a correspondingly good story. Most of it was due to his newspaper contacts since DC and past reputation. There was also the inefficiency of an overworked and overstretched Police Force. Anyway, in all serious cases of kidnapping the police were never the first to know because of dangers to the kidnapped victim. Further, the local police were usually quite thin on the ground and could not investigate all such cases.

Although he earned a sustainable income, the risks were high for those meagre rewards. Nevertheless he enjoyed the job, with its variety of people and places, and unexpected dangers. Yet, he persevered in the hope of getting some financial success eventually.

His favourite restaurant was Rosie's Café, just two blocks down the street from his office. He used that place a lot to get away from the pressures of business and considered that joint relatively safe.

'Rosie, let me have number one and a glass of bear,' Mallory said to the stockily built near middle-aged woman behind the counter. Then he walked over to the corner table to hide himself. He began to quickly scan through the Help columns of the pile of newspapers acquired from the slot-machines outside. He didn't feel like too much hard graft on such a sunny day and fancied some easy local jobs. He could see no suitable work, so left the pile of newspapers on the floor.

Rosie soon arrived with a tray and placed its contents on his table.

'Enjoy!' she said and left. He set his watch alarm for two thirty and took a quiet sip. The note from Doctor Langdon was still bothering him, so he had a hurried late lunch in order to be in time for that three o'clock appointment. He glanced at the address he had previously missed. It was scribbled in handwriting at the bottom of the note. He was once again on the move.

'He is waiting for you, Sir!' the smiling male secretary said and opened the door.

'Mallory, please enter! This is Professor Michael Cockburn, he is presently Vice President of Solarian Banking. We would like your assistance in a very confidential and delicate matter. Please be seated!' Langdon said.

Mallory remembered Michael Cockburn from the old days with Doctor Jeffery Longhurst who frequently visited his president (Jerry). Everyone called him Mickey then. That was when he assisted in planning their covert operations. He was always the one for demonstrating and issuing the special weapons and gadgets.

'Mal, how are you? I haven't seen you in a while!' Mickey greeted.

'You are quite a sight for sore eyes, yourself!' Mallory jested and sat in the nearest chair. Mallory couldn't believe his own eyes, for there in front of him stood a guy that looked at least ten years younger. He was dressed in the most expensive suit and wore a golden tie clip. The circular insignia contained a large diamond. His watch was also of solid gold.

'Anyway, Mal, a baby has been stolen from the daughter of our president. I mean the president of Solarian Banking. The police have been ineffective in finding any clues to his whereabouts, so we have decided to go private. We understand that you are one of the best investigators, if not the best and would like to employ your services to find the child. Assuming you agree to accept the job. Here are the relevant case files and my personal number.'

Mallory carefully scanned through the documents but couldn't refuse a job from old friends and colleagues he knew during the better part of his life.

'I accept!'

'In that case, you are to contact me the moment you find out any relevant information. And you are to keep everything about this case under strictest confidence. Here is something to get you started,' Michael said and handed him another envelope. Mallory opened the envelope and began to gaze at the leaf of special paper that looked like a cheque.

'Two... hundred thousand grand. Are you sure you haven't made a mistake?' Mallory exclaimed, still doubting his glaring eyes presently focussed on the handwriting in blue ink.

'No! We think it's reasonable!' Michael replied.

'I have done every gad dam job in Christendom, but never have I ever received so much money for a single one of those. You sure it's not too much?' Mallory stressed again. He was certain something was amiss.

'No, Mallory, the organization is a very wealthy one and we would like you to give it your utmost attention. Consider it your most important assignment since you left the President, and if you find the child there will be an extra bonus in it for you.'

'Wow! What can I say?'

'Well, do you still accept?' Michael replied in jest.

'Do I accept? Of course I accept! But, can't promise any quick results.'

'Just do your best. From what I've been told, your worst is better than most.'

'Is there anyone I can contact for more information? I need to have some background before I can create a mental picture in my head. I usually find most information in files to be the most inadequate efforts of others. It's usually some other person's opinion fraught with all kinds of biases and inaccuracies,' Mallory advised.

'Feel free to contact the police inspector that was originally on the case. He personally handled it, but was moved to another district three months ago. Here is his card. More information is in the file,' Michael replied.

'So many infant disappearances these days and the problem is on the increase. Some reckons it's because the population growth is slowing down, causing wealthy infertile people to take the law into their own hands. I once saw three kids imprisoned in a cellar by such a family. They had been stolen from different families and were being psyched into rejecting their own families. Luckily, we found them in time. They can only use those methods on older children. Those above the age of two and don't need to use that type of hypnotherapy on the younger ones. They readily bond with anyone,' Mallory said.

'Well, Mallory, thanks for helping out. Please keep me informed. I think that will be all for now,' Michael said and left the room.

'Mallory, he is one of the most powerful men on the planet. In some ways even higher than the president of the USA, so please take this assignment very seriously. A success here could take you to much greater heights,' Langdon said and Mallory viewed him in utter surprise.

'Doc, I take every one of my assignments seriously. And no one can ever be more important than our President,' he scolded, while looking his doctor straight in the eye.

'You know me, Doc, when I am given a job concerning kids I go head on. It's just the way I am. So if I am unable to get quick results, it's because there isn't sufficient information to go on, or I haven't proper leads to follow. Luck seldom enters the equation.'

'Anyway, Mal, please do your best and see what you can find out about these other missing kids. Here is a list I compiled recently from local patients. It's possible they were taken by the same people. Anyway, Mal, good luck!' Langdon said and they parted company.

For the first time since he left the job in DC, Mallory was pleased with himself, even to the point of showing Rosie a smile when he entered her café the second time that day. He knew he was known by a few important people in New York, but not among the biggest people on the planet.

He didn't like the idea of carrying that much money on his person, even in the safer form of a banker's draft, so he immediately made his way to a local bank to have it transferred to his account. After that important job was done, he went to his office to make a few calls.

'Carl, are you very busy these days?'

'No, still bumming around. Fancy hearing from you after all this time. It's about a year now, isn't it? How can I help?' Carl Marsden replied.

'I think I might have a job for you. That is, if you still have your firearms license. You sure you're up to it? You are not still on the grog, are you?' Mallory inquired.

'I left the detox centre a while ago and haven't touched a drop since. I still have my weapons certificate. I've got a part-time job now doing security guard for a local hotel, but the money isn't that good.'

'Ok!'

'Captain, is it full time?' Carl was eager.

'Nothing is guaranteed full time, but I can guarantee you a year and more if the work picks up and I think it will. So what do you say?'

'I say yes, Captain! You know me, always willing to accept a sensible command, particularly when it's for bread and from my old boss.'

'In that case, come to see me at my business address on Monday morning, then we can have lunch. Don't worry about transport, I'll foot the bill,' Mallory said and hung up.

'I wonder what Roseanne must be up to these days, since her

divorce? She used to be such a damn good operative and fighting machine, with a keen forensic eye. Where have I put her number? Ah, must be in one of my old diaries,' he murmured to himself and began to go through his desk draws. Then he turned his attention to one of the old book shelves.

'Ah, there you are.' He began to search through the previous year's diary until he found her number.

'Roseanne, is that you?'

'Mal, what a pleasant surprise. You are lucky to have caught me. I was just on my way out. What's up, Mal?'

'I have got a job for you, but if you are otherwise employed we can forget it,' Mallory said.

'Not so fast, Mal. What does it involve?'

'Security and lots more.'

'I see what you mean. Does it pay a lot?'

'More than most. Are you interested?'

'Yes Mal! I am interested! It's the type of work I prefer.'

'Then come to see me Monday morning. We can have lunch afterwards, and don't worry about travel cost.' Mallory gave her the address and hung up.

After Mallory had completed his calls, he went to reception to collect his messages and once more made his way to his favourite café.

'Rosie, darling, please get me a vodka on the rocks and help yourself to a drink as well.'

'Whoops!' she exclaimed, 'You are in a strange mood today. Have you had a windfall or something?'

'Something like that,' he smugly replied.

For the very first time in his life Mallory felt the wind of change blowing in his direction and realized with the right contacts he could quickly get ahead. All he needed was a good team that could handle their end and Carl and Roseanne were the best. If things went to plan he could visit his son, Andy, for a few days. He hadn't seen him for close to six months.

Nevertheless he worried his new employees would most likely be out of peak, being away from active duty for a while. He soon called his old army friend Chad. That number he always kept in his mobile. Chad was one of his previous lieutenants who had since become one of his closest friends. Chad could always find him weapons at quick notice and had a military training school.

'Hello Pal, it's me, Mal!'

'Mal! Long time. It's a pleasant surprise!'

'I might need you to do me a big favour. I have two new operatives that might need retraining. Are you up for a challenge?'

'Pal, just send them along and I will brush them into shape in no time.'

'I think you know who I'm talking about. It's Carl and Roseanne.

'Those two, eh! They used to be great operatives. Don't worry, I'll soon knock them back into shape. Anything else?' Chad replied.

'I think we must get together soon. I've a new operation coming up and might need some more gadgets and weapons.'

'Perhaps I should visit you when I get a break. Pity I'm so busy at this time. Most likely in the next couple of weeks, or so,' Chad replied.

'Ok then. See you soon!' Mallory disconnected.

CHAPTER 13

The chosen One

Lumak (Professor Jeffery Longhurst) and his wife Sarah had met the Petersons' during one of their visits to England. That was just before their disappearance to Eden, when their shuttle craft was assumed lost in space. The Petersons were an average middle-class couple that lived in Chessington, Surrey, England. Lionel Peterson was in his early sixties and his wife in her mid thirties. She was his third wife.

His only son, Doctor George Peterson, was from his first marriage. His mother had died years before in one of those unfortunate motorcar accidents. After that time George was brought up by his father and second wife. He had spent a significant part of his young life away in boarding schools and colleges. After passing his medical exams he decided to join the Red Cross to assist those poor unfortunate souls in war-torn areas of the planet.

The doctor had taken great pride in his work and cured many thousands of wounded and diseased individuals until his unfortunate turn. It happened during a missile attack while assisting wounded refugees near the Turkish borders. When death came it was instantaneous. He was just twenty five at the time.

Sarah had known the good doctor briefly when she was a mere teenager. That was many years before during the early part of the twentieth century. At that time she aided the Red Cross as a trainee nurse.

She had always wanted to meet the Petersons and thought her short visit would be a kindly reminder to his aging parents of a past she shared with their son.

Although his wife desperately needed a son, Mr Peterson was unable to fulfil his younger wife's desires, having had one of those irreversible vasectomy operations during a previous marriage. Lumak observed their need and advised them to adopt, but they were afraid of that option, with all the follow-up checks and visits by the so called caring establishment of the day.

Further, his age and heart problems worked against certain stipulations. Nevertheless Lumak bore them in mind for an arranged adoption through Solarian Banking.

On Eden.... Earth time, winter 2059 CE

The Grand Lord appeared from nowhere to Lumak in his vineyard and began to update his favourite Shadite on important matters regarding the future of Osmaron.

'Our calculations and observations have shown Sarah's second child to be the chosen one. There was an unmistakable fifth order tremor felt at the instant of his birth. In view of those developments and certain important stipulations regarding the chosen one, the child is to remain on Earth. He must not have any further contact or connection with us or his biological parents.

'The chosen one must be brought up as a normal Earth child, if certain prophecies are to be fulfilled. **"for Jull the patriarch will come out of the Cosmos and arise to tear asunder the serpents with the sword of power and truth"**. *You are therefore required to make the necessary arrangements to ensure he is brought up like an Earth child without any links with you or his mother until the time is right. He must never be contaminated by our protective ways and methods,'* The Grand Lord commanded.

'But my lord, he is my son and it will be difficult to take him away from his mother. She loves the little one dearly,' Lumak replied.

'Yes, Sut. I realise the problems, sadness and pain, but the survival of the whole of humanity and others are at stake. Isn't it said that, God once gave his only begotten son to save mankind? Well, that job has not yet been done. What we are doing here is not of any lesser importance and the child will not die. He will just be away for barely twenty years. After that time he can be reunited with his parents and you both may continue where you left.

'My Lord, this will be very difficult for both of us!'

'Would you sacrifice all life throughout the universe for a large dose of a parent's love? She will get over the loss in time and will

be told when the time is right. In the mean while you are to construct a full proof plan. One that will foil any police investigations. You are to find him good foster parents so that you may keep a remote protective eye on him.' The Grand Lord was insistent and he had to obey for the good of all.

Lumak was distraught. He could not imagine his son being fostered to strangers. There was also his poor wife Sarah to consider in all this. She would in all probability never recover from the loss, but he couldn't prevent prophecy. The Grand Lord would not risk all life in our universe for the sake of a single human child or its loving parents.

It was then that Lumak remembered the Petersons and their wanting for a child. Someone to take the place of George Peterson. They were two of the most stable people he knew and would obviously have made the best parents. He also realised there were many unlawful organizations that stole children for a growing European market. He engineered a birthmark by tattooing the baby just underneath his navel and took several photos of him and his mother together. That mark would be his means of identification if things went wrong. It was quite common at that time for parents to mark their belongings and tattoo their babies. Those methods served well for police identification.

He subsequently approached the Petersons and told them of his supposed illegitimate child that had lost his mother at childbirth. Lumak made the story quite believable. They were very happy to take the child after a written agreement was signed. He contributed two hundred thousand pounds sterling for the immediate upkeep of the child. His wife Sarah never knew anything about the arrangement.

At the appropriate time he approached a few criminal individuals in the underworld through a third party. He offered them a large sum, with a one-hundred thousand dollars bonus, after the job was completed satisfactorily. That price was over triple the going rate at the time. They accepted his conditions, the child was stolen at an opportune time and delivery made.

The Petersons were an isolated couple, so registration was not a problem. Certain forgeries were made to prove the claim of a child she had while on a recent holiday onboard ship. Anyway, she was always slightly overweight and her claims could only have been rejected by close physical examination and DNA checks. The child was later christened George Peterson in memory of their original son of the same name.

Lumak kept in touch with the family by phone on a weekly basis. He soon created a private account in the name of his son. The account was held by Solarian Banking and steadily grew during the following years, to be released to him at the age of twenty-one. At that time Sarah's father Ben and others, including Michael Cockburn, knew nothing of those arrangements and thought the child to be genuinely stolen.

After several months had passed Ben realised the local police had lost interest in the case. They had no leads to begin with and whatever trails existed had grown freezingly cold. He could do little on his own to find the culprits and even less if the kidnappers were linked internationally. It was then that he was advised by the President of Captain Mallory Colman's investigative agency.

Mallory was contacted and given a large retainer. It was a job a poor GI could not refuse. At the time he didn't realize the dangers he would face as he entered deeply the dens of the underworld.

Soon Mallory was on track, but he was also followed by Michael Cockburn's detectives. They were also under pressure and wanted quick results.

CHAPTER 14

Mallory GI

Earth time... Spring, 2060 CE

Mallory Colman took the two notes from the receptionist on his way to his office, pushed the smudgy up-arrow button on the grimy side panel and waited impatiently. There was a buzz and then a ring and the elevator door opened. He pressed three, then entered the lift, still nervously glancing at the note.

'I would like to see you urgently. My office at three p.m. today, if convenient. Dr Langdon.' The other note read, **'do not forget the thirteenth, at five p.m.'**

Mallory folded then threw the first note in the nearest bin realizing he had already dealt with that one. He quickly glanced at his watch to note the date and time.

'What does he and his cronies want from me this time? I hope I am not going to botch the child's assignment. All this extra work is too much for a single guy. I just hope Carl and Roseanne accepts my offer,' he mumbled.

He had just left the scene of a crime where his client had almost blown the head off her two-timing boyfriend with a Colt 45. He had not yet recovered from the repercussions of that scene. He opened his office door and flicked his mobile phone to call the receptionist.

'Sandra, did you see this character when he left the message. Try and remember what he looked like?' Without waiting for a reply he took his second briefcase - the one with the hidden microphone and micro digital recorder and was again on his way back to reception.

'Sorry I hung up on you. I am in a bit of a hurry. Can you remember what the man looked like? The one that delivered this message? He was probably using a false name,' he asked, impatiently.

'Short, slim, slightly receding grey hair with a moustache to match.'

'Ok!'

'Why are you so nervous, Darling?' Joeanne, her friend, interrupted, while filing her redder than red nails.

'I had several shocks to my system today. I saw someone loose his head by a small bomb and another almost with a Colt 45. None of it pleasant. The bomb also took out another couple. They lost arms and legs. I just missed that blast by ten seconds. Thank God it was no one I knew. These days one can't be too sure who'll be next,' he said and Joeanne went silent.

'Gosh! What a day!' Sandra said and carried on her typing. She had seen it all before and was hardened to street crime.

'Keep my office keys in a safe place for me. I won't be back today. And you both be careful,' he said, as he threw Joeanne the bunch of keys which she snatched in mid air. Then he left by the side door to avoid the family and kids now fighting their way through the non user-friendly automatic rotating doorway.

He drove his aged, battered, Elepet car to the fifty-seventh street. Those cars worked mainly on electricity but could run on expensive petrol or ethanol in an emergency. There were fuel-celled, hydrogen driven and LPD cars, but they were too expensive and completely out of reach of the pockets of most people, including Mallory, until his present assignment.

He parked the vehicle in the lowest section of the multi-storey car park and stuck a handy 'INVALID' label on the rear window before visiting one of the tallest blocks in the vicinity. He could always fake a limp if the attendant was close by.

'I have an appointment with Professor Okeke.' He smiled at the female doorperson.

'Are you... just one moment... mister Mallory?' She glanced at his identification.

'Yes, that's me! Always at your service!' he replied in jest with a broad grin.

'Take the elevator to sixty fifth and second left along the right corridor.'

'Women!' he murmured, 'why couldn't she say turn right from the elevator and take the second door on the left. Perhaps I am getting too old for this sleuth lark.'

He walked down the plush-red carpeted corridor and entered an expansive office, lushly decorated. The beautiful female receptionist displayed the rosiest cheeks he had ever seen on a woman. He handed her his identification card with a holographic image and she slid it through a machine.

'How are you, Mister Coleman?'

'I am fine, thank you!'

'Your voice signature has been verified. Please take the third door on your right. They are waiting for you, Sir.' He had seen her before when visiting them in another hotel and realised she was part of their organization.

He entered another lush office that was laid more like a board room, with a long rectangular table.

'Ah, Mallory! There you are!' exclaimed the grey-haired one sitting at the head of the large conference table. His other twelve companions momentarily glanced in Mallory's direction while he took the second vacant seat at the foot of the table.

'I apologise for my late arrival, gentlemen.' Mallory fidgeted with his briefcase to retrieved a folder with some papers.

'Well, we are waiting! What has been your findings?' the professor asked, waiting patiently for a reply.

'It has not been conclusive and in all honesty, there are several aspects that still worry me. Although they may appear trivial at first, when taken together can add up to a form of conspiracy. However, real solid evidence will take time. The killer or killers concerned have evaded the police and are still at large. I saw three corpses today and the closest one had a donor card on his person, or what was left of it. It looked like the micro bomb was placed behind his head by a passerby, where it would do the most damage. But that bomb was far too powerful for the job. It also took out a couple of bystanders as well. So far over thirty lives have been lost this week alone.'

'This is truly terrible! Hal, anything you would like to ask Mallory?'

'Only a few questions! So these criminals are now using micro-bombs on young people for their organs?'

'Yes, Sir. I think they are now into organs!'

'Where was that incident?'

'On 22nd street in broad daylight. Their organization can't be too far away!' Mallory replied.

'What about street cameras? Are there none in that area?'

'Several when they are working. The police are less than useless these days. They do not have the funds or manpower!'

'In future, you may call me Dr. Hal, Hal Seaton. Watch your step, Commander Coleman. There are very bad boys out there!'

'Is there anymore information on this topic?' Okeke inquired.

'I think it's a large gang with influence in high places, but what gets me is their ability to bypass hospital security and steal organs for their own purpose. They must care very little for human life.

'Do you think there is a Doctor Frankenstein at large?' asked the professor.

'No, I think there is a thriving business in illicit organ transplants. Some wealthy people will pay any amount to live a little longer at the expense of others. While some barren women will go to any lengths to acquire kids, even to have a complete replacement womb and associated organs. It seams to me that the largest syndicates in organized crime have added organs to their shopping list. This is not the good old days of Professor Longhurst you know, when organs grew on bio-trees,' Mallory replied.

'Colleagues, may I suggest we allow Captain Colman another month to gather more information and compile his report. Shall we put it to the vote?' Okeke said and all thirteen hands were raised.

'We are for continuation. So be it!'

'In that case I will continue with this project and find what I can.'

'Thank you for coming at such short notice. Shall we say another visit on the thirteenth of next month?' Okeke said, with a European English accent.

'Mallory, as I said before, you are one man and there are many bad fish out there, so please watch your back!' Hal reminded.

'That's fine with me, Gentlemen and thanks for the encouragement.' Mallory glanced at Hal then stood up, closed his special briefcase, bowed his head to the thirteen elderly members and left. Anyway, why should he be overly concerned with the insane ideas of 13 old men while he was on a weekly retainer. There were many things going wrong with humanity and they wanted to find answers. Those answers they would supply to large organizations for a fee. Since Mallory was private and at the sharp end, his findings and advice were invaluable.

'What was the Group of Thirteen or Thirteenth Committee, anyway? Probably just another group of wealthy nutters trying to save the world. And why are they so concerned with organ donor fatalities?' Mallory thought, while following the quickest way out of the building.

He was himself concerned. Not only was every donor-card holder at risk. Many were refraining from adding their names to the registry for fear of supplying their body parts prematurely. If the present trend continued very soon there would be very few donors left and many innocent people, including children, could die for want of a simple organ transplant.

But why were they only choosing those with donor cards? It was probably because those people had been through extensive hospital checks. Their organs were guaranteed. They were mostly non-alcoholics and non-drug takers and after death such organs could be held in special solution for several weeks without refrigeration. But most of all, their profiles were in the computer system which was accessible by certain criminals.

'Anyway it was too easy to get a list of registered donors,' he murmured. If only the good Professor Longhurst was here with his bio-organ farms?' Mallory thought, remembering a time in his life, almost ten years ago, when he met the good Doctor Longhurst through his old friend Harry Lennox. That was the second time he met the doctor in almost 20 years. In all that time the doctor had never changed.

'At that time I was chief of security for the President and based in Washington DC. Then I had to follow president Gerald Fraser everywhere he went with two of my chosen assistants, Carl and Roseanne. Those were the best days of my life. It was when I met my wife and started my new job.' Mallory took a deep breath of regret.

'Before that I was a captain in the paras. Sometimes on special covert operations for my president. That was until he offered me the Job on a more permanent basis. Poor Jerry and all his friends, including Lennox, Sharon... All lost in space in some unfortunate accident...' Mallory contemplated for a while.

CHAPTER 15

The Green Chameleon

Dr. Hal Seaton never liked nano-bots. He regarded all such unnatural devices with dread and dismay. He realized the destructive potentials of those micro robots that could not be seen by the naked eye. Nevertheless, he also realized their benefits when used in a proper way. Over the years he had learnt that those created by Dr. Jeffery Longhurst were different and from a well proven design. Nevertheless he could never ingest them for organ repairs and such like. He could only tolerate them when repairing flesh wounds and damaged limbs. Those could all be controlled by his powerful brain implants.

Having spent years in Eden, he was now able to add them to his list of tools for physical improvement. Finally he was able to build himself a nano-bot suit. It was no ordinary suit, but one with incredible potentials. It was virtually indestructible, could change his appearance to look like anyone and could make him invisible. The only thing it could not do was take him away to another part of the planet. That process using portal technology could only be accomplished on Eden with the necessary powerful satellites and infrastructure, lacking on Earth. However with added miniature LPDs he could fly at great speed. All those functions being precisely controlled through brain implants.

While wearing it he became the proverbial perfect Chameleon. However there were limitations. The main one was the ability of the suit for only three changes. Further, the suit just had a lifetime of 24 hours, give or take 2 hours. So he had a limited window of operations. Most of these limitations were due to limited battery power. Fusion power not included in his first designs. Nevertheless, he had a large team of scientists working on those problems, on Earth and on Eden. The first on Earth to perfect any of those defects would get a prize of 100 million. Therefore good old Powell was chasing them for gold.

The Chameleon suit was in two parts, and outer and inner. To add it to his body he first had to fill his bath with a special gel. Ingredients of which were mostly available on Earth. The nano-bots had to be imported from Eden. He had his methods of camouflage during transit, in the form of clothes, of all things. While in the nude when the bath was full he would get in. A thin layer of that substance would grow over his skin for added protection, giving him a green colouration. That was the healing part.

After the green part was added he would stand under a specially designed shower, while the metallic nano-bots rained over his body. Without the special gel only his face would remain clear of the metallic substance. Finally he would clip on his special utility belt with battery power.

After completion no physical evidence would be left in his home for forensics. The police were not aware of such advanced methods and would dismiss such substances as makeup chemi-cals. They had been contaminated in that way.

Once enshrouded, he could change his appearance to virtually any person through his brain implants. All he needed was a photo or close sighting. However, he retained several standard formats in his implants. Those he could manipulate and use at will.

Finally, Dr. Hal Seaton was ready to take on the nasty criminals on Earth.

'Now, let's open the gates and let the wolves among the chickens! Release the dogs of war!' he yelled with fervour, with arms outstretched. He was not playing games anymore with criminals.

CHAPTER 16

A merciless Phantom at large

My God! I can't believe it! Boss, Harry and the President have gone missing in outer-space? Their shuttle is missing?' Hal could not believe what he read in the news that day. Then there was the micro-bomb incident. As far as he was concerned Okeke was right when he said the planet was going down the pan hole.

Nevertheless he realized the demise of all those good people was a put-up job for the benefit of mankind on earth. As far as he was concerned they were too clever and would most probably be on Eden now sipping cocktails and having a great laugh at the expense of poor mankind on Earth. That was because they had lost the fight at curing mankind of his ills and addictions. He was frustrated that he could do so very little in redressing the balance. He wish he could return to the days when Earth's population was manageable. When animals grazed peacefully in fields, while food and energy was plenty.

Hal was presently on Earth for another of the Group of Thirteen meetings, being the thirteenth member. That day as he entered his hotel sweet he threw his grey-haired disguise into a clothes basket in the wardrobe and poured himself a tall vodka on the rocks. For the first time in his life he felt lonely. It was like the whole world was falling apart and he could do nothing to save it from ultimate disaster.

'I must always wear those disguises while here on Earth. They will think I am another person if they know I haven't aged a day for almost 20 years.' He was very upset so decided to contact his old friend Powell.

'Hello, old friend! How was your time in jail?'

'Not too bad! I made a few more friends that can always be bought for a price!'

'Sounds good! I haven't had that pleasure yet. Anyway, it's nice to know I can count on you!'

'Are you still with our organization?' Powell asked.

'I am! I shall try to get you in again, if you want. We can always kill one of the old boys!'

'Leave it for a while. I need to get my life together first.' Powell replied.

'Pal, our world is going down the pan and I need your assistance to put things right. Don't worry about money. I can get my hands on millions, and billions if I have to.'

'What can I do to help?'

'Can you get us lots of Micro-Bombs through your people. I have some fish to catch. When I am finished they will all be floating on the surface in little bits!'

'You are serious!'

'Very! Those criminal bastards will pay dearly! I will wire you 10 million. That should get you settled!'

'Nice one! We can call this a permanent partnership to save our world! If you like?'

'Now you are talking!' Hal was pleased.

'It's nice to know we are back in business and much stronger than before!' Powell was intrigued.

'Also, try and find us some good scientists. We have some great work to do together. We now have the technology and money to go places and make a difference, Partner!' Hal said

It did not take Powell very long to find a good supplier of Micro-Bombs and a modified airgun for shooting them. Hal had no intentions of taking prisoners. He wanted to teach some criminals a lesson in public and hope they would get his message. His only problem with that operation were bystanders. He had to make sure that the explosive yield was just enough for each individual and no more.

Powell was also good enough, albeit through his adopted criminals, to locate the organ removal gang. Therefore their operation and movement were recorded by hidden cameras.

That day was virtual hell on the 22nd street. As the criminals showed their faces, they were blasted one by one. The scene was too gore for shoppers and pedestrians. There were five heads on the pavements with five torsos to match several yards away with blood spraying everywhere. The police was soon on the scene, with Captain Calahan leading the investigation.

'What happened here, People! Anyone saw anything?'

'Only a green guy. He laughed like he was mad and disappeared over there! I think he was mad. He was all green with red lips. He couldn't stop laughing!'

'Laughing like a bloody hyena. Perhaps he was the Joker. Well I am not bloody laughing!'

'Captain, we did a check on these guys. They were all top crims!'

'Charles, you think someone or something is doing our job for us?'

'If he is, he is doing it well!' Charles was smiling.

'Well, I just had a call. Our Mayor is not pleased!' Calahan said, while switching off the communicator.

'Anyway, it's nice to know someone or something is doing your job for you!' Charles grinned and left. Leaving Calahan in deep contemplation.

'It's not bloody funny. With this phantom about no one is safe.' Calahan was dumbfounded. There was virtually no forensics.

'I thought he only targeted criminals?' one of his sergeants said.

'At this time, I don't know who he targets. This could be the beginning of worse to come. I must have words with Mallory.' Calahan was not pleased and realized he had more trouble on his hands that he had bargained for.

'We found a green apple, Captain. It's been partly eaten!' Charles informed.

'It could be his calling card. Bag it for forensics!' Calahan replied.

All Calahan could find was a bitten apple. When the apple was tested nothing could be found. Not even saliva. Calahan realized his work was truly cutout in finding this Phantom Menace, or was he the Phantom Saviour?

Calahan was right in his prediction, that the Chameleon would be back. Nevertheless the streets of New York would be quiet for now. Hal was presently back on beautiful Eden, sipping cocktails with his everlasting friends; for he was a true Chameleon in both mind and body.

CHAPTER 17

No regrets and no recriminations

Mallory left the hotel to follow up some leads and heard a cops' siren from behind, so he carefully slowed at the lights. A large blue car suddenly stopped on the right next to his. The man behind the wheel showed a broad grin and signalled him to lower his window.

'Calahan, how nice to see you at such short notice. How are things in the precinct these days? Still climbing over dead bodies to get to your desk?' Mallory shouted through the noisy traffic.

'Very funny. I am laughing like a bloody hyena. You know, Mal, since I have known you, you've always been a cocky son of a bitch,' Calahan reciprocated.

'If that's the case it makes us both bastards!' Mallory replied. They always tried to get one over on the other. For Calahan it was probably a way of relieving his pent up stresses, but he always tended to pick on Mallory. It was probably because Mallory always gave as good as he got and was also at the sharp end.

'Anyway, cut the crap! Anything more I should know about what happen to those poor buggers this morning?'

'Sorry, I had a busy morning. I had to see some guys about a dog!' Mallory said.

'Yea, very funny! I just been to a scene with five bodies in bits. Notorious crims with their heads missing on the 22nd . That's where crims killed a guy for his organs. Wasn't that so?' Calahan continued.

'Really? It's new to me! You mean to say, someone is doing your job for you?' Mallory replied.

'Go on! Take the piss, mister private eye. Anyway, watch your back and keep me in the loop!' Calahan said.

'No more than I told you and your guys. If anymore comes to mind you'll be the first to know. Anyway, I'll give you a call, later.' Mallory continued.

'Don't you forget!' Calahan insisted.

'The criminal guys that did that job must have flown the coop well before the timed bomb went off. Your best chance is to check with Organ Storage down at the local hospital. I'm sure they have inside contacts for removal, storage and delivery. The ambulance could also be a fake, or diverted on route to a slaughter house or some suitable place with refrigeration. As for crims blowing up, that part is new to me. Have a nice day!' Mallory said.

'Dam organ robbers! Thanks for the info... call me later! And keep your nose clean!' Calahan shouted and sped off to the left at the lights.

'Wow! Now we have a vigilante killing of organ crims. I wonder if it's anyone I know. I should consider him a friend. I only hope he adds child-smuggling to his portfolio,' Mallory was ecstatic but always preferred to remain on the side of the law and order. His conscience wouldn't have it any other way.

Mallory had remained single since his divorce twelve years ago, with the occasional female friend and one-night-stands. The shock of that episode and the unstable times made him almost immune to the more serious relationship. Always worrying for the safety of a permanent partner while in his chosen profession was not good for business. Anyway, he always preferred his freedom as a bachelor and did not like the idea of explaining his actions and lateness to anyone, not even his caring mother.

For a brief moment he regurgitated the incident of the micro bomb that blew the head off a simple guy going about his normal business. That incident happened only because the guy was a registered donor. He wondered whether all such registered donors were at risk and whether he should take advantage and advertise his services for their protection.

Then he realized the crims in that particular branch would soon stop their operations and be running scared. Whoever it was had advanced technology and would always get away. That one was very careful and cared very little for such criminal pigs. They could never be safe again.

Being on the opposite end, he had found the steep increase in crime much better for business. The only problem was, criminals were more clever in planning and carried better gadgets and more dangerous toys. On the other hand, police were thinner on the ground and many were untrustworthy and corrupt.

Even so, he had known Calahan since his move to New York. He was always an honest and hard working cop, with his work cut out. Therefore he always assisted him with field information when he could. It helped in keeping the police dogs away from his office door. One thing a private detective never liked was cops moving in and out of his office every time there was a major crime in the area.

He removed his handkerchief and wiped his sweaty brow. It was another hot and humid day with 41 degrees centigrade in the shade and his little car hadn't any airconditioning. That novelty item stopped working years ago.

'I must get out of this damn traffic and place you on charge if I am to get anywhere today,' he muttered. He had forgotten to top up the small tanks with petrol and ethanol. They were used as reserves in case of emergencies, when battery power went low. Presently petrol was hard to get. Only a few pumps remained and they wanted payment well in advance to fulfill their daily quotas.

He cut through a few back streets and was soon in the small parking square at the back of his apartment. His apartment was in the basement where it was always quiet and cool. It was more like a cave than a home, but it was his cave. Then he plugged the little car into its power charger.

'Oooh!!! Back playing up again!' he whispered to himself. His back was always painful when he sat for long periods in the old battered car with its less than orthopaedic back rests. The after effects of that bullet in the back for his president remained a constant reminder and needed frequent massaging and medication. He went into the kitchen for a glass of water and took a pill from the container on the thin shelf over the fireplace.

'I hope I'm not due for another spinal operation? No implants either,' he murmured.

Mallory went to one of the kitchen cupboards and collected some seed for his favourite macaw. She was about ninety and always wanted more than her fair share of attention.

'How are you today, my little Daisy?' he said and the parrot reciprocated by gently pricking his finger with her beak. He had taken her with him after leaving his wife. Originally she was called Poly, which he considered too ubiquitous for parrots, so he changed her name to Daisy.

'My little Daisy! Little Daisy,' she said, repeating his last words.

'Thanks a lot for that friendly greeting!' he rebuked as he redrew his finger from the cage. It was not blooded. Then he opened the cage door and freed her.

'What a morning! I sometimes wish I was back in the past with good old Lennox, Chad, Carl, Roseanne and of all things, Daisy. What a beautiful intelligent computer she was, with the most sexiest holographic figure I have ever seen. Pity she wasn't real. At least that was what she showed us on the mobile and coms. We had a lot of fun in those days with Doctor Longhurst's special gadgets and weapons. That was why I changed your name Poly to Daisy... To remind me of those great times.'

The parrot flew across to her perch and began pruning her feathers.

'Funny how life changes and people go their separate ways. Some die the most horrible deaths while others take bullets in their backs for others. Anyway, the limp in my left leg went a year ago and I am almost back to normal, but for the occasional pain and cramps,' he said with more regrets and sadness. He was presently digging himself a big hole, going no where fast and didn't know how to pull himself out. The phone rang and he went to answer.

'Yea, Mallory!'

'Dad it's me!' Andy yelled.

'My son! How are you and school these days?'

'I am fine, Dad. I'm changing school. Mum decided to send me to a better one.'

'Do you like it. I mean, will you be happy there?' Mallory asked.

'I think it's a great place. Anyway, when are you coming to DC?'

'To tell you the truth, Son, I don't know. I will try to make it next month.'

'Dad, you said that last month and the month before that.'

'Son, I can guarantee that I'll be over to see you within one month from today, and I always keep my word.' Andy was satisfied with that reply.

'In that case, see you in about 4 weeks.'

'You to, Son,' Mallory replied and hung up.

Suddenly Mallory worried that he would not have time to get flight tickets and presents. Taking time off between assignments was going to be a major hassle. Nevertheless the boy had called him three times in the past week. He had to make it this time and plan for at least a couple of days in his schedule.

'I am not hungry and in no mood to cook. I'll get a takeaway later,' he thought aloud.

Mallory slumped in the large settee to watch television and soon fell asleep. When he awoke he just couldn't stop thinking of the good times he had in the past with a few loyal colleagues and friends. He would give anything to have them back.

He thought of his old friend Professor Lennox and the times they had together. That was when he was with Chad, Carl and Roseanne doing covert operations for his president, until overwhelmed with sadness by their sudden death in space and fell asleep again.

CHAPTER 18

Bio-farms

Several years before... Lumak's ranch, North Dakota

'Mallory! Don't look so glum! This place is as tight as the Pentagon. We have lots of super sensitive security androids all over the place, so your president is absolutely safe.' An enthusiastic Lennox said.

'It was my first time on that ranch in North Dakota. I had to check the place out for myself before I was convinced it was secure enough for golf and fishing. When I saw the many towers around the multi fenced periphery, I realised the place was tighter than Fort Knox. Then there was the intelligent computer called Clair. She kept her eyes and sensors on everyone and everything within the perimeter.' Mallory recalled.

'Please follow me to that large dome over there, Mal. I want to show you something of interest. But promise me you won't spill your guts all over the floor afterwards. Anyway, if you do you will have to clean the mess up yourself,' Lennox jested, with his usual sarcasm. Harry Lennox had always been a good friend but also a keen leg-puller.

It was a long walk through some of the largest and most beautiful flowers Mallory had ever seen. Some were several feet across with every pattern and colour imaginable. There was one that he had never seen before. That one had the petals with stamens around the head and another flower in the centre waiting to be opened.

'This is my pet flower. It's what you call a flower within a flower, within a flower. As it grows the previous flower is discarded for the new one in the centre. That way we can have a new flower a day with different patterns and different colours. What do you think, Mal?'

'I think it's bloody marvellous and it's got a very pleasant perfume!'

'They've all been specifically designed to please. This one

creates a different scent for each flower.'

'It's about the most pleasing thing I ever saw!' Mallory sniffed.

'Don't inhale too long, the perfume intoxicates!'

'Really? I must really get one of those!' Mallory was ecstatic.

'Mal, you've seen nothing yet. These are all bio-engineered for the average garden and require minimal care. They will even prevent weed from getting too close by releasing certain toxins. The toxins are not dangerous to insects and bees love them. We can control their colour, form, texture and fragrance with certain chemical additives in the localized soil.' They continued onwards until they arrived at the entrance of the largest dome.

'This environment is completely sealed from the outside. The plants inside are further contained within their own bio-chambers. This is necessary if we are to prevent cross-contamination and viral infections.'

'I see!' Mallory said, somewhat confused.

'Please follow me into the decontamination booth. It will simply scan you and check for every kind of bug. There is also a sniffer several times more sensitive than a dog's nose that will detect any illness you carry and do a complete analysis, while finding a suitable method for cleansing.'

Mallory was subsequently scanned by a device resembling the head of a Martian alien weapon. The type used in 'War of the Worlds' to melt tanks with its strange beams. However in this case it sniffed his body with a super-nose. Finally he was flooded with green rays of light. The door opened as Lennox read off all his ailments on a screen.

'I see your wounds have almost healed, but there is some scarred tissue. I can have it removed for you if you wish.' Lennox said. Mallory was amazed by the levels of technology in that place. However he declined the operation, not wishing another few weeks of recovery in hospital. Then they continued towards another building within the same dome complex.

'What's this? Plants with fleshy leaves and blue veins? Bloody hell! Bio-organs... for fruits!' Mallory exclaimed.

'These are what I call "the trees of life". This one grows a particular type of heart,' Lennox replied.

'Hearts.... Hell, there are hearts on each of those bloody branches... pumping blood. How is that possible?' Mallory inquired as some previously unknown type of disgust came over him.

'I warned you that you might be sick,' Lennox said, with a grin of success on his long face.

'I had no idea that such a thing was possible,' Mallory replied, still flabbergasted.

'They take in oxygen through their leaves which act more like lungs. They have their roots in a bio-soup that is continually fed with specially prepared nutrients through that large tube over there. The whole place is completely sealed from contaminants. That is why the robot had to check you over. We have trees for every conceivable organ. What we haven't developed we have found unnecessary for human survival.' Lennox felt triumphant.

Mallory stood, completely bedazzled, but filled with curiosity and admiration, while watching trees upon trees with numerous hearts like apples, pumping away on every branch. There were close to one hundred hearts on that one tree alone and there were countless rows of hearts, kidneys, livers, lungs and other types of trees, all alive and producing their relevant body functions.

'When the time comes for harvesting, their stems are simply tied and cut in the way you do a baby's umbilical cord. Then they are stored in a special refrigeration unit until they are called for transplantation. The stems simply grow another set until the tree gets too old or becomes contaminated by bacteria. Each tree can last for two years, supplying us with over two thousand organs on average over that time. We have plants for every possible blood group.'

Mallory's initial feelings of disgust had turned to admiration for the scientists who had engineered actual living plants for the purpose of saving lives. He continued walking through the rows of organ plants but could not see a brain plant. He dared not ask Lennox the reasons why. Mallory didn't know if it was scientifically feasible or ethically acceptable, or that no one there had even considered that particular option. Then again, it was quite difficult to transplant a complete human brain and he concluded it was because the body and its organs were for the benefit of the brain and not the other way around.

'I'm not through with you yet, Mal. Follow me this way!'

This time Mallory followed him out of that massive dome enclosure towards the main research laboratory. It was a neat little hut with its own miniature piano and other bits of furniture including toiletry.

'This program has been one of my greatest achievements. Geib where are you?' Lennox shouted.

'Over here!' the small creature shouted back.

'You are pruning your feathers again?' Lennox inquired.

'I have a slight itch. I don't think it's a parasite,' the bird replied.

'I would like you to meet a friend of mine by the name of Mallory. You may call him Mal.'

'Please to meet you, Mal,' the bird said. She stretched her little hands out for a handshake and Mallory did likewise.

When greetings were over they left and went back to Lennox's office.

'I thought I've seen everything, but never could I have ever imagined a parrot with hands and wings.'

'I know, Mal. It's not easy for natural evolution to do it that way. In most cases as we adopt to changing circumstances and environments, Mother Nature can only use what's already there and extend their functions for the improvement. This is one of the reasons why birds do not have hands in addition to wings. However, with genetic engineering we can accomplish virtually any change by gene-splicing. And her offspring will be the same.'

'Wow man! You people are like gods!' he just couldn't imagine a flock of such parrots in flight.

'We think if it wasn't God's will we wouldn't be able to do it. Anyway, Geib stands for "Genetically Enhanced Intelligent Bird". She has also been thought to play the piano professionally and does great renditions of Bach and Mozart. This is all accomplished without the use of Brain Implants and special drugs. Mal, we never realized the so-called lower animals had so much potential on their own. All that was required to get them going was the right equipment, diet and training. By the way, she has an IQ of 125 and is quite clever with it. That's a lot for a bird that can live close to 200 years,' Lennox said and Mallory was amazed.

That was a long time ago when Lennox, Professor Longhurst and Jerry, his president, was alive.
Mallory pondered those thoughts before getting up and ordering himself a Chinese. He always wished he could turn back the clock to those times of incredulity, pleasure and romance.

CHAPTER 19

Boomerangs to Bazookas

Mallory was no soft touch or slovenly sleuth. His military training had thought him a more methodical and direct approach to field work. In so doing he seldom paid much attention to security systems, fences and front doors. He was always equipped with a special range of gizmos and gadgets. His tools of the trade as he called them. Those included a range of electronics that could bypass those difficult security systems. When technology failed brute force always won the day.

And that was not all. He packed a range of effective weapons, from his ever faithful Browning Auto to a more silent miniature dart gun with capsules that released neuro-toxins on impact. He always carried a miniature compressed air dart gun for silence or when the others failed. It was equally effective when the darts were tipped in certain poisons or included small bladders filled with certain neuro-toxins. Those he could collect from certain friends in federal security.

During his time in the president's service he had accumulated several such weapons and devices from Michael Cockburn. Although mainly experimental, he had adapted many to his type of field work and placed in storage until needed for special assignments. He had saved many small compressed canisters of nerve gas that could temporarily quell a party of over one hundred almost simultaneously.

Therefore his basement armoury contained everything from bazookas to the latest machine pistols including a range of primitive weapons like boomerangs.

Mallory was also a licensed collector. It was another big favour, Jerry, his past president did for him. Jerry was then head of the ballistics committee, whose sole purpose were to stop the indiscriminate use of firearms. Nevertheless he didn't mind allowing responsible collectors and those in security.

The current state laws prohibited the use of all such dangerous weapons. Those laws had existed since president Gerald Fraser

(Jerry) came to power. In those days guns were freely available and riots, street fights and massacres were common. The death rate from the use of such weapons had increased to incredible levels before then. That figure included many innocent bystanders, children and law enforcement officers in the course of their normal duties. Something had to be done and very soon a bill was passed. Afterwards the President gave an amnesty of one month. During which time all dangerous weapons were to be returned to the nearest police station, no questions asked.

That day coincided with the second of May, now a national holiday. Therefore no one had an excuse for not returning their weapons.

After that amnesty, the penalty for anyone carrying a weapon without a license was life in prison and that penalty could be increased to one of painless execution by injection if the individual had an unsavoury violent past. After that first amnesty there were random police checks and soon the majority of weapons were handed in. He allowed another amnesty a year later and soon there was an annual holiday called Amnesty Day. During that time many would freely return their remaining weapons with no questions asked. They would simply drop them into the security bins at specific secured locations.

Despite those severe laws, weapons were in great demand on the black market. Therefore Mallory's armoury would have been considered a treasure by any underworld dealer. Despite those changes, many criminals had moved on to more devious methods and weapons like Micro Bombs in envelopes, the small and silent irretraceable dart gun, Nano-bot devices that could deliver poisons directly into the blood stream and others.

Mallory became a weapon's collector after the death of his most devoted girlfriend thirteen years before. They had just decided to get married and planned a celebration on the very day it happened. She died during one of those unpredictable riots. Despite his later marriage to Andy's mother he had never recovered from that loss.

She had gone to the local shops to buy some groceries and got caught up in the cross fire on her way back. Since that time he had given most of his free time to his collecting hobby and his pet parrot. In some small way his armoury kept her memory alive.

He realize the pattern of life on Earth was changing from bad to worse and knew not why, so he decided to arm and protect himself as best he could. Even so, his new profession was not the most ideal for long term survival.

'My darling Elizabeth. I am so sorry for the way you left me!' he thought whenever he entered his armoury and glanced at the photos when they were together.

CHAPTER 20

Mallory and partners

There was a knock on his office door and Roseanne entered.

'Hi, Captain! So much for your impeccable security!' An excited Roseanne slumped on the visitor's sofa just in front of his desk. She was tired and sweating.

'Roseanne! How are you, my girl? I heard you recently got divorced. Sorry to see you also suffered that common experience.'

'Yea, it didn't work out! You received my wedding invitation and didn't show!'

'I know. I am sorry about that. I was not in town at the time. It was necessary to tail a client's wife all the way to California. But you did receive my little gift and my sincerest apologies?'

'Yes! I did! Some little gift. I still have a few bottles left.'

'You haven't changed a bit! Just as lovely as ever!'

'And you? Same old office, eh. I thought you would have made it to Long Island by now,' she replied, sarcastically.

'Don't let looks deceive you, my girl. This place is just a front for the police and other creepy-crawlies. It gives them some place to visit whenever they think I am linked to one of their crimes. They have such a flare for the melodramatic. If I didn't, they would be searching everywhere else, including my home. My motto is, always give my assailants free access to the information they desire and that information happens to be exactly what I want them to have. It's always kept in this place at easy reach. These days I make it a point to visit all my important clients at posh hotels and in secret.'

'Pity about Jerry and our other good friends dying in outer-space like that,' she said with sadness.

'Yea, I can't get over it. We lost Doctor Longhurst, his wife, Sarah, my good friend Lennox and a few other great people I knew personally. I found that situation much harder to take than my divorce. But I saw Mickey recently. He is now a director of Solarian Banking and one of the most important men on the planet.'

'Wow! Solarian Banking is the most powerful organization on Earth. Anyway, sorry for bringing the matter up,' she replied.

'You know, things were never the same after the changes. I found the new brass a constant butt in my ass. Anyway, my little accident gave me a good excuse to leave the service. What was your excuse?'

'I got married and pregnant, but I had a miscarriage and lost the child. I heard Carl was kicked out because of his drinking on the job. I haven't heard from him since.'

'Yea, he had it hard at that time too. I think he is now off the grog, though.' Mallory continued.

'I hope he is getting it together. Life is too short.'

'It must have been hard for you during that time. Anyway, my girl, let's talk some business. I have a few big jobs on, at least half a million bucks worth and I need a couple of good ex paras I can trust. There is danger involved, so if you decide to take the job, you'll be sent on a few weeks special training. I have an old friend who's got a school for that purpose. Someone you know, but I'm not going to tell you yet and give the game away.'

'That's great, Mal!'

'You'll be given a ten percent partnership share in the business and more if things improve on both sides. However, the partnership will be probationary, to commence at the start of the next financial year. You will also earn a monthly salary. The total should add up close to two hundred grand a year when things begin to move. There are also the occasional perks, like gifts from happy clients for a job well done and so fourth. Those we share equally, but they must be gifts and not part of our fees or bonus promises.' Mallory said.

'Really, Mal?'

'Yea! All in all, I think you could make well over one hundred grand in the first year. However, I can't give any guarantees.'

'Whoops, a partnership as well! What a nice guy you have become, Mal. I've been looking for such a job since I left the President's employ. Anyway, it's much better than working for Pal Bunny's Club as a waitress. Is there much danger involved?'

'The main job involves a kidnapped kid. It's for Mickey, but it's not his kid. There could be some danger, but I think no more than usual. Anyway, I shall have you both well tooled for the big jobs. A good friend and I have been working on a few gadgets over the years, so when I am through with you, you'll make Catwoman look more like baby Cupid,' Mallory grinned.

'You mentioned another person. Anyone I know?'

'Yes. I am expecting Carl to join us.'

'You mean Carl Marsden, the drunk mountain climber?'

'Yes! Like you, he has had his own share of problems, but took to the bottle instead. He tells me he stopped drinking six months ago.'

'It could be risky if he still takes a sip during work. Could endanger us all? But if you say he is ok that's good enough for me.'

'I know. That's why I called him here this morning, so we could both look him over and have a chat as well.'

There was a knock on the door and Carl entered.

'Hello, Captain...! Roseanne! The receptionist told me to come up!' Mallory shook his hand and Roseanne did likewise. Then he slumped next to Roseanne.

'And how are things?' Roseanne asked.

'Much better, thank you! You look good yourself!' he replied.

'I know what it's like. We have all been put through the mincer some time or another, but we must learn to fight back if we are to survive in these awful times. I am one for letting bygones be bygones, but I must have a good team if things are to work with us. A team that I can trust on a twenty-four-hour basis. So if anyone isn't up to scratch, that person should tell me now so I can make other arrangements,' Mallory stressed. Then he went on to explain the salary scale to Carl and he accepted.

'Now... can I have your ammunition permits.' Both retrieved their papers and handed them over. These two I shall keep here in a safe place. Your identity cards will be ready for you by the end of the week, so please get me a couple good photos sometime today. I shall also inform the local police and the FBI of their whereabouts and your new jobs with me, in case any of you are arrested while on duty. I have a good mate in the police by the name of Calahan, Captain Calahan. We help each other sometimes and he can put a good word in to get us out of tricky situations, but we can't always guarantee his assistance.'

'Sounds good, Mal!' Roseanne replied.

'Unfortunately, problems with other services happen occasionally, and we have to be prepared. Carl, as I was telling Roseanne before you entered, I want to make you both ten percent partners in this business. With perks, you could both earn well in excess of one hundred grand in your first year. Although I can't guarantee anything, I do have almost a million in the books now and could complete a lot more if I had more help.'

'That sounds fantastic to me!' Roseanne exclaimed and Carl agreed with a double nod and glaring eyes.

'In that case, I would like you both to complete these forms. One for the job and the other for the local police. The partnership papers can be signed after I collect them from my lawyer. They have to know that you are now involved in Alpha-Omega Securities, for the records. Those pieces of paper can save us a lot of time in false arrests and misunderstandings. I am sure you don't like hanging around crowded police stations while they search your files when you have important work to do,' Mallory said.

They completed and signed the forms and he placed them in a small wall safe on the side of the old revamped gas fireplace. That safe was concealed behind a false wall which was almost impossible to find. The main safe was over the fireplace and in full view of everyone, but behind a small oil-painting.

'Now you know where they are hidden. And in case you ask, I never keep large sums of money or jewellery in this place.

'Nice to have you on board. Now we can go to lunch.'

'Rosie, I would like you to meet two colleagues of mine. This is Carl..! Roseanne! They will be working with me from now on, so take good care of them for my sake!'

'Nice to meet you both!' Rosie greeted and they ordered her special dish of the day.

'I have known Rosie since I arrived in New York. She can sometimes be very helpful and the food is quite good.'

'Yea! The smell of fried onions always gives me an appetite!' Carl said.

'You might want to know why I use this place for meals? Well, I'll tell you. It's because Rosie keeps an eye on all suspicious characters coming into this joint. That makes it safe from attacks and bombs, and makes me feel less insecure. Any of my enemies will think twice about trying anything in here with so many people moving in and out.

'What about Micro and suicide bombers?' Roseanne asked.

'Our present criminals are not religious, with notions of life in paradise after martyrdom. They will probably all go to hell anyway. To them there is little to be gained by killing innocent bystanders, unless there is some gains, like internal organs for the transplant market.'

'From what I read in the news, they wont be doing that anymore with The Phantom about!' Roseanne interjected.

'You have a valid point,' Carl said.

'People are calling him The Phantom?' Mallory inquired.

'Some are also calling him The Green Chameleon! He can also become invisible.' Carl replied.

'Anyway, I have special detectors that will sniff most explosives, and miniature radar that can detect any new changes to the place other than wood and people. It can search any lesser or denser materials from a fixed reference, and that reference can be changed from wood to glass, plastics or other materials by the simple press of a button. Those devices can also scan a body or object in full 3D.'

'Yea! But nothing can detect the micro stuff. I mean nano-bots,' Carl said.

'Yes, but they are seldom used these days by small crooks. Too expensive!' Roseanne replied.

'Anyway, these days one can never be too careful so I am going to have you both wired as soon as you've been on the course. I can't have any of my operatives becoming premature stiffs.'

'Yes, I agree! And it's getting worse! I think the gangs have recently taken over our streets. It's mainly because our law enforcement officers have become too ineffective due to all those human-rights, bad sentencing and corrupt corps,' Carl said.

'In that case more power to our Phantom or Green Chameleon, or what ever he is called. We could do with some help in clearing our streets,' Roseanne replied.

'Yep! Poor Calahan and his honest guys can only do so much when their hands are tied and the Mayor is always on their backs for results,' Mallory said.

'Not to mention general government cutbacks,' Roseanne added.

'Much changed since you last saw action. Equipment have significantly reduced in size with more sophistication since Nano-bots and microids came on the scene.' Mallory advised.

'So we have a little learning on the job,' Carl replied.

'Talking about microids; I had a call this morning from a large private hospital. Apparently several of their specialists operating robots have turned to dust, grey dust. One did it during an intricate heart transplant operation. Luckily for the poor patient it had just completed the stitching process. One robot have survived though. That's the one they kept in storage for a year or so. Looks like some kind of microid bug or virus. If the trend continues, we'll have lots more calls and hopefully lots more work of that type. They want us to investigate, in case it was tampered with. I jokingly told them they needed a microid doctor to put Humpty Dumpty back together again.'

'I suppose even he and the king's men couldn't put those Humpty Dumpties together again, and good old Doctor Longhurst and all his men are no longer on the scene,' Roseanne interjected. They couldn't help seeing the funny side of that sentence.

'It's a bad thing Professor Longhurst disappeared during that space voyage. Presumed permanently lost in space. Now there is no one with any real knowledge of microid technology to stop the spread of such a bug, if one exists,' Carl said.

'Anyway, that one will be your first case. I think it might be a good idea for one or both of you to get some library books on microids and begin studying the subject. It could be a money spinner if it were known that we were specialists in prevention, anti-contamination or infection prevention. Those robots are owned by the largest companies who wont mind parting with major bucks.'

'Interesting job!' Roseanne was enthusiastic.

'Nothing too difficult for two ex paras, eh. Just observation and questioning until you get a feel. That should get you back in the mood for some real work. Well then, do you both want to tackle this one?' Mallory asked.

'Yes, please! When can we start?' Roseanne was keen.

'I shall call them and say to expect you tomorrow morning at ten a.m, if that's ok.' Mallory retrieved a mini cellular phone from inside his jacket. It was no larger than a tie clip. He had the receiver part well hidden inside his ear without any wires.

All the main controls, including Mallory's main computer was on a thin broad belt around his waist. It also held his special gadgets. The belt itself was made from a special type of latex that looked exactly like his own hairy skin. The material absorbed shock impact and gave searching fingers the sensation that it was just soft fleshy tissue. Once installed, such equipment could be concealed from all types of detectors. Through his mobile station, as he called it, he could communicate to anywhere on the planet and use his main office computer for locating places and information. Nevertheless all his technology was about Class 3, while Solarian technology was Class 5 and above. That technological difference spanned about 100,000 years of advancement. Therefore he could never compete with the Green Chameleon or Phantom.

There was also a bullet proof vest of the same make for the upper part of the torso, but he seldom used that one, unless his life was seriously threatened.

'Is that Doctor Alison Morley.... This is Mallory from Alpha.... Can I send two of my security people along tomorrow at ten a.m., to check your robot's... remains?'

'That will be fine!' The doctor replied.

'It's all arranged. You are both expected at the hospital tomorrow morning and I would like your report in the afternoon. Here is the address and the name of your contact.' Mallory scribbled the details of their visit on a small pad.

'In the mean time I shall arrange your training. When you return from your first assignment, I will show you how to work the computer and simplify your reports. The computer uses speech recognition, but it will need a little time to get used to your different voices. It's not Daisy, but it's good enough for our purposes.' Mallory continued.

They remembered the intelligent computer, Daisy, and smiled.

CHAPTER 21

Microid infection

The Mount Pleasance Cardiovascular Clinic was situated on a hill overlooking Jersey City. It was set in several acres of beautiful gardens and one of the best in the area for heart transplants. It included an extensive convalescing home for those needing more intimate care on a twenty-four-hour basis. The beautiful gardens and recreation facilities were designed to aid quick recovery. Being one of the most auspicious hospitals in New York State it had a reputation to maintain.

At that time all the best hospitals utilized Microid Robots for greater precision and less operation trauma. Those robots, being of a nano-bot design, were twenty times faster than any human. They could make very small incisions within major organs, were infinitely more precise and had a more thorough map of the human anatomy all the way down to molecular levels. They could miss the smallest capillaries and nerves during complex operations. They were so accurate, they could even join or repair nerves and neurons. Therefore any loss of such equipment could have taken the medical profession back by at least half a century.

Since the unfortunate and publicised demise of Professor Longhurst and his other colleagues, who were responsible for bio-organ farming and Microid Robots, a virus had quickly spread through those farms killing off all the bio-trees. His robots were the only ones that remained in tact but the doctor's people were no longer around to service them.

One week after that catastrophe in space, several violent fires occurred in his main laboratories and domes. Perhaps by a gang that wanted to remove his advanced systems from the planet, but no one really knew the reasons why. During those fires the main buildings for maintaining such equipment and computers were destroyed. After that unfortunate tragedy, all supplies of bio-organs began to diminish and dried up a few months later. Soon after all forms of bio-organ transplants were once again depend-ant on donors which were presently at a relatively low level.

Several decades before microid robots were introduced in medical theatres for operations. All associated equipment had become a lot more complicated as a result. Complex pinhole operations that once took a day could now be completed within minutes, with the resultant reduction in blood loss and other discomforts to the patient. Not to mention their quick recovery.

Therefore it was not long before they were used by all the major hospitals in the northern hemisphere. Some hospitals became fully dependant on them, as they could be linked directly to their master computer systems for costing and maintaining a more thorough database.

Because of those reasons, experienced human surgeons soon became rear. Nevertheless the more backward countries still used the old methods and had improved their skills during the intervening years.

It was therefore to great surprise and even greater dismay when those large organizations found their microids had began to crumble into dust.

'We think they may have passed their sell-by dates, but how can we acquire new replacements when the original supplier is no longer with us,' said a disheartened doctor Kennedy.

'Yes, I am afraid that course seems unlikely, because their creator was lost in space with those who knew most about such things. The production plant was later burnt to the ground and after that time several distributors went out of business. May I suggest that you keep their dust in separate sealed containers. Just in case they can be revived at a later date,' Roseanne advised.

'Perhaps you can arrange storage for us until they can be revived. If at all possible?'

'In this case, we can!' Carl said.

'I am afraid all we can do at this time is look around and interview the people who witnessed the incident. Then we can decide whether it was caused by sabotage or some form of microid infection. In the mean time, may I suggest the good one be kept in its sealed container until every bit of the others have been cleared from this place. After they are properly contained we should place them in storage. That will further reduce or prevent any chance of viral contamination. And please ensure your people do not contaminate the microid dust with dirt or foreign bodies. They should also wear nasal filters, in case it can spread to humans, but I think it highly unlikely,' Carl said.

'No one is allowed in that area. Would you like to observe the one in the theatre? I have the key here. We sealed that area off and cancelled all difficult operations for the time being. Several patients are at risk, therefore we would like this problem resolved as soon as possible so we can commence our scheduled program. If not, we might have to send them to another hospital,' Doctor Kennedy said.

'Yes, Doctor, I am aware of the urgency of the situation. However, this problem might take some time to resolve, so may I suggest you quickly get hold of some foreign specialists in your field until we find answers. You should call your local senator and explain the problem to him. If that fails, call the relevant embassies and explain your situation to them and mention money. That word usually does the trick with those from developing countries,' Roseanne said while the doctor shook his head in dismay.

'We would also like to take some measurements of the dust pile before it's cleared up,' Carl said.

'Here are two nasal filters. Please come with me,' the doctor said as they followed her down the main corridor. The theatre was situated at the end and could be entered through two large sliding doors.

Although they opened automatically, they were under computer control, which prevented entry during operations or at other unscheduled periods. She slid her card-key into the slot and it opened.

'Here it is!' She pointed to the grey pile on the side of the special operation table. Being an operating theatre, the place was as clean as a whistle.

'You will have to excuse the smell. Most of it is to do with the microid remains,' the doctor said.

'I see what you mean. It smells like sulphur and rusty metal,' Roseanne replied, while adjusting her facials and trying to keep a straight face. Carl soon withdrew his retractable tape ruler and began to measure the pile and other important parts in its vicinity while taking photos of the scene. Roseanne took notes, reviewed several videos and finally drew a rough sketch of the room.

'Is this the only point of access?' Roseanne asked the doctor.

'Yes, except those four windows, but they are always kept closed. The computer controls the air circulation to this area and the vents are too small for anyone to enter. The air comes from the top of the building and is thoroughly filtered and checked before entering this area.'

Their operating theatre was on the fourth floor, with no fire escapes close to that part of the building.

Finally they were to interview the three doctors and two nurses that were at the scene.

'David... we gave him the name David after one of our co-founders... he had completed the final stitching to the patient's heart and continued to seal the small incisions. He... Please excuse me!' she cried while taking a handkerchief to her nose, 'he... the moment he completed the final stitch we could observe a sudden change in him. Then he took the stance of a statue, followed by an increase in temperature. Then he began to tremble and overheat, with bits of his face dropping off in the process. The scene was quite shocking.... I feel like I am going to throw up,' Cathy, the senior nurse said as she ran off to the ladies room.

'Luckily, he had the good sense to withdraw his hand tools from the patient, but the operation had been completed by then and the patient was functioning correctly.' Dr. Kennedy said.

'It was almost like he knew something was going to happen and hurried to complete the operation. Is there such a thing as a caring virus? One that ensures its host does not endanger human life before a fully blown infection sets in?' Dr. Simon said.

'Stranger and stranger,' Carl remarked.

'When I checked the dust pile there were no clothes within the powder. Don't they usually wear clothes?' Roseanne asked.

'No! Not during operations! It's more hygienic that way. That's because they have to be thoroughly disinfected each time and the process could be very time-consuming if they had to change each time. He just enters the microwave shower and the process is completed in seconds. However, the nurses dressed him in the past for parties and special occasions. He was treated like one of us. Well, he worked ten times more than any of us and deserved an occasional break. We could take him almost anywhere with his Portapak,' Dr. Barbara said and began to cry.

'I am sorry to ask these questions, but we have to get to the bottom of this and we haven't dealt with microids on such a personal basis before,' Carl said.

'One more thing: they are controlled from a microwave unit. Where is it now?' Roseanne asked.

'It's in the ceiling, close to the main light. I think he was controlled by three separate units for greater safety,' Dr. Kennedy said.

'If you don't mind, we'll have to visit the theatre again and have a last look around before we leave. Now, if there is anything else regarding this case that you think might be important to our investigation, please let us know. This is our card. You may call us on that number, day or night,' Carl said, while handing them some of Mallory's business cards.

By two p.m. they had finished their investigation at the hospital and decided to have a late lunch at Rosie's, before making an appearance at the office.

'Mallory left just half hour ago. He went back to the office,' Rosie said. They placed their order, paid their money and went to a corner table.

'What do you think? Three robots fragmenting almost at the same time and at three different locations. Do you think it could be coincidental?' Roseanne asked.

'No way! I am sure it's a computer type virus that can be triggered by an external stimulus. Either that or they have an inbuilt timer. I wonder what strange sounds, smells or radio wave sequences took place in that hospital on the day of the operation. Perhaps it was just an inbuilt safety procedure that was triggered when a part of the system began to fail? Either that or it was set to trigger when the microid reached a certain age,' Carl said.

'I think the first option might be the case. You will recall that most of the others within the city fragmented at different times. However, those that were in close proximity went down together, except of course, those that were isolated. So it couldn't have been due to random system failure or age. The chance of all three falling apart at the same time after twenty years of active service must be near impossible. Then again it could be a combination of all three, depending on environment and circumstances. The doctor was a super genius and those microid robots are highly intelligent,' Roseanne said.

'Do you think the good old Professor Longhurst could have put a delayed bug into those microids when they were created? Sort of inbuilt obsolescence to guarantee future sales of his products? One that could be transmitted to others in the vicinity once triggered through microwave or some other means?' Carl asked.

'Yes, Carl, I think you are on the right track, and he would have done it in such a way not to attract attention by people like us. Perhaps a range of different viruses that can be randomly triggered by different stimuli, but why in such a manner. It doesn't sound anything like the good old Doctor Longhurst I read so much about. He always put people before money and ma-chines. The man was a bloody genius and a perfect saint in every sense of the word,' Roseanne said.

'Perhaps one of his unsatisfied cronies put a spanner in the works to get their revenge,' Carl said.

'Why after twenty years? Anyway, if it's as devious as you think, no one I can imagine could ever do a thing like that,' Roseanne replied.

'I wish I had the answers to that sixty-four thousand-dollar question, but I still think your idea about the inbuilt bug and external triggers to be the most likely cause. Now, all we have to do is find the reasons why. He could have done it for some other more important and overriding purpose. You know... he was a very clever person, even clever at predicting the future.'

'It would be nice if he left information about those robots in a book somewhere. Even an old manual,' Carl said.

'No! I think the main building burnt down taking all that information from us. It is said he was a super genius in every sense, with an immeasurable IQ. Whatever he did could have been for some overriding purpose and there are no library books. All his work was covered by strict patents. Anyway, who on Earth would understand any of it now,' Roseanne replied.

'I wonder what that purpose was? I suppose we better show our ugly mugs at the office,' Carl said and both placed a tip and left.

Ohhhh! Finally the return of the prodigals! How did it go?' Mallory asked.

'It went like a dream. I thought I lost it, but the moment I began looking the place over and asked a few questions, the old skills surfaced. Mal, this one is a great mystery, with many puzzles,' Roseanne said as she began to explain their findings.

'Sounds interesting. I want it all in the database, including your final assumptions. By the way, I had another call before lunch. It's exactly the same problem in another hospital. This time, it's in Manhattan.'

'Another! They are dropping like flies!' Roseanne exclaimed.

'Would you like to take that one on as well? You both seamed to have done so well today. I think you've cracked it,' Mallory said.

'Yes, please!' Roseanne replied, always revving to go.

'In that case, I think you both deserve a month's pay in advance. Just in case you could do with a little extra cash this week, and now, let me show you both how to use my ingenious computer.'

'That will be great, Mal!'

'This little AI piece of important hardware was my going away present from the President, and top of the range then.' Mallory handed them two packets, each containing five thousand dollars.

'Wow! I haven't seen that many notes in a very long time. Are you sure, Mal!' Roseanne was ecstatic.

'You guys deserve it!'

They spent all of that afternoon learning everything they could about the computer. When they were confident enough, they sat at two separate monitors to enter their data. It took them a further two hours to compile their first reports. They were amazed by the professional look of those documents. Even the bad grammar was appropriately corrected. The complete document had been compiled from somewhat haphazard verbal utterances.

'You guys are a lot better than I thought. When you get used to the keyboard and mouse I shall teach you a few easy tricks. Anyway, she has a full dictionary and can analyse sentences better than a person with average education. This can be done in English and eight other commonly used languages, including Chinese. Functions include auto translation if required, so she is a beauty once you learn how to use her. Even so, this computer could never be as good as Clair or Daisy,' he said and they remembered those clever computers and wondered whether they were still around at the manor.

CHAPTER 22

A strange encounter with an incredible car

Mallory had cashed the Bankers Draft and felt more financially secure than he had since leaving the White House. His main task ahead was in improving his business. He knew that with clever criminals about, he had to acquire the best protection for his new operatives. He also realized special protective suits and devices did exist in the past when he went on covert assignments, but he had been away from such activity for many years.

Nevertheless his immediate requirement was to change his battered elepet transport to one that would get him in and out of traffic more quickly and without the constant need for electric charging, petrol or ethanol fuel.

'I can now invest in a used LPD Roadstar and save the other one hundred and fifty-grand for sundries and running expenses. For once in my pathetic life I can take to the air in a super car and be truly mobile again. Not being held up on some bumpy road tooting my horn in lengthy traffic, while on an urgent assignment with power running low,' Mallory thought, while struggling out of his apartment sofa. He used it as a temporary bed when he was extra tired.

'It's a nice day! A nice day!' Daisy his parrot announced. He drew the curtains to observe the almost clear sky with bright sunlight everywhere.

'Sometimes, I do believe you just pretend you are a bird,' Mallory said and open her cage.

'Pretend! Pretend!' she said and flew out, dropping a feather at his feet. It was then that he remembered the strange parrot Lennox showed him. It had hands in addition to wings and could play the piano like a concert pianist.

'We shall never know exactly how clever you guys really are or how you see our universe. Not until we can get into your heads

and sea it exactly as you do,' he said looking at the bird,
  'Exactly! Exactly!' the parrot replied and he agreed.

LPD Roadstars were the best available means of transport. They could travel through the atmosphere as efficiently as they could on land when there was less traffic about. They added much greater mobility, being able to leapfrog above buildings and cars within laser controlled air lanes and at great speed. Presently the population of New York was 22 million and rising, which made any form of surface transport a virtual nightmare, with criminals and pickpockets everywhere. Many used the dense crowds as cover for their crime. But a good LPD Roadstar eliminated most of those problems.

They also had a manual override with inbuilt guidance controls for following the laser skyways at higher altitudes and at even higher speeds. Despite those facilities, many preferred remaining closer to old terra firma.

With auto-routing and satellite guidance, those computer cars could find their way about much more efficiently than their electric or fuel driven counterparts and didn't always require light to find their way about in the dark.

The old petrol and later, Elepet cars, were becoming collectors' items, since most of the major manufacturers had turned their attention to Linea Progressive Drive technology (Lpds). Those new types of transport with their special drives could nullify the effect of gravity and focus inertia to cause motion in any given direction. Their drives were based on hydrogen fusion and used pure hydrogen for energy. Such cars could travel across the globe in minutes instead of hours. However intercontinental flights were seldom made with LPD street cars. Those vehicles required special insulation, oxygen and air pressurization for the space-ways which were at higher altitudes. Further, a special pilot's license was required. Intercontinental passengers could journey on large shuttle craft in better luxury and comfort.

The door buzzer rang and Mallory rushed from the kitchen to answer the door phone. He was in the middle of preparing himself an English breakfast.

'Who is it?' he shouted tiredly through the door intercom.

'We have a delivery for you, Sir!' the male voice shouted back.

'Give it to security for me!' he replied, hoping to get rid of the nuisance. He was not expecting a parcel and had never received anything at his home address in months.

'No, Sir, I can't do that! It's a car! A new Roadstar and you are to sign for it!' he insisted.

Mallory immediately began searching for his clothes which were strewn about the living room. In another moment he darted towards the elevator with his shirt unbuttoned.

'It must be a mistake. Who could have sent it?' he asked the uniformed driver.

'The name is on the docket, Sir!' the driver replied.

'Solarian Banking...' the address read and he immediately signed the square and was briskly given the top copy.

'Solarian Banking? It must be on loan from them. Someone may have seen my old and battered Elepet banger, and decided to take pity on a poor overworked investigator. But what a bloody surprise,' he said to himself while moving closer to the vehicle.

'Those people must really mean business. That little nipper must be some important...' he was going to say "son of a bitch" with out-of-control excitement but held those words back. He slowly walked around the new vehicle admiring its contours while touching its every curve like he would his favourite woman. Then he slid the Micro-card key into the door and it lifted vertically with a slight hiss.

'Please enter!' a voice said and he sat into the nearest padded seat. The control panel slid to one side as the seat adjusted itself to his posture. It was one of those very expensive dual models that could be used throughout the planet. It also included extra aerodynamics needed for intercontinental flight.

'Please enter your voice print by saying a few of your favourite words,' the voice said.

'You are the most beautiful car in the whole wide world,' he replied.

'That will do. You may use "the most beautiful car" for future voice identification. Now, you may place your right hand on the illuminated pad while looking at the rear mirror for visual identification,' the voice again said and he followed its instructions.

'What a security system and it's fully voice activated. What a bloody car!' he exclaimed in astonishment still not quite believing his fortune.

'My poor mother would sing in her grave if she could see me now.'

'Would you like to drive, Sir?' the voice asked.

'No...! Why don't you take me for a spin instead. Not too far though?' The car shot vertically like a bullet, almost flattening him against the soft reclining seat in the process. Although he tried his hardest to connect his safety harness manually, he could barely have moved his hands. They appeared to weigh a ton due to the extra gravitational forces.

As if by magic the seat began to take his shape and a flexible metallic harness slid around his body. There were some more adjustments. He felt more comfortable but still compressed. Then a type of anti-gravity field came on and he felt normally seated again, even when the car was still accelerating. The car suddenly came to an abrupt stop and began a new course towards a large satellite.

'Sorry, only limited anti G's in this model!' the pleasant male voice said and Mallory remained silent, shocked and amazed by the incredible speed. The clever car was obviously impressing him of its tremendous capabilities.

'What a beautiful sight,' he said as he watched the globe of Earth beneath, and not too distant, the shining outline of satellite Eta. It was the second largest artificial satellite orbiting Earth. Both images filled the screen in his car.

He was about ten thousand miles above Earth and wondered how he could have travelled that great distance in under fifteen minutes. Here he was gazing at one of the best views in the Solar System.

The experience made him feel at one with God. He wondered how long the Roadstar would have taken to Moon-base, but kept that thought to himself in case the car decided to take its meaning literally. He wondered how much oxygen there were on board, how much was left and whether the Roadstar would have withstood the rigours of space over that journey.

Mallory was a trained pilot and had at times taken his place in the cockpit of fighter bombers, although more in helicopters. That was before he joined the paras, seeking more adventure on land with a team of commandoes that were well trained in every conceivable method including hand-to-hand combat. To him, that was much better than throwing bombs from great heights or dodging missiles at lower altitudes. Anyway, these days those explosive jobs were done by clever drones with operators thousands of miles away. Using remote viewing they could even be controlled by kids in a games scenario. They wouldn't know if they were killing a real person in that particular game.

However that Roadstar was something else. Never before had he experienced such extreme acceleration. He wondered what other surprises the car had in store for him.

The car continued to career towards satellite Eta which was even at a higher altitude until he could observe the small image of satellite Gimbal rising from Earth's terminator. Gimbal was the largest of all artificial satellites ever built. It contained a three-kilometre diameter sphere that constantly rotated within two outer rings, that were themselves in constant precession. Its motion was truly spectacular when observed from Earth through a telescope. The internal surface of that satellite contained a large city with several of the best hotels, lakes, small forests and parks.

Both satellites, Gimbal and Eta, belonged to Solarian Banking and were doubtlessly the greatest engineering feats of mankind, although built by robots.

The car came to a sudden stop and was slowly pulled into Eta by an invisible force with a greenish glow. Mallory was stunned by its reality, for never in all his existence had he experienced such strangeness. He found his body being pulled in different directions within the car, while under the influence of some strange nullifying energy beam.

The car entered three consecutive docks. At the final dock several operators dressed in white overalls approached. One carried what looked like a large weapon. The car door opened with a depressurization hiss.

'Please remain seated while you are decontaminated,' said the one with blue collar stripes. The gun was pointed and radiation flooded the car and its contents.

'Please follow me,' he continued and Mallory was escorted to a nearby elevator, but did not complain. He was too curious. He could observe many robots and androids assembling and carrying out repairs on delicate equipment. When the elevator stopped its doors slid open. He was taken to a most comfortable waiting room. It occurred to him that the whole satellite had almost normal gravity throughout, while no space suits were used by anyone.

Just ahead of him was a transparent screen with a view of Earth. Its image was stationary, making him think it could not have been a direct view since the satellite was constantly rotating. Any view from that position would have been of a constantly shifting globe.

Towards the left of the screen was a large fish-tank with several colourful carp swimming about. A figure dressed in cream with winged multi-coloured insignia on his left shoulder was feeding them with a brown substance. He suddenly stopped and glanced in Mallory's direction.

'Mallory, please join me over here. Come and see my fish,' Ben said. Mallory briskly walked in his direction.

'I am pleased to meet you, Mallory. You may call me Professor Khan or simply Ben if you wish. Please help yourself to a glass. It's fresh orange juice. I am non-alcoholic and a strict vegetarian.'

'Ok! Thanks!'

'I was given these beautiful creatures fifteen years ago by a Japanese friend. They will live pass a hundred in this artificial environment, with virtually no diseases.'

'They are really quite beautiful. How are you able to feed them when you are away, on Earth?' Mallory inquired.

'I could have rigged an automatic feeder, but they are too dear to me. So I have assigned one of my look-alikes... an android that was made in my own image, so to speak. They are unable to tell the difference and he is quite competent at his job.'

'Wow! I see what you mean.'

'Now, let's talk business. Shall we?' Ben said, as they both moved towards the large transparent screen and began to view Earth.

'Motion compensation has been added to the image by our Macron computer. Truly a beautiful planet. Don't you think?'

'Yes! I do!'

'By the way, it's my grandson that you have been assigned to find.'

'I see!'

'The car has been thrown in to aid your search. It's an older model, so you are welcomed to keep it once you have signed the relevant release documents. My grandson is quite dear to me, so no expense will be spared in the search. However, there is another important matter I would like to discuss and it concerns human survival on Earth.' Mallory took a sip and swallowed hard in anticipation.

'There is a crisis brewing in the wind. One that will eventually tear the human race apart and you have been chosen to assist in their survival.'

'Really?'

'You have recently met with the Group of Thirteen? Well, they are harmless enough. Just another so-called save-our-world committee of wealthy industrialists and bankers. They are not happy with the way things are going, but have little teeth to implement relevant change. Then, there are the conservationist and others doing likewise, including extremists, willing to resort to any type of force as an alternative. Some of those are even affiliated with the largest crime syndicates on the planet, but most of them wouldn't sacrifice a thing they owned for our beautiful and loving planet.'

'You are very right!'

'To cut a long story short, our scientists have found a human disorder, call it a deadly targeting disease, if you like. It will eventually cause the complete extinction of all human life on Earth within a few generations.'

'What the...?'

'Yes, I'm afraid so. Once infected by the disease, it cannot be treated, neither can it be eradicated from Earth within a normal lifetime. Luckily for some, it has not completely spread to all individuals yet and tend to somewhat refrain from affecting the young before puberty. But you see the problem. All humans beyond puberty will never be able to bear offspring if infected. This situation will lead to the mass extinction of our human race well within a period of one hundred years or so.'

'My God! You can't be serious!'

'I am afraid so. This particular Terminal Disease appeared in China about ten years ago and has since spread through Asia and Europe, while working its way across the globe. It will continue to spread to other parts of the globe by tourism and such like. We are now working on an antidote, but it can only be administered to the young if caught in time. Only then will they be able to have children.'

'What a bloody shocker! What am I to do? What can I do to help?'

'When the time is right, you are to take this report to a national news agency and make these findings generally known to mankind before the disease becomes too well established. The knowledge of this plague will undoubtedly lead to more immediate cures. However, we of Solarian Banking had to warn Earth of the impending disaster and you appear to be the best person for that important task.' Mallory patiently listened to every disturbing word.

'Sorry, Sir, but don't you think such public knowledge could be disastrous once tests were available and people realised they couldn't have kids. Every young family could become targets for kidnappers and con men,' Mallory replied.

'Yes, Mallory, I do realise the problem, but everyone has a right to know. It would be deceitful and unethical if we did otherwise. Honesty is essential here. The patient must be told of his ailment irrespective of the consequences. Only then will society be able to formulate a proper survival plan.'

'I see what you mean, but it's going to create no end of problems!'

'Do you know what will happen when this news is made public? Well, let me tell you. First of all there will be disbelief. Then tests and confirmation. Those with young children will realise their vulnerability and find safety in numbers well away from the major cities. You are to assist those as best you can, but it will not take place for several years yet, so you have time to prepare. I am sure most families will give you a small fortune if you found them safety. Some of the money you make from such ventures through our organization could be used to aid the poorer and less fortunate families.' Mallory continued listening to the strange story from the professor, with trepidation and bewilderment, but took the folder from him.

'This is really bad news! I shall have to consider all this. I mean, what you just said about the end of humanity. My God, this whole thing is almost unbelievable. Any way, when will be the right time to release this!'

'Immediately after I speak to the press on this topic!' Ben said.

'I would like your advice on another matter, however. Microid robots are turning to dust in many of our major hospitals. Is there any way in which we can revive them or even acquire some replacements? I ask, because I am concerned. Such failure in hospitals mean suffering for many unfortunate patients. Can you help?' Mallory asked.

'They can only be revived for two years at most, I am afraid. Many years ago, Jeff... sorry I meant Professor Longhurst, decided that there was a small probability of microids getting into the hands of gangsters and criminals. That was one of the main reasons why they could only have been programmed during production. Because of that reason they were given a disruption code sequence that could be initiated after they had completed what was considered a useful lifetime. However, the viral codes could also be transmitted to others of a similar programming within close proximity. The microid virus can only strike after the robot or android had completed its current task. Thus preventing premature failure while in the middle of an operation, for instance.'

'I see!'

'Some things do not live forever, you know, and it just so happens that their operational period have come to an end. In order to revive them you will need a Revitalizer and some Constructor Microids. You must mix them with the original sample in precise quantities; like flower and salt when making bread, if you get my meaning.'

'I think I understand?'

'I shall contact the chief of engineering and see if he has a spare unit and microids. After you have thoroughly mixed the sample, simply point the funnel part of the device towards it, then pull the trigger as you would a gun,' Ben said.

After a few seconds had passed an engineer entered and handed Ben a container the size of a shoe box. A large can of Constructor Microids had already been placed in the trunk of his car.

'Here you are.' Ben handed Mallory the item.

'I must pay you some money for this device and the microids,' Mallory said, feeling awkward at Ben's generosity.

'Personally, I do not deal in money, but if you wish to make recompense, please concentrate your efforts in locating my grandson and assist us in our future programs towards Earth. This will include finding us the occasional pair of endangered animal or plant species. We have created a refuge for them on another world that is unsuitable for Earth humans,' Ben said and Mallory nodded confusedly.

'One final question before I leave. You didn't even call that engineer. How could he have known of our conversation?' Mallory asked.

'Friend, between you and I, we use brain implants that allow us to directly communicate with each other and the wider world. Call it a type of telepathy if you like. However, like any complicated system, it takes some getting used to and I can't say any more than that,' Ben replied.

'Gosh, some technology you have in this place,' Mallory said, completely aghast by the idea, although he could see the purpose for efficiency's sake.

The meeting was terminated and a somewhat confused Mallory was escorted to his car by the original supervisor.

CHAPTER 23

A new reality

Eta, was shaped like two inverted elongated pyramids on either side of a rotating tubular toroid. The toroid was held to the central pyramids by a large hub through several spokes. The toroid contained the main laboratories, while the central pyramids were used mainly for accommodation and recreation. The spokes contained the transportation systems and passages to and from those areas.

A large elevator took passengers from the docks, at the two extremities of the stem, to that area. The stem contained accommodation modules throughout its length and breath. That part constantly rotated in an anticlockwise direction, giving those areas a sense of gravity. However, LPD type devices were used to focus gravity throughout the structure at approximately 10 metres per second squared.

Mallory kept his eyes on the massive structure as it slowly receded from him and couldn't get the bewildering thought of mankind's extinction out of his head. Suddenly he realised the significance as a type of fear he never knew before welled up within him. Then Ben's grandson came to mind. Even the wealthiest human child in the universe shrunk to insignificance by comparison. A once complete planet of humans, never to be seen or heard of again in the history of the universe. What a catastrophe of all catastrophes. He always sensed something was wrong and now he knew exactly why. Thank goodness the Green Chameleon guy was taking out the worst criminals like there was no tomorrow. He obviously had inside knowledge of worse to come. But he was fearless and hated them to a point of revulsion. I wonder if he lost a love one like I did by the hands of such crims.

He could imagine dead cities overgrown by weed and infested with all forms of insects, rodents and smaller mammals. There would be cockroaches and vermin of every description taking whatever advantages they could. The whole world once again being covered by forests and deserts, the way things used to be before man's presence was felt by the eco-sphere. But there had to be survivors. Those in the forests who lived in remote places well away from the cities and isolated from modern civilization. But if the plague was air and water borne even those would be infected in time and the disease had already been around for a decade. Perhaps encircling the globe several times since. God alone knows how far it could have spread in that time.

Without an antidote everyone was doomed. He wondered whether he had the disease, but realised he would not be able to tell until suitable tests had been developed. Many scientists would be sceptical at first. His main concern was for his son, Andy, but he was still an adolescent and susceptible to a cure if one could be found in time.

After all, he was just a modest investigator and despite a few old friends in Washington DC and the publishing business, hadn't that much clout. Perhaps the famous Group of Thirteen could help spread the bad news? But they only saw him on the thirteenth of each month and never held a meeting in the same hotel more than once. Always notifying him two days in advance.

'Why thirteen?' he thought aloud. He also thought about Ben and his alien technologies, including what he said about a different world like Earth for animals, but not suitable for Earth humans.

'What other types of humans were they suitable for? Perhaps he meant uninfected types,' Mallory mumbled to himself, utterly confused and bemused by his first visit to Satellite Eta.

This time the car landed on the top of his apartment building, in a small area that was reserved for those rear occupants with that type of transport. He had to make that fact clear to reception, to permanently book that space and immediately descended the elevator to the lobby.

When he arrived at his apartment he was famished and decided to prepare a large breakfast before visiting the office. It was to be the original English breakfast with lots of coffee and double bacon and eggs. He sprayed black pepper and ketchup on indiscriminately. He never felt like drinking alcohol when he was in such a distressed state. He only had an appetite for food. Lots of food.

'I'm going to be very late at the office today and the guys haven't got a key. What a bloody morning. Have I been dreaming? First, a present of the car I always wanted and then the worst shock of my life. A car that moves faster than any aircraft and a satellite with a controllable gravity beam unknown to Earth. They even have the technology to revive microids and carry brain implants. They must be another of those breakaway human groups.' He place some seeds in the parrot's cage.

'With all those advanced robots and androids, Solarian Banking must be some incredible organization. Now I know what the doctor meant when he said Mickey and Ben were more important than the President. But how much more? Good God, what are we dealing with here? What are they really?' he constantly chatted to himself, then switched-on the small radio on the kitchen sink to add some more tangibility to his flustered world. After breakfast he decided to hide the folder until his next meeting with the Group of Thirteen, but took the small container with the microid revitalizer and made his way to the special car park on the roof of his office.

Mallory was worried about the Terminal Disease, but also of the repercussions should he be blamed for the release of Ben's information prematurely. He had to find a way to do it on the quiet and incognito. He knew of a few important people in the business, so he listed a few numbers in his diary for calling.

'Car, Please take us to my office. Let me show you,' he said as a small computer screen slid out of the dash board with a thumbwheel. It was voice activated, so a keyboard was not necessary. He simply moved the pointer to the street involved and spoke to the computer giving it the full address.

'Got it, Mal. Is there an available park on the roof?' the car asked.

'There is usually several blank spaces, so help yourself!' Mallory replied.

'Don't bother, Mal. I have checked the address given. There are six vacant spaces,' the car replied and they were off. When he arrived back in the office Carl and Roseanne were nowhere to be found. He handed the office keys to the receptionist and told her to expect Carl and Roseanne and left to follow up on his other plans.

CHAPTER 24

A new base

The experience of that morning had knocked Mallory off balance and in the process, his innermost senses to the core. Within that new model of reality he could see himself participating in a global purpose, where he was the captain at the helm taking mankind to a safer shore through the worst storms ever encountered.

There was so much to do that required much planning. He didn't want to tell anyone of his experiences that morning, or his new purpose in case they thought he was going loopy. After hearing such a tale, who would ever dare trust him as a detective again.

He viewed his cramped office and immediately got on the phone to a local estate agent.

'What have you got in the way of commercial premises?'

'What type do you want? I have lists and lists of the damn things. Don't you know we are in the middle of one of the worst property slumps since the late thirties? So we can give you almost anything you desire at a most reasonable price and with a better than ninety-five percent mortgage, if you wish,' the agent said, enthusiastically.

'How much can I get for a deposit of a hundred grand? Let's say, one-hundred grand cash on the nail,' Mallory said.

'About three million to be on the safe side and you don't have to pay a cent for the first year,' the agent replied.

'Can I see a few? I can take you around in my Roadstar if you like. It will save us both lots of time,' Mallory said.

'When can you make it?'

'Right now, if you don't mind.'

'You've got our address so I'll be waiting?' the agent said and Mallory immediately ran out of the office.

'I have prepared a list for you. It contains some of the best properties in one of the quieter areas, just outside the city. They have their own car parks and are fully licensed.' While they walked towards the car Mallory got close to his door and pressed his fingers on the glass and the doors lifted vertically.

'What a bloody car you've got here! Must be worth five million at least? This model was reserved for a few VIPs, including the President. I know, because I read all about it on the bulletin a year ago. Cars are one of my hobbies and Roadstars are top of the league,' the agent said. Mallory was astonished by that knowledge. He thought it was a G model and in all the excitement of the past few hours, hadn't notice the LX plate near the front grill. The LX was a top of the line model and worth ten times more than his original estimate.

'What an expensive present,' Mallory thought.

They viewed four buildings in the areas he preferred but he fell in love with the third one. It had four floors with its own elevators. The fourth was reserved for offices and had been suitably partitioned. The other three floors could have been used for any purpose, baring certain legal restrictions.

'I shall take this one,' Mallory said, pointing to the picture on his sheet.

'In that case, let's get back to the office and finalize the deal.'

When it was ended, the agent shook his hand and handed him the keys. Then he went directly to the building to look it over more closely. This time he parked the Roadstar on the roof.

'Thank you, dearest Solarian Banking. Without your helping hand I would never have got this far ahead in such a short time.' Mallory kissed and slid the card key in the lock.

The building needed cleaning and slight touching with paint, but it had a sound structure and much potential with some surrounding land for future expansion. It was ex bankruptcy and previous occupants had vacated only recently. At least within the last year.

'Wait till I tell Roseanne and Carl the good news,' he thought.

When he returned to the office they had also returned from their assignment and busy with their reports.

'Ah..., there you are! Stop whatever you are doing! I have an important announcement to make and I need your undivided attention, because it also concerns you.' They stopped their keyboard operations and sat on the sofa in front of his desk.

'We have known each other for a long time. Haven't we?' he asked and both nodded in agreement.

'Well, if we are partners, that means we are also to trust each other and never mention any matters concerning our business to anyone, and that includes our best friends, wives and husbands, unless of course they are also part of the business. Because, they can innocently mention something to someone and those few words could get in the wrong ears,' he stressed in no uncertain terms.

'We understand the implications, Mal. After all, we have been fully vetted by Pentagon security in the past,' Roseanne replied.

'In that case, what I am to tell you is absolutely confidential and must never leave this room.' They nodded in agreement again, but with utter curiosity.

'Our human race is becoming extinct. I mean, the whole human race, all over the world. It's to do with some bug in the land, air and water that is being transmitted to everyone. It shows no symptoms and stops childbirth completely. In one hundred years from now there will be no one left if an antidote is not found soon. I suppose that is one of the reasons why children over here are being stolen and sent to places like Europe and Asia where the plague started over five years ago.'

'You are not kidding! Are you?' Roseanne said, impatiently but with sadness.

'We don't know to what extent it has spread throughout the planet. In particular North America, as no one over here have tested for it. Solarian Banking have carried out tests and as far as they are concerned, some of the grown-ups over here are infected. However, children before the age of puberty are immune and could remain that way if we had an antidote.'

'You think there is a cure or antidote?' Roseanne asked.

'Solarian Banking is currently working on one, but they are not sure when it will be ready. So you see our problem.'

'You mean... I might never have any kids of my own?' Roseanne interrupted, with utter astonishment.

'I don't know...! We live in a big city and those types of bugs tend to spread uncontrollably in such populated environments. Let's pray it hasn't travelled this far yet,' Mallory said.

'What can we do?' Carl asked, sympathetically.

'Very soon we move to our new base and make plans to assist young families. We also have to recover those kids that have been stolen with a squad of specials that are trained in the latest art of combat. Young women will be tested as soon as possible by a set of trained nurses from our organization. We'll try to keep them on a special diet and isolated as best we can from exposure to the public. All those factors I must discuss with Ben. He is the one with real power and also the President of Solarian Banking.'

'This is very bad news,' Carl said.

'Professor Bengizara Khan (Ben) of Solarian Banking?' Roseanne found the whole situation quite unbelievable.

'The very same! All this could be another money spinner for our security company, but I don't want to profit at the expense of the poor and suffering. We could create a special charity fund where a large percentage of our profits could be used to aid such victims. After all, it's the human race we are talking about here,' Mallory said.

'We need a master plan. People must be told of this Terminal Disease for the scientists and others to become interested enough to find a cure,' Roseanne replied.

'Yes, I have been given the same advise by Ben. I have decided to make the relevant facts known to certain important people on the thirteenth of next month. When I am sure the bad news is getting around in the higher levels of society, I shall quietly slip it to the press. Then all hell will break loose. Hopefully by that time our organization will be ready to take advantage of the situation. Anyway, there is another matter I have to discuss with you.'

'Another one?' Roseanne inquired.

'Not another bad one?' Carl inquired.

'No!'

'Thank goodness for that!' she had as much as she could take.

'Fellow partners, I have just bought us our own building for three and a half million bucks. It will be used for our new offices, storage, medics and training. In future we give special rates, including insurance, to anyone wanting to store their microid dust with us, and we charge a fee of fifteen thousand dollars to defragment and revitalize any dead microid. What do you think of my idea?' Mallory said.

'I think your idea is bloody brilliant. But how are we to put them back together again from dust?' Roseanne inquired.

'I have been given a special device and microids that can do the job for us. Mind you, the process will only last another two years, but that's enough time for them to train human surgeons. That will also be the limit of our guarantee,' Mallory replied.

'I'll believe it when I see it. Sounds too far-fetched for me!' Carl said, smiling and Mallory slowly withdrew the strange looking gun from its container.

'If you think this is incredible, wait till you see my new car. This gun transmits a neutralizing code by microwave. First you have to thoroughly mix the dust with a small quantity of what he calls Constructor Microids. It's the bluish powder within a container in the back of my new car. The relative quantities are given on the label.'

'Your new car, Mal! What kind is it?' She inquired.

'You just wait and see!' he replied.

'Regarding our robot piles. Hopefully, the dust will begin to reform into the original microid, warts and all, immediately afterwards. You just point it towards the pile of dust like so and pull the trigger like you would a normal gun. Then the Microids become alive and take form. Like bringing Lazarus forth from the grave. There is an included video training manual that can be displayed on the little rear screen and the whole thing is driven by a mini nuclear power-pack. However, you must be sure that all the dust is present within its field of view before pressing the trigger.'

'That sounds bloody scary, to me. I hope it doesn't affect people,' Carl intimated.

'No! It doesn't! Don't worry about details, we'll have a special rig set up with an electric mixer. Moulds could be installed in our new place for that purpose. This gun can be fitted above the microid target and controlled by computer. That will save the operator lots of time,' Mallory said. They were astonished by his incredible ingenuity.

'That puts us out of a job,' Carl said.

'No, that makes you more busy, because the moment I am sure we can handle real numbers, I shall send our brochures and emails to every hospital and large organizations in the land. By that time we'll be wearing our Specials uniform. Then you will be attending those places to receive their microids and advice them on future changes. So don't you worry on that score.'

'What's next?' She inquired.

'I have something else to show you. It's a present from Solarian Banking. I met the big chief today on Satellite Eta... and what an operation they have on that satellite. They make our technologies here on Earth look like kids play.'

'You went all that way without an expensive shuttle?' Suddenly she became excited.

'I did! And did you know that my Roadstar was pulled into the satellite by an invisible beam and I couldn't do a thing to stop it. Even my brain was affected. It's like they are another race of... people.'

'Sounds so bloody cool and exciting!' Carl said.

'Anyway, he gave me that microid toy and he simply transmitted a thought to the guy in stores without even moving his lips. We could do with some of that stuff, you know.'

'You actually went to satellite Eta today?' Carl asked with astonishment.

'My new car took me there. It's fully automatic and voice activated. It's worth at least five million. That is what I was told by the estate agent who sold me the building,' Mallory replied.

'Where is the car now?' Roseanne asked, equally curious.

'It's on the roof, twelve floors up. Why don't we take the lift and you can see for yourselves?' They could not wait and were soon out of the office and on their way to the topmost floor. They were so excited, they couldn't contain their emotions and left all their work behind.

'This place is mostly unused and handy for me,' Mallory said.

When they saw the beautiful silvery car, they couldn't believe their eyes.

'It's so large. How many can it seat in comfort?' Carl asked.

'Just eleven, but there is lots of space for food, oxygen, water and other necessaries for intercontinental and even planetary trips. You can have my old car if you like, until you can afford your own Roadstar. I shall be signing it over to the company, anyway.'

'What a beautiful vehicle!' Roseanne said, as she slid her fingers across the very slippery bodywork.

Mallory used the card-key this time and slid it into the almost invisible door slot. The doors lifted and they were amazed by the comfortable upholstery and panel technology.

'I call him, Oscar, after an old buddy in the air-force. That was before I joined the paras. He was always in a hurry, but was also extremely good at his job,' Mallory said.

'How fast can Oscar go?' Carl asked.

'I don't know for sure, but we probably did about forty thousand miles an hour average when we visited Eta. He took under fifteen minutes to make the trip of over ten thousand miles,' Mallory replied.

'Whoops! You really have a space ship here. Retractable wheels, expandable fins, for finer atmospheric control... and God knows what else. We must take her for a good spin one of these days,' Carl replied.

'Yes! But it's a him and I suppose he came with the works. And we can go for a little spin right now if you like.'

'Really?' Roseanne was ecstatic.

'Oscar, take us to the new factory!' Mallory said.

'Yes, Mal,' replied the car to their utter amazement and in a perfect male voice. The car shot vertically and made a few complicated manoeuvres. They thought they were on one of the monster rides in one of the larger fun fairs. Before they could count to one hundred the car had settled down on the roof of their new building and the relevant doors lifted. They didn't know what to expect and never had a speedier flight in all their lives.

'Now you know why I call him Oscar,' Mallory said as they slowly recovered from the shock and began to drag their shaken bodies out of the car. He opened the door and they entered the large building.

'You also have a percentage in this place, you know, but you will have to put a percent of your profits into paying your share of the mortgage, but not for another year. Anyway, we can discuss that matter later.'

'Are you really serious, Mal?' Roseanne could not believe his last words.

'I couldn't be more serious! Well, what do you think?' Mallory said.

'Our own company? I can't believe it. So bloody posh we have become. This place can easily hold five hundred people. Are you serious about asking us to join you in this... enterprise?' Roseanne asked again, with disbelief written all over her face. She still couldn't accept the implications of their own business within their own premises and in such a short time.

'Well, we are going places together and I think this is a trip you shouldn't miss. Also, I think you guys brought me the luck I've been waiting for. Since you arrived everything has changed for the better,' Mallory replied.

'Captain Mallory Colman, I love you!' Roseanne said and hugged and kissed him.

They viewed each floor in turn and Mallory decided to take them to Rosie's for another late lunch.

'This is one place I'll miss when we move from this area. I suppose we'll have a canteen at our place as well. We can still hold on to the old office as cover. It might come in handy for certain operations. Anyway, you can both handle the microid side of the business from now. For that program I think the first floor is ideal for our new program. What do you think?

'I don't know. I haven't given it much thought, to be honest,' Roseanne replied.

'Yea! I think the ground floor can be used for reception, security and some storage. The roof should only be made accessible to senior members of staff,' Carl said.

'Why don't you both work something out on paper and I can get the builders in to make the necessary changes? When the tests and antidote becomes available, we'll have to administer the stuff, so we'll need some form of surgery and a complete floor for distribution. Then there is the missing children's section, other odd investigative and security jobs. It's a pity the police are so thinly spread and fully employed with all the crime about these days. What do you think?' Mallory said.

'As for crime, I think our Green Chameleon guy is taking care of that for us, but he wont be around forever,' Roseanne said.

'It's all too fantastic!' Carl replied.

'Are you certain they will find a cure?' Roseanne asked.

'It's quite probable that Solarian Banking already has a cure, but they have to go through the motions and let us find out for ourselves; otherwise they could be accused for supplying medicine under false pretences. Anyway, how can they already have a cure when no one knows about the disease. When the disease is officially listed, only then can they make a statement to the medical fraternity about a tested cure,' Mallory said and Roseanne's eyes lit up with hope.

'We now have five piles of dust. That should bring us... seventy-five grand,' Carl said, with a twinkle in his eyes.

'Say fifty-four grand. If we let them have the first one at fifteen grand and decide to do the others at say... eight grand a piece, if they are all processed at the same time. People tend to make quick decisions when they are given a discount on quantity. That will prevent them from holding on to the others or putting them into permanent storage until they are needed. Better eight grand now, when we need the money and it prevents a second and third call to the customer's premises. Not to mention storage facilities and other inconveniences.'

'Yea! I like the discount idea,' Carl replied.

'By the way, we also charge for storage. And that price doesn't include the investigative part of the job, so they must be kept separate when billing the customer. In future, jobs will have to be broken down into different categories and that one includes investigation, microid engineering, storage and sundries like delivery.'

'Yea! Very sensible!' Roseanne was enthusiastic.

'First thing tomorrow, you must find out about warehouse prices and insurance for such items, because we don't want to over-charge our customers. I sometimes find it a good idea to send them separate bills on each item as it's completed. That is better than putting it all on one enormous bill,' Mallory said and they both agreed.

'When do we go for training?' Roseanne asked.

'From next Monday, for two weeks. I contacted Chad from the car and both your names are already on his list.

'You mean we are going to see our old mate, Chad?' Roseanne exclaimed.

'Yes, the same. We've always kept in constant contact. I suppose because of his military facilities and suppliers. I think we should also have a small gym on the ground floor of our building after it's completed. Perhaps until we build a larger one on the grounds. The next thing I have to do, is introduce you to some gizmo's and weapons. And we need better communication between ourselves and the main company computer. I will ask Ben about those items next time we meet,' Mallory said.

They patiently listened to an enthusiastic Mallory and wondered whether he was the same person they had met only a few days before. In just those few days they had moved so far and wondered whether their luck would last, or would it all come tumbling down on top of them.

In any event they had already benefited from his plans, even more than ever before so they were sure that if anyone could accomplish their goals that person would be Mallory Coleman.

CHAPTER 25

Ben visits the President

Earth time.... Summer, 2060 CE

'Mister President, Professor Bengizara Khan is here to see you. He is in your diary for three p.m,' the female voice announced via his desk intercom.

'Please send him in, Rachel. I shall be waiting in the study, and I do not wish to be disturbed during our important meeting!' Nicholas Wilson said and immediately left for his private study. Then he began reorganising his desk as if awaiting an important visit from supreme royalty. He pressed a concealed switch within his desk, above the first right-hand draw. A hidden lid slid open to reveal a small black box. Nick, as he was called by his close buddies, was addicted to his so-called gadgets and gizmo's. That particular one was given to him by Shadite Lumak. It supposedly quelled all bugs, recorders and listening devices in the local area of his office.

During the period of his presidency, the White House had been frequently cleaned of bugs, but he could never be sure how efficient that process was and could take no risks regarding his future conversation with Ben.

There was a tap on the door and Ben walked in, dressed in his cream suit with the Solarian winged insignia pinned to his white satin lapel. Presently Ben boasted a beard, but never looked his true age. He was a brilliant scientist and Solarian, although originally from Earth. Solarians could live forever with minds over ten times more advanced than Earth humans. As a matter of fact, what it took us years to learn a Solarian could learn and analyse in seconds. Such were the powers of their minds that we were like mice by comparison.

Although he had the most beautiful golden palace with his own fief the size of a small continent on planet Eden, he spent most of his time on Earth taking care of his many charities including

Solarian Banking and BioLive.

'It's great to see you again. How is Sarah and the others these days? Particularly Jerry and Sharon?' Nick inquired.

'They are quite fine and Jerry sends his regards. Sarah has adjusted well to the painful circumstances of the kidnapping and is still hopeful. Pity she had to return to Earth to have the child. However the change in environments has helped her to forget. The others are on several important projects of an interstellar nature.'

'It all sounds so exciting! Sometimes I wish I was over there instead of here!' he jested.

'I am presently the only one assigned to Earth, with Mickey as my second in command.'

'Oh, yea! Good old Mickey,' Nick replied.

'Despite everything, I still find it extremely difficult to tear myself away from this world, awful as it may be. I have to ensure certain plans are set in motion and organize the antidote distribution. I am currently based at Sol-Newton. From there I can take portals to the main satellites and most of our branches on Earth.'

'Yea, that one is going to shake our human populations,' Nick replied.

'This brings me to the Terminal Disease problem. We are now at the point of informing the public. The necessary information has been given to one of your citizens, a Captain Mallory Coleman. He was chief of security here once and well recommended by Jerry. Mallory intends to release the information some time this month, after he has given it time to simmer on the scientific grape vine.'

'Really! That soon?'

'I'm afraid so! Several billion antidote capsules and powders are already in storage ready for use. The program of Fertilate housing, for want of a better word, has commenced in many suburban areas. Sol-Newtown and several other sealed environmental domes are now prepared and are awaiting their first occupants. So our program is well on target.' Ben continued.

'Let's pray that the amount of violence is kept within controllable limits when the news break. I shall be one of their main targets for a quick solution, which I shall not be able to deliver on time,' Nick replied.

'There is also the problem of distribution through schools and town halls. Not everyone will be given the real antidote. After all, we only wish to save 500 million.'

'How will you choose your subjects?' Nick asked.

'We have records of virtually every individual on the planet. Each gun can analyse one's genetic code and immediately relay information to our Macron computers. Then the vaccination gun will be updated and only the placebo given.'

'Thank goodness during this process most of our genetic deviants will be removed as well. And they wouldn't have a clue.' Nick was pleased, knowing that within 100 years there would be almost no criminals left on the planet.

'Jerry wants you to pay special attention to his son, Donald, his sisters and some other good people. Here is a list. Sarah has also added a few names to it and we must not forget Mallory, his family and those he recommends for initial treatment. We would also like you to assist him as best you can, for he is honest, clever, keen and energetic. Personally, I think he is the best man for the job,' Ben said.

'Do you think we are still clean? I mean, from the bug? Not that it matters to me and my wife anymore. We have already had our quota of children. I think two is more than enough for any family these days,' Nick said.

'I think most in this country are still free from infection. Recent tests have shown a 10 percent contamination in New York, 20 percent in Florida and only 5 percent in Washington DC. There are a few hot spots within cities like Los Angeles, but the national average is still below 10 percent. That level will not increase significantly in one month. Things are not so good in Asia and Europe, where the average is over 50 percent and now rising exponentially. However, everything seems to be going to plan.'

'When the time comes I shall have to give a good speech to the nation and nominate you as chief bio-physicist of the year. After that, I am sure you will be nominated for the Nobel Prise. That announcement should release the pressure valve and calm the people,' Nick said.

'You can always count on me and move to Eden if things become uncomfortable here. But I am not too sure whether your wife and kids will agree to that arrangement. Even if you tried your hardest to explain it to them. I for one have always hated air transport and even more, being transposed in one of those confounded inter-dimensional portals. However, the aging process will dictate those changes and we are always free to choose.'

'Pal, if I didn't have the enormous responsibility of being leader of this great nation, I would be on Eden tomorrow. Because of this pandemic my presence here is needed now more than anytime ever,' Nick said.

'I think, when the time is right you will have to explain it all to them, but not unless it's absolutely necessary. They will have many friends and contacts and it's not going to be easy to leave all those people behind. That's why we created accidents in the past to cover our trails.

'Nevertheless, it will be quicker by portal. I shiver each time I enter one of those cubicles. During the process I feel that I have departed this life and in a kind of milky limbo between heaven and hell, until I awake at the other destination. When that happens, which is usually in one of the vertical types, I feel my legs buckle under the sudden weight of my body and have to immediately compensate to prevent my knees taking me to the floor. But I can just about grin and bear it whenever absolutely necessary. It's probably just a matter of practice making perfect. Nevertheless, the kids think it's the best thing since sliced bread and jam.

'Yea, typical kids. No thoughts of danger, whatsoever,' Nick was amused.

'Whenever I visit Eden, I always return a new man. The last time I returned with a brand new brain implant which enhanced my abilities over ten times, adding a few additional doctors to my brain in the process,' Ben said.

'Why don't you remain here with us for a few days? Alison and the kids will be very happy to see you. This is also a quiet period for me, so we can play a few holes together. Anyway, I would like to have a break now before the shock of the Terminal

Disease begins to rattle my office chains,' Nick said.

'In that case, I accept, Mister President. A little golf will get the blood back into my cheeks. However, I shall have to send for some suitable clothes and clubs,' Ben replied.

In less than fifteen minutes a special messenger called to deliver Ben's request.

CHAPTER 26

In search of a child

After ensuring his partners were competent enough in taking care of their side of business, Mallory decided it was time he began his search for Sarah's child.

Initially he didn't know where to begin. The meagre leads he had compiled from the file and police inspector Rod Nixon, had led him to a house of ill repute. That place was in the French quarters of New Orleans and one famous for shadier ventures.

Her name was Marlina DeCosta. She was a tall and voluptuous blonde temptress with one of the most beautiful figures Mallory had ever seen on a woman. It meshed well with her seductive manner. Her whole charisma oozed sex. She reminded him of a once beautiful Hollywood actress he admired. That actress lived in the previous century. Her image had been placed in a particular magazine commonly read by his long departed girlfriend.

'Mal, my darling,' she said, 'please follow me into my boudoir for our private chat. Would you like a drink, tea, coffee, gin, vodka, brandy?' she spoke with a foreign accent and he turned his head meaning no. Then she sat on the comfortable settee next to him.

'In that case, how can I help?'

'I am looking for a stolen kid that was taken about six months ago. There could be something in it for you, if you help me. Whatever you say will be kept strictly between us.'

'How much, Darling?' she inquired.

'If the information leads to finding the kid, you can name your price. There is at leased half a million in the kitty, so you get my drift.'

'Wow! So much for a little nipper. Some will kill and take life in jail for a small fraction of that sum. You know, Darling, six months is an awful long time to find a lost child. He could have been sold ten times over in that time. As a matter of fact, he would have been sold before he was taken and sent to Europe or Asia, depending on his looks and cultural background.'

'Yea, I know!'

'Adoption papers can be forged and computer records altered. Some of the people involved have many contacts in high places, and there are ways, you know. Legitimate papers would prevent nosey neighbours from asking too many questions initially. After the first year the child would be accepted by everyone.' She said

'That's a likely possibility!' Mallory listened patiently.'

'The other way is for the potential mother to pretend pregnancy and go away to have the supposed child. Then after a week or so she removes the padding from her belly and returns unconcerned with the new baby. Then it could be christened and registered in the normal way. That method is usually full proof, but will only work with babies of a certain age. Anyway, most of the wealthy families that require such heirs to their property live sheltered lives in large manors, farms and estates, so isolating and holding on to a kid is never a problem.' Marlina continued.

'I see!'

'Is there anything different about the child?' She asked

'He has a small birth mark just below his navel. It's the size of a small button, but shaped like a triangle. Someone may have seen it while changing him,' he replied.

'Leave it with me, Darling. Here is a key to my safety deposit box and an address to visit. Memorize its contents and burn the note. I shall place any information I find there, and don't let me down, Darling.' She took him to the door.

The car was already waiting for him at the front of the building. Many scruffy children were looking it over. Mallory threw them a twenty-dollar bill, saw them fight over it and flew off.

He spent some time working through the controls of Oscar, to familiarize himself with his many features. One of them was a miniature transmitter that could be linked with his own cellular system. Oscar's powerful computer could now be in direct communication with him virtually anywhere on the planet. Therefore all his future interviews could be remotely recorded by the car.

Oscar could also pinpoint past criminals and inform him of

suspects in the vicinity, including unexpected dangers, by warning him through his hidden earphone. He could also use Oscar to contact the office or to contact one of the other operatives in an emergency and talk with them via his powerful transmitter. It was then possible to give an excuse to leave a potentially perilous situation before the threat had time to develop. He soon found Oscar's menus in such operations to be quite extensive.

'You know, you are one incredible car!' he commented, but Oscar remained silent.

After his visit to New Orleans he felt drained and hungry. There was also his new partners to consider, so he decided to return for lunch.

'What a city. If not for the great wall it would be completely submerged by now,' he thought as he left Oscar.

'Hi, Rosie! Let me have a couple of your best donuts and coffee.' Mallory handed her a twenty-dollar bill and she stared at him in admiration.

'Have you won the national lottery or something? You look quite spectacular in that grey outfit. Are you looking for a delightful woman as well?' she flirted, humorously.

'Nice to see you in such a cherry and frank mood. I am looking for a six-month-old kid at the moment, but you'll do in the mean time.'

'That young, eh.' She gave a broad smile.

'Is everything ok with you?'

'Thanks for the kind interest, but how can a thirty-eight-year-old woman ever compete with a baby. In reply to your second; just the usual business and end of year tax problems. Running a café is no easy matter, you know. One constantly has to keep an eye on everyone, from customers to employees, and workers are so damn untrustworthy and unreliable these days.' Rosie said

'I know what you mean. Anyway, if you need my assistance you just shout in my direction,' he said and a broad affectionate smile came over her face. He took the tray and went towards a corner table. He quickly scanned the table for bugs and such like before making himself comfortable.

Mallory had not yet recovered from his strange experiences of the previous week, including the incredible force beam that emanated from satellite Eta, which was still quite vivid in his mind.

'In just two weeks three separate jobs, and in all probability interlinked in some way to Solarian Banking. The strange story of the Terminal Disease, to the equally strange character, Ben, with his incredible technologies.

'He also happened to be the grandfather of Sarah's lost child and was also without doubt the most wealthy person in the world. Then there was the microid problem and a simple solution, thanks to Solarian Banking.

'Solarian Banking seemed to be the pivot, but how and why, and where did the director, Michael Cockburn, my doctor's friend, fit into the picture. Perhaps he was just a messenger boy, but whose? In that case, why did Ben have to see me personally? Was Michael working for another party? Anyway, I was told to deliver my reports to him and would continue to do so until Ben told me otherwise. After all, he made the first payment and would make the last.

'The gift of the car was obviously Ben's idea. A sweetener for making the Terminal Disease known to the mass media and to aid in the speedy discovery of the child. However, why did Michael not give me the car at our first meeting and why did Ben supply that himself? Perhaps he wanted to see me in person. To judge my sincerity and capability?' Mallory thought.

Mallory soon gave up trying to unravel the complex jigsaw of past events. He thought of Roseanne and Carl, on their first day of military training and would like to have been there to surprise them.

The following day he flew off to New Orleans and went directly to the safety deposit box where he found an envelope with "To Mal" written on it. He opened it and read its contents.

'See Joeboy Hazard at the Paradise Club, Miami. He will have a few answers.'

He was soon on his way back to the car to make the trip.

'Where on Earth is Paradise Club?' he said aloud and a voice spoke in his earphone.

'Mal, it's two streets away from another one of Marlina's places. It's in the basement,' Oscar replied.

'I didn't realise you had every nook and cranny in your memory banks? You are a bloody gem, you know,' he replied, but Oscar remained silent.

After he arrived back at the car they were soon on their way to Florida. This time he decided to take a route close to the scenery.

'Take it easy over this area, Oscar. I don't want the inter-state cops on our back,' Mallory warned while Oscar watched his speed.

Very soon they had landed and were travelling along one of the main routes in the city.

'Oscar, this place is so hot,' Mallory complained.

'Let me turn on the air conditioning. Sorry, Mal, but I didn't realize you were susceptible. It's all to do with global warming. This part lost much of its land area to the Atlantic. Although the inner city was ringed to prevent further flooding, humidity is very high. Severe hurricanes had also taken their toll,' Oscar said.

'Yea, so I read. But It doesn't stop me sweating like a pig!' Mallory replied.

'Sadly, it will not remain ringed for long. It has to be evacuated within twenty years. Too much water, I'm afraid and too many hurricanes.' Mallory was concerned, but could do nothing for such a major catastrophe.

'I think we should find a vacant spot on one of the large hotels and book in for a while to cool off. Most of these places are virtually empty this time of year. These days people only come here in early and late spring. Summer is too hot and autumn is the hurricane season,' Mallory commented. Then Oscar took to the air once more.

'Mal, I found a spot on a local hotel,' Oscar said and in a moment he was descending over the spot.

CHAPTER 27

Rough games

'Mal, I am certain we are being followed. It's a black Cadillac... out of state number. Here is the registration. Would you like me to take it further?' Oscar advised.

'No. Leave it for now. They could be on our side, to keep an eye on me. Anyway, I like giving them a little rope.'

'Why rope? Do you want to tie them up?' Oscar inquired, innocently.

'No. It's just a figure of speech. When you want to see how far someone will go before they make a mistake. Then I can find out on whose side they are on, or what games they are up to.'

'I have noted that figure of speech for future reference.' Oscar continued to follow their present route with the other car barely in sight.

Mallory thought anyone with a name like Joeboy Hazard would be rough, tough and at least six feet tall. He could be involved with drugs, prostitution, gambling and any other unsavoury occupation, including child snatching. He made sure his weapons were as inconspicuous as possible in case he was searched.

He arrived in one of the derelict areas of Miami and walked towards a steel padded wooden door.

'Who are you?' came a voice from the door phone.

'Madam Marlina sent me!'

The lock buzzed and he pushed it open. He entered a large plush basement bar through another strong door with crimson velvet decor and went directly to the tall muscular African-American barman behind the counter.

'I would like a word with Joeboy Hazard. Is he around?' The barman turned away briefly still wiping the counter with a damp cloth.

'Who wants him?'

'Tell him I am searching for a lost child and there could be a very large reward if the child is found. I am a private investigator.'

The barman pressed a concealed button under the counter. A small slim effeminate looking Caucasian with dyed blonde hair entered through the make-believe curtains. It concealed the door to another most private room.

The supposed male was dressed in a blue glittery outfit that clashed perversely with the red of the room.

'Mister Hazard?' Mallory inquired, surprised by expectations. This guy was only a small squeak and in no way what Mallory expected. His name seemed to fit the barman to a tee.

'I am Hazard. What do you want?'

'I am searching for a stolen child and was told you could help...'

'That much I overheard,' he cut in.

'I need to locate him.'

'How do I know you are not a cop, snooping around.'

'Here are some identification. You can run a check if you like,' Mallory replied, handing him a biometric card with his photo but with a false identity. Joeboy scanned the image for a while carefully observing Mallory's features. He was satisfied and nervously handed him back the card.

'It's a kid from a very wealthy family.' Mallory had never seen a criminal so nervous.

'The Phantom must have rattled his cage,' he murmured to himself.

'You want to snatch him back! We might be able to give you some information, but we can't assist you in acquiring the child. We would lose our reputation if anyone got to know that we snatch our own kids back and it will cost you dearly to arrange such a deal. How much are you offering?' Joeboy said with little reservations.

'There is five hundred grand in the kitty, but you can have fifty when we find the child.'

'Let's say a compromise. Because I don't know you from Adam. Let's say seventy-five grand and I shall give you something positive to go on, but I need ten grand up front,' Joeboy insisted.

'Have you got a D-link?' Mallory asked.

'Yes, behind the counter. Max, get him the unit.' The barman retrieved a device with a small keyboard and slot for inserting a card. Mallory checked to see if the sealed unit was tampered with, then slid his credit card into a slot. He dialled several codes. That method was more secure than others.

'What's your access code?' Mallory asked, but Joeboy took the unit from him and begun to enter several numbers, including a different name and ten thousand dollars were transferred to his account.

'Come to my office. I will give you a note to take to the girls. It's run by one of my partners. They handle the kids and will know who he was,'Joeboy said and Mallory followed. Joeboy realized Mallory was genuine, since not many coppers would part with ten thousand grand so readily.

Mallory did not like this Joeboy. He reminded him of everything he found disgusting; like a scab on the face of humanity, but he had to put up with the humiliation if he was to find the child. His so-called office was more like Marlina's boudoir, with three luxurious settees and there were two boys about the age of ten waiting around.

'A paedophile among other things. I wonder if those kids were stolen as well?' Mallory thought. Joeboy gave a gesture to the boys and they disappeared into another room.

'One of the main routes to Europe is via Canada. They use legitimate LPD cars and change their plates across the border for Canadian ones. Those steps evade the laser guidance systems which are linked to the police on both sides of the border.'

'I see!'

'Here is my partner's address. I shall call them first to inform them of your visit, Captain Mallory Colman,' he said and Mallory was surprised that he had already ran a check on him, or else Joeboy's lips would have been sealed from the moment he entered the building, and even worst could have happened.

'It's easy to get travel papers from Canada to London. Then you are in Europe and free like a bird in the tree. There is now a growing demand in Europe and Russia for Caucasians and other types in other places. People in those countries are finding it difficult to have kids, so we try to maintain a balance. They reckon it's because of another sex bug like AIDS. That one started just before the turn of the century and took many lives, but has now been more or less cured. This new one just stops all human reproduction. It reduces sperm count to zero and destroys female eggs, but it hasn't arrived here yet. Keep this information to yourself. We don't want everyone to realize the problems. We might lose business. As they say, ignorance is bliss.' Joeboy stressed.

'Yea, I will.' Mallory didn't realize others knew or even guessed about the Terminal bug.

'Anyway, here is some more info. Marcus Darling owns a Café close to Chinatown. Pay him a visit after you have seen the girls. He handles the despatch side of the business, but be careful. He is not a very nice person when it comes to strangers,' Joeboy said. Suddenly he became very helpful and Mallory thought it was something he discovered about his past.

Mallory realized Joeboy had been extra helpful in his case and wondered whether they had met somewhere before. Perhaps he had done some work for one of his bosses in times gone by or maybe he was scared of the Phantom or Green Chameleon. He realized they were one and the same person.

'I deal with Marlina, so if you have any useful information, drop it in to her and she'll get it to me. As I said, I am not interested in you, your associates or business. I just want to find that particular kid. I shall get you the balance of the money the moment the kid is found.' Mallory said,

Before leaving that building he called the local police through Oscar. It was not long before the place was crawling. The kids were soon taken away, but Joeboy was no where to be found.

Mallory was intrigued, so remained on a local roof with Oscar to observer the action.

'Come on Mal! Get out of here quickly. I have some crooks to kill. This whole area is due for demolishing. The waves were going to take it anyway. I am just speeding the process. Watch your back, Mallory!' The Phantom said, and flew away towards the building he just left. When the police saw him they left. Not long after Mallory heard two pops and realized two heads were off. Then Mallory decided to move quickly.

'Oscar lets go high!'

'Yes, Mal!'

In another minute and that whole area by the sea had disappeared into the ocean amidst the largest blast he had ever seen.

'Mal, The Sea Front has been destroyed and most likely, so is Joeboy and his associates.'

'Then he observed a green streak in the sky above. The phantom made a few spins and circles aerobatically and was away in a flash.

'Good! That will save me a few grand!' Mallory replied.

'The Phantom knew my name and warned me?' Mallory murmured.

Mallory left the place as quickly as he could, with a few sheets of paper in one hand. On arrival he scanned the information into Oscar's memory.

He was soon on his way to another building. This time in the red-light district. It was five storeys high and once used as a normal hotel. That building had since been converted to a gambling casino and the upper floors converted for legal prostitution and other vices. The whole operation was covered by law and functioned under the new name of Plaza-Plus Hotel.

Since the stricter firearms laws were passed those areas were legalized to take violence away from the streets. Furthermore, drug addiction was no longer a serious problem since the introduction of Cofines. They were a range of drugs that could make one feel almost any way they desired without any side effects. Each capsule and its effects could be identified by its coloured bands. They were readily available from drug stores and machines at low prices.

'Can I see Clair? My name is Mallory Colman.' The receptionist lifted the receiver and pressed one of the many buttons on the keypad several times. A muffled female voice replied, then asked who the visitor was.

'Send him up to the third floor. Someone will be waiting near the elevator.' Mallory walked towards the closest elevator and wondered whether most of that outfit was owned by Joeboy, deceased. Nevertheless many of those houses were owned by large syndicates who used people like Joeboy as front men.

'Please follow me, Sir!' a beautiful girl beckoned, as he got out of the elevator. She had the figure of a model and here again he wondered whether Marlina had a hand to play in that part of the business. He was taken to a comfortable little bar with expensive decor.

'Please to meet you, Mallory. My name is Clair,' she greeted, with a smile.

'I think you know why I'm here.'

'I shall talk to my girls. If such a kid was here, they will remember.' Clair buzzed another room and another girl appeared.

'Nora, pass the word around. We are looking for a child about three months old with a small triangular birth mark just below his navel. He was dispatched about six months ago. Tell the girls it's urgent.' Nora immediately left the room.

Clair nervously offered Mallory a drink and he accepted.

'Make it a small whisky on the rocks. Buy the way, The Phantom only decapitates men. He has a soft spot!' Mallory said and she was more at ease.

'One...One of our main handlers died recently. She was shot by her boyfriend during a lover's quarrel. She may have been the one responsible, but we always keep coded records. We also run a legitimate nursery in the basement. Anyway, we have to follow certain formalities for tax purposes, so if he passed through this house we'll locate his records.' She remained nervous.

This time another girl appeared. She was blonde, and supremely attractive, with a face and figure like another famous actress. They tended to model themselves after those actresses and actors. Most had on-going cosmetic surgery to enhance their bodies and looks.

'Madam Clair. I remember the child. He cried an awful lot. "Little Jimmy" that was what Alison called him, God bless her soul. He was always crying, so we got him one of those little pink rattles which he liked to hold and play with,' she said.

'Thank you, Joan,' Clair said with authority and dismissed her with a flick of her risk. Then she went to a small computer terminal and nervously pushed a few keys. She jotted some more information on a piece of paper.

'See Marcus Darling. Give him this note. He'll be able to find the exact route of that particular dispatch through his computer, and he knows my signature.'

'Thanks a lot. If you should require my investigative services at any time, please give me a call.' Mallory handed her one of his cards and smiled.

Mallory was escorted out by Clair and he was soon on-route to Marcus Darling's place.

CHAPTER 28

Marcus Darling

'Marcus Darling. So who is this Marcus Darling? Could be a right old darling, by the sound of things. Seems I am expected there as well,' Mallory murmured to himself.

'He is in charge of that faction, Mal!'

'What faction is that!'

'Children Smuggling. The police have been tracking him for a while now, but he remains as clean as a whistle.' Oscar replied.

'Ah, so you understand our little metaphors. "Clean as a whistle", "Enough rope to hang". Nice to know, you'r getting to know your stuff, Oscar!'

'I am trying! While scanning the police criminal database!' Oscar replied.

'Take me to Chinatown. Lets get there before the Phantom. I must have words with this guy before he loses his head. To this guy Marcus's place,' he said to Oscar and the car was off like a shot. They ended up at a large worn-down block, just on the outskirts of town. He could observe several multistory blocks in the distance being battered by the waves. Most were partly submerged by the rising waters. In those criminal areas, door numbers were rear and people could only locate others by word of mouth.

He entered the entrance displaying Chi Lings Import Export. There were just two Chinese men inside. That place was made to look the part of an ongoing business in spices and other oriental foodstuffs. There was a single computer terminal with two filing cabinets, three old dusty desks and three torn typing chairs.

'Is Marcus about?' Mallory inquired.

'Who Marcus?' asked the older, grey-haired Chinese male individual in broken English, with a strong Cantonese accent.

'Mister Darling!' Mallory added.

'Wha dona you sai soy,' the old man growled.

'Out the door, and second on your right. It's the green door,' said the younger man in perfect American English with a local accent. On his way he expected to be ambushed, but nothing happened. It was like they knew he was coming.

One of the more intriguing parts of Mallory's work was to do with the variety of strange and dangerous people he occasionally met in the course of his inquiries. It was probably the thought of not knowing what was around the next bend that kept him going so relentlessly. Nevertheless curiosity was known to kill the cat and he sometimes wondered when his turn would come.

His impression of that last place, its smells and its occupants were not a pleasant one. He was sure those two were not involved in any legitimate type of business. They had given him the information too easily.

Recently he had decided not to take along any weapons. Being skilled in many forms of martial arts since his military days, gave him an edge in dangerous situations providing he could show good identification and kept his cool. He was quite capable of taking care of himself, although not against guns and more subtler weapons like poisonous darts and toxic sprays.

He was in constant communication with Oscar, who monitored all conversations and was programmed to detect the slightest danger. That made him feel more secure. He realized that even if he was searched, the micro transmitter and receiver in his ear and other equipment in his belt couldn't easily be detected. Anyway, they seldom removed clothes for the more thorough visual checks, so he was relatively safe.

He opened the green door and entered. He was immediately greeted by two tough hoods waiting just behind the entrance. They firmly held both his arms and frisked him, taking his wallet in the process.

'Why are you guys so sensitive!'

'You could be the bloody Phantom for all we know! He is also called the Chameleon because of a knack for changing into other guys! He can change his appearance in a flash!'

'Surely not his clothes in a flash!'

When they were sure he was clean of weapons and gadgets, they took him over to a small chair and spun a nylon cord around him and the chair. Then his ankles were tied together with a shorter length of cord.

'You wait here while I get the boss!' said the smaller of the two and he left the room.

'Is this really necessary? Where can I go, anyway?' Mallory grunted, trying to see how taught the rope was. He soon realised that he was helpless and tied like a portion of lamb for the oven. A short stubby man soon entered the room through Venetian blinds.

'You disturbed my game!' he barked, 'Anyway, I am Marcus and I hear you are looking for me.' He removed a large cigar from a box on his desk. Then began to crop its end before lighting it.

'Yes! I am a private eye by the name of Mallory. I was told by Clair that you would assist me in finding a child. This matter does not concern the cops and the reward could be worth your while. That is if we can find the kid,' Mallory said, tauntingly while handing the paper with Clair's signature.

'Why are you interested in a single kid?' he growled.

'I was given a job to find a particular kid that was taken six months ago from some important and very wealthy people. Good money is involved, so I took the job. Anyway, I always like to see my cases through when I take money. That applies to everyone or I can lose my reputation. I suppose those ethics apply to most in my business.'

'How bloody honest and noble of you,' Darling growled. Then gestured to his two colleagues to untie Mallory, to which they immediately complied.

'One can't be too careful these days with the bloody Phantom about! Let me see his ID!' he barked and the smaller man handed him Mallory's wallet. He quickly checked its contents.

'You appear to be who you say you are. You say six months ago? That's a long time. The bloody trail is now as cold as ice.'

'Are you going to help?' Mallory stressed, sympathetically.

'I will help for two hundred grand, that's double the price of a special male kid and also double the risks. I will accept fifty grand now for setting it up and the balance on completion of the job. You can use my D-link.' Marcus got one of his men to collect the machine. He plugged it into the phone line and local power point. Then Mallory transferred the money into his account.

'You operate a computer with Email?'

'Yes! Why?' Mallory replied.

'I will send the information by encrypted Email with a special key. The key you will have on a piece of paper. You are to read the odd digits from right to left. That way it will be in your computer and hidden from prying eyes. It will also contain a one hour self-destruct virus code. Make sure you decode and erase the email before it disappears from your computer, or it might take some of your main programs down when it goes.' Marcus scribbled the number down and handed him back the small piece of paper with the key for deciphering the information and he was quickly shown out the building.

This time the Phantom was nowhere to be seen, so he assumed he was working in another area. Mallory kept close to his office after he left Marcus. Within two hours the computer blipped, as it received the special data. It was filed under the name of "My Darling". The r in Mr was changed to the letter y. He wondered whether that had anything to do with his chosen pseudonym. Those criminals were quite clever at hoodwinking the legal system and Marcus appeared to be the king of such deceitful methods.

The data included the name of his main contact in London, England. It was the one responsible for that end of the traffic in young children in that part of Europe. Even so, Mallory realised he had a long way to go before the child was recovered.

He now had to get his travel papers in order to visit England, which would take him the better part of two weeks due to strict regulations.

CHAPTER 29

Mallory - business and romance

Mallory was in the office working late when the phone rang.

'Hi! I thought of calling you, to let you know how we are doing,' Roseanne greeted.

'How are you getting on, my girl?' Mallory was surprised.

'Everything is fine, but the going is hard and painful. Carl is also doing quite well with similar complaints. He went to the clubhouse with a few of his friends from the course, while I stayed in to read a book on assertiveness, of all things.'

'You have more than enough of that!'

'And a lot more. I have blisters in places I never dreamt was possible. I didn't realise I was so rusty and my body was so out of trim. Anyway, just three more days to go. We have the toughest assault course tomorrow and the survival one after that. Then we remain in barracks to complete the defensive martial arts before the written test.'

'I am sure you will make it with flying colours, if you survive.'

'Ha! Ha! Ha! Very funny!'

'I might have to leave for England after you return from camp. I will be over there for about three weeks. It's to do with the stolen child, I am trying to locate and recover. It's one of those tricky assignments.'

'Would you like to take along a female companion on that trip to assist?' she asked, jokingly.

'But you will be too tired and crippled to make it even to the car, with all those aches and pains?'

'A girl can very quickly recover if she is invited on such a trip, and I always wanted to visit that particular ancestral country.'

'Have you got your papers ready?'

'No. But that shouldn't take too long to arrange, and Carl can handle our outstanding appointments. I am sure he wouldn't mind if we asked him nicely.'

'Ok. Let me have whatever papers you've got and I shall push it through. It should take a week if you have your birth certificate and photos. Less if you still have your old passport and isometrics. Finger prints and other checks are only for first-timers. It's not required for us.'

'Thanks, Mal. I can do with a break when I am through with this course, and I haven't been anywhere for over ten years. Anyway, anything will be a holiday compared with this torture. You wouldn't believe, lots of companies send their top executives here for business holidays. I can't see why?'

'They must use the easier side of the ranch with Exec. facilities like sauna, bubble bath and massage parlour. Not to mention the extensive golf course and facilities. I am sure you will survive even the snake pits. Just keep away from the rattlers, they are the worst,' he replied and she giggled.

'I can't stand creepy crawlies and snakes, even as a child and I'm real scared of large spiders. Anyway, take care. I've got to go,' she said.

'In that case, I will see you soon, chin up and say hello to Chad for me,' he said and hung up.

Mallory was not the type to fall in love, because of his reckless life style and the dangerous nature of his work, but Roseanne was now in an equally dangerous profession and those two cancelled each other. For some reason he always had a soft spot for her, even when they worked together at the White House and she probably had similar feelings for him, but he was married then and little interested in extra-marital affairs.

Over the weeks he had found himself being drawn ever closer to the woman. She, like most vulnerable women of her age that wasn't hitched, had a few major setbacks and disappointments in their lives and needed time to put things back into perspective.

He had seen the relief in her features since she joined his outfit. Before that she was like a lost soul, not knowing exactly where she stood in relation to the future. Now and finally, she had a little security and was beginning to make some of her own choices in her life. Incredible the things a little money could do.

She had just passed thirty-four, five feet nine tall, beautifully put together and always very positive in her actions. When she wanted something, she went for it and that single quality made

Mallory admire her. That admiration had turned to fondness. However she also appreciated his attentions and assistance, even when he was twelve years her elder.

Training Camp was just outside the city of Scranton, which was about one hundred kilometres from New York as the crow flies. Chad Collison was owner and an old friend of Mallory since military days. Both being very close in the paras. It was said that they saved each other's lives at different times when they were on a special mission in Africa.

After their return to the states, Chad's father died from a heart attack and left him some money which he used as a deposit on the training camp. Despite large summer profits, the bank loan was large and it would have taken him several more years to repay.

The camp was divided into two sections. The first, the tourist part, for those holiday-makers and company executives. Those that wanted golf, fresh air, trekking, horse riding, rock climbing and some aspects of survival training, but with their accustomed luxuries.

The more serious part or professional section dealt with security and military training on several of the specially designed survival courses and fire-ranges. There were indoor activities like the martial arts and boxing. In some cases the training was as tough as received by the best fighting troops during combat training. Therefore only ex military types with a good medical record were accepted in that section. In particular, those with previous combat and survival experience.

Chad enjoyed training others and did quite well financially out of his business in the peak summer months. During that period he was always over-booked, with more groups than he could handle. Most of it being due to his reputation and recommendations by the tourists board and others.

When Roseanne and Carl arrived, Chad gave them his best accommodation and made sure they were thoroughly coached through each training session. But he also saw to it that they received his toughest training, because they worked with Mallory and he didn't want any of them to come to grief when they went back into the field. After their six days were up, he called Mallory.

'Mal, it's Chad.'

'What's up, Pal?'

'Things couldn't be better with me at this time. During this period of the year I tend to have more bookings than I can handle.'

'In that case, why don't you branch out a little? Build another similar camp elsewhere?'

'Not enough money yet to invest in such a scheme. Most of it is still tied up with the initial bank lone. I would rather not take out another before I've repaid the first. When I bought the place my dad's money was just the deposit,' Chad replied.

'I will go half with you and get you a loan as well if you decide to run it, baring your extra salary and commission, of course. You could pay it all back in a couple of years max. You just find the place. Anyway, think about that one for now.'

'Sounds interesting!'

'I might need your advice on another matter. We have new headquarters and I was thinking of including a small training area in the building. I need your advice on equipment. Why don't you visit me when I return from England? Then we can do some real talking about business as well.' Mallory said.

'I will plan to do just that and let you know. When I decide it will be for a couple of days at least. Whenever I visit the big rotten apple, I always like enough time to sample some of its dirty fumes. Reminds me of the battlefield and what I am missing when I am away from camp,' Chad said and Mallory laughed.

'Don't give me that! I know you always hated the city and most of all, New York. But my friend, there is lots brewing in the wind. I mean real big stuff involving the whole human race, and I don't know the half of it yet. Anyway, I'll tell you when you come.'

'You sound quite serious! Is it to do with our Green Chameleon friend?'

'I am very serious, and it's not about our intrepid Phantom!'

'Anyway, my main reason for this call was to let you know how your two operatives are doing. Although they were a bit rusty, I soon knocked them into shape. That girl Roseanne is better than a lot of trained guys and she's got a good aptitude. They both passed, but Roseanne was the best. Carl is still recovering from, you know what, but is also trying his best. I will fax you their details later, during the week. They should be on their way to you. I gave them the afternoon off.'

'Also send me your fee. We all have to earn a living, you know,' Mallory replied.

'Later! Leave it for when I visit. There may be some little favours you can do for my business in the future. You being in the big city. Anyway, got to dash.' Chad hung up.

Roseanne and Carl arrived at the office later that day.

'You both have a lovely tan. Like you've been to Miami for a fortnight. How was your holidays?' Mallory jested.

'Some Miami holiday, indeed! I feel like my arms and legs will drop off any minute. I will say one thing about your friend, Chad Collison, he is a sadist and probably a masochist as well, and Carl will agree with every bit of that observation,' Roseanne said as she slumped into the office Settee.

'It was hectic and sometimes even dangerous, but we got through all six challenges and passed the written test. I think we now have a clean bill of health and are also fully combatant, Sir!' Carl said and saluted, but suddenly placed his hand on his back as if in severe pain and also slumped in the settee.

'Seeing that you both are so dead beat, why don't you take the rest of the week off. It's not the busiest time of the year and the microids can wait until next week. A good rest should relieve those aching muscles and stretched sinews?'

'I see our Phantom guy was in London recently? Ten crims lost their heads!' Carl interjected.

'Yea! He does his rounds every month. I met him recently. That was before one of the old docks in Miami went up. He could have taken out over a dozen then!' Mallory replied.

'I wonder what drives him? How does he get away with it!' Roseanne said.

'Most likely he uses very advanced technology,' Mallory replied.

'Thank goodness he is on our side!' Roseanne said.

They both decided to follow Mallory's advice for a long rest and left early that day.

The following day he was visited by Roseanne. She went to give him the papers and photos for her new passport.

'Are you sure you want to have me along?'

'Yes. I am sure. Why the sudden doubt?'

'I am feeling a little guilty, thinking perhaps I talked you into it. I sometimes get over excited about such things these days. It's probably a phase I am going through,' she replied.

'Say no more, my lady, on that topic. I would dearly love to have you along. This is going to be mainly a business trip, but who is to say we can't visit a few places as well. I have to find that stolen kid and you are going to be my backup. What do you say now?'

'I say, I would love to tag along as your backup, dear captain.'

'Why don't you let me take you to the theatre sometime, perhaps tomorrow? The break will do us good. What do you say?' She suddenly realised he was asking her for a date.

'I would like that very much, Mal,' she replied, feeling wanted and appreciated as if by the boss of her gang.

'In that case, let me drive you home. I feel like a break from this place, anyway.'

Over the next few days Mallory took Roseanne to several venues. Both enjoyed their time together and had become fond of each other.

Mallory was careful not to rush the relationship. He realized she was still quite fragile and scared emotionally from her previous marriage.

CHAPTER 30

Terminal relief

On the thirteenth of that month mallory visited the Group of Thirteen and gave them a file. Okeke briefly scanned through its pages then passed it over to Dr. Hal Seaton. Hal was now dressed in a lawyer's suit.

'So Mallory, it appears there is a pandemic disease about! Do you think it was mainly responsible for global unrest?'

'Yes, Sir! And things will get much worse. If not for The Phantom, crime would also be endemic at this time!'

'Mallory, keep on your good work, but watch your back!' Hal interjected.

'Now we know the true cause, we can pass your information over to our scientist!' Okeke said. Mallory was soon out of that hotel and went back to his office.

When Mallory received the passports and realized they were visiting Europe, it suddenly dawned on him that the Terminal Disease was rampant in that part of the world. He had to do something to safeguard himself and Roseanne from the infection, but how could they have received the antidote before leaving for England. He realised that his doctor knew Michael Cockburn and if Ben had it, so also would Michael. He immediately communicated with Doctor Langdon and informed him of a new and important development on the case of the lost child. Then they arranged an urgent appointment with Michael to discuss the matter.

That meeting was just a ploy, use to ask Michael for some antidote. Since he was on a job for Michael Cockburn, any risk that was far beyond the call of his normal duties was questionable, so he was well within his rights to reduce those outside risks.

When Mallory visited his doctor's clinic that morning he was eagerly awaited by Michael Cockburn and Doctor Langdon. He gave them a report on his recent enquiries and supplied him with an up-to-date file. Michael was pleased with the progress made in only a few days. That was a lot more than what the police and FBI had collected in months.

'This is incredible news. Is there anything else I can do for you to speed things up?' Michael asked.

'Yes! There is a little something. Call it reducing a serious risk, if you wish. However, I would like to mention it to you in private. It's supposed to be top secret information.'

They excused themselves from Doctor Langdon's presence, went out of the office and were standing in the hallway.

'One of my young female partners and myself are visiting London next week, to follow up our investigation on the child. I am also aware that the Terminal Disease is endemic in that part of the world. Because of that reason, would it be possible for us to have some Terminal Antidote for the trip?'

'You know about that matter as well?' Michael replied, absorbed by astonishment.

'I assumed that was the case, because of what Ben told me, and knowing you guys, it would have been ready several years ago. He also said I could assist him in distributing the antidote when it was ready and gave me a file to release to the press. I have since given some of the information to the Group of Thirteen, in the hope they will spread it around at the scientific levels before I called the press.'

'Wow! So Ben has told you about it?' Mickey was surprised.

'Yes, I think I am the chosen one.'

'Know something, Mal. You are one incredible investigator. You must however understand that the antidote cannot be released until the disease is generally known, for obvious reasons.'

'I am aware of all that, including the legal ramifications and I am not going to use it on anyone, except my partners and myself,' Mallory pleaded.

'In that case, although it's a big risk on my part, I shall arrange a small delivery for you in a few days. It will contain the necessary equipment and capsules, to be taken once daily. But please keep it to yourselves. You will however realise that it will not work if the recipient is already infected.'

'Is there a testing machine as well?'

'I shall also send you one with the necessary instructions, and an article I wrote for The Times on the Terminal Disease. You may use it for the press publication when the time is right.

'Is that all, Captain Colman?' Mickey said, showing much respect in his manner.

'That will do fine for now, thank you, Mickey,' Mallory replied and they both returned to the office to rejoin Doctor Langdon.

'I am sorry for leaving you out in the cold like this, Doctor, but it's a very sensitive matter and I don't know the levels of your involvement. Anyway, I shall let you know after Mallory has completed this job. Far too much is at stake at this time,' Mickey apologised.

'Don't worry about it, Pal. If I was involved I would most probably have done the same,' Doctor Langdon replied.

After just two days Mallory had received a packet from Solarian Banking. It was delivered by private courier and contained two hand-held devices resembling plastic guns and three containers of capsules. One had what appeared to be a blue nozzle with a perforated flat front and the other in red, with a pointed nozzle. The instructions told him that the red one was for testing. It included an inbuilt analyser and readout screen.

The blue one contained two large retractable cylinders that were filled with the antidote and the placebo. Both units also included the necessary sterilizing fluids to prevent further contamination by the units themselves. However all those that were tested negative would be prescribed the antidote capsules. Those already infected didn't matter anyway, since they would receive the placebo, which was probably a neutral substance like a saline solution.

The vaccination was not a permanent cure and would only prevent infection up to a period of three months or so in a highly contagious environment. Therefore it was necessary for all the few selected to take daily medication or live in specially secured areas where their water supply or foodstuffs were mixed with the antidote, for easy distribution. The main purpose of those vaccination guns and testers were to make the initial selection and add those numbers with their names and addresses to the computer database.

The following morning Mallory called Roseanne and Carl together for another serious chat.

'I have something important to tell you both. We have received the antidote for the Terminal Disease. It's just enough for us three. You must understand that this knowledge must go no further. Far too much is at stake here.'

'I thought it was not...not ready yet and you... you really have the stuff?' Roseanne exclaimed, with tears of happiness.

'I did tell you that even if they had it, it would have been kept a secret until the bug was publicly known. Now you see why I decided to buy the large building. Anyway, here are the devices and the instructions. It's self explanatory. There is a computer disc as well that explains everything. You two will be my first guinea pigs.'

'Really!' An astonished and unhappy Carl exclaimed.

'Now, I want you, Roseanne, over here!' Mallory said and she went over to join him behind the desk.

'Should you be doing that? I mean... shouldn't a qualified nurse be using that equipment?' Carl queried, nervously.

'No! We have to do it ourselves. Information about this stuff must not leave this room. However, in order to be fair, I shall do Roseanne, she will do you and you will do me. That way we all share the risks and get some practice as well,' Mallory said, with a glare of dare-you in his eyes.

'I still think we should practice on a pig or sheep before we try it on ourselves,' Carl insisted, still scared out of his wits about the strange equipment. He never liked needles and such like.

'Mallory had to dispel the trepidations felt by his two companions, so he took his jacket off, folded his left sleeve and pressed the nozzle against his upper arm. Then he pressed the trigger. There was a hissing sound and then a buzz and finally the small screen lit up.

'TERMINAL DISEASE NOT PRESENT,' was displayed, with a further blinking icon at the bottom of the screen which read,

'PURGE AGAINST DISEASE, IMMEDIATELY.'

Roseanne and Carl were soon convinced. The device didn't even draw a drop of blood in the process. It simply analysed a thin layer of skin tissue. Then Mallory took the other gun and did exactly the same thing, but this time there was a quick hiss as with the release of gas. The screen on that one also lit up, giving the patient's number, which in that case was number one. Then it requested his full name, date of birth and address. Mallory gave those particulars verbally and the screen reset for the next patient.

The unit kept a full record on all its patients and was designed to be used by anyone. The complete process would have taken less than twenty seconds under normal conditions. After the main vaccination was given, special tablets had to be taken on a daily basis to enhance the effect.

Roseanne couldn't wait any longer. She rolled her sleeves and went closer to Mallory for her shot. She was scared in case she got a 'TERMINAL DISEASE PRESENT,' indication, but was also clear of the disease. She couldn't believe the results and danced around the room several times.

'I'm clean! I'm clean!' she shouted joyfully.

Carl was next, but wasn't too bothered one way or the other. He preferred the bachelor's lifestyle because to him, children and wives were a form of imprisonment. Nevertheless, he was also negative.

'That's great! Now I'm a 100 percent free man again!' he exclaimed.

'Ah! That's fantastic news, we are all 100 percent free of the bug. That is what I expected. We are well away from city hot spots and lead single lives, so we come less in contact with the infected. But we must remember to take the capsules every day. We have enough for about three months. That amount should do us for now.'

Mallory handed both their supplies of antidote capsules. Then he took Roseanne home.

'Since we leave on Monday for England, I had to get the antidote before then, knowing the levels of infection over there to be a lot higher and not wanting you to be infected,' he said, affectionately.

'You are the best man I've met so far, you know? Always so thoughtful and considerate. If only I got serious with you before my marriage to that moron, George, would never have happened,' she replied, disappointingly.

CHAPTER 31

Calahan's dilemma

Captain Calahan from the local precinct was checking the house of another female fatality, when Lieutenant Charles Collins followed while reading the local paper.

'Seems to be a straightforward enough killing. Her violent boyfriend had enough of her two-timing and blew her head off with the shotgun and ran! Now he is nowhere to be found!' Calahan said

'Seems that way captain. A cut and dried case!' Charles replied, unconcerned.

'What can you do, other than thoroughly check the scene!'

'Forensics is already on the job in the bedroom, so not much to do!'

'Ok, I know you have something on your mind. Please give it to me!' Calahan said, in expectation of some important news.

'Our green friend is back on the job. Now he targets child kidnappers. Two crims lost their heads in another precinct yesterday, the 25th.'

'That is not good? Let me see that paper!'

'Here! Read all about it!' Charles showed a happy grin.

'My God! Doesn't he ever stop!'

'He could be targeting all criminal categories up the ladder? Every time he targets those crims, crime in that area drops below 50%.'

'You mean, up the ladder to god! You guys seem to love and appreciate the freak. One of these days he will get caught. Then what?' Calahan was not pleased with the Green Chameleon's fame. To him he was also a criminal for taking the law into his own hands.

'This give you guys a break. Don't plan your retirement or long vacations yet. He wont be around forever.' Calahan was not amused. He had never seen his precinct so relaxed for a long time. It was like the Green Chameleon was doing all their work for them. However, his present case was just an unexciting rare violent domestic dispute or so it appeared.

Calahan was in the canteen sipping his rear cup of coffee with two donuts awaiting his undivided attention when Lieutenant Charles Farrow, his second in command, tapped him on the shoulder and placed a note next to the saucer.

'I think we got him! He just took out a couple kidnappers in the Bronx! They got him pinned down!'

'Let's go, sirens blazing!' Calahan shouted.

'Take my LPD. A donation from Solarian Banking!' Charles said. Three police cars plus one new LPD Roadstar tore through the crowded streets.

'A gift from Solarian Banking? How come I knew nothing about it!' Calahan inquired. He was in the front passenger seat with three police in the back.

'A recent delivery. I thought I would test it for you, Captain!' Charles said and smiled with guilt.

'Thanks, for testing it for me. Now can I have it or is more testing required?' a stern Calahan inquired.

They were soon at site, with local police firing all their rounds at the greenish figure. Bullets ricocheted off his body in all direction just missing the captain.

'Stop firing! Stop firing this minute! Bullets reflect off his body. He must be wearing a special suit!' Calahan shouted. However the Green Chameleon remained where he was. Apparently he had enough fighting.

The local captain came forward to have words.

'Hello Captain Lyle! Sorry we had to thread your patch like this. We have been after this guy for a while now. He tends to disappear when he has enough,' Calahan apologised.

'Then you can take over and do the paperwork! Good thing we work for the same Mayor!'

'Thanks for your cooperation! I owe you one!'

'A big one!' Lyle shouted and signalled his men to leave.

'Come on guys, we are out of here! Leave it to Batman and the

Green Joker!' He added on the way out.

Another bullet rang out, but missed the target.

'I said stop firing! You idiot! We want to capture, not kill him!'

'Sorry Captain. The men are eager, nervous and touchy.' Charles said. Then Calahan shouted at the Green Chameleon, to give him an incentive.

'Surrender now or we start firing again!'

'Dam it! Dam it! Dam it! I lost all screening power! Bloody battery! Gone flat again!' Hal, the Green Chameleon, was not please. His only option was to surrender and fine some way to escape.

'Ok Calahan, you win!' Hal had no choice, so he held his arms high, while the local police went forward to handcuff him.

'Are you going to read me my rights.'

' There is time enough for that. Let's take him to jail!' Calahan replied.

'Nice to meet you, Green Man! You have created quite a rumpus!' Charles greeted.

'I have been doing what you guys are not allowed to do! Eliminating the shit from this planet. Get with it Calahan. The whole world is falling about you. There will be nothing left in 50 years or so!' Hal said, and Calahan knew he was right.

'Charles, take him to the van. Treat him kindly, but make sure he doesn't escape again!'

'On it, Captain!'

The Green Chameleon (Hal) soon turned his attention to one of the female officers and blew her a kiss.

'So delightful and cute!' Hal said.

Hal was soon made comfortable in one of Calahan's jails on 22nd precinct. The moment he entered that station he was made comfortable and taken a table with a tray filled with food and drink. They were all over him, asking for autographs. However there were no reporters on the scene.

'I can't use backup for invisibility, so I have to find a power-point and recharge,' Hal mumbled, while observing the area in detail.

There were no power points in jail. Nevertheless he knew his fingerprints and DNA from saliva were controlled by him through implants, with numerous criminals to choose from, so they could never database him that way. He realized they were like little mice compared to him. Yet he was intrigued by it all. Neither could they place his image on file. His face was just a green blurry blob with red lips that could be adjusted at will. They couldn't remove his disguise when it was all part of his body, with the exception of his trunks. Therefore his escape was planned for the interview room.

Calahan was sat in his office pondering over a suitable present for his wife's birthday and security of his jailed captive when there was a knock on his door.

'Come in! I hope it's important!'

'Captain! I would like you to see something!' Carol went to his computer terminal and began to press keys. Calahan couldn't believe the charts on screen. Child smuggling had dropped 50% and organ stealing by 100%. Then she brought up a world map and showed him the global effects.

'All that happened because of The Phantom?' she stressed.

'There is no doubt, Captain! And look, he has been in Paris, London and other important cities.'

'How can he be in all those places at once?' Calahan was intrigued.

'He targets them on different days. We are on the 22nd . London, 23rd . Paris, 24th and so on. There is one on the 15th, in Los Angeles. This guy wants to save the world and us from nasty criminal gangs.'

'And he is doing a bloody good job!' Carol said.

'Captain, I want to see my kids grow up in a better world. If they live that long. You must let him go for all our sakes. He is accomplishing what we could never do. He has no politics or laws to obey. He is as free as a bird in the tree!' Carol was concerned.

'Calahan scratched his head for a while, knowing Carol was right. But he was a lawman and had taken the oath.

'Follow me Green Man. It's time for your interview!'

'You should let me go! I have no gripe with all you good policemen and women. I think you do a grand job, with all the crims about these days!'

'So you do speak English?' One of the police women inquired.

'That and every other language on the planet. Is there a power-point so I can charge my cell phone?' He inquired in jest, but she smiled and remained silent.

'No need, use mine!' Charles advised, but Hal refrained. He was also a hygiene freak.

'When he entered the room the first thing he could observe was a power point, so he marked that spot. Then he observed a pamphlet on the wall with 'Human Rights" written in bold print and began to laugh.

'Human rights! What a laugh! So because of human rights the main camera is off? I can't complain, first time I've had human rights on my side. Yet, all I see around me are human wrongs. You guys are really nuts! Yet, I love you all!' Hal had a good laugh.

'Please take a seat!' Calahan said with three officers looking on.

'I must say Calahan, I am impressed by your considerations! But I think you got the wrong guy. For all you know I could be a copycat!'

'You know, if it was up to me I would lock you up and throw away the key!' Calahan said, putting on a brave face in front of his subordinate officers. Then Calahan left the room for a while.

'Charles, I have a call to make. Take over!' Then he walked over to his office.

Calahan did not know what to do in the circumstances so decided to call Mallory.

'Mal, it's Calahan!'

'Sorry I didn't return your previous call. Had to visit a few places!'

'No matter! We have your Green Man at the station.'

'You have? You sure it's not a copycat?'

'I am sure!'

'Then my advise to you is, let him go. No one will know the

difference between him and a copycat. Calahan, since he was on the job how many good people you think he saved?'

'Thousands, perhaps!'

'That guy is a godsend. Pity he had to blow them up like that. Anyway, it's better them in the morgue than filling up your station. Although I don't agree with such violence, he only targets the worst criminals who deserve his treatment. Anyway, I don't think he is one of us.'

'What do you mean, Mal?'

'Calahan, there are things happening that I can't mention about. Not even to our President.'

'That bad?'

'Pal, this guy could be from another world?'

'You mean a little green man from Mars?'

'No! I mean a big green man from another place, so leave it alone for now. Anyway, I think he is on our side. Remember, our military would do the same with orders of "Shoot to Kill!"'

'Yea! I got your advise. Good practical advice and know one will ever know he is not a copycat!'

'How can anyone know with his disguise?'

'Thanks for the advice, Mal! We must go for a drink sometime!'

'Will call you!' Mallory hung up.

Calahan was back in the interview room. For some strange reason, Hal's belt buckle was invisibly plugged into the local power socket charging itself.

'Charles, words please!'

'Yep!'

'I want you to do the interview. But I think he is a copycat. The information don't add up. A similarly dressed person could have taken his place during the excitement at the Bronx. You might have to kick him out of the station. I can't stand people wasting our police time.'

'I understand, Captain! I shall tell the bastard where he should go and kick him out the station!'

Then Charles went back into the interview room to put on a show.

'Bloody bastard, wasting our time all this time! I should lock you up and throw away the key! Guys, he is a bloody imposter. Things got switched over at the Bronx, so the Green Chameleon is still at large!' Charles exclaimed.

'I have been saying so all this time! It's a good thing you realized I am not the guy you are looking for. Now, can I go home and have a bath? All that dried paint is giving me an itch in difficult places!' Hal said. Then he pretended to drop a pen from the table and in the process plugged his buckle into the belt on his waist. He just had enough charge to change clothes and return to his apartment. Even so, he remained his original self while in the station.

Charles and his other officers soon escorted him to the door and had words.

'Bloody nutcase! Don't you ever show your green slime and ugly face in this precinct again!'

'Thanks for the hospitality. It's been a laugh!' Then he ran away and was lost from view. Hal was soon in his apartment and slumped on his bed.

'That was a close call. I must do something about that battery. Perhaps I should use two instead of one. Yea, but I think those guys let me go on purpose.' He pondered for a while before entering his bath to become normal again.

'Sir, the Mayor is on line!'

'Mister Mayor!'

'I heard you guys caught the Green Chameleon. Can I visit sometime?'

'No need, George! He was an imposter; a copycat! Trying to benefit from the infamy! There are lots of these nutters about, waiting for the right opportunity!'

'Sad to hear that. Let's hope we catch him soon?'

'Yes, Mayor!'

That day, when Calahan checked his fingerprint and DNA profiles he was surprised to find they belonged to a known criminal that died several years before.

'So you are truly The Phantom. Very good luck,' Calahan muttered.

CHAPTER 32

To England we journey

Mallory collected their papers and made arrangement with a hotel recommended by Michael Cockburn. That hotel was in England near Croydon and owned by Solarian Banking. In fact lots of the major hotels were presently owned by that company globally.

'Carl can handle the business in our absence and the builders are on schedule at our new place, so everything should be moving when we return. This makes it the ideal time for us to travel. I hear the weather in London is great this time of year, almost tropical,' Mallory said and Roseanne was even more excited about their trip.

'Please don't go right now. Stay a while and we can have dinner together. I must thank you for the antidote and other things. But most of all, I would like to spend some time with you. You are always too much in a hurry these days. Like you are avoiding me,' she said.

'Avoiding you! I didn't realise you felt that way. I didn't want to crowd you too much. You know how it is. Anyway, if anything, it's probably the lonely bachelors life I've grown use to all those years.'

'You can never crowd me, even if you tried. And if it's due to habit, I will have to take you in hand from now.'

Mallory handled Roseanne with kid gloves, never pushing his attention too far and when he pushed, he always held back until he received the appropriate response from her. He didn't want her to lose affection and run off in the opposite direction if he became too overwhelming. Nevertheless they had lots of fun together over the following days.

When her passport arrived she was even more ecstatic and relished their visit to the great city of London, England. He gave Carl the necessary briefing, made him know that he was fully in charge in their absence and they were ready for the journey. He subsequently booked his time with the hotel in the outskirts of London. Then both did some New York shopping together.

On the morn of their departure Roseanne looked spectacular in a blue suit, hat and matching handbag. She was waiting in the lobby of her apartment building for Mallory to arrive. He soon entered and looked her over with admiration, before giving her a peck on the cheek.

'God, Woman! You look like a queen and your perfume! I hope Oscar likes it,' he said in jest.

'Who is Oscar?' she inquired in innocence and suddenly the penny dropped.

'You can't mean that bit of circuitry and metal called Oscar?' she exclaimed.

'Don't you knock my Oscar. That guy has the most discerning eye and incidentally, he has the ability to smell,' Mallory said and she was surprised.

Like a model gentleman, Mallory assisted her with the cases and dumped them in Oscar's large trunk.

Oscar's doors lifted and they entered. Then he made sure her harness was taut but comfortable, before instructing Oscar to leave. That aspect didn't matter too much, since Oscar tended to switch the artificial gravity when certain G-force limits were exceeded. The harness also adjusted to the most comfortable position during flight.

'Oscar, please take us to the hotel on the destination card. Make it the shortest route and no heroics please. I want Roseanne to enjoy the trip, but don't take too long,' he said.

'Mal, the most direct route to your hotel is via Gatwick Airport and our ETA for optimum velocity is just after 25 minutes. We should arrive there at one-fifty-seven, p.m., Greenwich Mean Time. Drinks and snacks are available in the rear compartment.' Mallory didn't realized that Oscar was stocked with food, but he let it go for now.

'Thank you, Captain Oscar!' Roseanne replied.

The route would take them about twenty miles above the surface, where Oscar would connect with one of the main space-ways to the east. Then they would accelerate to an optimum within their lane until instructed to change speed or direction. All those instructions were carried by the guidance lasers that controlled the lanes.

When they arrived over London the car would take one of the main landing spirals to Gatwick. Basic authorization checks would be carried out by laser beams during transit. Although those beams were use for guidance, they carried information to and fro via geostationary floating space platforms at much higher levels. GPS was also available for pinpointing their position at all times and comparing with other traffic. They received information from the shuttles and cars, so they relayed the data to other platforms and ground bases.

Because lasers were line-of-sight communication, there could be no errors or noise during transmission. It also eliminated channel crosstalk, as in the case of radio waves. However journeys to foreign countries required further checks of their vehicle and its contents on land by customs officers before being given the all-clear. There was still some drug trafficking in Europe and penalties were high for contraband.

It was the first time that Roseanne had been at that altitude in any transport. She was quite apprehensive at first, but soon became used to the reduced gravity when they approached a steady velocity. All said and done, she found the flight quite comfortable compared to the one she had several years ago on a large passenger shuttle on-route to Australia.

When they approached the Gatwick spiral, Oscar made a sudden dive to follow the narrow space corridor towards the airport terminal and she almost threw up after the spin. He had to take advantage of a space in the constant stream of traffic. London was still one of the major cities in Europe if not its capital and most came to London for business, tourism and gambling.

From high altitude they could observe two great walls around the inner city. The southern wall contained all buildings south of the Thames and the northern extended along the Thames, but was not yet complete. They looked like the great wall of China from space but in miniature. Most of the southern regions of England was flooded by the rising sea and only so much could be protected by the ingenuity of man.

On arrival, Oscar and their cases were thoroughly searched for weapons and other restricted items before given the all-clear by the customs' officers. Then their personal documents were electronically stamped and Oscar sped away towards their hotel.

'This country is so green. It's like an Alice-in-Wonderland fairytale, with beautiful meadows, vales and the occasional river. Why so green?' she said.

'Lot's of rain I suppose and a very mild climate despite changes in weather pattern. It's a truly beautiful country. Global Warming has also improved the climate over the years, at the expense of some of the shoreline. While in our country there has been more freakish weather, with more than average hurricanes, tornadoes and reduced rainfall.' Mallory said.

'Yea, it seems that way!'

'To think most of our ancestors once came from here and Ireland,' Mallory added.

'I think the English must be a neat and tidy lot compared to us, but most of all, they are survivors and I am proud of my heritage,' she replied.

'I am afraid, this is also my first visit to this beautiful land. While I am here, I would like to combine business with pleasure and soak up as much of its history and culture as I can,' Mallory said.

'I do hope you don't mind me tagging along.' She was holding his hand.

'I couldn't really enjoy any of it without you by my side.' Then she held his hand even tighter with affection. Strangely enough, there were not many LPD cars travelling the airways. But there were numerous electric cars on the many motorways below. Occasionally they would pass large arrays of solar panels and wind driven generators.

'Are these large domes in the distance also owned by Solarian Banking?' she asked.

'Some are tropical bio-farms, others are holiday camps, parks and zoos, but most are owned by them. Whatever they don't own outright they have large shares in and the rest they are not interested in. These massive structures were built by their robots about twenty years ago during the boom years. At that time they were built at twenty times faster and cheaper than could have been by any skilled human worker, and they will last for many centuries to come,' he replied.

'We seem to be the only ones up here?' Roseanne asked with curiosity.

'Yes. I suppose we in the States are partly to blame for that discrepancy. Many years ago when Professor Longhurst was still around, we were given the option to franchise LPD's to the rest of the world, but the government decided to get more revenue from those exports. As a result, the prices soared in these countries and drove them to use other methods. Mainly because of those reasons, England and most other European countries became self-sufficient in energy. Old gas stations and pumps were converted to quick-chargers and ethanol. They have also got super-clean coal-fired and nuclear power stations, not to mention wind, wave and solar. All that gives them what they need in electricity and make electric cars the ideal form of transport.' Mallory replied.

'I suppose that's the reason why this country is so clean?'

'That too! Also nowadays some cars can travel as far as five hundred miles without a single charge. It's all to do with more efficient batteries, tires and better aerodynamics. Now only the large passenger airlines and shuttles use LPD's. Anyway, LPD's are now extremely costly items. They have to be exchanged or primed every ten years, and that process can cost several thousand dollars each time.'

'What are these great fields I see ahead of us?' she asked.

'Those look like cane. They are a bio-engineered type of sugar cane that can grow in colder climates. They are optimized for high grade ethanol. The extracted sugar and fuel is mainly exported to our country and parts of South America. It's not as polluting as petrol. It's also suitable for rum and some other drinks.'

They soon arrived at the car park of a large hotel. It was at the outskirts of Croydon. Many came out to view the incredible car that landed from the sky and to say hello to the two supposed wealthy Americans.

Mallory was surprised by the attention paid to them by the hotel staff and wondered how they knew so much about him. Then the manager asked them into his office. He shook their hands and handed them their keys and a folder each, containing local tourist attractions. There was also a wine list, menu and other relevant lists for room service.

'I hope you both have a most pleasant stay with us. Should you wish anything, just call reception and it will be done. We have reserved two of our best suites for you and madam on the first floor.' He buzzed the assistant to have their cases delivered to their rooms.

The hotel was set in beautiful grounds with an adjacent golf course.

CHAPTER 33

Summer and romance in London

Mallory decided to take advantage of the good weather and spend some time with Roseanne viewing the sights of London together.

In just three days they had visited most of the special places from museums to The Tower. On the last day they visited Tower Bridge and later walked along the Great Southern Wall.

'Wow! This sea-wall is so high. Pity no one can see a thing beyond them,' Roseanne complained with sweat pouring down her cheeks.

'It's one of the prices we pay for Global Warming. These are just 50 feet high and the waters will rise to about 200 ft within 100 years. So this is just temporary, no thanks to the little rock hitting Antarctica. I reckon most of London has another 50 years before it's completely submerged,' Mallory said and she was saddened by that fact.

'Good thing the meteor, Little Solo, didn't hit New York or some populated part of the planet?' Roseanne became uncertain of their future and held him tightly.

'Don't you ever leave me!' she said.

'Never!' he replied.

Finally, they visited Regent Street for some shopping, then dumped it in Oscar and went off to Tower Bridge.

'When I am in places like this, I sometimes think of my son and the fun times we could have had together,' Mallory said.

'You mean, Andy? I met him once in DC. He must have been just three then and I thought he resembled you even at that age. The eyes and nose. She was calling him at the time. It must be very difficult when you are so far apart. How is your wife now? I hear she got married after you left.' she replied.

'She met some local doctor guy. She was always a very nervous woman, perhaps she carried a little baggage from her childhood. Her father was one of those brutish alcoholics. Anyway, she was nervous about the job I did and also for the boy. She wouldn't even allow him to visit his friends a few streets away and never allowed him to enter water and learn to swim. I haven't seen them for six months. Anyway, but for my son, the rest is just water under the bridge.' he said with no regrets.

'How appropriate,' she said while looking over Tower Bridge into the wider flowing Thames below.

'Nevertheless, we get on well together. Don't we?' Roseanne nudged him.

'Yes! I suppose like a house on fire. I never thought it possible for two people to have so much fun together, and I can talk to you.' He said as he took her hand in his and gave it a gentle squeeze. He began to utter something but held his breath.

'You were going to tell me something?'

'I was going to ask you to marry me then, but I stopped short.'

'Why did you stop?' she asked, with disappointment.

'I don't really know. Perhaps I didn't want it to be a thing of the moment. After all, we have only been really close like this for a week or so, and marriage is supposed to last forever. I suppose I still have a few scars from my previous.' He said.

'That also applies to me, but it shouldn't stop us from moving forward,' she replied.

'Well, when I ask you and if you say yes, I would like us to have a reasonable period of engagement before we take the plunge. I can't afford too much turbulence and complications in my life at this time, from any direction, and perhaps you feel the same?' He said.

'You've been single for far too long. But you do like me?' Roseanne was saddened and disappointed by his last comments.

'I like you very much and I am getting fonder by the minute, so let's savour these moments together and Que Sera, Sera. If we are to go that way, so be it, and we should try not to make the same mistakes again.' Mallory was full of nostalgia.

'I am all for Que Sera, Sera. What will be, will be,' she replied.

'Do you think these great walls will last?' he said changing the topic.

'They must have put a lot into building these structures. I thought we were never going to see walled castles and ramparts out of history books, but history has a strange way of repeating itself,' she replied.

'Yep! Now we are fighting the waves! But this is only temporary, Love. They reckon Global Warming is a lot worst than anticipated. As temperature increases to over 3 degrees centigrade, the waters in this area will rise by at least 250 feet in another 200 years or so and the effects of Global Warming will remain with us for several thousand years. By then the UK will change into a few more islands and be reduced to less than two-thirds its present area. That is when almost all the ice melts. The worst will be the increased temperatures in tropical areas, leading to more deserts,' he replied.

'What are you saying, exactly?' she inquired.

'I am saying that all these coastal cities will be submerged eventually, if nothing is done to slow the process. All habitable land areas throughout this planet will shrink by at least 30 percent over the next 50 years. There is enough ice in Greenland and Antarctica to bury us under by at lease 200 feet. Almost as high as our tallest buildings.' She was totally shocked by that knowledge.

'My God! We are in such big trouble!'

'It's all to do with human over-population.' Mallory was convinced.

They went to a popular local restaurant near the river and enjoyed a romantic evening together before calling Oscar for their trip back to the hotel.

'I think I've had enough travel for one day. So when we return to our hotel we can sample the bar and get acquainted with some of the natives,' he said and she agreed.

CHAPTER 34

Lumak informs Ben about the child

Lumak had received an urgent and coded message from Michael Cockburn on Earth. **'Your presence is required on Earth immediately. It concerns the child.'** Lumak dropped whatever he was doing to make the trip. He told Sarah he had urgent business on Earth and took the nearest palace portal to their North Dakota manor.

'What could ever be that urgent!' he complained, while breaking off another of his important missions. Nevertheless, all matters concerning his son overruled all others. He soon realized he couldn't use the original Doctor Longhurst persona and created another.

He wore a new disguise as one Doctor Charles Mansell. Unlike his previous persona, Doctor Jeffery Longhurst, Charles was cleanly shaven and twenty years his elder. Lumak was very good at carrying off such personality changes and could readily transform through his incredible brand of technologies. To him, wearing a new body was almost like changing clothes.

Since leaving Earth, Lumak was very careful when showing his face in public places. After all, the famous Doctor Jeffery Longhurst was supposed to be dead, since their shuttle accident near Mars, and many would recognize him as such. Therefore it was necessary to wear a few disguises during his infrequent visits to Earth.

On arrival he immediately contacted Michael Cockburn and gave him his identification code through implants. That was not really essential as only Michael and Ben had such brain implants on Earth. Lumak always tended to be thorough and precise in his endeavours. Brain Implants placed Solarians within their own Virtual Worlds where they could perform and communicate hundreds of times faster than normal speech and vision.

'What is of such great importance... to take me all the way to this world?' he asked. Michael was surprised by the new form of Lumak.

'I am sorry, Siend, for any inconvenience caused, but I couldn't find an easier way. Your father-in-law did mention the situation to me and I had no choice in employing Mallory. But I didn't realize he would get this far so quickly.' Michael was apologetic.

Solarians always use Siend to address their superiors, in particular their Supreme Councillors. It was equivalent to Lord. Metra-Siend or Grand Lord was reserved for Supreme Beings.

'Why did you employ him in the first place?' Lumak asked.

'Ben had decided to employ someone, and I thought it was the best way to keep an eye on the situation,' Mickey replied.

'In that case you should continue your surveillance.'

'By coincidence, Siend Ben... also acquired his services on a full time basis to locate the child!' Mickey said.

'There is no such thing as coincidence! It is the way of the Greater Purpose!' Lumak replied.

'Anyway, I have two of my best operatives tracking him and we think it is only a week at most before he finds the child. Therefore, I thought it important that you knew of those developments immediately.' Mickey continued.

'It is indeed a very important development and quite unfortunate. Now I shall have to tell Dad the full story. I hope he accepts it without too much fuss and doesn't decide to spill the beans to Sarah and others.' Lumak sent an urgent message to Ben, while patiently awaiting his arrival at the manor by fast shuttle.

'Ah, Dad, you received my message. Thank you for coming immediately,' Lumak said and Ben wondered who the unfamiliar individual was, for they had never met before.

'Father, my disguise is much better than I credited,' he said and Ben realised it was Lumak, his son-in-law in another of his strange disguises.

'I am here on a brief visit and Sarah sends her love. The matter that I am about to discuss with you concerns my lost son. I think you had better sit down and prepare yourself, because you'll be completely shocked by what I have to say. However, I would like you to promise me that whatever transpires, you will leave any decisions in this matter to those above us. They are the ones that know what is best for our universe in the long term.'

Then he placed a small black box on the table. It began to transmit dreadful images of Javols decapitating humans and other animals on the nearby wall. Then he went on to explain the future invasion of Earth by the Javols, who had already decimated the complete galaxy of Andromeda.

Ben listened to the strange story with disbelief, but knew that his daughter's husband was not one for tales, despite his some-times strange way of doing things. Then Lumak went on to explain the position of Earth in the greater plan and finally the birth of a great profit that would one day save the Galaxy of Osmaron (our own galaxy) and the greater universe from the Javols.

'You are trying to tell me that the great profit, our Messiah is here and now?' Ben asked.

'Yes, Father. He is in the form of our long lost son. He is the little one that was stolen. It's just that he was not really stolen, just misplaced for a while until he came of age.'

'Not really stolen? Then, where is he?' Ben insisted.

'He is where I can find him. I shall tell you only if you swear to keep his whereabouts from his mother and all others until the time is right... which will be about twenty years from now.'

'That's a long time to wait and I don't like keeping such secrets from my daughter. However, I shall promise not to reveal his whereabouts, only if I am allowed to see that he is safe.'

'I shall take you to him and introduce you as my older brother after I have changed my disguise. You may keep an occasional eye on my son, and your grandson, in my absence. If you think he is in danger or trouble, you must take immediate action on my behalf. This situation is also quite painful for me, but I must obey the ruling of the Grand Lord and his Council. In any event, you are never to become directly involved in his welfare and family life, because of your direct association with us. It's a matter of divine prophesy! Nevertheless, you may pay an occasional visit like an uncle in passing, or perhaps, an occasional friendly voice on the phone, but any more familiarity might distort his natural development,' Lumak stressed.

'If I had known before, I would not have assigned the man Mallory to locate him. Mallory is now in England and from what Michael says, is quite close. I shall have to recall him immediately and that part will be extremely difficult, if we are to prevent him asking too many questions. After all, why should he be suddenly requested off a case that he has almost solved. Not to mention the costs incurred in the process?'

'I see, and the truth might be much too ridiculous to be believed by him and others. In that case, don't you think it may be necessary to get him on our side. This Mallory... was he not the one that used to be Jerry's chief of security?' Lumak inquired.

'The very same,' Ben replied.

'From what I understand, he was a very well mannered and disciplined member of Jerry's staff. Can you get him here to the manor... in order to debrief him.... I wonder if he is clean of the disease?' Lumak inquired, with an air of uncertainty. Then Lumak wondered: 'He must also be part of the Master Plan. Too many coincidences!'

'I am unsure of all those factors, but he was given the tester. He wanted to have the test and vaccination before going to England.'

'You mean... he already knows of its existence?'

'Yes. He figured that much out for himself. I have also made him instrumental in spreading the knowledge of its presence and its distribution in North America. The man is very persistent, has very good principles, a high intelligence and a knack for solving problems. I suppose these qualities are the reason why he got so far so quickly in the investigation of the child. I do believe, at present rate, he will find the child within a week.'

'Where is he now?'

'We have traced him to a hotel in the outskirts of Croydon, England. It happens to be one owned by our company. Michael has been tracking his every move from the start. He has informed the hotel of his importance to the company and to make him comfortable during his stay.'

'In that case, I shall have to see him immediately,' Lumak insisted and vanished.

CHAPTER 35

An angel from God?

Mallory and Roseanne got back to the hotel late that evening. When they arrived they were interrupted on their way to the elevator.

'Sir, there is someone here to see you. He has been waiting at the bar for some time now. His name is Doctor Charles Mansell,' said the formally dressed male receptionist.

'I wonder who it can be? It's no one I've heard of before and no one knows we are here?' Mallory said, looking at Roseanne and showing concern.

'Could be one of Mickey's people wanting an update on the child,' Roseanne replied.

They went towards the bar. There at the counter was a man in a deep blue suit sipping a cocktail.

'Are you Doctor Charles Mansell?' asked Mallory.

'Yes, I am the same. And you are Mallory Colman, I presume?'

'This is my friend and colleague, Roseanne. What is all this about?'

'I have come from Professor Khan. It concerns the little child you seek. Can we discuss this matter in greater privacy?' Lumak, now disguised as Charles, asked.

'I suppose you could use my room, upstairs,' Mallory said and they left for the first floor.

'Now, what's on your mind?' Mallory asked with a worried Roseanne sitting next to him.

'Before I commence the more serious part of our conversation, can I ask you both a few personal questions?' Lumak said.

'I suppose that will depend on how personal your questions are,' Mallory replied.

'Not that personal.'

'In that case, please shoot.'

'Did the antidote tests work right for you both?'

'The answer to that question is, yes. The tests showed us to be negative on all counts, but we can't be absolutely sure the test equipment was fool proof at the time. Machines do fail occasionally, you know, and it was delivered by courier without having been tested after delivery. Even so, what does it have to do with you... and how do you know of such personal matters?' Mallory said.

'Thank goodness for that. I think we can safely assume that your test results were negative. The next question I shall ask is an even more ridiculous one, but you must be patient with me and humour this poor old man.'

'Ok, I'm all ears!'

'Do you believe in life on other worlds? I mean what you would consider alien life?' Lumak inquired.

'I suppose... in a way. But despite many so-called UFO sightings, no one has yet met anyone publicly. So I think most of it must be either hallucinatory or fraudulent, and I would rather reserve my judgement until I met such a person, human or otherwise,' Mallory replied.

'What would you do if you came face to face with such an individual? Would you go quietly insane or take the incident in your stride like any intelligent individual would?' Lumak asked.

'I suppose I would remain quiet, but shocked out of my bloody wits. I suppose those feelings will also apply to most people,' Mallory replied.

'The reason why I asked you those questions, is because this matter is very delicate. I have to take you both into my confidence before I can explain them in full. There are a few things you should know before you resume your search for the child. But you must promise me that you will not divulge any of our future discussions outside of this room. What I shall now show you concerns all life within the known universe,' Lumak said. They stared at the old man as if he was as mad as a hatter. Nevertheless although they were slightly tired from their daily adventures they decided to remain patient listeners.

'I don't know much about you, but I need a drink. Do you need one, Darling... and you Doctor?' Mallory asked. Both shook their heads and he decided to place an order with room service.

'What are you drinking, Doc?'

'Vodka and tonic, please!' Lumak said and Roseanne left for her room, to put on some more comfortable clothes. Mallory removed his jacket and tie, and Lumak his jacket. They waited for Roseanne to return and when she did, so did the waiter with the drinks, glasses and ice bucket.

'Now, we can relax and listen to what you have to say,' Mallory said. Roseanne got up and began to pour the drinks.

'The child you seek is the Son of Destiny. The one that will save mankind and others within our universe from.... Let me show you what I mean.' Lumak retrieved the small black box from his coat pocket which he placed in the middle of the table. He gently tapped the box and it came alive in a splash of multicolored lights that extended towards the nearest wall. A moving three-dimensional image took form, but there was no sound.

The picture first consisted of beautiful scenes of a world. However, it was not Earth, as there was no grass, just a thick violet moss that covered areas of the land like a carpet. Although the trees were mainly green, they were all alien and beautiful.

'This world is called Caefon. This is what it used to be like just over three thousand years ago. As you see, it's populated with humans not too unlike ourselves, but with six fingers and two thumbs. They were known as the Andromedan Ancients. It's in the galaxy you call Andromeda, over two million light-years away.'

'You are having me on! No one can travel that distance to Earth in a lifetime. Not even to our galaxy. It's impossible!' Mallory stressed and poured himself another drink.

'That trip was made in a single day, and I can take you there within seconds if I so wished, but first, please observe the projected image,' Lumak said, and they both observed the images intently and couldn't believe what the doctor said.

'This is what became of that beautiful world.' The scene changed to that of a large city with people going about their daily business in a very advanced society. The technologies were beyond anything they had ever seen. Then the scene changed again, showing several objects of many shapes including others with large batlike wings hovering in the air above. They were able to take the form of any life-form of an equivalent mass and were very intelligent. Missiles and lasers were firing from every direction towards the creatures, but they appeared to be unaffected by those weapons.

The creatures suddenly darted towards a crowd of people and began to systematically decapitate and absorb their remains in the most gory manner. Although the poor humans fought vigorously, the monsters seemed to enjoy the ferocity of the attack and duplicated their bodies in the process, to go elsewhere and reap more havoc.

When the nightmarish recording came to an end there was not a single human or animal left on Caefon. Most of them had been eaten and the few remnants soon died from disease in the ensuing decades.

'Gracious Lord!' Roseanne exclaimed and immediately rushed to the bathroom. Mallory felt equally unsettled and sickened by the very realistic gore images. They were both completely shaken in their innermost cores and had to take a breather. Mallory poured himself and the doctor two tall drinks.

'You mean to say all that really happened?' Mallory asked.

'Yes Mallory, All that really happened about three thousand years ago and the monsters are presently on their way to our galaxy, and will do the same to us.' Roseanne returned from the bathroom with tearful eyes.

'Sorry I had to put you both through this, but I had to tell you the truth and perhaps you might wish to join us in the future in the fight against these alien monsters. That is Caefon now and the monsters you have seen are called the Javols. They are microid in design and are composed of Nano-bots. There are many such life-forms throughout the universe. They were initially created by intelligent creatures like us and because of a flaw in their design, went their own way after destroying their creators. Independent Nano-bot type life-forms have always seen biological types like us as a threat and will go to any lengths to exterminate all such threats. They have been on their way to our galaxy since that time and are now less than one hundred and fifty years away from Earth.'

'Seems like we have a real fight on our hands,' Mallory replied, with fear written all over his face.

'Do we have a chance?' Roseanne asked, equally fearful.

'Yes! We have a very good chance, but long term plans have to be followed precisely. It's like a complicated jigsaw that has been put together since the pass three thousand years and will go on being assembled for perhaps another thousand years in the future. If we are not properly prepared, this whole galaxy could be overrun by Javols and almost every race exterminated in the process. Those they cannot use for food will be imprisoned and used for some other undesirable purpose. To them we are little more than fodder,' Lumak said.

'This is most horrible. How do you know all this? I suppose you are going to tell us next that you are not of this world,' Mallory replied.

'Can I use your bathroom, please?' Lumak asked and Mallory showed him the way.

The elderly doctor left, but it was a younger and infinitely more powerful person that walked through the door towards them. He was dressed in a black hooded cloak that did not reflect any light, nor did it cast a single shadow. When he dropped the hood behind his head, he resembled a young man in early thirties.

'I am Lumak, Shadite. Sometimes known as Professor Jeffery Longhurst. I am not of this world and was sent by one of the Grand Lords of this universe to ensure Earth plays an important role in future events.' Then he faded into nothing and faded back into himself.

'Oh my God!' Roseanne exclaimed.

'Our powers exceed anything that you can ever imagine. In this form I can travel anywhere within the known universe within seconds. I am impervious to any force or missile and can never die.' Mallory and Roseanne remained stunned in their seats by the aberration.

'You are really an alien... from another world. With godlike powers, to travel anywhere?' Mallory asked bravely, partly in a daze.

'Yes, Mallory. I can go anywhere I choose, almost instantly. I cannot grow old and neither will I ever die. I am like an angel. We were born and trained to serve the Cosmos. In some ways I am very similar to you, in the job you do. But I am here to help mankind and our galaxy in the long term.'

'So Doctor Longhurst and others like my good friends Jerry, Harry Lennox and others survived the shuttle disaster, after all?' Mallory asked, with a smile of affection.

'Yes, they are all happy on a paradise world called Eden. It's the most beautiful world in our galaxy,' he replied.

'That's incredible news!' Roseanne shouted and almost jumped out of her seat with happiness.

'What would you say if I told you that there were beings in this galaxy that are billions of years old? Beings that are above us in every conceivable way. They are also involved in the survival program.'

'That's truly incredible!' Mallory was intrigued.

'What if I also told you that I dealt directly with a Supreme Being. The one responsible for this part of the whole universe. One that has existed since the beginning of time.' Lumak said.

'I would say that was one of the most incredible things I've ever heard. I have never believed in an all powerful, all knowing one called God, and neither do I believe in any type of religion. Because I have seen and witnessed too many terrible and painful things in my relatively short existence. Things that I think any reasonable god would never have allowed,' Mallory replied.

'Our Grand Lord is not involved in the day to day activities of the individual. He likes his subjects to be free to develop in their own preferred ways, and neither will he take sides. He is only concerned in the broader cosmic survival plan. What we call The Greater Purpose.'

'I think I see your point. But I wish things were better.'

'Yes, all that will come in time. Life on Earth is more to do with the haphazard way people live, combined with the natural order. And that brings me to the other projection,' Lumak said, while retrieving a second box from his Shadites cloak and placing it on the table.

'This is the way things will be on earth several decades from now. However, the scenes here are of a local world I previously mentioned, called Eden within Solaria.'

This time the pictures were of a most beautiful and uncontaminated world. One that Roseanne and Mallory would have associated with Heaven. If there was ever such a place. There were beautiful golden palaces and a crystal city with many humans going about their daily duties, but whatever moving transport there was, it was only restricted to the city complex. Every individual was under thirty years of age and beautifully built.

Humans travelled to and fro via portals which were installed in every house. They simply entered a cubicle and were instantly transferred to their destination. The scene changed as the camera entered the largest palace and Mallory was surprised by the people he could observe seated around the large dining table. They were talking and laughing in a familiar manner, and they included Jerry and his wife, Sharon, Jeffery Longhurst, Lennox, Meron and many others he could recognize. Those he and others had regarded as lost in space when part of their shuttle exploded, but they were twenty years younger than when they were on Earth.

'You and Roseanne can visit planet Eden if you wish and also be young again. We have the technology to do almost anything to promote happiness, longevity and painlessness,' Lumak said, but the film continued. This time they could observe numerous flowers of every conceivable colour and large multicolored fairylike insects that were collecting the nectar while obtaining those and other nutrients.

'Oh, my darling! This place is so beautiful,' she said while holding Mallory's hand.

The sky was a deep blue and there was no pollution anywhere in that near perfect environment.

'This world is really an Eden. It was named by Gerald Fraser. That was on his first interstellar trip over two decades ago. That is what can become of a world when all its members pull together for the common-good. Jerry, The President, is now a member of the controlling council and owns his own palace and protectorate state, and there are thousands of such areas on Eden.'

'Fantastic!' She was almost speechless.

'You see, it is Earthly man and his greedy self-indulgent ways that should be blamed for most of the dreadful things that can be experienced here on this world,' Lumak said. They nodded in agreement, completely overwhelmed by the beautiful images.

'But why did they have to disappear like that?' Roseanne asked.

'They had to make a clean breast of things. If anyone on Earth knew of Eden, it wouldn't have lasted five years. Your property developers, prospectors, and God knows what other greedy idiots, would have ruined that beautiful world in much the same way as they have done to your Earth. Those that live on Eden are of the same mind and purpose. We should all be responsible for life within its every habitat throughout the Cosmos. Because of our high levels of perfection and singular purpose, crime does not exist on Eden.'

'I see,' Roseanne replied, but couldn't see how.

'Would you like to meet Jerry again?' Lumak said.

'I don't know how we can. It's all so incredibly confusing. Can it be arranged?' Mallory asked, almost as if in a daze.

'Almost anything can be arranged. Even a visit to Eden. Concentrate on your special work for now and I shall send you a message through my father, Ben, at the appropriate time. My father seems to have a high regard for you and so also does Jerry.'

'That's quite reassuring,' Mallory said.

'I shall now give you the address of the child. When you check him, you will find his birthmark. Then you must contact his grandfather, Ben, immediately. However, under no circumstance should you inform the Petersons' of your true identity. You are just someone sent by his real father to deliver a present. You may get the boy a little toy on my behalf. After you meet the Petersons, you will realise he is in a good home.'

'We shall, Doctor! I only want to see the end of this caper,' Mallory said.

'For reasons that I cannot explain to you at this time, you are never to mention anything concerning the boy to anyone except present company and his grandfather, Ben,'

'I understand,' Mallory replied.

'And now, I must leave you both. Always do what is right and you will win the fight,' Lumak said and slowly faded into the air. Mallory and Roseanne was dumbfounded by the whole ordeal.

'Wasn't that a ghost, Mal? How could anyone appear and

disappear like that?' Roseanne inquired, perplexed.

'A very advanced technology that we cannot even comprehend. Perhaps millions of years in advance to ours,' Mallory replied.

'Do you truly believe in this Eden planet, and what he showed us about the president and others?' Roseanne asked.

'What would anyone like that gain by lying? Anyway, I always wondered why that shuttle disappeared in the way it did. Now I know. So good old Jerry survived after all?'

'It appears so!' she replied.

'Darling, I need another stiff drink and don't mind me if I slowly get drunk in the process. I've got to collect my thoughts on this one before I go quietly insane,' he said.

'Do you realise what time it is? It's three in the morning and time we both went to bed. We can have a long discussion at breakfast tomorrow.' She collected the glasses which she put on the tray. Then she made sure he went to bed and tucked him in.

'Ok! The first thing I shall do tomorrow is call Ben and verify what this guy said. Then we can make new plans.' Then Mallory slumped unto his bed completely overcome by exhaustion.

Nevertheless he still had to carry on with his investigation. There were several loose ends and many had already been paid. To break off now would have made those criminals suspicious.

CHAPTER 36

Conrad Alexander

After recovering from the initial shock of meeting Lumak the Shadite in their hotel room, Mallory decided to do as advised. He had to continue the pretence of searching for the child.

His next contact in the underworld was Conrad Alexander. That man was tall, muscular and fear inspiring. He had started his career as a lowly pimp com bouncer and steadily progressed through narcotics and later on, to the more lucrative enterprise of paedo-smuggling. Conrad was the last link in the European chain of child-smuggling. Like a few of the others in his business, he also operated an import export business as a front. Of all things, he also dealt in babies nappies (Diapers) and women's fancy underwear.

After Mallory had breakfast with Roseanne that morning, he had a lengthy discussion with her about their strange experience with Lumak the previous evening. However, whatever happened, he had to continue the search, or at least make it seem that way to everyone concerned, and in particular, the criminal organization. They would ask many questions if he suddenly disappeared from the scene or refrained from paying them their dues.

'Despite everything that had occurred, I shall have to visit Conrad. He will be expecting me today and soon after that, his cut. If I fail to show he'll see it as a betrayal and contact his friends back home. After that, my life won't be worth a rusty dime. They are highly organized and can be very nasty if they suspect the slightest thing or detect the smallest discrepancy. I'm sure they think I already know too much about their operations. So I shall have to play along for now.'

'Sounds very dangerous, Darling?'

'Yea, I know. Danger is my middle name and taking dangerous risks, my game. At times like these I wish I had the Green Chameleon to watch my back!'

'You be extra careful today, our Phantom friend is probably working streets back home now.' Roseanne replied in jest.

'Yea, I will. You just remain here at the hotel for the moment and carry your cell-phone in case I need you in a hurry. Here is the number of a car-hire company. They will take you anywhere in a hurry and they know their way about the city.' Mallory handed her the card.

'If you are sure, Darling,' Roseanne replied, knowing that Mallory always knew the best way to tackle a problem. Anyway, in that particular case two could be a crowd and hamper the delicate operation.

Oscar took Mallory to a place in the East End of London. It was in one of those converted warehouses close to the northern Thames Wall. Conrad's business was in the worst part of that area and on the first floor.

As he entered, he was quickly frisked and his wallet removed and checked.

'We can't be too sure these days with the Phantom about?' The smaller of the two said.

'Selton Park Hotel. That's a very expensive one, isn't it?' The largest of the bouncers jested, while reading one of his cards.

'Let him in, boys! We have business to discuss!' Came a voice from the adjacent office.

'Please come this way, Mister Mallory Colman, I presume? And you are on time!' Conrad said while glancing at his watch and Mallory grunted 'yes!' showing dislike for being searched in such a manner. Then Conrad took him into his office while the two bouncers remained outside.

'Sorry for the close search, but these are bad times with the Phantom about. He killed several of our street guys recently. If you wanted a clean kid... I could have got you one at a quarter the price. Why is this one so bloody important?' Conrad asked in a near cockney accent.

'His people want their son back and they don't mind paying, so I took the job. Now I have to follow through,' Mallory replied.

'If we knew before... we could have snatched him back for you or swapped him over with another and his adopted parents would have been none the wiser.'

'The child has a special birthmark which would have made that plan difficult to operate. Similar babies can look a lot different to parents who have grown used to them, even for a short while, but thanks for the suggestion,' Mallory replied. Conrad soon realized Mallory was always ahead of him and his wild suggestions. It was an attitude he seemed to dislike.

'In that case, it will cost you two hundred grand to locate the child.'

'But we have already agreed a sum of one hundred,' Mallory reminded, realising that present company was not the most scrupulous of men.

'That was before. If these people are so bloody rich they won't mind another hundred grand, and I want one hundred big ones up front. The other hundred to be delivered after you find the child. And try not to double-cross me. Do we have a deal?' Conrad spat and put his arm forward.

Mallory remained still for a moment, considering whether he should shake the hand of such a corrupt and perverse individual. He also realised a handshake was their way of clinching a deal, so he took his hand and shook it. As far as Conrad was concerned a deal without a handshake wasn't a real deal.

'You've got all the information you need in that folder. Everything about the kid is in there. Make sure you don't mention any of this to anyone, or you are one deceased Mallory Colman. You hear me!' he snarled, handing him the brown folder.

Mallory had to make a bank transfer of one hundred thousand international dollars. That was the standard currency for transactions between international criminals because of the sometimes severe fluctuations of local currencies. Then he would commence his search for the child.

Mallory thought everything was signed and sealed and was on his way back to the hotel. On the way he stopped off in Croydon to do some shopping. Then he made a call to his office in the States.

'Carl, it's me. How is everything?'

'It's not too bad. I had a few phone calls regarding more microid failures. One hospital lost three in a row. They wanted us to collect and store the dust for them. I told them to put the remains in bin liners and we would be along to collect them in a few days. We can't do much until the new building is ready, so I can have them collected and stored in the office temporarily. Seems your add is working, so we'll be quite busy with Microids over the foreseeable future.'

'Pal, that is small fry compared to some things we'll be doing together in the future and you don't know the half of it. We'll talk the moment I return. Anyway, I've got to disappear. Roseanne is probably waiting for me at the hotel.'

CHAPTER 37

The kidnapping

Roseanne went to do some local shopping in Croydon. On her way back the cell-phone rang.

'Madam, it's the hotel. We have two gentlemen waiting for you in the lobby,' the male receptionist said.

'Who is it this time?' Roseanne thought and tried to contact Mallory but couldn't get through.

She wondered whether something bad had happened to him and hurried. When she arrived one of the ushers pointed her to three plain clothes gentlemen in the lobby. She went over to meet them.

'You are Mallory's woman?'

'I am Roseanne, but I suppose you could address me as such. What has happened to him?'They remained silent for a moment before the taller of the two began to speak.

'Nothing too serious. He is in a bit of bother and we think you can set things straight, but you'll have to come with us, immediately!'

Without even asking who they were or any identification she followed them to the car.

'Are you the police?'

'No. We are not. Let's say you are our security in a business deal, and you are not to act strangely. Just remain where you are and be quiet if you know what's good for you!'

'Am I kidnapped?' Suddenly she was quite concerned.

'No! Kidnapped is too strong a word. Call it a temporary change in hotel accommodation. But, I am afraid ours could never compete with the famous Selton Park,' the little slim one said as the car sped off towards London.

The taller one lifted the car-phone receiver and dialled a number.

'Boss. We have the girl. It went like a song. She didn't suspect a thing. We are now on our way to the hide-out.'

'Good work, Gill, keep her on ice for now!'

It was then that Roseanne realised she was really kidnapped. She immediately decided to switch off and hide her small personal cell-phone. She began to hatch an escape plan and assumed they knew nothing of her past training with the FBI. Then she could take whatever little opportunity was offered and escape when the time was right.

Nevertheless she was going to follow the demands of those criminal idiots for now and learn as much as she could about their organization. Even so, her first problem was in finding out where she was being taken. She was not familiar with the roads or streets of London, so couldn't memorize landmarks to name.

Roseanne was sitting at the rear with two men on either side. Although she was not tied up they watched her every move. She realized she had to do something to retrieve her cell phone and place it in a more appropriate hiding place before they searched her handbag. Having observed the young driver in front, who was seemingly only concerned with dodging traffic, her only immediate concern were those two with her at the rear.

At an appropriate moment she pretended to be very nervous and opened her hand bag to retrieve a packet of peppermint.

'Be careful little lady! Make no sudden moves!' said the one with the yellow floral shirt.

'Its only peppermint. I don't smoke and tend to use it when I'm nervous!' she explained, while opening the purse.

She timed the diversion and dropped the little packet of peppermint on the floor when the car made a sudden swerve. While she fumbled, she switched it off and placed the small cell-phone within her cleavage, gently tucking it into her bra. Eventually she retrieved the items from the floor, took a peppermint and offered the packet around, but both men refused.

'I am sorry, but I am a little nervous. I have never been kidnapped before,' she said, judging the situation.

'Yea, Yankee woman, you seem to be too nervous! Let's have a look at that bag of yours!' The one in grey suit said and pulled it from her. He emptied its contents on the floor and thoroughly went through them. He could find no phone or dangerous weapons, so scooped the items up, including her purse, and place them back in the bag. Then he handed it back.

'American bitch, where is your mobile?'

'I don't have it. Left it back in the hotel on recharge. You can always take me back to collect it!' She shouted back.

'Must say, Woman, you have lots of spirit. You just remain still! If you move from your space again, I will let you have some serious pain!' The little one with the missing front tooth advised in no uncertain terms. He was cleaning under his black finger-nails with a small retractable blade. He smelled of motor oil and could have been a motorcar mechanic.

She was still not sure what trouble Mallory was in. Any sudden moves by her might have compromised his position, so she decided to go along for now until better informed.

They took her to a workshop in the East End where she was handcuffed and chained to a small metallic pillar. Close to where she stood were a brand new sleeping bag and a box of groceries. She viewed her dirty surroundings with its pungent smell of engine oil and realised they had planned the whole episode in advance. Her stay would be a long and uncomfortable one.

Mallory had to do some shopping that morning before visiting Conrad again to arrange the transfer of a hundred grand. When he completed the transaction, Conrad lifted the phone to contact someone. Then he handed Mallory the phone.

'This is Mallory. Who is it?'

'I am afraid we have your woman. She would like to talk with you,' the voice said.

'I am sorry, Darling. They came to the hotel and told me you were in serious trouble. I thought they were undercover cops. I will be ok, Mal. Just do what you have to. They...' She was suddenly cut off.

'Your little lady has been snatched by us. Just our guarantee to ensure you don't split on us before you pay the balance,' Conrad said.

'But she is an innocent party in all this. Why don't you send one of your guys to keep an eye on me instead and release her?' Mallory pleaded, but Conrad always had his way in such matters. Conrad was one of those sadistic people who loved to see his enemies squirm in the muck and for some reason didn't like

Mallory.

'I am sorry mate. Your girl remains with us until you find the child and give us the balance of our money. I've already carried out my side of the deal by giving you the information.' Conrad insisted. Mallory realised his mind was implacably made up. Yet he persisted.

'But we had a deal!' Mallory complained.

'For all I know, the moment you find the kid you will take the first flight out of here and split. The deal didn't mention anything about your woman, one way or the other.' Conrad continued.

'You could tell your colleagues back home and my life wouldn't be worth a dime,' Mallory pleaded.

'That might well be, but I shall still be out of pocket by a hundred grand and the woman guarantees my full share.'

'You better just keep your gorillas away from her and make her comfortable, or you and your boys won't live to see another Christmas!' Mallory shouted, seething with rage.

'Threats, threats, Mallory. That will not help the situation,' Conrad replied, confidently.

'You just hurt a single hair on her head and you and your guys will pay dearly!' Mallory stormed out of that place like he was possessed.

Somehow he had to locate Roseanne. Once her whereabouts was known, he could put together a rescue plan to get her back. As always with kidnapping, one was never sure whether the episode would end satisfactorily after the ransom was paid and there was Roseanne's life to consider. He also realized that with 100 grand at stake Conrad would do his best to keep Roseanne alive, but there were no guarantees with criminals.

Finally Mallory had to consider the child in all this. If only he could have got a pretend child to mislead Conrad into thinking he had completed that part of the job, then he could pay him the full amount and get her back. Even then, there were no guarantees. Also, the Petersons had to be kept well out of this complex and delicate operation for the sake of the child.

He hoped Roseanne still had her cell-phone. Then she could contact him and they could trace her call through Oscar. However that process was highly unlikely, since she would doubtless have been relieved of her bag during the snatch. Even so, crooks always felt more comfortable when their valuables were close at hand. So he reasoned their hide-out would be within a five-mile radius of Conrad's office.

'Oscar, do you know the frequency of Roseanne's cell-phone?'

'Yes! I think I have a record, somewhere. Here it is.' Oscar displayed the details on the screen.

'Keep it handy. We might have to use it in a hurry, and make sure that line is kept open. Be prepared to locate her position the moment she calls.'

He parked the car at the top of one of the larger car parks and waited patiently for her call. It was in the late afternoon when the phone rang.

'Mal! Mal!' Came a quiet female voice.

'I am here, Love. Describe to me where you are.'

'I am in what appears to be a workshop. There are just two of them here at the moment. They handcuffed and chained me to a pillar, but I am all right. I've got to go now, someone is coming!' The phone went dead.

He didn't have time to say another word, but she knew he had received some information to go on. Whether it was enough could be another matter. She would try again when they left to do whatever they did.

'I have it. It's about two miles from here,' Oscar said and the small screen lifted from the side of the dashboard to display a map of the local area. It showed their present position in blue and Roseanne's position in a blinking red circle. With the use of Satellite Imaging the local buildings and roads could be seen on screen in clearest detail, with pedestrians and vehicles.

'How did you do that?' Mallory exclaimed.

'I am also linked globally to a range of satellites. So when I received her signal I sent out a search command,' Oscar replied.

'Believe me, Oscar. You are the most clever car I've ever seen, and thank you for finding her so quickly,' Mallory said, but Oscar remained silent.

'Now, all we have to do is get her back, and...' Mallory caught his breath for a moment, thinking of revenge and then he thought of a better plan. He was never the type to take such criminal intent lying down and knew the police were too busy to be concerned with his problems. Anyway he could show no evidence regarding a kidnapping. No ransom had been asked for or given and he had only recently arrived in London.

'I have to silence that rat's nest, permanently. If they remain alive and the word gets around they will hunt me down for sure, and there is the special kid to consider in all this,' he thought, hoping that Conrad hadn't informed his other colleagues of the kidnapping. Mallory thought that Conrad and the other members of his gang were working independently. With such criminals there was little to be gained by telling others and sharing the spoils.

CHAPTER 38

Roseanne's rescue

Mallory thought for a moment and soon found the answer. It was to do with a drug. One that rendered certain brain functions temporarily inoperable and also gave the patient permanent amnesia. If his idea was to work he had to administer the drug by dart gun in reasonable dosage. The criminals would soon become his amnesic patients and Conrad was the first project on his black list. He considered that method the most humane from several other choices, including killing them outright. But hopefully without blowing their heads off with micro bombs. After all, he was not the Green Chameleon that blew heads off without question.

He imagined Conrad begging and grovelling for pity with outstretched arms before the drug took effect. He would completely ignore the rascal's pleas for mercy until he fell in a useless heap on the floor. Then he would recover, not knowing who he was or where he was. Not even being able to recognise his closest family and friends, and the effect was permanent. Mallory's problem was getting the drug and gun in time.

'Perhaps Ben might help,' he murmured and immediately asked Oscar to contact Ben, which he did.

'I require your urgent assistance to fumigate a nest of vipers, but I don't want to kill them. Just give them a loss of memory. They can then be rehabilitated and become useful members of society. Could you get me two fifty millilitres of Amiterol and a small repeating dart gun, for about twenty mills a shot, at a distance of say, ten metres?'

'Leave it with me, Mal. I know just the job. It's not Amiterol and is a lot more effective for a much smaller dosage,' Ben said. A moment later Oscar sounded a mild alert.

'Mal, I am to collect a package from Eta. Could you wait here for me while I take the quickest route?' Mallory knew exactly what Oscar meant and did not wish to be flattened like a pulp against the seat by those excessive g-forces. When the door lifted,

Mallory got out as quickly as he could. When he glanced behind him the car had already disappeared in a gust of air and on his way. Within seconds it was a mere speck in the horizon. Oscar was soon back with a small package.

'Oh, Pal, some bastards are going to pay dearly for taking me on,' he mumbled.

Conrad was surprised to see Mallory back in his office so soon and wondered whether he had found the child. Once again the two men searched him, checked his wallet and sent him through to Conrad.

'You've got the balance for me?' Conrad asked, fully confident in himself. He realized he had Mallory where he wanted him, since he would have done virtually anything to save his woman.

'I have it, but I need a leak. I pretended to be a travelling salesman in kiddies' toys to get to the kid and needed to get some stuff for him. Then I had too much tea at their place. He is definitely the kid I'm looking for. All I have to do now is get him back. Have you got Roseanne here for me?' Mallory inquired, but instead Conrad pointed in the general direction of the toilet.

The small gun had been carefully taped to his under belly, just above his genitals and could not be easily detected by a quick and simple body search. He pealed the tape off and assembled the three parts of the gun, took the capsules of micro syringes from his belt and inserted them into the magazine. Since each capsule contained 12 darts, there were more than enough in the chamber for the remainder of Conrad's gang. When he entered the room, Conrad showed him a chair.

'I suppose we better talk business. When you transfer the money I will tell you where she is. And don't keep me waiting too long because I can't guarantee my boys will keep their hands off her much longer,' Conrad said and sat down.

After those words Mallory was fuming with rage, but kept his feelings to himself as best he could, saving his energy and concentration for the delicate operation ahead. Instead of documents, Mallory retrieved the weapon from his pocket and fired point blank at Conrad's neck. Then he swiped him a fierce blow across his head and he slumped quietly in his chair, with his head still resting against the desk. Then Mallory half opened the door.

'He wants one of you boys.' The tall one walked towards the office, unsuspectingly. As he entered, another dart was fired and another knockout blow, and he was in a pile on the floor.

Mallory was well trained in the martial arts and knew how to knock out any person with a single blow across the neck.

'You are also wanted,' he shouted through the slightly opened door and the other bouncer, who was now standing close to the main door, was curious enough to follow. He was the one who always took pleasure in searching visitors. Another dart was aimed and fired but this time he lunged at Mallory. He began to struggle with all his strength when he observed his other companions in a state of dormancy.

'It's a very bad day for you, Pal! You are going to eat some shit. How did everything go to nasty so bloody fast!' he said.

'It's you that's got the shit, so why fight it!' Mallory replied.

He pulled the dart from his neck, and lunged towards a grinning Mallory. Mallory played a little cat and mouse with him, by enticing him to take a fist to his chin, but he missed each time and eventually staggered to joined his companions on the floor as the drug took effect.

Mallory realised that when they woke from their short sleep they would not be aware of anything, other than being alive in a strange office. Neither would they have recognised their companions and present environment. He wanted to permanently divorce them from their present criminal careers and associates. However the major part of that job was done.

After everyone in that area was silenced, Mallory removed his fountain pen, unscrewed the nib and pressed the clip. A needle-like device protruded from that part of the pen. He entered that part into a slot near the combination lock of the safe and numbers were displayed at the other end of the pen. A small laser scanned Conrad's left eye with the 8 digit number. He entered the numbers on the dial and a clunk could be heard. Then he released the lock and the thick metal door opened. The safe was full of money in packs of 100 dollar bills and EU notes. He took 200 grand, then another 100 grand for his troubles.

'You wont be needing this any more. Never ever renege on a deal after a handshake... 100 grand of this dirty money can go to a suitable children's charity,' he murmured to himself, realising they would never be back to that office again.

'I think it's time you guys found some new careers. You, Conrad, I shall drop into the nearest launderette. Your mind has been washed clean and now it's your clothes. I must do a professional job.' He removed all their personal documents and identification, and assisted Conrad down the flight of stairs to a local launderette. A poor elderly woman was doing her laundry when he walked in with the seemingly drunk fellow.

'Sorry, my dear! Too much to drink, I'm afraid! His wife will kill him if she sees him like this. Could you give me a hand to remove his jacket?' Soon all his clothes were being laundered with the exception of his underpants. He gave her some paper money for any further expenses and she was thankful. When he returned, he called Oscar to the building and loaded the remaining villains into the booth. Then he took them to two distant parks and dumped them in the middle of each.

'Beautiful weather we are having! Have a nice day, sucker!' he said each time as they journeyed to the next bench. Every gang member had a note tied about his neck, It read '**Please take pity. I am due for rehabilitation!**'

Finally it was time to visit the hide-out. That operation would be more difficult and risky because Roseanne was more vulnerable while chained to the pillar. He had to formulate a plan and get some tools, including powerful bolt cutters. The latter were a simple matter once Oscar located a nearby hardware store.

'The problem is, getting those two or more out of the way before I can get to Roseanne and remove her cuffs. I think I've found a way, but it will have to be very swift on my part,' he muttered.

He soon arrived at the workshop's entrance. It was in an area that consisted of many garages. The workshop was the last building at the end of an alleyway. He checked the rear entrance and found it was secured from the outside. There was only one exit at the front. The gangsters had chosen their hideout well, but with only one escape route.

He silently parked his car several metres away from the main double door of the garage, opened a bottle of alcohol and began to splash its contents throughout the door's surface, including the framework. Part of the metal shutters had been lifted at the time and could not have been easily shut from the inside. Mallory lit a match and threw it at the door. Then he threw a brick towards it to arouse its occupants in case they were asleep.

He could soon hear turmoil inside as fear and smoke began to spread.

'What the bloody hell is going on outside. Keep your eye on the bitch while I have a look!' The tall one said.

'Ignore it! It must be kids playing games,' the other said, while the one with the knife moved closer to Roseanne. Eventually the smoke built up and they began to cough and panic, leaving Roseanne for a while.

Very soon afterwards a latch was released and the first head showed its ugly face. Mallory was ready and waiting, and immediately fired a dart, which found its almost stationery target. One of his panic stricken companion, not knowing what the danger was, decided to run for it, but he also took a dart. This time Mallory aimed for his lower torso, which was not as effective on a moving target as the neck.

As he exited through the alleyway, Mallory quickly got into Oscar and he was soon cornered close to the other end. Mallory had to quickly finish him in the same manner. He didn't want to take too long and was not sure whether the fire would spread and engulf Roseanne, so he approached him and as he attacked, kicked him between the legs. While he grinned with agony, Mallory smashed him in the face. The recoil of that blow also took its toll on Mallory's fist. Nevertheless he cracked his knuckles and stretched his fingers before dumping both villains in the back of Oscar. Then he ran into the building to assist Roseanne.

'That's more than enough excitement for one day. I must say, I won't give much for your new accommodation and friends,' Mallory said in jest, while approaching her with the large pair of cutters.

'I thought you would never find me in this rat-infested hell hole, but thank God you received my call.' Roseanne said and hugged him. Both handcuffs were released and she was free, although sore and hungry.

'I could eat a horse, Darling!'

'What happened to all those groceries I saw back there?'

'Did you see the old camping gas cooker? They expected me to cook my own meals and I refused.'

'So the kidnapped woman also went on hunger strike in defiance. I can't top that one.'

'Yea, I preferred to remain chained until my rescue. Why should I cook for them as well?'

'It's nice you had such undying faith in your rescuer,' he said.

'I always thought you would rescue me,' she replied.

'What a pong?'

'Yea, this place really stinks. It gets into every bloody thing!' she exclaimed.

'Don't worry my lovely beauty, you may have stepped in the shit, but you came out smelling like roses,' he said and Roseanne smiled.

'Some roses! This stink will remain with me for a week!' she complained.

'Is that all of them?' he inquired.

'No! There is one more. He went to get some take away,' she replied and they both went to hide behind the door.

'In that case, it seems we have a free Chinese, so you don't need a horse after all,' Mallory replied with a grin. As the criminal entered she kicked him in the groin and he went down holding that part with both hands. Than she slammed him one across his forehead and he went out like a light.

'Payback can be a bitch, when its done by a real bitch! Now I feel great!' she said and Mallory was surprised by the way she took him out.

'I see Chad did a great job training you guys.' She steered at him with keen determination, as if she was ready to take on the world.

Then Mallory darted him in the buttocks. He was also dumped

in the back of Oscar.

'Well, my girl, too much excitement for me. Let's get out of this place. We can have Chinese later. Anyway I have to drop your friends off on-route. If we delay they might recover and think we are their parents,' he said and they hurried towards the car.

'And I need to wash this oily filth off my body. Three baths should help!'

'It was all my fault, you know. They found our hotel address on one of the cards I carried, but they will not bother us anymore. They are going to have permanent amnesia from now on. I hope it will permanently change their lifestyles,' Mallory said, while Oscar sped off in the general direction of Croydon.

'I think I was also partly to blame, Darling. I thought you were in trouble with the police, and gave little thought to who they were.'

'No problem. I would probably have done the same,' he replied.

Although the doors were still smouldering, the building was mainly brickwork and the chance of a major fire spreading was minimal. However Mallory dialled the emergency services and gave them the address, and a fire engine was soon on its way to that location.

'Oscar, please land on Mitcham Common. We have to drop off some more cargo,' he said. The car soon landed in an isolated area of the common and bodies were dumped on two separate benches. They would revive in due course when the effects of the drugs wore off.

'Which one of these rascals would you like to kick in the teeth before we leave?' Roseanne declined when she saw the placid state of her captives. Then he stuck the rehabilitation signs around their necks.

'How did you manage to get them all like this?' she asked.

'I asked Ben to get me some Amiterol and a dart gun. You know, the drug that induces permanent amnesia. It's sometimes used for rehabilitating violent criminals, before they are dispatched to a new life. Well, I decided it was time those five were rehabilitated. I think the stuff Ben gave me was much more advanced, with less side effects and at least 10 times stronger.

'Are you ok, now? They didn't try any funny business...?' Mallory said and she smiled.

'No, Darling! They wouldn't dare!'

'Anyway, that's one episode I won't like to repeat in a hurry, but you are safe and that's the main thing.'

CHAPTER 39

The Child is visited

They were soon back at the hotel, had a thorough shower while licking their wounds with antiseptic and plaster. Although they were slightly inconvenienced by the ordeal, they were experience operatives at the sharp end of business, and still had work to do. During the ordeal they had grown much closer together. While the adrenalin rush brought back memories of more serious encounters in the services.

'I've got to call Carl later today. I have to see what's happening back at the office and we'll have to make arrangements to see the child,' Mallory said.

'If it's the last thing I ever do, I've got to meet this Son of Destiny for myself and hold him in my arms. If he is that important to our future, we should always keep an eye on that family. You never know... someone might try to kidnap him again,' Roseanne replied.

'Unless we get rid of the whole criminal organization, permanently. What do you think?'

'Whatever you want, Darling. But it might be a little more difficult giving them all amnesia. They seem to have a worldwide network, and another even worse one might spring up soon afterwards.'

He immediately contacted the Petersons and told them he was in London for a brief visit and had to deliver the child some presents on Mr Longhurst's behalf. They accepted his reasons and told him he could call the following morning.

'What did you get the child?' Roseanne asked.

'How did you know I got him something?'

'I had a peep while you were outside. I also got him some things, but I left them at the hotel desk before...'

'I got him a large tree. One of those things you build with blocks. You start with the trunk, then the branches and after that you add the pyramids, spheres and other colourful shapes for the fruits and leaves. I have been told it can be extended almost indefinitely. The salesgirl also said it's useful for building cognitive perception abilities and aptitude. Next time I visit I have a good excuse to take him some more blocks. By then, he'll be a little older, more clever and perhaps more appreciative of my attention.'

'It's a good thing you didn't get him a toy car, booties and a bib, because I got him those. I find it almost impossible getting presents for kids that age,' Roseanne replied and he nodded in agreement.

'It's probably because you never had one yourself!'

'When do we visit him?'

'First thing tomorrow. If everything is all right... After I contact Ben and give him a run down on the investigation. Then on our return to the states, I put it in writing and hand a copy to Michael Cockburn. After we return home, I will pay the others off and this case will be filed and placed in a secured vault. Anyway, we'll be back here again soon enough.'

'What do we do over here in the mean time? I mean, after we visit the child?' she asked.

'I don't know. Perhaps more of what we've been doing before. I didn't realise how much I loved you until you were in danger. Then I knew I couldn't live without you,' Mallory replied.

'Really?'

'Yes! Really!'

'I must say, although I knew I was in serious danger, I always thought you would rescue me. Like my knight in shining armour. Instead, you created a smoke screen and scared them out of their wits and out of the workshop. Now, they are wandering all over the country not knowing who they are or where they are. Some knight. I sure wouldn't like to have you working against me,' Roseanne said and they broke into laughter when they saw the funnier side of her rescue.

'Those armatures sure deserved everything they got and I'll do it exactly the same way again. I was damned upset when he so blatantly told me that he kidnapped you and there was nothing I could do about it. No one ever tells me that and gets away with it. Fancy playing such a damn trick on me after we had a handshake to clinch the deal. Now I know for sure that there is no honour among villains.'

'Regarding the bit about getting hitched together officially. I accept!' Roseanne said and Mallory put his arms around her and they kissed passionately.

'I also got you a little present.' Mallory took a small blue case from his pocket. She opened it and was enthralled by the most beautiful engagement ring she had ever seen.

'It's.... It's, incredibly beautiful and so delightful, my darling.' She kissed him again. He removed it from its velvet cushion and placed it on her finger.

'There you are. Now you are 100 percent woman again and it suits you. Now I feel like the luckiest guy in the world.'

The Petersons' lived close to the Chessington Dome. It was one of the largest indoor adventure parks, with many features and facilities. That one was also owned by Solarian Banking and contained numerous buildings for their commercial affairs. It also held the European head quarters for Sarah's numerous charities. One could observe the BioLive sign for miles.

Due to his recent heart problems, Mr Peterson had taken a part-time job within the dome. He was presently a senior supervisor in one of the administrative departments. This position was made available to him by Lumak, who was the real father of the child, Son of Destiny. It was quite handy for the family, partly because it was local and mainly because it was not as stressful as his original career in sales within the chaotic city of Central London. Lumak also had some of his own security working in the area that could keep a constant check on the family.

On arrival they introduced themselves at the door and were ushered into the lounge.

'How is Jeffery these days?' Mrs Peterson asked. They had never known their true identities and had never linked the shuttle accident with them.

'We saw him before we left. His wife Sarah was not with him then, but they are both fine. He is unable to break from a special project at this time. We decided to take our holidays here this year and see the sites. He gave us these presents to deliver. It's our first time in your beautiful country, you know. He also wanted us to say hello to the boy for him,' Mallory said.

'He is presently asleep, but he should be up soon for his feed. I hope you don't mind waiting?' she said.

'This is a lovely and most comfortable home. Can I see your garden?' Roseanne asked.

'Yes! Of course! Please come with me.' They both followed. From there they could see the great dome barely a quarter of a mile away. It overshadowed everything in that area, but did not cast shadows. Instead it was more like a bright jewel, reflecting light throughout the area.

Their garden was quite large and she was obviously a keen gardener. There was another garden facing unto theirs and Roseanne checked the area, wondering how easy it would be for someone to enter from that direction. However because of the positions of the houses, any wandering villains would have been easily detected in such a closely-nit residential area.

'You have never thought of moving to another more secured area to live?' Roseanne asked.

'Why should we? We are well known in this area and the dome is handy for my husband.'

'So generally speaking, you both feel happy and secure here?' Mallory asked, following Roseanne's line of questioning. He was thinking of the Terminal Disease and Antidote Distribution.

'Why all these questions?'

'We were just a little worried. We hear of so many kidnapping of children these days and the situation is getting worse. We wouldn't like anything to happen to the little one. We are also in security business back in the states, so if you require any assistance or equipment, we know of organizations that can help.' Mallory apologised.

'Why don't you come to New York on a holiday sometime and stay with us? You will always be welcomed?' Roseanne said, breaking the present trend.

'Because of his medical problem, my husband has been advised against long flights. Something to do with his blood circulation and thrombosis.' Then they heard a child cry and she immediately went to a local room.

'Here is my little George!' she said. 'Would you like to hold him while I get his bottle?' Roseanne took the child from her while Mr Peterson remained to keep them company. The boy was very playful, liked it when his tummy was gently tickled and Mallory and Roseanne bonded immediately with him. Mallory made sure his birthmark was the correct one and where it was supposed to be. Then Mallory opened the box and started assembling the first part of the tree and they were curious.

'Everyone should be given a proper start in life, and he is only a little nipper.' Mallory said.

'Don't worry, we can move it to his play pen later,' Mr Paterson said.

When she returned, Roseanne handed the baby back and he was already sucking from the bottle.

Mallory had placed two small positional indicators in two of the building blocks of the tree game. They would occasionally transmit information pulses that could be picked up by one of satellite Eta's large dishes. That way they could always keep tabs on the family's movement. The batteries would last 5 years, by which time it was hoped a better method would be found.

When he finished building the tree the child couldn't keep his eyes away and was soon crawling towards the beautiful object.

'Ahhhh! He loves my present!' Mallory exclaimed. After having a cup of tea and cake with the couple they decided to leave.

'What did you think about security in that area?' Mallory asked.

'I think the whole thing was very cleverly thought out. No one will ever suspect such a normal caring family for anything and the area is filled with many elderly people, nosey neighbours and a few CCTV cameras, which is much better than the best security systems,' Roseanne replied.

'The only factor that worries me is the health of the old man. What if he took a turn for the worst or even died on us.'

'His wife is still a young woman and will probably remarry,' Roseanne replied.

'That's exactly what I mean!' A worried Mallory stressed.

'In that case we must keep a tighter leash on the child.'

After they left the Petersons that day, Mallory was relieved that his current investigation in England was finally at an end, but even then, he wondered whether it was only the end of the beginning of that particular episode.

CHAPTER 40

An important announcement

It was late afternoon when they arrived at their hotel. That time corresponded to mid morning in New York, so Mallory decided to contact Carl on the bedroom phone.

'Carl, it's me. How are things in your neck of the woods?'

'Things have gone quite madly over here in your absence, but I am coping. I could have contacted you sooner, but I didn't want to be a nuisance. Anyway, the President's Secretary for Internal Affairs rang. They wanted an urgent meeting with you. I told them you were in London and would be back in a few days.'

'Wonder why?' Mallory worried.

'The news of the Terminal Disease is flying fast and wild down the grapevine and has found its way to the White House. Apparently some clever doctor in your Group of Thirteen took your words literally and went searching for the bug. Well, he found it in almost one in ten patients, as you have said he would. Apparently it's a lot more prevalent in club goers and those with an active social night life. I suppose such people come in contact with many others in the course of a week.'

'Yea!'

'Anyway, I think you should return here as soon as possible before pandemonium breaks loose, and some of these officials are quite powerful.'

'I see what you mean!'

'I had no idea things had moved so quickly. I will have to release the documents to the press immediately. Carl, expect me in the office sometime tomorrow. I will see you then.' Mallory hung up. Then he went to Roseanne's room and tapped on the door.

'Come in!' she yelled and he entered.

'Sorry, Love. We have to leave for New York tomorrow!'

'So soon?'

'Yes. It can't be helped. Too much is going on back home,' he said.

'If it can't be helped!'

'As it's our last day, I would like to take you to somewhere special in the morning. You'll have to decide where, because I want it to be your treat.'

'Can we visit the old palace? I mean Buckingham Palace? I have always dreamt of going to that place and wondered what it used to be like living in those days... When it was alive with royalty. We can observe the beautiful paintings, jewellery and ornaments together.'

'Ok! We can go to the palace. After that I will take you to one of the best restaurants in the city. The rest of today we can stay in the hotel and relax a bit close to the television. I still have a few aches and pains from you know what. Anyway, the cases can be packed later tonight.'

'Ok, Darling!'

'I was hoping to remain here for another week, but Carl seems to have more than he can fairly cope with at present.'

'With the exception of my kidnapping, I had a most wonderful time. So don't you feel disappointed about anything.'

'That's fine, Love. You be happy and comfortable today. Whatever you want just ask, and I mean anything,' he replied.

'In that case, I want you to come over here right now.' He slowly approached her expecting the very worst, but instead she grabbed hold of him with one of her special Judo locks and kissed him.

'Oh! I wish every black-belt taught Judo like you.'

'You've seen nothing yet!' she said and released him.

That evening was spent in front of the television in Roseanne's room, with the occasional call to room service, until the television program changed abruptly.

'We interrupt our current broadcast for an important announcement!' The screen immediately changed to a laboratory scene.

'The presence of a deadly global virus has recently been brought to our attention. The consequences of this new pandemic could be catastrophic to humanity. It is one that inhibits human conception.

'For a more comprehensive report on this recent discovery, we visited one of the largest bio-laboratories in the country to interview the director; one Professor Bengizara Khan.'

The scene changed again to Sol Newtown Dome in North Dakota.

'Professor Khan, why has this rather dangerous virus only now been discovered, when it has been present on several continents for many years?' the reporter asked.

'I cannot answer that question. All I know is that the virus involved is not easily detected. The carrier, being so similar to normal skin bacteria would have eluded our best doctors and scientists. Once it replaces all normal skin bacteria, a complex virus is released to invade the genitalia and prevent conception. A type of sexual cancer if you like, that manifests no outward symptoms. It was discovered by our most sensitive computerised equipment while doing some basic tests on cancer patients,' Ben said.

'Professor, will this disease affect every person in our country?'

'At present it affects just over 50 percent of Europe and Asia, and is quickly spreading to continents like America, Africa, Australasia and associated islands. It will affect everyone in Europe within a few years. It spreads by touch, water, and air, and can remain dormant until conditions become favourable, or a human host found.'

'How can it be stopped?'

'The virus can only be prevented by inoculating the very young before puberty or catching older, productive couples before the infection has progressed beyond 10 percent on their bodies. However that latter situation is highly improbable as the disease will spread from 10 percent to fully blown within a period of just two weeks. Once it's at that level, I mean the full-blown stage, nothing can be done and those infected will never procreate again. It causes too much damage to the genitalia. Because of the contagious nature of this disease most males will be unable to produce sperm or females initiate fertilization. The strange virus that causes the real damage works on both sexes equally. The virus that does the real damage is a very small part of the bacteria involved.'

'Is there an antidote for those few that have not yet been infected?'

'Yes! We at Solarian have currently produced a suitable antidote. However it is still undergoing stringent tests. It will take another three months or so before it can be released for general use. That one can only be administered to the very young and those that have been tested negative. This is because there will only be a limited supply at that time.'

'People, you've heard the eminent professor. There is no simple cure or advice at present, but as more information is released, so you will be informed.

'Nigel Thompson, for CLT News, signing off.' The original program continued.

'What did you make of that, Darling? Ben has released the information here... so soon,' Roseanne said, astonished.

'There must be a darn good reason for it. Now I have to return and face the music, whatever happens,' Mallory said.

'You better watch your back and be careful you don't become a scapegoat in their complicated plans. Ben could be using you in all this, so be extra careful,' she advised.

'I think I know the game plan. It seems to be the only way they can get it out to the public without creating a global riot. That way, people will grow used to the idea over several weeks. He has also given them hope, by saying he has a working antidote. I bet he's been planning for this time many months ago and already acquired large stocks of the Antidote.'

'You mean, this whole thing was contrived by him to make more profits,' Roseanne said.

'Could be, but I don't think he is that type of person. He already owns half the planet, and screwing the human race for an extra buck is not his style.'

CHAPTER 41

Back home

After they returned to the USA, Mallory took Roseanne directly to her apartment, then he went to his address. He made an important call to an old friend he had known since the days of Jerry, his president. He was called David Anderson.

He was now with the Daily Observer, which had over the years become a national news outlet, in printed journals, E-mail, Internet and computerised news. Those could either be viewed on television, small notepad, mobile phones and others. Those types of media were global in scope.

Journals printed on paper were far too expensive for the average person to buy, even when trees were specially grown for that purpose. Therefore paper was recycled time and time again until the quality sagged. At that time most people relied on computers, television and cellular phones for news bulletins and important information like news and weather broadcasts.

The Daily Observer had its main offices in New York with branches in Europe and the Far East.

'Hello, Dave! Guess who?'

'Ah, don't say. It's my old pal, Mallory Colman. How could I ever forget that voice, even after... five years?'

'Are you as popular in your outfit now as you used to be then?'

'Is Vice Editor big enough for you!'

'Congratulations! I knew you were keen, but that's something else, Pal. I might have a big one for your paper, and I would like it to go international as soon as possible.'

'Whoops! Sounds like you've got something real big!'

'Have you heard anything on the grapevine regarding a national health problem. Well, it's now at presidential levels?

'What are you saying?'

'Pal, I am not going to say any more over this line.'

'When can we meet?'

'Can you make it to my flat right away? I have just returned from London and haven't visited my office yet. I would like to get this thing off my chest before I begin work.'

'Yes! I suppose so. Let me check my diary. Can I take my personal secretary along? She is much better at shorthand and operating the laptop and recorder?'

'That should be all right, but no photos please. I want my name kept well away from this story when it breaks.'

'In that case, I am on my way,' David said.

David and his beautiful female companion arrived one hour later and she was as efficient as she was sensual.

'So you never got hitched again?' David asked.

'I intend to soon. I got engaged a couple days ago in London,' Mallory replied.

'Congratulations, Mal! I am now on my third, with five kids and they are happy.'

'Congratulations!'

'So what's this all about, Mal?'

'I've got a file to show you. It's from the President of Solarian Banking. Read the first few paragraphs and tell me what you think.' Mallory handed him the file.

David read several sheets and handed them to his assistant who quickly glanced through them.

'This is dynamite! Who gave you this?'

'The head of Solarian Banking, Ben, himself. They discovered the bug while carrying out standard blood tests on cancer patients. Then purely out of curiosity they tested healthy people and found the bug was endemic in Europe and Asia.'

'It's a bloody knockout! I am completely shocked!'

'Didn't you receive any feedback from England yesterday regarding his lengthy interview on television? Pity I couldn't have recorded it at the time.'

'Since this new president there has been a lot more press censorship. Not everything from Europe is freely available over here and there are high penalties for rule breakers. Anyway, don't worry Mal, we have our sources,' David said.

'Can I take this file away?'

'Yes, Pal, it's yours. Just make sure it goes national as soon as possible and keep my name out,' Mallory insisted.

'If what I just read can be proved... but when it gets public there might be trouble. It's difficult to predict how mister and missis average, not to mention the in-betweens, will react when faced with that type of knowledge. Knowing that they might never be able to have any kids will be quite a blow to normal couples, particularly newly weds. There might even be riots. Now I see why this thing is being kept from us. Tell me one more thing, and don't say another word if you don't have to; is there an antidote?'

'I have very bad news for you in that department. Those that are already infected have no chance whatsoever. Only kids before puberty and those that are not yet infected can be saved. They can be inoculated and prescribed an antidote for life or until they decide not to have any more kids. The antidote itself will be fully tested and ready in about three months. This is one of the main reasons why everyone must know as soon as possible.' Mallory realised he had followed Ben's exact words on the London program. Nevertheless he also knew it would have taken several months to organize the necessary testing and distribution of the antidote.

'It's worse than I thought. However, I think I understand the situation and the reasons why you want it to go national. What if everyone was infected by this disease before we found a suitable cure? Our leaders are damn negligent if they knew about this before. I shall make that point clear in my article.'

'Now, that's the David I used to know. Give it your best shot. It's important for every member of the human race to know where they stand if we are to save some,' Mallory replied, realising at last that David had already lit the fuse.

David also had much to gain from his paper, since it was breaking news and he was the only one with that particular angle.

'Will you have access to the antidote?'

'I should be distributing it,' Mallory replied.

'That's very good news. Let me know the moment it's ready, Mal. I suppose everyone will be tested?'

'Yes! But only those below the age of forty-five. Couples will be selected by the age of the youngest female partner.'

'That's very good news. I've got to leave you now. Got to see my boss and make a few calls, if I am going to get these pages to press. We must get together for lunch sometime soon.' David handed him one of his cards. Then bolted out the door with his assistant in tow.

Mallory then decided to visit his old office. The following day he and Roseanne had much shopping to do.

'This is unexpected. I thought you guys were coming back tomorrow,' Carl said, but got up to greet Mallory.

'I didn't want to miss the real excitement,' Mallory replied.

'Anyway, are you coping ok?'

'Just about. What I can't handle I file under Hold. This is the Hold file,' Carl said and retrieved a very thick tray with several folders.

'Don't worry. Things will be back to normal in a week. Just manage as best you can for now. The experience will be good for you. It's now also your business as well, so you have to handle the reigns when needed.'

'No problemo! Buy the way, Calahan called and left a message, something about the guy that called himself the Chameleon was an imposter.'

'Ah...! so our real Chameleon is still at large!' Mallory was pleased with that outcome. He was beginning to hate those criminals since London, but was limited in what he could do.

'By the way, Pal, Roseanne and I are getting married.'

'Congratulations, Captain! I knew she always fancied you, but I didn't realise how much. We must celebrate sometime soon.'

'We shall, and I want you to be my best man. It's going to be in about a couple of weeks, after we move into the new building.'

'I will love to, Mal!'

'Did you see this morning's news? Well, I brought you a paper copy. Dave, the Editor, sent me that one specially. I released the file yesterday, so very soon all hell should break loose in Washington. I am sorry, but you will have to hold the forth a little longer.'

'I kind of enjoy being boss in your absence. It's just the amount of work. Not to mention the phone.'

'Here is an agency. Call them now and get a couple temps. They will do the processing and other work for you in half the time. I have used them before and they are very good. Just tell her it's for Mal. Now, Pal, I've got to finish my report on that kid today. I can tell you all about Roseanne's kidnapping next time we have a meal together,' Mallory said and went towards the computer. It was much quicker by voice and Dictaphone, leaving Carl in wonderment about missing out on some London intrigue.

'Kidnapping?' Carl wondered what it was all about.

He left early for Roseanne's department. She was busy cooking when he arrived. At that time his mind was set on discussing their future wedding.

'I was thinking. Why don't we set an early date for the wedding? With things moving the way they are at present, if we don't do it now, we might not be able for a long time. We could keep it as simple as possible. What do you think?'

'Whenever you think, Darling.'

'No! It's not what I think. It's what we both want. Why don't we spend a little time this evening and discuss things like, the ceremony, invitations, reception and such like. So that we can get the ball rolling?' he said and she remained silent while preparing the salad.

'Are you having second thoughts?' he inquired.

'No!'

'What then?'

'It's not that. I don't have any real family or friends in New York. My only sister is now living in Chicago. I don't think she'll be able to make it either.' Roseanne was saddened by that fact. He went over and hugged her.

'That's not a major setback, you know. I don't have much family left either. Just my son and friends. We'll just have to do with what we have and invite a few local friends and colleagues, and the Pastor of course,' he replied. She smiled and wiped her tearful eyes.

The following morning the Terminal Disease had made head-lines in that particular publication and many others. Mallory was excited when he saw the bold print on the screen. That particular one included his article. It read, **"Most Deadly Pandemic**

Terminal Disease Discovered," with a detailed map showing the spread of the disease throughout the entire globe, with a smaller contour map of the world showing the most infected regions and the flow of human carriers.

Even Hal, The Chameleon, was pleased. That meant he could stop chasing criminals and create a better plan.

'So... At last! My friendlier bug is out of the bottle. I must plan a more efficient method next time. Thank goodness I'm not on Earth anymore, with a great lab and planet of specimens to choose from. There is also the Virtual Chambers. But I must do the dirty when the time is right. That will be when all survivors receive the Terminal Antidote. After all, I don't want to kill the innocent when I can help it.' Hal muttered.

The news had taken many by surprise with little time to slowly arouse public awareness. But once it did there were announcements and interviews about the Terminal Disease throughout the entire day.

The following day the phone in his office rang. It was the Secretary for Internal Affairs.

'Captain Mallory Colman?'

'Yes! That's me!'

'You are to visit Washington DC, immediately! The President is holding an important meeting at the White House. It's a matter of national importance and security, so you must not, under any circumstances, discuss this and any other conversations you will have with us from this moment on. Not even that I spoke to you! Do you understand?' the Secretary insisted.

'Yes, Sir. I fully understand the implications. You can expect me there tomorrow,' Mallory replied.

'The meeting has been reserved for three p.m. We shall see you then,' he added and hung up.

'Bloody hell! I hope I am not in the deep soup because of the early release. David promised he wouldn't mention my name,' he thought and was soon on the blower to David.

'You are sure you haven't included my name in any of your correspondence?'

'Yes Mal, I'm 100 percent sure. They must be bluffing. It's either that or most likely it's to do with a completely different matter. But I didn't, and it will not come from my office,' David stressed and Mallory was convinced it was to do with another unrelated matter. Even so, its occurrence on the back of the recent publications was suspicious to say the least. Knowing Mallory, he always took the path of least resistance, so in this case he decided to pretend complete ignorance and stick to his guns, come what may.

Anyway, he was just the messenger, but also realized unscrupulous politicians looking for scapegoats had a tendency to shoot messengers.

CHAPTER 42

Face the music

Mallory immediately got on the phone to Roseanne.

'Darling, pack some of your best clothes. We are off to meet the President at the White House first thing tomorrow. I'll be over to see you in about an hour.' He hung up, glancing at Carl.

'Carl, I have to visit DC tomorrow with Roseanne. Do what you can in our absence and please check up on the progress of the new building if you have time. We have to begin our move there next week.'

Suddenly it dawned on Mallory that he was in the Terminal soup up to his neck. He wondered whether Ben had planned it that way; to drop him in the deep end and let him take most of the heat when the information was publicised. It would be a way of introducing him to others of importance before passing the distribution and other more labour intensive parts of the operation over to him.

'What a bloody clever man you are, Ben. You must have figured it all out years ago. But how did you know I would be involved. Could be that you left that option open-ended, to be filled in at the appropriate time and I just happened to be the innocent sucker to have fallen into your trap. Either that or you think I have the right credentials for the job,' he thought, while entering Oscar.

He could be in big trouble with the Pentagon if they found he was the source of the information leaked to the press. He could be in it if he had breached any rules they considered compromising to national security. After all, despite what Dave said, he was the one that released the information to the press. Mallory was very apprehensive and nervous of the whole ordeal, to say the least.

Michael Cockburn and President Nicholas Wilson also knew the master plan, but was unable to give anything away to anyone, including his own congress and most of all, his Secretary for Internal Affairs. Any knowledge of the planned long term global population control of mankind would have been tantamount to betrayal of humanity and considered the worst kind of conspiracy. But this was not just population control, it was also the culling of humanity. Nevertheless they would act their parts well and let Mallory take the heat, with them throwing the occasional bucket of cold water on the flames when things got too hot. At least that was their worst case scenario.

Mallory and Roseanne arrived in Washington DC during the later part of the morning, parked Oscar in a known car park and made arrangements with one of his favourite four star hotels. He had known the proprietor since his previous assignment to DC and had dated his daughter on occasion. That was immediately after the divorce, but had to break off the relationship when he left for New York.

He booked two rooms for two days. One day for his appointment with the President and the other for himself and Roseanne. He wanted to revisit nostalgia and in the process, visit a few of their favourite haunts and see his son.

Once he had settled in, he contacted the White House staff and informed them of his arrival and availability for the afternoon meeting. Then he took Roseanne to the nearest shopping mall. They bought some clothes and some presents for his son, Andy.

'Love, I would like you to be with me at that meeting today. Just to hold my hand while I face the music. I shall tell them you are my personal secretary, if there is any opposition to your presence. That way, they will let you in. If I fail, you can view the gardens and revisit nostalgia by yourself,' he said. Roseanne had never seen him that nervous before.

'Don't worry, Darling. Those meetings always seem a lot worse than they are. They always spin that yarn about everything being confidential and relating to national security,' she replied. He already felt more at ease in her presence.

'Thanks for the pep talk and I love you,' he replied, squeezing her hand.

'This place hasn't changed a bit since Jerry's time. I was eighteen then and just one year out of high school. I got posted here because of my dad's connections and my keen interest in international intrigue. But I never made it that far. The closest I got was just a little undercover work for the agency on some unscrupulous immigrants that were affiliated with certain nameless Arab embassies. After that I was assigned to your side for a while. It was then that I really learnt about covert and surveillance activity.' Roseanne said.

'Yea, that was also a great period in my life!'

'After your accident and Jerry's disappearance in space, my heart went out of the job like most of the others. Now, that was one great president. Thank goodness he is still alive on Eden. After that, I found my husband and made the biggest mistake of my life,' Roseanne said.

'Let's not dwell too much on the past. We've all been there and made those types of mistakes one time or another, but we learnt from them.'

'Yes! We sure did!'

The meeting was held in the Roosevelt Room. The President stood up the moment they entered and began introducing them to his other three guests.

'Mallory!'

'Please to meet you, Mister President! This is Roseanne, my fiancee. She is also my business partner and secretary for the day. She has clearance from her previous work in security here. I hope you don't mind her presence?' The President, Nicholas Wilson (Nick to his friends), took Roseanne's hand, then he shook Mallory's.

'Don't worry, Mal! That will be all right. Let me introduce you to some important people. This is Michael Cockburn, Vice President of Solarian Banking, who you have already met. Malcolm McKenzie, my Secretary for Internal Affairs and Professor John Friedman, head of Bio-research at Princetown and also a close friend and advisor.'

'Please to meet you!' Mallory greeted.

'Now, with the introductions out of the way, perhaps you and Roseanne could seat over there, while we get through a few questions about this Terminal Disease crisis.'

'No problem, Mister President!'

'We'll appreciate your input on a suitable method for solving our present problems of social unrest... Also any ideas relevant to the possible weakening of national security, while the population becomes more concerned about their individual welfare and begin to demand immediate testing and inoculation.'

'I'll do my best, Sir!'

'Whether we should administer a dummy antidote or placebo in order to engender hope until the real thing is ready, or begin testing immediately for the bug and delay the antidote for as long as we can, until it's ready. Those are the types of questions for which I would like immediate answers. However, this will be an informal discussion and notes may be taken,' Nick said.

It was Malcolm who stood up next to speak his mind.

'Mister President. The latest information coming from our sources in London, show a general pandemonium in Asia and certain areas of Europe. The more religious groups are taking it more seriously. Strangely enough, the UK have remained relatively calm, but it's still early days since Professor Khan's undesirable statement to the British press,' Malcolm said.

'I think it was quite necessary to inform the public at this time. So Professor Khan was correct in giving that interview,' Michael interrupted, but Malcolm continued reading his notes.

'I believe we should accept the UK model as a pattern for population behaviour over here, although perhaps, slightly more aggravated. No thanks to the idiot who released the news of the disease to the press here recently. We've contacted the paper involved, but their memo stated that the file was delivered by an unknown courier from an unknown source. We are almost 100 percent sure the document involves Professor Khan (Ben) and his organization. What have you to say for yourself, Michael?' Malcolm probed.

Michael Cockburn stood up to speak as Malcolm sat.

'From what I have been told by our own security people, the file in question had been mislaid. However we believe it was stolen by one of our competitors and leaked to the press to give us unfavourable publicity throughout this country. Even so, in light of Professor Khan's recent interview by the British in London, we consider its release somewhat relevant and less than premature.

With the knowledge that our own mass media was certain to have it in print by tomorrow at the latest. Anyway, why keep such important information from the public when everyone has a right to know. After all, this is a democracy!'

'Mister President. That's a cop out and cover up, if ever I heard one. I have it on good authority that Solarian Banking is fully responsible for the release to our press. Furthermore, a security breach was made and I find any talk about the judicious time of that release to be irrelevant,' Malcolm stressed.

'Gentlemen and... ladies, the damage is done. Please... no more recriminations. The patient is already infected. Let's put our heads together and turn our attention to a possible cure,' Nick insisted.

Then Mallory stood up to say his piece.

'Mister President and colleagues. I have already prepared a plan. Although at present it's in a rather sketchy form. I am sure it will produce the desired results. The basic plan also includes the effects of immigration and imports at present levels. Which depends to some extent on how thoroughly we immunize our own people. Further, once they are immune, more contamination from outside sources will be ineffective. Therefore, we should completely ignore that area of concern for now,' Mallory said and sat down.

'Let's hear some more of your plan, Mallory?' Nick asked and Mallory again stood up.

'The first thing we need is a speech from you, Mister President, to the nation. Such a speech could also be intended for our neighbours and those abroad. Basically, you should inform the nation of the presence of such a disease. Stress the point, that the infection is minimal and at under 10 percent of our present population at this time. Also mention that you have authorised the commencement of tests at all major hospitals, town halls and schools.'

'Yes! Go on!' Nick insisted.

'At present, all those travelling abroad should be inoculated and those entering, tested and inoculated as appropriate. I can't say I like the idea of deporting those entering our nation with the disease, but that might be our only option other than isolation and quarantining for three months or so. Those could be our initial options until we have completed the process of assessment. During that time we can plan the Antidote Distribution and begin the inoculation program. Testing should not be a problem at this time.'

'Please, go on!'

'Those initial measures will calm the population for a reasonable length of time, and they will not expect a program to be implemented immediately, because of the time needed to organize a suitable campaign. Obviously, those that are infected will not be aware of their inability to have children for many years. Nevertheless I do believe it wise to tell everyone the truth.'

'Yes, Mallory. I agree,' The President said.

'With just under 10 percent of our population infected, that level will not cause us any great problems in the immediate future. My basic calculations, which also takes into consideration those that have passed their fertile years, give us an infected population of barely fifty-five million. Taking similar factors into consideration, we need only inoculate less than two hundred million, including children. Most of the children and students can be processed by their schools and colleges in a relatively short time, given the right staff and equipment. Others above those ages and below the age of forty or so may be tested and inoculated at town halls and other public places.'

'Sounds quite practical,' Michael said.

'I am sure we could handle that figure, if we first sent them properly worded leaflets through our appropriate local state departments.'

'Yes! That method is quite practical,' Malcolm said with confidence.

'I carried out some tests myself and the process took just twenty seconds per individual. I used a standard Solarian tester that was quickly modified for this disease. I was hoping a modified version of the standard inoculating gun could be quickly mass produced for schools and such like. Anyway, I'm sure Michael can supply us with the necessary equipment for our customs.' Mallory said.

'Michael! Can you?' Nick inquired.

'Yes, Mister President,' he replied.

'Those are my basic ideas on the subject, Mister President,' Mallory continued and they were utterly surprised by his ingenuity and modesty.

'You are something else, Mallory. You have doubtlessly given much thought to this problem and have come up with great ideas. Do you think you can handle such an extensive program? I mean on a national level?' Nick said.

'I don't know, Sir. I've never done anything that big before, but I will give it my best shot,' Mallory replied.

'You needn't worry about funds and such like. We have a budget set aside for such situations. It's called the Disaster Fund. However, with all the multi-state disasters these days due to Global Warming, there is never enough when we need it. You might have to move quickly after my speech, because I will have to say weeks rather than months for the initial testing program,' Nick said and Mallory nodded his approval.

'Michael, could your organization really assist us in this thing?' Malcolm asked, now tranquil after Mallory's few informative words.

'We are quite willing to assist Mallory in his efforts, but we must have a free hand in this, with no red-tapeism or outsiders poking their noses about,' Michael said.

'Perhaps I could be seconded to Mallory, just to assist him in the more technical areas. That way, I can report directly to the committee on progress and funding. That is, if Mallory doesn't mind my presence,' John Friedman said.

'Mallory, what do you say?' Nick asked.

'We shall be very pleased to have the eminent Professor John Friedman on board, but purely on an advisory basis, and for dealing with relevant government departments,' Mallory replied.

'In that case, I shall conclude this meeting and arrange another for after my national speech. My press secretary shall inform you at the appropriate time. All relevant details have been recorded and transcripts will be available from the relevant departments.

'Perhaps you, Mallory, and Roseanne can visit the White House tomorrow for dinner with my wife and myself,' the President said and the meeting was ended.

'I thought I was for the fryer, but they didn't even suspect the press release was my idea on Ben's prompting,' Mallory said with a glint of surprise.

'That's probably how it was planned by Ben, with everything precisely timed to the second. He must be a very clever genius. He even made sure Michael was there to defuse the situation. To take attention away from you and place the ball in the court of some imaginary competitor, knowing that the whole thing will be very difficult to prove one way or the other. And they can't blame the UK for wanting to know more about the disease, so that lets you off the hook, Darling. I think you are dealing with very clever people, with almost alien intelligence,' a very clever and astute Roseanne advised.

'Yes, I think the genius, Professor Jeffery Longhurst is also behind this, but we must remember he is on our side. You know, if these characters are so damn clever the whole of our planet must be in a kind of vice while being prodded and coerced in whatever direction they choose.'

'We can only do our best in all this and hope everything turns out for the best,' Roseanne said.

'If I know anything, that's only the calm before the storm. I've got a strange feeling that our new building will very soon be inundated with all kinds of people and equipment, as we become a major depot for distribution on a national scale,' Mallory replied.

They had a most pleasant dinner with the President, who immediately took a liking to the couple. He also realised Mallory was the correct person for the job, when he observed the rather ineffective and naive attitude of his Secretary for Internal Affairs on the day of the meeting.

To him, Mallory was a straight forward and down-to-Earth person. One he would sooner trust above the majority of his senators. Above all, Mallory appeared to be his key for remaining in the White House over this tumultuous period. However President Nicholas Wilson knew a lot more about the Terminal

Disease than he was letting on and Ben, the president of Solarian Banking, was one of its chief instruments and planners.

As Lumak (Professor Jeffery Longhurst) had previously planned, the antidote was to be released when the infected human population throughout the planet had reached an average level of 49 percent, which was presently the case. In Lumak's complex mathematical models he could predict precisely those values and place his human variables to take control when necessary. However, their minds were so advanced and clever, that the human variables tended to appear as and when needed. It was as if the process caused a certain causal vacuum to appear at the appropriate time that attracted the right people when they were needed. It was all part of what Lumak called The Greater Purpose. As far as Lumak was concerned, within the Greater Purpose there were no coincidences.

It was so planned that the most highly developed and ecological countries would have the less infected population, thus causing less unrest in those countries that were expected to provide a lead so that others could retain a measure of faith in those countries.

Because of the isolation of England and other islands in those regions, the disease didn't spread beyond the 49 percent when the announcement was made. While at that time, China, India, Russia and those local countries with higher per capita populations, were 65 percent and higher.

CHAPTER 43

Terminal Chaos

One week after the president's speech to the UN, there was general pandemonium and panic in the majority of countries throughout the world. Somehow his speech tended to give more weight to Professor Khan's interview, which had taken place over a week before.

Once they realised the disease had started from the Asian continent. Those countries were unduly blamed by most of the others. They were blamed for gross negligence in their testing methods and utterly slow in the release of such crucial information to the west. It was a known fact that many of the more serious influenzas and other deadlier flue viruses tended to come from that part of the world, so past reputation in those areas didn't help.

It was thought that if news of the disease were made available sooner, the impact on global communities would have been less traumatic. Enough time would have been available for their scientists to develop a cure before it became pandemic.

The leaders of those Asian countries argued that they were themselves ignorant of the disease, which showed no symptoms and required very advanced technologies in its testing. Which had not been available in their respective countries.

The extreme ecologists were placing all blame squarely at Mother Nature's door. They argued that the human race had outstepped its bounds and human population growth had well exceeded its planetary limits. Due to those and other factors which were human related, Mother Nature had stepped in to redress the balance by creating an ingenious method by which the system could be brought back to normality. In that case they were partly right, the only difference being it was not from the hands of Mother Nature, but from the hands of a few clever Solarians who were in many ways much more powerful than Mother Nature. Nevertheless, they were all part of Mother Nature's realm so in effect came under Mother Nature.

Some of the more extreme Christian-based religious organiza-tions commented that it was the sign of the times foretold in the scriptures. Armageddon was upon us and the second coming of Christ had arrived. If only they knew how true to fact they were, concerning the Son of Destiny.

In certain parts of India, where the disease was highest because of the greater sociability of its people, they were worried about the stigma that would be attached to those non-productive families, thus creating yet another unwanted social caste.

However when they became aware of the implications, the governments of most countries suddenly turned their attention towards their young children, who were considered their only hope of long term survival. They were their only true means of investment for the future, if they were to prevent invasions by neighbouring countries as their population aged and declined. There was therefore much prejudice, and suspicions flourished through many corridors of power. Those new changes signalled the birth of the Fertilates; those few capable of bearing offspring soon to be assisted by the state.

Organized crime saw it as a new opportunity that couldn't be missed. Suddenly they realised an immense market in paedo-smuggling and other related crimes throughout the planet. Many unscrupulous governments ignored the problem when it worked in their favour. However many were still fearful of the Green Chameleon or Phantom who still roamed the city streets.

Mallory had given the Terminal situation much consideration and soon came to the conclusion that all wealthy fertile couples and their families would have to be isolated sooner rather than later. Many would have to be rehoused well away from highly populated areas of cities, if they were to avoid a new outbreak of child snatching, kidnapping and other associated crimes. In that respect, the job was truly immense without forceful legislation. People were stubborn and seldom wanted to leave their family homes and lands because of any disease.

Further, there was also the problem of round-the-clock security and the constant administering of the antidote which would be more effective if such families were all in one enclosed place, or in clusters of such secured communities. Then the antidote could be supplied with tap water, milk and other foods. Mallory had decided to discuss those matters with Ben the next time they met. He sent an urgent message to him for such a meeting, and he agreed.

'Mal, I would like you and Roseanne to visit me at the Sol-Newtown dome to discuss those matters. You should realized by now the sensitivity of this problem in light of recent decisions at presidential levels,' Ben said in the secured email.

'What's it, Darling?' Roseanne inquired.

'Ben sent us an invitation to Sol-Newtown.'

'That's fantastic! I always wanted to visit that place. Did you know it's one of the greatest wonders of the present world. It's the largest environmental dome on the planet and stretches in height through several layers of clouds. Within its structure are the highest multi-story buildings on record,' she said and he was intrigued.

'Ok. I'll say yes for you!' he shouted. She left what she was doing then kissed him on the cheek and left.

Mallory and Roseanne were invited to the Sol-Newtown dome for the day, during which time they would be shown around its production and storage facilities. Afterwards they would be invited to lunch. Then it was hoped most of his questions would be answered.

The President had decided to give his speech in the United Nations building, thinking that venue to be more appropriate. That was because his message concerned the whole planet, its countries and their representatives. Afterwards he gave orders for strict customs control on all visitors, with the exception of nationals, VIPs and important business people. Those few were to be exempted from such controls pending future developments. But they would be tested and inoculated as appropriate. As a result of those measures the tourism industry came to an abrupt stop until suitable testing could be implemented at ports and airports throughout the land.

All transportation systems were to be constantly fumigated and radiation cleansed before collecting passengers. This also included air transport. It was hoped those methods would further reduce the spread of the disease.

Many countries soon followed the USA's example with strict border controls and suchlike, until appropriate measures were found to quell public unrest. There were the usual lobbying and complaints from the tourism industries and affiliated businesses. In any event they were told it was a matter of national security, which overruled any grief they might have. However those initial tough restrictions also deterred child smuggling during its imposition.

Mallory, Roseanne and Carl had moved into their new building and each given their own plush offices with assistants and computer terminals that were linked to a brand new and powerful computer system. That one was of the latest technology on Earth and not of Solarian design.

Very soon thereafter the microid robotic plant for reviving androids were up and running with storage facilities. That part of their operation brought in much capital and was presently the only one in the world for such repairs. Ben let Carl have his own way in that regard, knowing that those revived androids and robots only had another two or three years before permanent meltdown.

Mallory had got one of his old technical friends to assist in the production of more test guns from the original sample. However they soon found the guns could only be assembled by special robots in a clean-air environment. Those robots were in extremely short supply on Earth and incredibly expensive to buy, so he contacted Ben to explain his dilemma and was told all his problems would be resolved after his first visit to Sol-Newtown.

'Darling, when are we getting the proper vaccinating guns. Our program is ready and waiting,' Roseanne complained and Mallory was surprised the most important part of the program was ready. The leaflets had already been distributed throughout the land and several awareness campaigns had begun, so Roseanne was worried. They had so much to do and didn't know whether Ben had such a large supply of the needed equipment. Because of those reasons he couldn't make any plans or give dates to the authority and that aspect of the program worried him.

Carl was now quite competent at his job and soon made general managing director. He handled most of the nitty-gritty, while Mallory, Roseanne and Professor John Friedman prepared their national plan of operation for the distribution program. It included the purchasing of all items by the government and organizations like UNICEF from Mallory's company at rates that he and his partners had decided on. His main problem was to begin the ball rolling with enough stocks of the equipment and drugs from Solarian Banking. As main agent, he was also required to sign an agreement with Solarian Banking on legitimate usage, prices and such like. Since he was the only one involved in the States with direct links to Solarian Banking, he had little worries from competitors.

CHAPTER 44

Sol-Newtown dome

Mallory had decided to move in with Roseanne at her flat. That decision was partly because her apartment was in a more suburban part of the city, but was mainly for security reasons. He was worried about the ripples he created with the gang in London. They had lost one of their main connections in Europe and he was not sure whether their American counterparts were after him to settle the score. He knew a lot about their operations and was sure they would soon be on his tail to tidy up loose ends. Despite those worries, the couple also wanted to be together.

They had set the date for the wedding and decided to keep the whole affair as simple as possible for security reasons. Despite Mallory's lack of any personal religious beliefs, he insisted on having a proper clergyman to conduct the ceremony with all the usual trimmings, including dress for Roseanne's sake.

In expectation of their lives together, Roseanne was very happy. Her life had apparently taken a u-turn for the better but she genuinely loved and cared for him.

They had a very important appointment with Ben at Sol-Newtown and Mallory insisted that they looked their very best. So it took them over two hours to prepare for the ordeal of meeting the most important individual on the planet.

Mallory was dressed in one of his best light grey suits and Roseanne in blue, with a distinctive silver broach pinned to her lapel. She also wore pearl earrings and carried a simulated leather handbag to match.

Both looked spectacular and even Oscar, the car, had a good shine and looked forward to the trip to North Dakota. That was his old base so he knew friendly cars in the area. All such artificial intelligent systems could develop a type of conscious-ness peculiar to most intelligent life-forms and were sometimes curious of their environments. However unlike us and those without brain implants, they could automatically download their thoughts and experiences to others.

They entered an elevator to the roof of Roseanne's apartment and were soon on their way. It took a leisurely half hour to complete the trip, while watching the changing scenery on-route.

As they approached the massive Sol Newtown structure, they were awed by its immensity. The dome measured just over three kilometres in diameter and over one kilometre into the sky. It extended through several layers of clouds.

Through its glittering transparency they could observe many multistoried buildings, the most central of which reaching the very top of the dome, acting like a type of support. It was in many ways like a modern city centre that expanded throughout the dome, but designed to make efficient use of sunlight. Nevertheless it was completely sealed and isolated from the planet's atmosphere with a positive pressure in case of leakage. That way no unwanted bugs or viruses could ever enter through its structure.

As they moved closer, several robots could be seen like insignificant moving specs throughout its structure making minor repairs and adjustments. Those intelligent machines were assigned to the structure since its construction about twenty years ago.

Since the pressure within the structure had to be maintained a fraction above the outside atmosphere, constant inspection and repairs prevented leakage. The robots were also used for cleaning the many large panes of transparent flexi glass in order to maintain a high level of sunlight within the structure. Thus minimizing the enormous power-drain from the internal fusion generators.

There were many entry and exit points or docks at different levels throughout the dome's hemisphere. They were built in pairs and coloured blue for entry and red for exit, but all approaching vessels were usually controlled by the dome's own landing computers. They would choose the closest and most vacant one for each arrival.

Oscar dived towards the topmost entry point and was shuttled through three sealed chambers. In that area the car and its occupants were thoroughly disinfected within a type of mist.

Mallory and Roseanne were taken away by two humanoid assistants and placed within a local room where their clothes and jewellery were removed and scanned by machines. Then they were cleared by the sensitive scanners. Finally they were taken to a cubicle and left there by themselves. There was a blinding flash of white light and the door opened in another place some distance away.

'Mister Mallory? You are expected. Please follow!' the young lady said. They followed her to Ben's office.

As they gazed through the transparent windows they soon realized they were over one kilometre from where they had landed a few minutes before. Both were astonished by whatever mode of transport that had taken them to that building in under a second; for they could clearly observe the central building of their arrival in the misty distance.

'Are we still on Earth, Darling?' Roseanne whispered.

'I've never experienced anything like that before. This is definitely an alien environment, and they are all so friendly. I think we are going to have to remember our manners while we are here,' he replied.

Both remained utterly bewildered and couldn't stop wondering what possible means of transport had taken them that distance in the blinking of an eye, and yet they were still in one piece.

'Mallory and Roseanne. It's nice to see you again,' Ben said, while firmly shaking their hands.

'I do appreciate your efforts in finding my grandson, but was somewhat annoyed by Roseanne's ordeal with those criminal idiots in London. However, I suppose that's all behind us now.' Ben spoke in perfect English.

Still daunted by the immensity of the structure and the strange technologies within it, they felt like little kids on their first day in class and in the presence of a master teacher.

'Thank you for having us here at such short notice. This place is truly incredible and immense,' Mallory said.

'Please make yourselves comfortable. We have an awful lot to get through today. However, before we begin, I think we should have some light refreshments.' Before he finished his sentence two humanoid assistants entered the room with two trays of drinks and cakes.

'They are what you would call androids. Most of the people you see about us here are androids. Programmed to maintain this environment and take care of all visitors,' Ben said, leaving both Roseanne and Mallory astounded by that observation. They could not detect any difference between those artificial people and normal humans.

'There is another matter that you should both know and keep to yourselves for now; we do not use elevators and cars within this structure. We are much too advanced for that. We utilize inter-dimensional transposition at all points of entry and exit. We call the system, portals. They can rotate you to any point within this structure in normal space-time. However, you should not worry unduly about those means of transport. They are flawless in their operation and can save much time getting you from points, A to B.'

'Really?' Mallory replied with overwhelming curiosity.

'From here, I am able to journey to Eta, Gimbal, our domes in Europe and on Mars, and to planet Eden, which is over twenty light years away. As a matter of fact we have many of such portals strewn across the galaxy and have little need for space ships and such like. So you see, my friends, you are now in a different world to the one you have been accustomed,' Ben said. They gazed at him in awe and disbelief.

'All this was built by robots?' Roseanne asked, as she surveyed the spectacular and ornate environment with golden statues and beautiful items of art, somewhat bewildered and overwhelmed by it all.

'It's not pure gold, is it?' she exclaimed.

'Yes! They create such beautiful objects. Interiors like this can be assembled in one fiftieth the time taken for an equivalent team of the most efficient humans, including myself. Robots are not affected by ill health, the time of day, coffee breaks, wages, unions and such like. They are controlled by a master Macron Computer. They are a lot more intelligent than humans. We have planets that only produce automatons, some a lot more intelligent than humans like us, but that's another story. As for metals like gold. we have planets of gold. When you visit Eden you will find most of the structures there to be made of pure solid gold. It's a very stable metal and does not readily rust or decay. But we cannot supply large quantities of such minerals to Earth, it would destabilize the financial institutions,' Ben replied.

'If that's the case, why are there so few robots in our cities and industries?' Roseanne asked, trying to dig some more information out of Ben.

'One day it will be done. When the population of Earth has reduced significantly and mankind becomes a more humane and caring species towards all life, the environment and himself. The presence of advance robots would only aggravate the problem further and speed the wanton decimation and destruction of our world by the unscrupulous and deficient.'

'I see!' Roseanne said, hardly believing her own sanity.

'Did you know that our planet could only at present sustain a global population of just five hundred million humans, indefinitely? Presently there is over ten billion. As we exist, we should also consider the habitats and needs of those with whom we share the environment, or it could be taken from us and given to someone more acceptable to the system.'

'I did not know that!' she said.

'Well, I cannot, in anyway, speed the process of the death of our world by the supply of any more robots,' Ben said in no uncertain terms and Mallory nodded in full agreement, but Roseanne didn't fully understand the long term implications.

After they had tea, Ben took them to an outside cubicle where they transposed to an immense underground area.

'We are now almost one kilometre beneath the surface. This vault was created by Jeffery for the storage of all Terminal Disease or TD associated products. Here they are held before distribution.'

They could observe hectares upon hectares of racks and large refrigeration units. There were enough to serve the needs of billions of patients, with testers, vaccinators and capsules.

'Wow! What a sight for sore eyes!' Mallory exclaimed and Roseanne took a deep breath.

'The chemical products are in constant production within this dome and elsewhere. There is enough her to supply ten billion people continually for five years. The testing and vaccinating machines are manufactured, assembled and tested on Eta and Gimbal,' Ben said.

Mallory and Roseanne were astounded by the enormity of everything in that area and wondered how long ago Ben and others had known about the disease to have planned and prepared so thoroughly for its arrival.

Afterwards he took them to another building where they were issued nasal filters. While there they could observe numerous rows of robots and automatic machines producing the chemical capsules in quantity.

Finally they returned to his office.

'Friends, I am afraid Earth will never return to the planet to which you have grown accustomed. Far too much damage has been done to its eco-sphere to sustain any long term stability on a global basis. All that will happen from now, is more extinctions and more extreme changes in its weather patterns globally.'

'Really?' A disturbed Roseanne interjected.

'However, we shall attempt to repair the planet as best we can after the effects of the human population becomes negligible. That level will be attained after the population has reached the five hundred million mark, in about one hundred years from now. Afterwards, we can reintroduce many of the now extinct life-forms and create a new and more perfect order. A system in which everyone, including its now extinct life-forms will be happy and fruitful,' Ben said and Roseanne remained silent as if in deep concentration.

'I Thought we were going to have a great problem locating equipment and antidote in the required quantities, but you have it all here,' Mallory said, surprised.

'Before we can start the ball rolling, however, we must first sign a mutually binding contract. Then you can have all of our present stocks, if you so wish. Nevertheless, every country must be limited to its quota, which can under no circumstances be exceeded. The Macron computers will ensure that those limits are followed precisely. After the appropriate time a computer virus will be transmitted to all the vaccinating guns. From that moment the antidote will be supplied directly in water supplies, food or directly in small capsules. That is the main reason why it is essential that all Fertilate families are isolated.'

'This has been well thought out and planned!' Mallory interjected.

'Every quota is related to population size, effective agricultural areas, natural resources, population growth, children per capita, and so on. For instance, our present quota for the United States and Canada is fifty million, and that limit can never be exceeded. All others must die naturally from old age over the ensuing years until the global five-hundred-million limit has been reached.' Ben continued.

'I see!' Mallory said.

'Personally, I am saddened by the whole affair, but these drastic measures cannot be circumvented or appeased in any way. Mankind knew of this problem almost a century ago and completely ignored it and its consequences, praying that it would go away by itself. Well, it is now far too late for that. It hasn't been spirited away by any of their primitive gods or miracles. Those drastic steps must be taken if our planet is to survive the immediate future,' Ben said and Roseanne swallowed hard to relieve a lump in her throat.

'Billions of people will disappear. All our cities like New York and Washington will...' Roseanne said with tears in her eyes and Mallory hugged her to console her.

'Darling, it's all right. Mankind has always survived and this time he will have a better future,' Mallory comforted, but she still sobbed a little and wiped the tears from her eyes.

'All major coastal cities like New York will disappear under the ocean within a few decades, so please don't worry unduly about those changes. Global warming will get much worse and continue for several thousand years without our assistance.' Roseanne contemplated his words and realized he was right. This global problem was all due to inconsiderate mankind and his reckless over population of our world.

'Please follow me. There is something I would like you to see,' Ben said and they followed him like lambs to the slaughter.

Ben took them to an adjacent room and as they entered, the whole place came to life as a scene expanded to engulf the entire room.

'This is a virtual simulation of what our Earth will be like after its conversion. There will be no changes to the general sociological structure of humanity. The things you now appreciate and love will be present and in finer detail. Crime and other detrimental genetic defects and disorders will be almost nonexistent. Everyone will have the freedom to develop in whatever creative ways they choose, with no cost to themselves or their families.' As Ben spoke the scene unfolded into a most beautiful world where even some of the old monuments and buildings had been preserved and used for schools and universities.

The roads and motorways had been planted over while most of the now fewer population, lived in great palaces, with hundreds of acres for wild life and vegetable farming. All of Earth's manufacturing had been sited on dead worlds like the Moon and Mercury. However Mars was left untouched for some unknown reason.

The great deserts on Earth were gradually receding and suitable weather patterns brought back to normality by large orbiting satellites. They reflected sunlight in certain areas to compensate for extreme temperature variations elsewhere. There were massive stations on Earth that controlled humidity and ozone levels. Not to mention the orbiting array of Magnetic stabilizers that focussed the solar wind in a manner more beneficial for the planets life-forms and its biosphere.

The weather pattern could have been controlled within very narrow limits by the large Macron computers. Soon the rain forests were emerging again even stronger than before, with their wide variety of flora and fauna.

Throughout that world could be seen the most advanced robots carrying out building and conversion processes. The whole scene was so enchantingly beautiful, like paradise on Earth.

'This is an image of the future. One that I am sure you will both live to see,' Ben said.

Mallory accepted the principles and modus vivendi of that world with open arms, but Roseanne couldn't dismiss the expressions of ecstasy shown in his features. She realised it was probably where he always wanted to be.

'One day soon you will visit Eden and see for yourselves,' Ben said and took them back to his office.

'We have decided to make you responsible for all distribution within North and South America, and associated islands as shown on your territorial map. That area accounts for a residual population of only one hundred and ten million people.

'Initially, only those passed by the test may be given the Anti and that initial number will have to be further reduced through the following decades until they reflect the numbers on your list.

'All supplies will be given to you at zero cost, but you can only supply to major governments and legitimate charities that are responsible for groups that are outside of government control. Under no circumstances can supplies be duplicated to any single distributor.

'We have set prices for equipment and capsules, but they can only be hired for a maximum period of two months. After that time they must be recalled and reprogrammed or they will be neutralized.

'Most of the monies accrued must be reinvested for expanding this operation, and another Special Operation that we shall discuss in the future.' Ben handed Mallory several sheets of plastic paper.

Mallory and Roseanne spent some time glancing through the documents and raising the occasional question with Ben. When all their queries were answered, Mallory and Roseanne signed the documents.

They were now officially partners with Solarian Banking, but with full control of their own business. Nevertheless they were to supply monthly reports to Ben on progress and deficiencies, or to contact him or Michael in emergencies, until their computers were interlinked.

CHAPTER 45

Old habits die hard

When they returned to New York that evening they were still numbed by their experiences in Sol-Newtown. They also realized that the Solarians were not Earth's humans in the strictest sense. For some reason, they were thousands of years more advanced than any Earth people they knew. Their minds and bodies had been improved to a high level by genetic engineering and other means.

'You were right, Love. They are not us, but represent the future. That whole program must have been planned several decades ago, even before the disease was known to anyone in the normal world,' Mallory said.

'So you think the Green Phantom could be one of them?' Roseanne inquired.

'He must be! That's why he cares so little for Earth's criminals. Their laws are not the same as ours. So to him it's like terminating a few rats without conscience. How do you feel when terminating rats or mice?' Mallory replied.

'I see your point!' she said.

'Then, why is he on our side. I mean, saving us from those nasty street criminals?'

'I suppose he is here to save us from ourselves during this period of unrest?' Mallory replied, but was none the wiser.

'So you seriously think the Solarians began this program years before?' Roseanne was confused.

'Yep!' he replied.

'But that is impossible? How can anyone plan for something that doesn't exist. Could the disease have been engineered and released by them? If it's the case, that will answer a lot of questions,' a perceptive Roseanne said.

'It could have been the most humane way to reduce human population on that enormous scale. I don't know whether I should curse Ben and his organization, or welcome paradise on earth,'

Mallory replied.

'The whole process seems completely out of character with the humanity we know so well. We are like pigs that enjoy wallowing in the muck occasionally. Can you imagine a world with no villains, sickness or deficiencies of any kind? Where robots do all the menial jobs while we concentrate on our own mental and physical developments, and those of our children? What if one of our children decided to follow a different path or was born with a deficiency? What then? Wouldn't he or she be ostracized or punished in some way? There is lots we have to learn about their methods before we can commit ourselves to any long term program,' Roseanne said.

'What if they had the technology to change the human body to any levels of perfection, both physically and mentally, without the patient feeling any great difference or inconvenience in the process, other than a higher level of consciousness and fulfilment? That type of advanced technology could also apply to the deformed child and even to the lowly animals.'

'You think that's possible?'

'Anything could be possible with their levels of technology. Anyway, a few years distributing the antidote won't change matters one way or the other. So we can leave any final decisions for after we visit Eden,' Mallory replied, realising how practical and caring Roseanne really was.

'You know, those portals they have. I was thinking... If we had them now, there would be no need for roads, motorways and congested traffic. With those things we could cut pollution by a significant amount. Why haven't they released it to us, knowing it would make our lives much easier?' Roseanne asked.

'I suppose the population would further increase because there would be no accidents, and the reduction in stress would further reduce heart problems. All of this adds to more population growth and longevity, and the damage to our world is already beyond repair by our means,' a practical Mallory replied, with a broad grin.

'It's not that funny! I know that Earth is close to disaster, but even so, I find the whole thing very difficult to accept.'

'I think you are doing exactly what humanity has always done.

Trying to improve matters by procrastination. This is why this planet is in such a mess at present. People always want improvements without looking at the broader picture and doing a bit of long-term planning.'

'What are you saying, Darling?'

'I never once heard anyone mention a thing about overpopulation or a method to reduce human population growth. They have always had their heads in the sand.'

'We never thought the world would change about us. After all, it's a very big place!'

'The question is, what could anyone have done to save humanity from itself. Thank goodness they cared enough to have taken the time to reason the problem out and to have found answers. We might not like the results, but how could anyone have permanent answers if they didn't take into consideration the same thing happening again, say in a thousand years from now. This time the patient needs a more drastic operation if he is to be cured.' Mallory continued.

'Yes, cured from the Terminal Disease and bad weather!'

'Anyway, you can't make an omelette without breaking a few eggs.'

'Wow! You are really on their side!' she said.

'I'm not on anyone's side! Perhaps the whole philosophy of our lives could also be placed on the scrap heap. It could well be that we humans are unsuitable for this universe. Sort of an outcast, even a plague or planetary parasite that eventually eats its way out of house and home and in the process, ends up killing its host, namely our planet. A freak creature of evolution, always looking for emotional arousal at any costs. A fly in the ointment that eventually screws everything for the sake of its own selfishness, indulgence and self-importance.' Mallory was furious.

'You have really gone off humanity in a big way!'

'Yes! I am truly disgusted with Earth's humans! I think the system they propose will keep the human race and Earth surviving for a very long time in the future. Perhaps forever. However, if Earth's populations continue to increase at present rates, we face extinction in but a few centuries.' Mallory continued.

'Extinction?'

'Yes extinction! We live within a complex food chain. When the lower life-forms go, we are next. With the correct amount of self-control and population control, we could have lived indefinitely without unduly polluting and decimating our world as we are still doing, and when we talk about Heaven, isn't it a similar kind of place to Eden? Why do we always want to have our cake and eat it? You think God will allow such morons in his beautiful heaven to screw it all up for him.' Mallory complained vehemently and Roseanne was stunned by his attitude.

'You know, you are beginning to sound just like Ben. You must realise that even with perfection there is always a price to pay somewhere down the line. I would like to know what that price is before I commit myself to any of their long term programs,' Roseanne replied.

'Ok, Love, you've made your point. If you make a list of all your nagging questions, I shall try to get us to Eden. Then we can put those questions to whoever is in charge. But you should also realize that they have little to gain by saving us. Earth has virtually no resources left and no real wealth as a planet. All the antidote supplies they have accumulated on our behalf must have costed them a tidy fortune and is freely given to us, to save our race from extinction,' Mallory said.

Roseanne just couldn't keep up with Mallory's arguments on the subject so she decided to differ and leave it at that.

'Changing the topic, Darling, where are we going to put all that Terminal stuff? I don't think all the warehouses in New York will hold that much?' she inquired.

'It's a lot simpler than you think, my dear. We despatch directly from Sol-Newtown for our immediate needs by computer linkup. Our main problem will be how to store and handle the returns, because after every ten thousand patients or two months use, they have to be returned to us for reprogramming and recharging. At that time they will be connected to our computers for updating our database files. Then they must be returned to their original operators. We'll have to see how things develop with Ben's assistance and perhaps arrange delivery through the postal service. I think the maximum storage will be 3 months,' Mallory said.

'I am not in any mood for cooking. Shall we order some Chinese?' she asked.

'Yes, Love. That will make a nice change. But no horses please!' he replied, remembering the last meal they had in Mitcham Common after dumping some criminals for rehabilitation.

CHAPTER 46

The program begins

Mallory and Roseanne realised that Earth's technological growth was being deliberately stifled in order to limit environmental damage and other detrimental factors. The planet had been cocooned like an unsuspecting larva until one hundred years or so, when it would be released from its confinement and like the proverbial caterpillar, be transformed into a most beautiful butterfly. And now, it was far too late for anyone to do anything about it, except of course, to save a few lives.

During that period of global readjustment our world would undergo drastic changes due to the rising oceans and seas. Even the walled city of New York would be partly covered by the rising waters of the Atlantic ocean within barely 50 years.

They also realised the tremendous powers and almost alien intelligence of the Solarian planners. Those minds were little interested in the here-and-now. Their vision of Earth's survival was more cosmic in scope and considered over an incredible time scale. And that was not all. Ben had given the impression that he and everyone in the organization would be around then - over one hundred years in the future - to assist the process.

It was also obvious to them that although Earth was held back in many ways, the world Eden was progressing in leaps and bounds, with technologies that anyone on Earth couldn't even have imagined. That place was probably an Eden in the truer biblical sense of the word or even better.

During the following weeks they spent much time organizing their new premises and installed another new computer system with associated standby power for the complete building. That unit was another black box with several large electrical terminals for making connection to the building's supply. Both items were supplied to them by Michael Cockburn, who wanted their system to run efficiently and without any hitches. They assumed it was some type of fusion generator, but the writing on the cases was in a type of language unrecognisable to them.

The system was fully automatic and soon interlinked with the master Macron computer in Sol-Newtown. Despite those improvements, advanced robots could not be used outside their organization on Earth, so over one hundred young people were interviewed, tested and given the antidote. Then they were trained for the task of administration, including handling all manual aspects of that side of the operation at head office. Several nurses were recruited for both part and full-time in attending schools and other public buildings to assist in the training program.

Many operators were subsequently trained, then sent out to train others in organizations like schools, colleges and hospitals to use the equipment and supply the correct dosage of the antidote. Most of those factors had already been determined and pro-grammed into the special vaccination guns.

After the initial tests and vaccinations were given, there were three basic forms of the supplied antidote: capsules, a concen-trated liquid additive which could be mixed in food and drinking water, and powder. Capsules were supplied initially in plastic containers, each holding one hundred. This was for three months supply. However they were only given to those who had passed the initial tests.

There were also placebos of the same type without any visible identification. Those could be detected by a special device. Once patients were identified and placed in the system, labels could be inserted on the containers with the patient's name and number for repeat supplies.

The Terminal program was run very much like a military campaign, with large computer generated maps. Those showed zones, cities and towns with their schools, colleges and hospitals. In those places were areas reserved for trained operatives and assisting nurses.

All information was readily available on the operative's own small portable computers and to the public through the mass media and the Internet.

The program was supported by local broadcast networks that

would informed the local population zones of times when they were to be tested. That initial program was handled in much the same way as an election campaign.

Regrettably, Mallory also knew that the master computer would be correlating all received data for criminal tendencies and serious genetic disorders. Those and their respective offspring that failed the computer criteria would be given ineffective placebos that looked exactly the same as the antidote capsules, but kept separately. The ignored would in time be infected.

Because the uninfected were well in excess of Mallory's quota, selection would continue from the worst cases towards those that were near perfection, until his quota was filled. Then that quantity would be maintained. All others that were outside and not infected would be given the placebos for a limited period until they became irreversibly infected and the process discontinued.

From that moment on, Earth's population would be divided into two types of humanity: the survivors and the condemned: the Fertilates and the Infertilates or Infilates. That way, it was hoped, most of the criminal and other deviants would be eliminated from humanity once and for all time. However there were exceptions to those rules.

Testers and vaccinators were recalled for priming and reprogramming at the end of each three-month period or ten thousand patients, whichever limit had been exceeded. That aspect ensured the computer was constantly updated with names and addresses. Even so, Mallory knew that data was constantly downloaded from those guns even during operation, so the process of returning them was probably a safety feature.

At just fifty dollars per day per tester or vaccinator, it was estimated that over one thousand patients could be done in a single day per gun. The average cost per head worked out at four cents each, which as far as governments were concerned, were peanuts.

Mallory charged fifteen dollars for each container of one hundred capsules. Most of that cost went on postage and handling. Nevertheless he was always conscious of assisting his fellow man, so a large part of his profits were saved for assisting

Fertilate families by rehousing them well away from city limits.

CHAPTER 47

Trouble brewing in the wind

Mallory had risked everything, including Roseanne and his own life to find the Son of Destiny and after he had attained that goal, was told that his efforts had been unnecessary. Nevertheless after his return to New York he had to keep his word and pay off Marlina and the others, mostly criminals that were involved in the search.

Those payments he made by bank transfers for services rendered and hoped it had ended his association with the criminal fraternity permanently. But dealing with such unpredictable people was much like aiding the devil. One never knew where they would next surface.

He wondered whether the whole episode had been forgotten and laid to rest. That was until he received an urgent call from Carl. It was late in the evening and made to Roseanne's apartment so she took the call.

'Yes, Carl. I shall get him for you.' She called Mallory to the phone.

'Mal, someone or persons unknown, have broken into our old office. They smashed everything... the furniture and filing cabinets have also been turned over. It's like they were searching for information. Anyway, they left a note for you and it doesn't make pleasant reading.'

'Please read it, Pal?' Mallory asked.

'It says: **"Mallory Colman you are one dead son of a bitch"**.

'I told you it was not nice and it was written in red paint. I suppose to symbolise they wanted your blood. I thought I should call you immediately after I got out of the area as quickly as I could. I am now on my way home. If you need me to come over, just say the word.'

'No, Pal, don't worry. Go home and have an early night, you deserve it. Anyway, I've got some thinking to do and plans to make.'

'In that case, I am on my way home, and you be extra careful.'

Mallory was dismayed by that call and wondered whether the price on his life was anything to do with the trouble in London. Perhaps old Marcus Darling or their boss was tidying up a few loose ends. Many people in that criminal organization could now consider him to be one knowing too much and therefore a very poor risk. So much for honour among villains, or so he thought.

He had to gather more information about the contract, so he decided to check Marlina's safety deposit box for any scraps of information that she might have left him.

He explained the situation to Roseanne, who was equally dismayed and was advised to take greater care in her movements to avoid another recurrence of their terrible experience in London. Even so, he assumed they did not know about Roseanne.

'From now on, we organize better security about this department. Whenever you leave this place I always accompany you. I don't quite know what this is all about, but we are not going to take any chances. If they are after me it's possible they might want to get their hands on you, if only to lever me into one of their traps. Anyway, this place should be safe for now. If they have anything on me, it will include my home address and that building is quite secure, with cameras and guards,' Mallory said.

'In that case, you will have to take me shopping today. I'm not going to waste any more money on telephone orders. The groceries are always delivered late and they sometimes include the wrong items, or extra discounted products,' Roseanne complained.

'We take Oscar. That's the safest way and he can keep an eye out for us.'

He wondered whether he should return to his apartment for a brief period and await his enemy there, but he was not sure whether there was going to be one or many. If it was an open contract several would be after his life and only the successful one would claim the bounty. However that factor depended on how many people knew of the reward. If they were clever enough they could breach security. From then on it would be between him and the enemy. He was also on home ground, so had a good chance of survival until the next time.

His apartment was the most likely place because they could have found that address by checking through his bank and other official records. His concealed armoury was also located at that address with an extensive range of weapons and ammunition. He also realized they could plant someone to follow him to Roseanne's place, but that was not possible with the keen eyes of Oscar, who could spot such cars even in dense traffic.

He now had a big problem and in the middle of a very important campaign concerning the survival of humanity. He would have preferred an immediate solution.

After some extensive shopping that morning he took Roseanne to his apartment for selecting some weapons. While he was there the phone rang.

'Mal, it's Chad. I have been trying to contact you since yesterday. I only have your apartment phone number. Anyway, I have decided to take you up on your offer and visit you tomorrow for three days. I hope you don't mind my visit at such short notice?'

'That will be a great surprise, Pal! Don't worry about a thing. I shall be at the airport to collect you. What time is your flight in?'

'It's in the morning. I arrive ten fifteen at the airport,' Chad replied.

'Got it!' Chad hung up.

'That was Chad, Love. I told him he could spend some time with us. I hope you don't mind?' Mallory said.

'No, Darling! After my painful experience on that ranch of his, it will give me the greatest satisfaction and pleasure, to see his face after one of my hottest curry dishes. That will even the score between us,' Roseanne said, in no uncertain terms.

'You are a right old darling when you see your chance for revenge, aren't you?' Mallory replied as he held her in his arms and kissed her passionately. Then he took her into another room, pressed a hidden button on the door frame and a large area of the partition lifted to reveal another smaller room.

'I had these changes made after I bought this place.' Then he took her to the other side of the room. He flicked another hidden switch and the whole place was alight in fluorescence. The room gave the appearance of an office, but the three walls were inconspicuous. Yet they were three times thicker than their natural widths. He pressed yet another button and the wall surfaces began to fold upon themselves and move along concealed top and bottom rails, thus revealing several rows of weapons.

'What are all these photos,' she inquired while observing the framed pictures on the wall.

'Someone I knew before I got married. She was very dear to me... but lost her life during the fuel riots.' He was sad but shied away from the painful topic.

One of the walls contained modern weapons, another antiques and the last, an assortment of ammunition and explosives.

'You remember Harry Hallett in engineering? He made this place for me. He is very clever like that and also with electronics. This is my famous weapons collection. I probably have enough here for a medium size army, with night eyes, body armour and grenades. What do you think?'

'It's bloody incredible. Are you licensed for all this?'

'Yes! I've got a special collectors license. Jerry helped me to acquire it, although he himself was always against guns and explosives. You know, he instigated the strict ammunition laws we have today.'

'Yea, I know!'

'I want you to select a couple of your favourite hand weapons. One for your apartment and the other for your handbag, and I am going to do likewise until our present threat has been eliminated. They are all programmable to the individual by DNA and imprinting.'

'What's that little one over there? Can I have that one and perhaps one of the silent dart guns?' she asked.

'That one is a special to be used in the palm of your hand. However, I only have a limited amount of tranquilliser capsules for it. The other capsules create a bloody mess when the target explodes.' She was intrigued. He removed the small streamlined weapon and another small tranquilliser gun and place them in a box.

'Don't worry, your license covers everything, including those of alien design,' he said while glancing at the smaller weapon with a grin.

The following day while on the way to the airport to collect Chad, he stopped off at Marlina's safety deposit box to see whether she had left him any important information regarding his present predicament. There was only a small note that read: **"Darling, I heard on the grapevine someone has a contract of one hundred grand on your head. So you be careful."**
'With everything that's happening. That's all I need,' Mallory complained in disgust. He tore the piece of paper into several bits on his way out and threw them into the wind.

Although the Phantom had reduced street crime significantly, getting to the larger gangs were much more difficult. Nevertheless many of the larger criminal organizations depended on their street gangs for organs and children, so they suffered greatly. Crime in those areas had dropped well below 50% in many cities, globally. However the larger organizations had gambling, prostitution, slavery and other illicit but lucrative ventures, so they would bide their time until the Phantom was captured or got tired.

CHAPTER 48

Chad and Ben's visit

Chad arrived at the airport on schedule and was assisted by the airport robot-trolley. Those trolleys were programmed to take passengers and their luggage to certain pre-programmed destinations within the airport perimeter. Oscar soon had the trolley under his control.

'What's this, Mal? You didn't tell me you had a Class A Roadstar?'

'It's the XL model and top of their range,' Mallory replied, happily smiling.

'I know, Pal. This particular model was only used by young Presidents and wealthy Solarian bankers. Where did you find it?'

'It's a very long story. If you stick around long enough you'll learn all about it one of these days. I am going to take you to Roseanne's pad. You can have the small room. I am also staying there at the moment. That's since our engagement.'

'Congratulations! I didn't have any idea. When is the happy day?'

'In a couple of weeks, we hope.'

'That's very good, Mal, and you look good yourself on whatever she gives you!' Chad said and smiled.

'I just feel comfortable with her around and we both love each other and get on together like a house on fire. Still the same old Chad!' Mallory replied.

'I understand! I feel the same way about my Elaine. Pity I couldn't take her along. I told her it was going to be a short business trip, but I'll still have to call her every day, and you haven't met my two lovely kids.'

'Don't worry, I'll visit your family soon enough,' Mallory replied.

They soon arrived at the apartment but Roseanne wasn't there. She had gone to the office to assist Carl with the campaign.

'You can unpack when we return. I've got something important to show you.'

Mallory left the cases in the hallway and were on their way to his campaign headquarters. The moment Mallory walked through the door he was greeted like a famous pop star. Since his appearance on TV he had become very popular and that knowledge worried him. Many young people were still waiting to be interviewed by Roseanne and Carl on the third floor, so he took Chad to the ground floor to show him the microid operation, then to the other floors.

'Wow! All this technology makes me think I'm on another world in another galaxy,' Chad commented, while observing the advanced equipment used for reviving the microid robots and androids.

'You've seen nothing yet, Pal. Anyway, this is our present set up. Let's go back to the third floor.' They took the elevator.

'Mal, is all this really your operation? I mean, including this whole building?'

'I have eighty percent, Roseanne ten and Carl ten. We are now the sole distributors for the Terminal Antidote within North and South America,'

'You are? I heard the President's speech, but thought the man was insane. You can't take politicians too seriously these days. Is all this for real? I mean the Terminal Disease?' Chad inquired, perplexed.

'Yes! It's for real, my friend. And it will effect all our lives for centuries to come.' Mallory took him through the third floor while showing him the rows of computer terminals with their operators and communicators.

'This is the hub of our operation. Here we can handle over five thousand calls each day. We also have charitable organizations working on our behalf.' Then they walked up to the fourth floor.

'This is where we have our own offices.' Mallory then called Roseanne on the internal system.

'Roseanne, come up and say hello to Chad. And tell Carl on your way.' Roseanne passed the interview over to her assistant. She told Carl and they were on their way.

'Hello, Chad, it's good to see you again,' she greeted.

'Same here. I see it, but I don't believe it. You guys have some operation here.'

After the introductions and greetings were over Mallory explained his personal problem to him.

Mallory went on to discuss their search for the child (never mentioning anything about his special significance). Then Roseanne's kidnapping and how he handled the London villains.

'They have a bloody cheek, to put a contract out on you, after paying them their dues. I doubt that the London kidnapping has anything to do with it. Someone high up in their organization over here sees you as a major loose end that has to be tidied, or in your case clipped off,' Chad said.

'I think that whole criminal organization should be destroyed from the head downwards. That way there will be less chance of the other parts knowing what hit them until it's too late. They must not be allowed to continue causing misery to poor parents, and their kids,' Carl replied.

'The Chameleon tries his best in reducing the street part of their organization, but removing the head needs careful planning. The minute you kill the head another one will take its place!' Roseanne said.

'Our Phantom guy is not too bad at removing heads,' Chad replied.

'Now, all we need is an action plan,' Mallory said.

They all agreed that something had to be done and it had to be drastic in its modus operandi.

That same afternoon Ben rang.

'Ah, Mallory. I would like to pay you a visit tomorrow afternoon, if it's at all possible. I am to see the President and thought of adding you next on my list. Is that going to be all right?'

'Yes, Sir, that time will be fine. Would you like any assistance from the station, or anything at all?' Mallory inquired, with excitement in his voice.

'No need for that. I have my own transport and assistance. Anyway, I shall see you then,' Ben said and disconnected.

'Love, Professor Khan is visiting us tomorrow afternoon. We'll have to organize something for him. What shall we do?' he inquired, nervously.

'We get this whole building scrubbed from top to bottom and organize some catering,' Roseanne replied.

They immediately got on the phone and sent the word around that they expected a visit from a VIP and everyone was expected to look their best.

Ben arrived as promised at three p.m. in a large black shaded LPD limousine accompanied by two eight feet tall Transmorphs, TMs for short. They were microid (Nano-bot) humanoids known as hunter killers. They had the ability to transform into any ferocious life-form for tracking an enemy. They were truly invincible as bodyguards and were unaffected by bullets and explosions, but that knowledge was unknown to all except Ben. Mallory and the others thought they were just super tough human bodyguards. Yet, they stood like Olympian gods of bronze in the bright sunlight.

Mallory and his group took Ben through the building from the ground floor up, while introducing him to senior members of staff in the process. Finally they took him to Mallory's plush office for refreshments and he was introduced to Carl, Professor John Friedman and Chad.

'I am truly impressed by your efforts here and must commend you all on a job well done. Are there any hitches in the program?' Ben inquired.

'No, Sir. Nothing that will cause us delays and we are constantly finding easier and more efficient methods of administration and distribution, with the aid of our computers,' John Friedman said.

'That's very good. Perhaps you could expand your operation on a global scale from here. There will be a lot more in it for you all. That will take the pressure off some of the most infected areas of Europe and Asia, and you can supply them at the same rates. However, it will mean a lot more training, but it will ensure the program is carried out in a most efficient manner, globally.' Ben continued.

'I see!'

'Anyway, you should give it some serious thought and don't

worry about money. I have about twenty billion in the kitty for this project alone and can find a lot more if needed,' Ben said. The others swallowed hard when they heard the number mentioned.

They continued the discussion for a while and when Ben's questions were exhausted he called Mallory to one side for a private chat.

'There is another important matter I would like to discuss with you. The time has come for you to form a special military squad, with the President's backing. I can give you two billion dollars for that outfit and whatever special equipment you need. It will be used mainly to seek and find stolen children and protect our young and fertile families, but later, to quell unrest, pursue criminals and decimate their organizations.'

'I see! I was thinking along similar lines, myself.'

'What about our friend, the Phantom?'

'He is not with us. I'm afraid he is an unpredictable loner. Once your people are out on the streets, there will be no need for him!' Ben said. Then Mallory realized the Phantom was not part of Ben's organization.

'This is an urgent program. Your first assignment will be to terminate the gang that kidnapped my grandson. You are to eliminate that Paedo-smuggling gang as soon as possible. They have too much information on you and my grandson. You may use whatever means you find acceptable, but they and any like them must be terminated forthwith for the sake of our program and the future of humanity. Far too much is at stake!' Ben stressed, in no uncertain terms and Mallory nodded in agreement.

'That's very good then. I am very pleased with your operation here and have decided to arrange a time for your visit to Eden, in the immediate future. I shall give Michael the necessary information when it has been arranged,' Ben added.

Mallory could not believe how the future had already overtaken his plans. Ben had already predicted those outcomes, even his problems with the gang and methods for their elimination.

'What a bloody genius to always anticipate my every move, even supplying me with the finances and most efficient methods to initiate those plans,' he thought.

Ben soon left with his two Primorphs and the limo flew off towards Satellite Eta.

'Did you see those guys. They were like Greek gods and completely out of this world!' Chad exclaimed.

'To all intents and purpose, they are... and I wouldn't like you to mess with any of them, Pal,' Mallory replied.

'What do you mean?' Chad inquired.

'Mickey once told me that there was a type of Microid hunter killer called Primorphs. I think those ones are the same. If I'm right, each one has the power to take out a complete city like New York all by itself. So, Pal, they are a lot more dangerous than the ancient Titans,' Mallory said and Chad remained silent and in awe.

CHAPTER 49

All villains must go

Mallory and Roseanne saw Ben and his two bodyguards off the premises and returned to their offices. After the others had left, Mallory called Carl, Chad and Roseanne together for an important meeting.

'Guys, we have another important project that Chad can assist us with. Ben and I would like to begin a special group of operatives for combatting child smuggling and other criminal efforts that will soon begin to affect our current programs globally. Therefore once our organization begins to run on its own, we can turn our attention to forming that special squad.'

'What special squad?' Roseanne inquired.

'A specially trained unit! We have to do something to stop those criminals now. If we don't, child smuggling will become endemic throughout this planet and our Fertilate families, who are the future of our world, will have a had time surviving. Once most people realise they will not be able to have children and heirs to their property, they will pay any amount for a child. Then any suitable child will be snatched for a price.' Mallory replied.

'And what about our friend Mr. Green Chameleon?'

'He is doing a great job, but he is just one man. I'm sure he will give this job up sometime in the future, when he has had enough. We need a large global force we can rely on, with trained operatives to penetrate and retaliate when the need arises. Our President also sees the need,' Mallory replied.

'Would any of you like your kids to be stolen? Never to be seen again?' Roseanne stressed.

'You heard the lady. Even national security is threatened by those scavengers and parasites that enjoy wallowing in human misery. What do you think would happen if someone stole the President's son for ransom or sale, or one belonging to some other important world leader? Countries would start blaming each other and very soon we could have an international crisis.'

'Yea, I agree!' Chad interjected.

'The buck must stop with a competent planetary squad who can operate within all borders. I know it's a tall order, but many countries will agree when they realise the alternatives. They now have us as their main source of the antidote, so we've got leverage,' Carl said.

'There is still a business in bio-organs on the black market. That one will also have to be traced and stopped. After all, we cant have our young peoples' heads blown off in the streets for the price of a few organs. For this to work, we need the latest in surveillance and ammunition. Perhaps Ben and his Solarian colleagues can help us in that department,' Mallory said.

'Therefore our Specials will have to be armed to the hilt and linked via satellites in order to communicate on a global scale. They must also be assisted by powerful computers to coordinate every action to the barest fraction of a second. They will require pretty effective body armour throughout. It will include, armed-wrist mini-rocket-launchers and high velocity ballistics with a high discharge rate. Our Specials will have to be the best trained in the land. We were once given armour like that on special missions for the President, so they must still exist. I think Mickey will know.' Chad said.

'Yea, he will!' Carl replied.

'So armed, it will not be advantageous to take any prisoners during a planned assault, unless it was a captive. Presently there is too much at stake in our survival operations, so we move up the next notch in aggression against the enemy. In future there wont be much left of them or their buildings, after the targets have been defined and we are through. If this is what you want, this is what you will get,' Chad added.

'That is exactly what we want. We take them out with extreme prejudice. Can you handle it for us?' Mallory asked.

'For that sort of operation, we'll need a brand new place, with plenty of acres for training, including forest and rugged mountains for rock climbing. Then we need to build special barracks and internal training areas for martial arts, competitions and such like. There will also be full-time doctors and psychologist stationed in camp. The main areas will have to be closed off from the public with electric fences and surveillance cameras to scan those areas. We'll also need armed airships with the latest equipment and weapons.'

'Sounds like World War 3!' Roseanne interjected.

'It could cost a fair sum. Perhaps even as high as one hundred million,' Chad said.

'Money is no problem. Make it a billion US if you like. You can have 10 million for your effort and 10 percent of whatever profits we make out of the deal. Which could be a lot more than your present operation. So leave the money side to me. You just concentrate on the best thing you ever wanted to do in your field. Make it the career of your life.' Mallory replied.

'What about my present business. Who will run it while I am away?' Chad inquired.

'Who is running it now?' Roseanne asked.

'My beautiful wife.'

'Perhaps you could train a few of your most reliable people and instal a good computer that can do most of the work for you. I can find you one if you like. Yes, we can get you a Macron computer and some very capable androids. Then we can pay off your debts and have your present place included in our training operations. That is, if you like the idea. The place still belongs to you and we will reimburse you for all training,' Mallory said.

'If you can do that, Pal, count me in. And I know just the place for that new camp,' Chad replied.

'In that case, make a list of what you need and I shall get you your first consignment within a month or so,' Mallory said.

'Why don't we concentrate on taking out the major gangs first, and initially train our Specials for those fighting tactics?' Roseanne interrupted, with the sole intention of improving Mallory's chances of survival.

Mallory's Terminal Antidote organization gradually expanded after everyone became aware of the disease and had grown to absorb the whole of his American territories and associated islands. Then he turned his attention to the other continents and islands, with the assistance of one of Ben's powerful Macron computers.

Stocks of the antidote were held in several underground depots and storage centres. They were located in North America, South America, Africa, Europe, Australia and Asia, so distribution was not a major problem. His main concern was whether current stocks and their production would keep up with the distribution program, which now served over five hundred million daily capsules and placebos.

The largest production plant was run by Jeremy Emil and his wife Karen in Turkey. That country had become one of the wealthiest on the planet. It had begun to improve since Lumak (Professor Jeffery Longhurst) left Professor Jean Claud Chairmowich and Jeremy in charge of anti-cancer serum production and bio-organ hydroponics.

It was Jeremy who developed the bio-tree on which human organs could be grown. For that ingenious living plant he had received his third Nobel Prise. They had installed portals in many secret locations within certain buildings and domes and could travel freely or transfer equipment at a moment's notice. They were all Solarians with powerful brain implants.

Ben had mentioned Mallory to Lumak's friends in Turkey and they contacted him for a short visit to assess his operation and get some helpful tips. However they also wanted to visit the USA for a break.

Jeremy had maintained the production of the anti-cancer serum, but had discontinued most of the bio-organ hydroponics, while converting those areas to antidote production. The large hospital in Sarah's country village had ceased the rejuvenation and longevity treatments since the onset of the Antidote distribution and was currently used for distribution in those areas.

Because of the toxic environment within those antidote plants, most of the work was done by robots. However Ben restricted their quantities whenever they were not strictly required. Once the precise quantity of antidote was known the production would be assigned to only a few factories.

Roseanne was shopping and getting things organized for her wedding, which had been postponed twice since. She hoped it would be third time lucky. It was now to be held in three days. More invitations had been sent out, so there was little chance of postponement.

Chad had returned home, but was expected back with his wife for the wedding. By that time it was hoped he would have ideas on the Special Squad, or SS, as they were jokingly called by Roseanne.

CHAPTER 50

Their new home

Mallory was still worried for his own safety and also Roseanne'-s, from the pending contract the gangsters had placed on his head. Therefore he decided to purchase a new house. Peace of mind was essential, with so much to do and accomplish in the immediate future.

'What are you so silent about?' Roseanne inquired. He was quietly reading a property magazine.

'Darling, we are going to look at a couple of properties today. I received some information from my agent buddy. He reckons this is about the best time to buy. I hope you don't mind the change, but it's necessary for security, and I think we need some more space for friends and guests.' Roseanne was ecstatic by the idea.

'I would love to, Darling. Is it local?' She merrily pushed four slices of bread into the toaster and continued making breakfast.

'You mean, you really don't mind? This one is about twenty miles away, in the suburbs. I don't want to continue living in the city if I can help it, and think you feel the same. Anyway, we can still retain our apartments for security reasons.'

A little later, after breakfast, Oscar was on his way to the first house. They observed the large and beautiful property from the air and Oscar landed just inside the gate.

'Is this the first one, Darling? This is not a house, it's a mansion and so lovely and beautiful,' she remarked.

'I am happy you like it. The gardener has the keys. I was told by the agent, John, to ask for Arthur. He might be at the rear,' Mallory replied, and they followed in that direction.

'Are you there, Arthur, the gardener?' Roseanne shouted and the elderly gentlemen stopped raking a new flowerbed and came forward.

'I am he, among other things. How can I help?'

'We have come to view the property and wondered whether you

had the keys?' Roseanne said, fascinated by the small and shrivelled figure of a man, but Arthur smiled.

'Please follow me. I shall be your guide and take you through every inch of this place, if you don't mind?'

'We don't mind!' she replied, beaming with enthusiasm.

He took them into the house and showed them through each floor, then the large basement. Finally he showed them the garden and a small part of the rear fields, with stables and horses grazing.

'You are quite a handyman, Arthur. Have you worked here long?' Mallory asked, admiring the many beautifully laid rows of every type of flower.

'Since Harry and Joan left. Joan is my daughter, you know. Anyway, they went to California after their business folded. After that time I decided to remain here, where my wife is buried. I couldn't bear to see this place fall to ruin, so I had an arrangement with the estate agent. This way the value of the property is maintained and I do what I like best, which is gardening. It's been empty now for a little over a year.'

'Well, you've done a very great job!' Roseanne complimented.

'I was getting to think this place would remain that way much longer, and now I might have to leave,' Arthur said with sadness.

'Well, Arthur, If we buy this place would you stay on and continue as its caretaker for us? I don't mind paying you for your services and extras for materials, of course. What do you say?' Arthur's face lit up, as he suddenly became a very happy man.

'I would like that very much, Sir!'

They left the house and went back to Oscar for their trip to see the other properties on their list.

'Do you think we should visit the other properties now?' Mallory asked, knowing that Roseanne had fallen in love with that place and the little old man, Arthur.

'I love this one. It has a unique character of its own and also a lovely gardener that reminds me of my dad when he was alive. But it will be very expensive?'

'Houses like these can't be easily sold these days, so I'll get it at a knocked down price. Let's get back to the agents and do some bargaining,' he said and they were off again.

'John, we have decided to have the property outside Trenton. The one with seventy-five acres,' Mallory said to the happy managing agent. Since the sale of the large office block to Mallory they had become good friends.

'That's great, Mal. I would have recommended that one to you, myself. It's three million and that's rock bottom. It was bought by the Brooks five years ago for six and a half. This gives you some idea of the state of the property market these days.'

'John, John... please! I've already bought a large block from you and intend to get many more properties as I expand. As a matter of fact, Pal, very soon we'll be in business together buying thousands of such properties. You have heard about the Terminal bug, haven't you!' Mallory said.

'Yea, I've heard!'

'Well, I am the guy for distributing the antidote across the whole planet. Therefore, I will want you to get in touch with your other pals in the business and make me a comprehensive list of housing throughout the country for those threatened Fertilate families. I have a budget of billions of dollars from Solarian Banking. In the mean time, this one is for me, so please get me your very best price,' he pleaded, in his attempt to drop the price as low as possible. He was always good at bargaining and enjoyed the process. This was also because he tended to have the last word and took pleasure in sealing a deal.

'Ok, Mal, what do you think is a good price?' John asked.

'Around two million, cash. I can have the full amount transferred right now,' Mallory said and John nervously took the phone and dialled a Californian number.

'Mister Brooks, a friend of mine would like to purchase your property for two million, cash on the nail within the hour. Do I say yes?' Then he turned to Mallory.

'He says he'll take it. It's better he gets two million today than wait for another year and risk further deterioration of the property and get the same amount or less for it. I've got all the legal papers here. The usual checks and conveyancing have already been made on that property, but you can get your solicitors to double check with the county office if you wish.'

'I've known you for long enough, Pal. Where do we sign?'

Mallory said and they signed the documents, but Roseanne's name was on the form.

He bought it in the name of Roseanne Marshall, which was her maiden name. It was hoped the new address would eliminate his connection with their previous addresses if checks were made by the villains through local authorities. In any event, they would still hold on to their old flats and use them for the occasional guests.

Mallory was sure no one other than his best friends knew of his association with their new offices and Roseanne's apartment. Neither did they know of his connection with the Terminal program. There was also the problem when interviewed by the press and his short appearance on TV, but that one was not a proper interview. However, they knew he was searching for a child and perhaps also knew the location of that child.

Nevertheless Ben had his own people in the local dome and satellite Eta had that area in Surrey, England, under constant surveillance. Therefore any changes would have immediately initiated a call from Ben, then he would have released his hunter killers on those would-be unsuspecting criminals.

Mallory was very careful not to expose himself unduly to hazardous areas in New York, Miami and New Orleans. After all, the gangs had their main operations in those parts and might have released his photos to their cronies. Anyway, the Green Chameleon had significantly reduced crime in that area and was still doing his rounds, although not as energetic and violent as before. That was mainly because those surviving criminals were not on the streets anymore and using different methods.

Mallory soon got himself a disguise kit. The mask was made of latex which stuck to the face and completely changed his features, but it was not exactly his complexion, so he communicated to the company and they decided to send an engineer to see him for a more precise fitting and colour checks. He was going to have several of those masks made for himself and Roseanne. If the idea worked he was going to pass much business their way. At least that was his idea at the time.

Mallory needed time to put his Special Squad together. Only

then could he fight his enemies on an equal footing. When he was ready, he would have his own contracts out on them and his henchmen would be his Specials. At that time his Specials would mow them down like sheaves of wheat.

For security reasons he would still retained the old office and their separate apartments indefinitely, until those problems had been resolved. He paid the occasional visit from the roof with Oscar's assistance to check on mail and such like.

Satellite Eta also had some very advanced scanners for tracking objects on Earth's surface, and soon, Ben assigned some of that power for tracking international villains. With all that was happening, Mallory wanted to find himself some paid spies within the criminal organizations. That way he could always be ahead of their plans. The problem was knowing who to trust. As usual, money was the greatest incentive and many didn't hesitate to change sides when the price was right.

The wedding was to be held at the rear of their new house, in a grassy area of the main garden. That area was the soul and joy of the resident odds-man, Arthur, who added landscape gardening to his many skills. A large marque was placed in the centre of the largest green. It was bordered by four narrow plots of flowers with pathways. The large lounge was reserved for the reception.

Two days before the wedding Michael Cockburn sent them a special package by courier. The package contained two blue metallic cards and an invitation with strange 3D images of scenes on Eden. It read: **"We look forward to your visit from the date shown. You are to visit us via Sol-Newtown."**

Mallory was ecstatic and immediately called Roseanne to give her the good news.

'It can be anytime after our wedding. Why don't we make it part of our honeymoon?' he said, but Roseanne was still slightly sceptical of technological angels bearing gifts.

'We'll see, Darling!' she replied, but she knew he really wanted to visit the paradise world of Eden and was more than curious about her first incredible adventures on a distant world.

CHAPTER 51

Tidying up loose ends

Mallory contacted his old office building by mobile-phone to check his mail.

'Any mail for me, Lovely,' he said to the young female receptionist by the name of Sandra. He had known both girls for a while. They had always gone out of their way to comply with his every messaging demands.

'Yes! There is a letter! How are you, Mal, I haven't seen you for such a long time?'

'I have been out of town for a while. One of those long-winded cases.

'Did anyone ask for me recently?'

'Yes! Twice. About three weeks ago and again five days ago. It's a guy in his early thirties. Rough looking with a scar on his right cheek. He wanted to know where you were and when you would be back. Like it was a matter of life and death. I told him I thought you were on a special assignment and wouldn't be back for a while.'

'Good girl. If you see him again or others looking for me, give them the same story. I think he might be one of the bad guys in my present case.'

'I am always happy to assist, Mal. You don't have a vacancy for a young and eager assistant?'

'Perhaps? You sound bored. Leave it with me and I'll arrange something for you, and the same goes for Chris, if she would also like a change. I'll also double your present salary. In the mean time, do me a favour. Slide any letters through my office door before you leave work today. Please don't forget. I might have to take a quick diversion to the office tonight. It could be very important.'

'Leave it with me. I will do it right away,' she said and hung up.

She didn't wait. She gave the phone to her assistant and took the elevator to Mallory's office and was going to do as he asked.

As she entered the office that day she was immediately gagged and pulled inside. It was a masked man that handcuffed and sat her down near Mallory's desk for interrogation. Sandra tried to resist but he was a strong guy that soon had her pinned down.

'You better stop resisting or I'll break something!' She calmed a little, once she realized she was under his control for the duration.

'Where is that bastard, Mallory!'

'I don't know! I am just the receptionist and don't follow our customers around!' She was adamant.

'You must know where he is! I checked most of his correspondence but there was not a single clue!'

'All I know is that he said he was on a long-winded job out of state, so he could be anywhere. He is a private investigator with jobs all over!'

'No one goes on jobs out-of-state without calling their office or their receptionist occasionally. If you don't tell me now, I'll have to break something and it will be one of your bloody arms!'

He uncuffed her and placed both her arms on the desk. Then began to lever them until the pain was excruciating.

'Ok! I'll tell you! I'll tell you!' she cried in utter agony.

'You are bloody lucky this time, nothing was broken! What! What!'

'He visited us recently and asked for his mail. We gave him some letters! That's all I know!'

'See! That was not too difficult! Where do you think he is now?'

'He said he was on a job out of town.'

'You know where he lives?'

'No! Guys like him always give bogus addresses. It's to do with their dangerous occupation!' she shouted back.

Here is 100 bucks and my card, if you should find out any more, let me know. There will be another 1000 bucks in it for you!' he said, while tucking the folded note into her bra.

'Ok, I'll try, but I can't promise!'

'I think you know a lot more that you are not telling. Perhaps I should lever your arms a little more!' he said, then she panicked.

'He told...told me... he would be back to collect mail later today!'

'That's my girl! See what a little pain can do!'

'Any idea what time?'

'He said about six!'

'You better get back now before your friend comes looking. You mention anything to your friend or anyone else and I'll definitely break something. So you know what's good for you!'

'I wont!' she replied.

She immediately got up and ran out of the office. A frightful Sandra was in no state to visit the desk downstairs so immediately left for the ladies room to collect herself.

Sandra realized she had gave too much away and knew they would be waiting for Mallory. Her only reprieve was to contact Mallory, but she hadn't any of his phone numbers. She didn't want to return to his messy office and check through his scattered mail, not knowing whether the guy was still there. Then she realized all customers were in her office files.

When she checked his file she found two original numbers and decided to call the first one.

Since he changed his phones, Mallory had transferred all the old numbers to Oscar, not knowing which of his old clients and friends would call. Oscar could always use his abilities to check such calls and transfer when necessary.

'Mal! I am in big trouble! I told him you would be back later. I think he and his friends will be waiting for you!'

'Who is it!' Mallory calmly asked.

'It's Sandra at the office, Mal! He caught me when I went to deliver your mail and wanted to know your whereabouts. He almost broke my arm!'

'It must be another one. I think these guys must work alone. Where is he now?'

'I don't know? He could have left by now. I told him you would be back at six and it's now about 3pm.'

'Stay where you are. I'm on my way!'

A fully armed Mallory soon arrived on the roof with Oscar and slowly made his way to reception.

'Switch your computers off! You girls are coming with me! I

have a much better job for both of you!'

'But Mal, we are not done yet!' Chris complained. After all it was only 4pm and they finished at five.

'Chris, Sandra was recently attacked in my office. I don't want any of you girls attacked on my behalf. I offer you girls jobs in my new business for a lot more money, so your new employer is me,' he said. Then he handed them 5 grand each. They couldn't believe their luck. Anyway, Mallory had grown quite fond of them and wanted them within his program.

'You girls now work for me. You can be my wife's assistants. Don't worry, where we are going is much better than this dump.'

'Are you sure, Mal!'

'Yep, but I don't want you girls ever visiting this place again. It has become too dangerous.'

'Whatever you say!' they were calm in anticipation.

They were soon taken by Oscar to his new home and introduced to Roseanne.

'Where are you, Love!' he shouted.

'Out here in the Garden!' she replied.

'I got two new assistants for you. Meet Sandra (Sandy) and Christine (Chris).'

'Please to meet you, Sandy, Chris! You girls are Mal's receptionist at his old place?'

'Yes, Roseanne, we are the same!'

'In that case, why don't we have tea together. You can start work with me tomorrow. I think you girls will like your new jobs and look great in your blue suits.' she said, and they were intrigued.

After explaining the whole situation to Roseanne, she wanted to assist as his backup. However he soon convinced her it was a one-man's job. Nevertheless she decided to go along and wait in Oscar during the operation. She could always assist if he was overpowered or wounded. Anyway, they were always in good communication via Oscar and no one else knew they were on the roof of the building.

As usual, Mallory wore protective vest along with his new dart gun and a few other items. His attitude was, that his office was untidy enough without having to clear up his enemy's filthy blood off the floor, so he wanted a clean resolution to that particular problem.

Mallory was not going to take any chances on this occasion. Too much was at stake. So he decided to take them out in the dark. That would give him the advantage while using infrared goggles and gasmask. He was soon on his way downstairs to the basement to switch off the main power. Then he entered the fire escape at the side of the building.

With heavy goggles and gasmask dangling over his shoulders, he slowly made his way up metallic steps while holding rickety rails.

He soon arrived outside his floor at the fire escape. At that point he slowly undid the lock until the door was free to open. That door was behind a small book case. Mallory had set things that way to prevent unexpected visitors from that entrance without his knowledge. He had placed a narrow slit at the right place to get a clear view of his office, particularly to his desks and fireplace wall.

Taking his goggles, he began scanning his office while noting the position and size of all warm bodies. There were 3, two stood against the desk with guns ready, while one sat in the chair behind his desk. He assumed the one in his chair was the person after him. The other two could well be his helpers for a small share.

Even though the electricity was off, they were non-the-wiser, since they intended to take him by surprise in the dark, having switched the lights off.

Mallory realized the whole ordeal was very similar to his London fiasco with Conrad and his two bouncers. However, this time they were all together. Nevertheless, he had taken along gas and smoke bombs for that very purpose.

Slowly he moved the fire-door. Then the bookcase began to move. He wanted just enough of a gap to throw a few cans.

As the first one hit the floor, they began to fire their weapons towards where the noise were. Then they were engulfed by dense smoke. They tried to take a quick exit but could not find the door.

At least not before Mallory dropped his gas canisters. Then Mallory closed the fire-door and waited. That nerve gas was quick acting.

Once he was sure the gas had dissipated enough, he entered the room to observe his quarry.

'You guys are very brave coming to my office like this without an invite.' Then he took their guns away.

'Love, they are as quiet as a lamb!'

'Darling, I was so worried! Thank God you got them! I am on my way!' she said. She soon joined Mallory.

'I think we have three more for rehabilitation, but I left the ID labels back in London.' he said, smiling.

'I am sure Oscar can print something!'

'Why didn't I think of that? Let me get the escalator working. I don't want to lift them all that way up the stairs and stretch my back!'

'Don't worry, Darling. I can give you a hand!'

'We can have a Chinese take-away after!' she said and he laughed.

'One down, I wonder how many more to go,' Mallory said quietly to himself, realizing there would be many more on his tail until he could neutralize the whole organization.

'Wish our Chameleon Phantom friend was here to give us a hand!' Roseanne said, while lifting the attached head.

'If he was here we would be using a shovel!' Mallory replied and they laughed.

That following evening Mallory took Oscar to the roof of that building and made his way to his old office. The place was in a much worst mess, with a few files and papers strewn all over. The only thing left alone was his hidden safe. He tidied the mess as best he could for appearance's sake. Then took some special documents from the hidden safe. He opened an important letter he had received days before.

'Please meet us tomorrow. Three p.m. at the Savoy,' he read aloud. The letter had the logo of the Group of Thirteen, but there was no address or signature.

'I almost forgot about you guys. I bet it's the thirteenth room of the thirteenth floor or some such puzzle. So much has happened since our last meeting. This time I shall tell you guys some facts you'll find difficult to believe. Perhaps I can use your organization in the future to locate some criminals,' Mallory thought aloud.

He took the letter and envelope and was again on his way to Oscar.

'I have observed an unusual vehicle parked at the front of the hotel. It has evaded the automatic parking system and displays a Miami license plate. Further checks have shown it belongs to one Charles Morang, a known small time villain. He and his companions, if any, could be staking out the building on your behalf,' Oscar said.

'Not again! Anyway, it's nice to see you have a sense of humour... on my behalf. He is probably here to make his killing of a lifetime and I mean those words literally. They are obviously waiting for me to show my face and when I am not looking, pop me one in the back. It's a good thing I didn't give up this office when I left. Now they think I am in the field on a difficult job. But they won't wait forever. I shall have to take him and his friends out soon, before he collects more leads. It's good the girls are not here anymore,' Mallory said. Then they left for home.

During the journey he asked Oscar to contact Marlina, knowing it was impossible for anyone to trace the call from the car.

'Hello, Marlina. It's Mallory. Is our call safe?'

'As safe as houses, when there isn't a hurricane about.'

'I called to thank you for the warning note.'

'That's all right, Darling. I think you must have stirred up a hornet's nest,' she replied.

'How would you like to earn yourself some extra doe as one of my informers? I am thinking of putting you on a retainer, of one hundred grand per year and good extras on information received. But you will have to make it good, because it's a large organization I am working for. It goes as high as The President. If you decide to accept my offer, we can use the safety deposit box and seldom meet in person.'

'That suits me to a tee. I was worried about my retirement, but you have given me a second chance. When you are ready, tell me what you want and I will give you a different box for leaving messages.'

'I shall do the money transfer soon, and you take care,' he said.

'And you, Darling. Watch out!' she replied and hung up. Although he disliked her type of business, Mallory had taken a liking to the strange woman, who tended to fancy every man she met. Perhaps it was force of habit from a long career of prostitution, but she reminded him of his mother, long departed. Marlina, despite her unfortunate way of life, was trustworthy. Perhaps she was just one of those from a good background that fell on hard times and couldn't make it back either through trauma, a lack of courage... or perhaps she was in the business too long to change.

The following morning he transferred the money to her account and called her from Oscar.

'I've sent you some money as agreed. I will also leave you an emergency number that you may use to get in touch with me. You must memorise it and then destroy all evidence.' Mallory said.

'I've left you the address of the other box. You must use it for your notes and also destroy my evidence. See you around, Darling,' she said and hung up.

Mallory had got a special number for Marlina which was diverted from an address accommodation to Oscar. Such a number was virtually untraceable. The note he sent her, read: **"Get me all the information you can on bosses of the child smuggling ring and bio-organ gangs. The enclosed number is a dummy. You must memorise this number and remember to subtract every digit from ten. That gives you the real number. The dummy number will take you to one of my answering services with one of my recordings, but it will go no further. Practice makes perfect."**

All Mallory wanted at the present time was to see his son before the wedding and introduce him to Roseanne. He didn't know how Andy would respond. Andy had never taken the divorce well and was more dismayed when his mother married his present stepfather.

Mallory wished he could have his son with him, but his mother had custody and any legal battle would be long and drawn out. The lawyers would pocket from the ordeal, not to mention more family turmoil which would be more unsettling for the boy. He wasn't sure he would have won out at the end of it all. He didn't want Andy to face any more trauma on his behalf, so he let things be.

At least, in a few more years Andy would be sixteen and have the legal right to choose. Even so, telling him about Roseanne might be a problem, but he had to visit him at his college before the wedding. Preferably with Roseanne present.

When he returned home that day, Roseanne was in the kitchen.

'Love, I've got you a little present,' he said and handed her a small box. She took it from him and opened it.

'It's earrings, how lovely, Darling.' She kissed him.

'I chose it myself. I had to buy you something to soften the blow.'

'What blow, Darling?'

'I've got to see my son, Andy, before the wedding and would like you to come along. I was thinking of visiting his college first thing tomorrow. Can you make it?'

'Yes! I suppose so. I will have to phone the office before we leave.'

'We can do it on the way.' he replied.

Mallory and Roseanne arrived in Washington DC in the early morning and visited the college to schedule a meeting with his son. After it was arranged, they waited patiently for his arrival in one of the private rooms. Andy soon appeared with a young teacher who left soon after.

'Dad, I got your message,' Andy greeted.

'Hello, Son! See, I always keep my promise,' Mallory said and embraced him.

'I have someone I would like you to meet and I've brought you a present. This is Roseanne, my fiancee.' Roseanne put her right-hand forward, but he declined to take it.

'Son, we are getting married very soon. We have a nice house in a beautiful area, so I would like you to visit us whenever you can. Just call me and I will arrange the flight,' Mallory said and handed him a card and a small package.

'Dad, I always wanted you and mum to get back together. When she remarried I felt terrible. Presently it's like I lost half my world. Now you are getting remarried and I feel like I am left out in the cold again and on my own,' he said with sadness.

'Sorry, Son, but that's the way things happen with most grown-ups these days. You've got to get used to the idea and make the most of your life. Think of it as having a larger family. You still have me and your mum, and two extra parents besides. Are you going to say hello to Roseanne for my sake? She is one of the best women in the world, you know,' Mallory pleaded.

'I am sorry dad, but that's the way I feel. Perhaps I will get used to the idea in time,' he said and went over to Roseanne to shake her hand. Then he bashfully turned away and ran towards the door in mental anguish.

'Don't worry, Love. He will get over it. He is probably having a hard time with his mother and step father at this time, not to mention the college regime. If only I could do something about his problems?' Mallory said with a sense of hopelessness.

They soon left the college and paid a visit to Donald Fraser's aunt, Julia. She was President Gerald Fraser's (Jerry's) sister. She had taken custody of Jerry's children after his supposed disappearance in space.

Donald was in the air-force and usually came home on leave around that time. His older sisters worked locally in the city.

They arrived at the house and rang the bell.

'Julia, how are you?' Mallory greeted and she was ecstatic to see him.

'What a pleasant surprise, Mal. Please come and join us. We were just having tea.'

'This is Roseanne, my fiancee,' he said and they shook hands.

'Mal, old pal. What are you up to these days, in the old apple?' Donald greeted, humorously.

'Not much these days in the apple. I have more or less curtailed the GI work and are moving to suburbia! This is my fiancee, Roseanne! We are getting married tomorrow afternoon. I visited

Andy to tell him the good news and while I am here, thought of looking you guys up and hand you some invitations.'

'Good God, Man! This is great news and she's got a great figure,' Donald replied, jokingly.

'Can you get Andy into the air-force for me? I am very worried for the lad. His mother has always been a nervous wreck and part-time alcoholic, and I don't know anything about his step father. Don't tell him the idea was anything to do with me. Just get him interested in it as a pal.'

'He was always interested in becoming an Astronaut. So I shall see what I can do. Anyway, he has always shown an interest in aeroplanes and flying, so leave it with me,' Donald replied.

'By the way, I would like you both to be at our wedding tomorrow. So I hope you can make it?'

'Why don't we both attend, Auntie? The change might do us good and it's been years since I visited New York,' Donald said.

'Folks, don't worry about transport, I have arranged free tickets through the airlines for all my guests. Just show them your invitations. I have an eighteen bedroom house with lots of space throughout, so no problems with accommodation.'

'You are not doing too badly for yourself these days, Mal?' Donald said with utter surprise.

'Not bad. When you come we can have a lengthy discussion about things in general, including some of my current projects.

'With a free travel pass who can refuse such an invitation, but please stay with us a little longer,' his aunt said, wishing for some local gossip.

They spent most of the morning at that house, until Roseanne decided to go shopping with the Roadstar, Oscar, which was another eye-opener for Donald and his aunt. Although Mallory had decided earlier to check on Donald and his family, he was slightly guilty for not having visited them since the supposed demise of their father. Now he knew Jerry was alive on Eden, but could not mention that fact without creating some turbulent waves, so he let things be for now.

CHAPTER 52

Glorious Eden

The Grand Lord's complex causal equations had predicted the presence of a tremendous force on Earth. That force was represented by the Son of Destiny. A narrow blip appeared in the final results of his temporal equations and calculations that predicted the birth of a great leader on Earth, and that part had since been fulfilled.

Within his powerful non-human mind, he also considered other constants and variables in the temporal matrix of those complex causal equations. He soon realised that any influence from outside Earth could seriously have affected the outcome. Therefore, he made it clear to everyone concerned that the child was to be brought up on Earth by normal Earth parents in order to maintain the correct type of environment and causal continuity. Because of those and other subtler reasons, Solarians kept well away from Earth until the child grew into responsible manhood. Thus leaving all future programs concerning that planet in the capable hands of Ben and his underlings.

The child's real mother, Sarah, and others, with the exception of Lumak his father, Ben, Michael, Mallory and Roseanne, knew not of the child's true identity. Those facts could only have been revealed to them when the child became of age, in about twenty years.

Lumak was presently arranging a trip for himself and Sarah to his home world, Kanaefon. That beautiful world within the globular cluster of Kalboron was just outside our galaxy of Osmaron. He was in the midst of such arrangements when he received an urgent communication from Ben over H-wave.

'Son, it's me... Ben. How are you and Sarah?'

'She is now much better. We are preparing for our trip to Kanaefon and she is looking forward to the break,' Lumak replied.

'I am happy to hear that. The reason why I called was to give you an update on the child and other relevant matters. The boy has been visited by Mallory and is quite happy and healthy. However his safety from a security standpoint disturbs me greatly. I have therefore decided to place his immediate vicinity under twenty-four-hour surveillance from satellite Eta. I shall also visit him occasionally to give him the usual presents as a friend of his father.'

'I see!'

'I think your chat with Mallory has paid off. He is now beginning to play an important role in our plans, with a view to assisting all our present programs within the public domain. He has also proven extremely resourceful and successful with the distribution of the Terminal Antidote. Over one hundred million have been treated so far and the balance is to be completed within six months on current projections,' Ben said.

'I always thought Mallory was a good and perceptive individual. Let him have what he wants. Is the boy in any immediate danger?' Lumak said.

'I don't think so. It is just a precaution. The gang's involvement has somewhat complicated things and may have left a loose end. Namely the knowledge of his whereabouts. That connection might have to be severed in order to remove any future problems from that source. I have advised Mallory to create a special squad that can be used internationally to remove such vermin from the Earth. That is his second mission.'

'That's very good thinking in light of the Javol's invasion of our galaxy. We have plans for such an outfit in the near future, particularly when the present Terminal situation becomes more volatile, but I thought... Anyway, everything is working to plan. His Specials have been predicted but I wasn't sure he would be the one. Anyway, Earth is now under your control, so do whatever you think necessary during this difficult transition,' Lumak replied.

'There is another matter, however. I promised him and his bride a short holiday on Eden, to remove some of their doubts about us and our intentions towards Earth. I hope you don't mind?' Ben said.

'Are they clean? I mean from the disease?'

'Yes, and they have taken all the necessary precautions.'

'In that case, they can visit us via Sol-Newtown. That way their bodies can be thoroughly disinfected on route. Long range portals will have their own inbuilt methods of cleansing.'

'I have planned their route in the usual manner for Earth's natives; through Sol-Newtown and Mars,' Ben replied.

'When are we to expect them?'

'In four days. Will you organize a reception at your end, and ensure them a happy time?'

'You do realise, of course, that we leave with one of the great ships for Kalboron one day after their arrival. Also, Bawaki takes the other ship to Tarran. Mind you, they are welcomed to join us on the two-week trip. However, if they wish to remain, they can stay in the royal palace. That way, they will get a clearer insight into our modus vivendi.'

'I wish you and my daughter a delightful vacation and please tell her I called,' Ben said and the H-Wave call terminated. The more advanced civilizations did not use radio waves. They relied on a type of communication that was based on symmetry and functioned at a higher dimension through the Quantum World. Further, very advanced civilizations never used radio waves for inter-stellar communication but utilized that more immediate type.

It was night time within their hemisphere on Eden. Their fief included the Eden Garden States and protectorates. At that time that part of the planet was bathed in reflected light from its two artificial moons. The one called Caefon looked slightly larger than Earth's moon, The other, an apparent opaque jewelled city that had arrived with the Grand Lord. It had since been placed in a geostationary orbit about the planet and remained poised above the Eden City. That one was a most beautiful crystal city in the sky that had been named Little Osmaron.

From the Little Osmaron satellite emanated a strange bluish glow that could be barely seen by the naked human eye and permeated all things within dimensions and universes.

It was one of those important days when members of the Grand

Council were brought together to discuss important matters of state.

Today's discussion in council included matters concerning Earth. In particular, the Terminal Program and methods to combat hostilities when many members of its populations realised they could never conceive their own offspring.

Lumak began the discussion by gently tapping on his attention button. Although a Shadite, he always took on the identity of Professor Jeffery Longhurst while in council.

'Madam speaker. May I say a few words concerning the present progress of our Terminal Program with regards to Earth?' he communicated silently through his implants without even the slightest mouth or head movement.

'You may speak, Siend Longhurst,' Empress Sarah said. She represented the position of chief speaker. Siend was a term used when referring to a senior councillor.

'Current reports show that almost all Earth's population are aware of the Terminal Disease. I have been told the antidote campaign has been promoted successfully. However, one problem remains. It relates to the proliferation of large criminal organizations about to take advantage of a growing market in child smuggling and other terrible crimes... as a direct result of the Terminal problem. This situation will doubtlessly place most of our Fertilate families at great risk.'

'Although intolerable, that was inevitable knowing Earth's humans.' she replied.

'As predicted, there is now an urgent requirement for a special international military force to counter the criminal upturn and predicted future unrest through varying sectors of society during the ensuing years.'

'So?'

'The man Mallory, who used to be Jerry's chief of security, is now in charge of that program. From what I have been told, he is quite clever and competent. If present successes with the antidote distribution program is anything to go by, he will show even greater success with his army of Specials; being more in his field. We are therefore obliged to design a range of class-three weapons for his operatives immediately, if they are to be successful in combatting our enemies.'

'As you know, most of that has already been done!' she replied.

'Finally, he is due here on Eden within one week. This is just three days after his marriage, so it is important that he and his wife enjoy a continuation of their honeymoon with us. During this time we should convince the couple of our motives and give them a very enjoyable vacation,' Lumak said. Those thoughts were transmitted through his implants to the group of robed councillors that were sitting in many circles on golden chairs with red velvet upholstery throughout.

That large chamber was called the Presidium and sat over one hundred individuals. They represented every group on Eden, including aliens. That place was ornately adorned and decorated with many strange sculptures and wall paintings within many of its recessed wall panels. There were also holograms of extinct animals and aliens sited on many pedestals.

Some of the councillors were not present in person and were represented by their simulacra. Their visual presence was only for the benefit of outsiders. The Presidium could readily create those images within their own minds in Virtual Worlds with the help of the large Macron computers. Yet, their simulacra were able to communicate and looked as real as their material selves, who were obviously communicating through the computers. At other times their Macron computers could communicate in their place. Those intelligent systems could be a part of their ultra egos for dealing with less important matters.

'Is the special child safe from detrimental influences?' Sarah asked, also realising the loss of her own.

'The child is safe. We have him and his family under twenty-four-hour surveillance. Mallory has been given orders to remove all detrimental criminal links with that family and is now making some of his own plans in that regard. However, he has since been preoccupied with several equally important matters. That is also one of the reasons why we are to assist him.'

'Ok, we shall!'

'Since we are unable to assist the child directly, we have to carry out all such operations through third parties and as indirectly as possible,' Lumak said.

'Any more questions on matters concerning Earth?' Sarah asked, but no buttons were pressed or thoughts felt.

'In that case, do we say yes to Siend Longhurst's demands?'There was a positive yes felt throughout the council.

'In that case, may we turn our attention to the Triog Desert, within the southern territories. Professor Lennox, what are your recommendations in this matter,' Sarah asked.

'Imperial Madam, soil and other samples acquired during our extensive studies and tests, indicate the desert and its indigenous life to have remained stable for over six thousand years. Its few and varied life have adapted well to that harsh environment during that period. Any abrupt change may cause them harm. Further, some marine creatures are beginning to crawl into those regions from the local seas. I think it's their first steps for colonizing the land. In those circumstances they must be given a chance to evolve naturally.'

'I see!'

'In our opinion, relocation is undesirable as life in those areas are in strict balance and will not readily adapt to other similar areas of our world. I have therefore recommended that any anticipated conversion of the Triog Desert to a more pleasant human environment be abandoned forthwith,' Lennox said.

'What say you Lord Meron our chief planetologist.' 'Mam, I agree with Lord Lennox's findings.'

'You have all received communication on this matter. I think we should now consider a vote. Since this matter more concerns, Councillor Meron and his planetologists, I shall require a vote of 50 percent or more from his group in order to pass the matter through,' Sarah said.

'Those for conversion may press the green button, those against, the red. Abstainers may indicate through their implants.'

Seventy eight percent were against and the desert remained with its present inhabitants. After several more items were discussed, they came to the last item on their agenda.

'Now we come to the item of recommendations. Who would like to air their points?' Sarah asked and a hand went up to get her immediate attention. It belonged to Jerry (ex president Gerald Fraser of the USA).

'Having known Mallory for some time, may I recommend him and his wife for a permanent home here with us after he has completed his task on Earth. That is subject to his acceptance, of course.' That other item was put to the vote and received 80 percent votes with 20 percent abstentions.

'Mallory and Roseanne is with us, it seems,' Sarah said.

'Any more recommendations,' she shouted, but there were no more.

'In that case, I call this meeting closed. It's nice to see our society in such a healthy, orderly and peaceful disposition, that we convene a meeting to discuss matters outside our more direct influence,' she said as she left her golden throne.'

Despite Sarah's loss and the ensuing trauma of the previous years, she had gotten used to the idea that her child was gone for good and hoped he had found a good home. Even then, Sarah hadn't realized that the Son of Destiny was her real son. She had convinced herself that he was still alive somewhere on Earth, but the shock had knocked her off perch and she was now a much sterner and less tolerant person towards Earth and its self-indulgent humans than before.

She fostered a natural hatred for all criminals, particularly those that stole children and so also did her father Ben. Luckily, there were no criminals on Eden or they would have been briefly taken away and reprocessed by the Psyrotrons into perfectly loyal subjects.

Princess Bawaki of the cat people were on her way to her home world, Tarran. She was to build her dream city there for her people. Both of the giant ships were to leave Eden at approximately the same time and loaded with extra equipment for that building program.

After Venusa's ship dropped off the supplies, Lumak and Sarah were to spend some time on Tarran before continuing their journey with Venusa's ship to the globular cluster of Kalboron.

Princess Bawaki's new city was to be called Ziona. The crew of Martia's ship included Jon, Lira and others of the young Andromedans who had decided to assist Bawaki in the building program. She wanted a city similar to those she had experienced on Earth during her brief stay at Sarah's country manor in North Dakota, USA.

Many construction robots had been acquired from Malik of Polok II, and the two ships were heavily laden with such machines and materials.

The city of Ziona were to be built east of Marawi City, towards the Zadi's border, on the shores of the Sadana sea towards the south east.

After completion, it would become the largest and richest city on planet Tarran. A jewel of the plains, with water recycling and air conditioning throughout. Bawaki had intended to use it as a centre for trade, education, entertainment and sport. During the intervening period, her mother had brought most of the savage clans together and life in general had improved significantly.

Having spent some time on Earth as a Shadite in human form, Bawaki preferred that type of city to the more advanced one on Eden and elsewhere. Her people were not yet as advanced as the others and even lagged behind Earth in many respects, despite their extensive training programs. Nevertheless her main concern was to her people. She was to get her cat people much closer together in matters concerning their survival.

After its completion, there would be several special schools, colleges, universities, arenas and hospitals at Ziona's perimeter that would be opened to all the clans of Tarran. Its peoples would come from the northern territories beyond the desert's rim and the most southern, beyond the Zadi's southern borders before the great southern deserts. The token fee would be the same for each clan member. It was hoped they would assist in its upkeep.

Bawaki was trilled with her enterprise. She couldn't have been more thankful to Jon and the others for their assistance in that most important project. Bawaki reflected on her past life and in particular the conversation she had with Shadite Lumak several decades before. She was young then and didn't realize it was possible to travel to the distant stars. Presently she was a Shadite and on a distant star contemplating their first dream city. How changeable the universe was and so she thought.

Lumak had continued with his previous desire for exploring ancient Hexolyte and Patriarch bases within Osmaron and elsewhere, with the aid of the Ancients Andromedan ship they called, The Ship. Nevertheless he hadn't seen his Speell Shadite friend Gemmi in all that time. She was presently stationed in Galaxy Triangulum.

After much searching Lumak had come to the conclusion that Osmaron was once the home base of the Patriarchs who had existed over two billion years ago. Their number of bases here far exceeded those of the Hexolytes in Triangulum and elsewhere. He intended to take up the investigation of such bases when he got back. He needed Shadite Gemmi's assistance and hoped she was not too involved in her own projects for The Greater Purpose. He found her to be the best company on such trips while her qualifications and experience were essential.

Since his meeting with the demon Neramon and The Ship's experience with the demon Hexil, he was quite worried that dangerous Hexolytes could be brought back to life by some ignorant scientist, or even by Javols; thus releasing another most evil predator species unto the universe.

Despite the passage of time - being over two billion years since the last upheaval - many of those ancient Hexolyte underworld bases were still functional, including their long range intergalactic portals.

Large containment tanks had been found in most of those underground enclosures. They were undoubtedly used for the imprisonment of Hexolytes, demons and other strange elemental beings and substances.

He had mapped the local galaxies and compiled an historical document containing records of his discoveries. Many unusual artifacts of that bygone age had been taken to Eden and exhibited within the Solarian Museum. That building was the largest of its kind in that part of our galaxy. It held historical artifacts and fossils dating back some six billion years. Most were of alien origin and it was thought, with the exception of those held in perpetual prisons, all species concerned were presently extinct.

CHAPTER 53

Mallory and Roseanne's wedding

There was a tap on Roseanne's bedroom door and she replied with a 'please enter'. He went in with a tray. It contained a haughty English breakfast for both with a mug of coffee.

'I do love this place and its surroundings. Makes me feel more relaxed than I have been for years,' Mallory said.

'Me too. You know, it's only six thirty. I suppose you are too excited to sleep.' Roseanne watched every expression in his tired features. She had a couple yawns herself and decided to pour two cups of coffee before drawing the curtains to let light in. Then she observed Arthur in best clothes feeding the birds.

'It's going to be our biggest day today. I hope everything goes to plan and there are no hidden surprises,' he said.

'You mustn't worry about such things. At worst, we can have a few late arrivals.' She went for a quick shower before getting ready.

He called the Hired-Help company for cleaners and the whole house was once again being cleaned and polished from top to bottom. He checked through the list of items and made a few mental notes, just in case he forgot something. Then he took his recently dry-cleaned grey suit from the closet and placed it on the bed where he could see it along with a matching black bow tie. Then he went for a shower.

It was now ten-thirty a.m. on the morn of their wedding, which was to take place at three p.m. on that Friday and Mallory was extremely nervous in anticipation of everything going wrong.

The many hired help and others had completed the sitting arrangements in the marquis for the main ceremony. Its use could be extended to reception and accommodation if space within the house became restrictive. All that depended on the number of visitors.

By now the makeshift bar had been arranged and filled with bottles and cans, and the many borrowed tables laid with table cloths, and serviettes.

All the original imitation Georgian furniture that belonged to the main dining room had been taken to another and would remain there until the reception was over. Arthur was busy giving instructions to all new-comers and assisting where necessary.

By one p.m. both were dressed and remained close to the main entrance to greet their guests. The caterers prepared an assortment of hors d'oeuvres and such like. Then there was the preparation of the main course.

The first to arrive was Carl and his girlfriend Joan. He was Mallory's best man. Then it was Chad and his wife, Sandra. Roseanne's sister, Claudia, appeared soon after with her husband and kids. Roseanne was ecstatic. Much later on, Donald, his aunt and Andy appeared in a large limo. Mallory hugged his son and thanked him for coming. Donald had obviously talked Andy around. However his mother and husband was not present.

There were thirty-two main guests and over two hundred associated colleagues and friends; much more than Roseanne had expected. The affair was cordial and joyful. Even Rosie, the restaurateur, had attended. She was beautifully dressed in white and blue with a broad rimmed hat of matching colour. The only one missing was Ben. He sent an urgent message saying he would be late.

The Pastor arrived just after 3 pm. Like Mallory, he was a Methodist. but Roseanne, although born into a Baptist family, was an agnostic. Both had turned away from religion since high school days and became sceptical of such views. A leaning that was further strengthened by their military careers.

The ceremony was a simple ordeal. It was held in the marquis at the rear garden. There they assembled, while the couple walked, hand in hand, towards where the Pastor stood with a classic record playing in the background. After they accepted their vows, confetti was thrown exuberantly, while the photographers continued fanatically. Then they led the guests into the house for the reception party. Soon after, the couple disappeared upstairs to change into party clothes.

Ben had arrived after five p.m. and apologised to the couple for his late arrival, then he gave a small speech to the guests. He wished the couple eternal happiness and fulfilment in all their pursuits.

Carl played the master-of-ceremonies enthusiastically, with the occasional military service joke. After the celebrations were over, several remained overnight to share the spare bedrooms.

The following day Mallory took Andy, Roseanne and some of his closest friends with Oscar to shop around the better parts of New York and bought his friends some presents. He also wanted to take some gifts to Sarah and others on Eden.

Once more Andy felt he was among family and friends. He appreciated his father's new home with its extra large swimming pool, beautiful gardens and horses. The horses belonged to the children of the previous occupants but were left behind with the house. He had given Roseanne a hug and kiss and wished them both a happy future.

'My son! My son! You have really grown up! I hope you enjoy horse riding, because one of the horses out there happens to be yours. All you have to do is choose between three. They are used to the saddle, so you shouldn't have any problems riding,' Mallory said.

'But Dad, I've never ridden a horse in my life!' Andy exclaimed.

'And you want to be an astronaut? You will have to get lessons, my boy. I hope your mother allows you that simple pleasure. Anyway, she doesn't have to know about your horse here and you can learn to ride later, when you come on holidays,' Mallory said, and Andy was less worried with the prospects of convincing his mother and father-in-law of his intentions.

'Don't look so glum. If you talk to her nicely I'm sure she will come around,' he said and Andy nodded.

'I hope you are right, Dad?'

CHAPTER 54

Eden, here we come

'I suppose you would like most of our honeymoon to be on planet Eden. How do you think we'll get there?' Roseanne asked.

'From what Ben said, we take a portal from Sol-Newtown to a Martian dome, and I suppose one from there to Eden. The whole process makes me a little queasy to say the least. I must be changing into a chicken in my old age. But I can't imagine all our body atoms being scrambled, transmitted, received and un-scrambled in the right way again,' he said and Roseanne suddenly became concerned. She was trying hard not to believe his last words.

'Wow! You say that like you believe it's real!'

'Yea!' he replied, with a false smile.

'What are you saying, Darling? You think it will have a permanent effect?' she inquired.

'In all honesty, I don't know. But Ben and others seem to use them on a regular basis, so they should be ok. I suppose we are like kids on our first train ride. Anyway, we used one once before, when we visited Sol-Newtown and we didn't feel anything, did you? If the procedure is the same, the experience can't be that bad,' Mallory said and Roseanne was little satisfied by that answer.

'I know how you feel, Partner. But I am not looking forward to my atoms being duplicated through space, and most of all, not during our honeymoon. There could be some lasting side effects and we might be completely different people when we return, including completely new bodies, with all those transformations,' Roseanne said, with bewilderment.

'From what Ben said, the atoms and other sub-particles are reproduced identically at the other end, while the original body ceases to exist. Apparently, the process happens to us all the time anyway. I mean, being transposed is like being kicked little by little into our futures. That's why there is a future in the first place. However, this time we are being kicked into a different space as well. According to Quantum Mechanics. Anyway, all matter happens to be waves of energy and all waves can be transmitted.'

'Really?'

'Yes! Ben reckons our physical bodies are like clothes that we wear while in this dimension. A corporeal body is needed to anchor us to this plane of existence. Changing bodies to Solarians is like changing clothes. They even have machines for that purpose. Apparently, we all exists in multiple states and in many multiple virtual universes, so I suppose we must go through similar transformations frequently.'

'If that's the case, why don't we see it?'

'We don't see it because we have just five senses and our brains are wired by evolution to ignore such changes. When we move our heads every thing in the outside world changes, but we still see the same world. A camera would show a different picture if you took a picture at an angle. That's why living in space under zero gravity is much more difficult than on Earth. Our brain is pre-programmed with over 80% of our perceived universe.'

'Are you sure? Everything appears normal to me!'

'Even if our universe shrank to nothing and expanded to infinity we would observe the same thing, because everything is acted upon equally,' he replied.

'I think I see what you mean!'

'Anyway, energy cannot be created nor destroyed. If an extra lump of matter suddenly appeared within our universe it would be instantly annihilated. The opposite process would occur if there was a deficit, and matter would be instantly created to fill the deficiency. That's the reason why it's not possible for anyone like us, made of electro-magnetic matter, can visit the past or the future within their own time-line physically in any particular Virtual Universe without paradoxes. However, a different process of matter creation is followed by the natural evolution of universes. That is where dark matter and dark energy can be utilized,'

'What are you saying?'

'I am saying that if we were made from a different type of

matter unknown to this universe we could visit the past without paradoxes, Anyway, coming back to your original question; our bodies will not change; we are just transferred, so we have the same bodies and causal history, with a slight blip or discontinuity in our existence at the time of the transition. Perhaps of less than a nanosecond duration. And what does it matter anyway, if our new body looks and works the same. What is important is our Identity,' Mallory said.

'Whatever you say, you are still going to have a problem getting me into one of those cubicles!' Roseanne replied.

'From what Professor Longhurst said in his book, 'The Glorious Cosmos,' on the subject of transposition, it's all to do with imposed symmetry. Two near identical symmetries can confuse the cosmic order or what he called the Primal System into making the wrong kind of adjustments. For instance, identical twins can sometimes feel each other's pains and people with similar minds can be telepathic. That is only because the primal system is confused by the causal players and attributes causal continuity in the incorrect amounts to those highly symmetric players. Symmetry is very important in our universe or multiverse.

'Those rules may even apply to certain crystals of high symmetry. He calls the process Cosmic Imposition, but are forms of symmetry in synchronicity.

'The fields and pseudo membranes of all similar type portals are of identical symmetry which can be adjusted and optimised by complex computers. It's a form of imposed symmetry, from the source to the destination, that can be fully controlled. Don't forget, at that higher dimension everything is at the same point in the universe. Material objects are only spread out in what we call space-time. If we remove time, we remove space and everything converges back to that singularity or common point.

'However, the whole process could only have been possible with the discovery of H-wave and higher dimensions. Because it would be extremely difficult, if not impossible, to optimize such distant units using electromagnetic radiation or any wireless transmission that travelled at the speed of light. It would have taken over twenty years for the portal on Eden to have received

the necessary signals from Earth.

'Both symmetries are apparently only slightly separated within the higher dimension, which I think is the fifth. That makes them vulnerable to each other's influences, but always from source to destination.

'They must use a similar method of imposed symmetry in the Quantum World for H-wave communication, which is almost instant in time anywhere within the homogeneous universe. That type of communication is similar to what they call Quantum Entanglement. With those methods and powerful computers, they mislead the Primal System into thinking we are in both places at once, like the identical twins. When in actual fact we are separated by vast distances. Then by fine adjustments in symmetry, we are held on Eden, and placed there in precisely the same forms as we are here.

'Obviously, inertia due to our initial velocities and other factors might have to be adjusted or damped at the destination end, depending on the stellar system and which part of the planet we happened to appear on. Since everything in the cosmos is in constant motion relative to other parts, such changes will be necessary. Perhaps those factors are compensated for during the transition,' Mallory said, with a grin of satisfaction.

'I didn't realise you were so well informed on matters of Trans-dimensional Physics and space travel?' Roseanne said, surprised at Mallory's in-depth knowledge of such things.

'I am just a layman who likes reading science fiction and such topics. Until we had that experience in Sol-Newtown, I thought the whole process was fictional. Now I don't know what is fiction anymore,' he grinned and she laughed at his candidness.

That night they discussed such matters late into the morning. Then they tiredly made love and fell asleep in each other's arms.

Mallory had already made up his mind on the place of their honeymoon. At first light he jumped out of bed and loaded his car with an assortment of drinks, cakes, chocolate and other Earthy items. Those he thought would be just in case there was a shortage on the beautiful world of his intended visit. Then he woke Roseanne, telling her to pack a large suitcase for one week's vacation to places unknown and he did likewise.

When they were finished filling Oscar's trunk, he handed the house keys to Carl who was up early and had coffee with them. Carl left soon after for the factory, as they called their new antidote distribution building. Then Mallory wrote a note for Andy and left him some money.

'Please give this note to my son and take care of this place for me while I am away. You may stay here in our absence, if you wish,' he said to Carl. Then they said goodbye to Arthur.

'Have a nice holiday and leave everything to me,' Carl replied.

Oscar could only take them as far as Sol-Newtown and would remain there until their arrival from Eden.

Despite Roseanne's fear of portal technology, she was very curious about life on Eden, wondering whether it was anything like the perfect picture Ben had painted. She also wanted to know what life on other worlds was really like. After all, it was their honeymoon and a little intrigue and excitement, with a few pleasantries would not go amiss, providing it was not like their previous escapade in London, when she was kidnapped by the criminal gang.

She also realised how excited Mallory had become since he made the decision. So she decided to play along and keep her fingers crossed, just in case things were not as clear cut as Mallory thought. Also, what if things didn't work out the way he wanted. She had to be with him to share his disappointments and pick up the pieces.

She loaded two of her own cases into Oscar and said a final farewell to the house and Arthur. Then Oscar leapt vertically into the dense morning clouds.

That Monday was not a very pleasant one and Oscar decided to make the trip at high altitude to avoid the mist and fog. He was finally well away from the stormy clouds. That way it took him just ten minutes to make the trip to Sol-Newtown in North Dakota.

When they arrived the great dome was covered in several layers of clouds. Oscar descended towards the topmost entry point or docking area. Oscar was left in a special parking area with a few of his mobile friends. They soon loaded their cases in a large Solarian trolley. With possessions and presents they were guided through the usual process of decontamination and purification.

Afterwards they were taken to a reception area which reminded Roseanne of one of the checkout points in Kennedy Airport. Mallory was left with a beautiful young female operator, who he assumed was an android.

'Can I have your destination cards please?' she asked and Mallory handed her both metallic cards. She glanced at the cards for a while. She had read every bit of information and checked his identity through the Macron computer.

'You may take the cubicle to the left, Sir. Bon voyage!' she said and handed him back the cards. He gave one to Roseanne. Both looked identical.

They moved hesitantly to the cubicle's door while pushing the trolley. It looked very similar to that of a standard elevator's door without push buttons. However the walls were translucent white. Apparently from that moment on the cards would be constantly interrogated by the computers during transit. They could also be updated during the trip whenever necessary while in their pockets and without their knowledge.

Such destination cards could relay information via a small screen or by voice. However the card was to be pressed against the ear to receive verbal instructions.

As they approached, the door automatically opened. The moment they entered the cubicle the door shut behind them. Suddenly they were flooded in light which penetrated everything including their bodies. It appeared to continue for several seconds until the door opened. They felt slightly disoriented as if their knees were not able to carry their full weight. However the moment they began to move their legs everything was back to normal.

'What a strange sensation!' Roseanne exclaimed, still slightly dizzy.

'I think it's something to do with the normalization of inertia. It only occurs for a fraction of a second. I think the effect will reduce as our minds get used to the change,' he said.

'Practice makes perfect, eh!' she replied sarcastically.

Roseanne looked Mallory over, making sure everything was where it was supposed to be. Then she removed a small mirror from her handbag and began to have a closer inspection of her own features.

'Is everything where it's supposed to be, my dear?' Mallory asked, with a broad grin.

'I don't think it's that funny, you know,' she complained and returned the mirror to her handbag.

The door opened unto a large basement. On the other side was the interstellar portals.

'Darling, I've never been on Mars before. Why don't we take a peek at the surface?' he asked.

'You mean... we are really on Mars!' she responded, nervously.

'Yep! Don't you feel a little lighter? I think these big portals are the inter-stellar ones they spoke of. This is why we felt different this time. Also, the light was stronger and appeared to last longer. It's probably because of the greater distance travelled and the greater inertia involved,' he replied.

'They got out of the cubicle and searched for an attendant, but no one could be seen. All Martian domes had since been placed on automatic. They left the trolley close to the cubicles and took one of the moving escalators to the surface.

'Look at this bloody place!' he exclaimed, overwhelmed by excitement. They were standing within one of the secondary transparent domes while gazing unto the Martian surface. The Admin Dome was the closest and largest of the Martian domes and formed the centre of that cluster of domes. It had been used for the mass evacuation of over ten million Andromedans from their now almost dead planet, Caefon in Andromeda, and from the dreaded Javols. All domes were accessible through sealed underground tunnels.

'Have you ever seen anything like this?' he said. Into the distance they could observe many small freighters flying across the Martian sky. They belonged to the miners in a distant dome that was owned by a mining consortium from the USA. Solarians had since halted all their mining operations on Mars.

'That over there in the distance must be Caefon Dome. The one Jerry, then our President, came here to inaugurate before his supposed tragedy in space. He christened it by that name, you know,' Mallory said.

'I know, Darling. Don't forget, I joined the security services before the incident,' she replied.

Caefon Dome was over fifteen kilometres away. Just beyond it they could just observe a raging sand storm. No trees or water could be observed as far as the eye could see, just a pink sky and reddish sand intermixed with gravel and boulders.

'How desolate. Even so, I find it has a charm of its own,' she said and Mallory placed his right hand about her waist.

'It's a lot more besides. I find this place to be quite romantic. I suppose one of these days it will all be transformed by technology into a less inhuman world?' he said.

There was a nursery dome to their right where robots cultivated several crops in added artificial lighting. They wondered where they were taken after harvesting.

After the couple had viewed enough from the surrounding platform, they decided it was time to make the trip to Eden.

'I wonder if they are expecting us?' Roseanne asked, now even more nervous of her mode of transport than before.

'They said anytime from today. We are just following their instructions. Anyway, they are highly organized and any delays or changes in the program would have been brought to the notice of the people in Sol-Newtown, so don't worry,' he said.

They pushed the trolley into one of the large cubicles. On its panel were several buttons and legends depicting destinations. Eden was the second on the panel from the top, Earth being the first. They were written in English as the first language, but there were other strange lettering unknown to them.

'Eden, here we come!'

'Here we go again!' Roseanne shouted, grabbing hold of Mallory by the waist and separating herself from the trolley at the same time. She didn't wish to be joined with the trolley during the trip, as in one of the old sci-fi movies she had watched, called The Fly. Showing a brave face, he held on to her to quell her nerves, but she soon pushed him away for the same reason. Then she regained her common sense and hugged him tightly about his waist. Finally she had both sets of fingers crossed behind him and prayed. There was a sudden flash. This time it appeared to remain longer than before. Suddenly the brilliance stopped and their eyes were normal again. The cubicle they observed was identical to the one they entered. Once again they felt the strange sensation of their feet giving way beneath them, but the feeling was soon overcome when the door opened and they began to walk.

Mallory wondered why there were no seats in the cubicles. However he soon realised that it would probably have made people too comfortable in transit. Perhaps there was a higher risk of something going wrong in that position, but he was not sure.

CHAPTER 55

On beautiful Eden

They pushed the trolley into what appeared to be a central station with many uniformed robots and androids moving about. They were obviously the security guards. While the couple moved along, a voice from the platform spoke to them.

"Please leave your trolley in this area and take the blue conveyor to the palace. You will be informed of further changes during transit," They did as advised. When they entered unto the conveyor two large rings shot out and clamped about their waists. It was not a tight fit, but prevented them from walking. Then the rings became excited. Their bodies became almost weightless and were lifted a few inches off the conveyor while they were propelled along its confinement.

They were now in the hands of whatever powers controlled the rings. It was a sensation they both dreaded, because they felt so helpless. When they got used to the idea they realised it was for their own safety. They thought their trip to the palace would be made more swiftly by local portals but their hosts had a different plan.

The moment they entered the sunlight, the long wondering conveyor glistened in the bright light. They were soon in the open air and utterly amazed by the tranquillity and beauty of the planet.

'This place is just one big garden. It's the sort of view one gets from a fairytale book. Can you smell the perfumed fragrance? The place is so incredibly enchanting. It looks like Alice's wonderland. Like it's begging us to stay. Its effects are everywhere and look at the flowers over there, how large they are. Those strange trees... How massive and so many beautiful colours!' Roseanne exclaimed, completely absorbed and utterly filled with excitement. It was like one of those massive illustrations on the cover of a science-fiction novel she had once seen, but could not remember the name of the artist.

'This is really Eden, not a bloody car, road or jet anywhere to be found. I can't believe a place like this could really exist. I can even hear myself think and I hear a slight buzzing in my ear. I suppose all our defects and impurities will surface in a place like this. This must be the most perfect world in the universe!' Mallory exclaimed.

They were moving towards the Royal Palace from the southeast, just east of Eden City and the space-port, which was furthest away. The city was barely five kilometres away to the northwest. It reflected the bright starlight like a glistening jewel.

Even from their distance, space cars could be observed hopping about the city's buildings, but they were confined to its immediate area. Just to their left could be observed two giant ships, each several kilometres long and about half that length in height. They were about seven kilometres away to the west and further in the distance were more ships.

'What are those in the distance?' Sarah asked.

'They look like massive interstellar cruisers; bigger than anything I have ever imagined. Could be inter-stellar or even inter-galactic passenger liners,' Mallory replied as a large insect-like creature flew past him and lingered a while in mid flight as if to say hello; to be followed by its mate. The creature landed on a giant yellow flower and both appeared to be talking to each other intelligently before tackling the nectar. Although they resembled giant butterflies from a distance, they were more like fairies with two tiny arms and legs, but with the most beautiful multicolored wings.

'Do you think we are in the land of Oz? I wonder if they are highly intelligent insects?' Roseanne asked, finding it all so incredible.

'I think they must be a cross between animals and insects, if that's the correct explanation. Because of the way they move they must be vertebrates. We must be like giants to them, yet they are not afraid. Like they know we are perfectly harmless. There can't be much violence and predation on this world,' Mallory replied.

'It's a good thing they are not on Earth, or they would be in cages by now and sold as pets. Look! Large domes in the distance!' She cried, excitedly, thinking her trip was approaching its end.

The conveyor suddenly snaked its way downwards towards a valley. They could observe several large buildings like universities on the hills as more valleys and hills came into sight. One of the universities had what looked like small lions, without tails playing football. They stood on hind legs and played the game quite professionally with almost normal hands with claws.

'And what do you think they are?' Roseanne asked, a little scared by the ferocious look of those creatures, but their faces were those of a cute domestic cat.

'Aliens, I suppose. From what Ben said, the universities here are used by several intelligent life-forms throughout the galaxy. I suppose many will be segregated to prevent them eating others and for their own safety, but those seem pleasant enough. Anyone that can play football like that, can't be all bad,' he said, with a grin and Roseanne smacked him one from behind. Yet, those intelligent predators seemed so out of place in that almost perfect world.

Soon they were passing isolated orchards of oranges and apples. Each different fruit were surrounded by canals.

'These must be originally from Earth and bio-engineered for climatic and soil conditions. They must also be neutral plants from an ecological viewpoint, and I bet they taste better than those on Earth,' Mallory said.

Those fields were attended by robots, with automatic sprinklers throughout the orchards.

After they left that area, they came upon rows of giant ferns. They were like the prehistoric trees that existed on Earth hundreds of millions of years ago and about fifty metres tall. There was an assortment of super giant trees with mossy leaves that resembled giant lungs.

Despite the enchanting beauty of the place, they had seen no large animals like horses and cattle, and there was no equivalence to grass. Just a mauve-like carpet of thick moss that covered the less densely planted areas.

From what Ben told them, the larger animals were kept isolated in their own dome habitats, free to roam as on Earth. That was to prevent cross contamination of Eden's own natural ecology, its indigenous creatures and their environments.

Planet Eden's sky was bluer than Earth's and its star bluish and more radiant than the sun, although a little smaller. It could have been further away or younger.

There was not a single cloud in the sky and they wondered if it ever rained on Eden. Nevertheless there were many canals and water appeared to be in abundance.

'I think honey bees would have a great time on this world. But I also think it's a great retreat from Earth, and we haven't seen much of it yet. There must also be deserts and unpleasant areas. Nature likes contrasts,' Mallory said.

As they came out of that valley, they could observe a large garden ahead. This time it was planned landscape gardening with flowers and trees in many rows and symmetrical shapes, with real grass within certain areas.

Just ahead of the garden was a most beautiful golden palace with spires of green blue and pink. There were seven golden domes with more spires. The central one was the largest and tallest of all. Just before the palace they could observe several horses grazing on a lawn of green grass.

'So there are Earth animals here, after all,' Roseanne said, joyfully, with a sigh of relief.

They soon realised their journey was approaching its end. When they glanced in the opposite direction, they could observe no other passengers on the strange undulating conveyor and realised its use was probably there for the benefit of the occasional tourists to gain a better view of the environment.

The conveyor approached an interchange with more conveyors branching in other directions and their rings slowed to a stand-still.

"You may walk from here if you wish by pressing the front of your rings or continue by ignoring this advice. Your path is the one directly ahead," the voice said in perfect English. They decided to stretch their legs a little from the confinement of the rings, so they pressed the central button and the rings unlatched themselves and spun off towards a small enclosure.

'What a clean method of transport. There can't be any pollution on this world. I have yet to see a wisp of smoke anywhere,' Mallory said.

'You mean, there are also no forest fires due to lightning?' Roseanne asked.

'If there are no clouds, there will be no lightning,' he replied.

'I have yet to see a large cloud in the sky. I don't even know if it rains on this world. The processes of this world could be completely different to those on Earth, depending on its age and the path taken during its evolution. Every planet can be completely different from another. It's probably to do with the adaptation of life to whatever conditions exist and not the other way around. But I think it's probably to do with both. There must be bio-feedback to ensure changes are not too abrupt, since it takes evolution a reasonable time to adapt,' he said and she agreed.

'A living planet!' She said.

'Yep! Both must adapt to each other!' he replied, excitedly.

CHAPTER 56

The royal palace

The journey from Earth to the palace had taken them the best part of two hours. They left Sol-Newtown at ten fifteen a.m. and arrived at a time corresponding to two p.m. on that part of Eden.

After they had walked about a hundred metres from where the rings separated, they approached a large Roman canopy with Roman pillars of solid gold. Mallory thought it couldn't be real gold, because each pillar was about six inches thick and twelve feet tall. Roseanne was not convinced either way.

At the furthest end of the long canopy they could observe several young people standing along a platform and realised it was their reception. The only one he could just recognise among the group was the now young president, Jerry, so they followed in his direction.

'Mallory, it's so good to see you!' Jerry cried out, taking his hand.

'This is Roseanne, my wife.'

'How was your trip?'

'It was quite a pleasant one, despite our initial fears of portals,' Roseanne replied as she took his hand. She remembered well his features, but he was now about 30 years old. The man she now beheld looked at least twenty years younger than when she was with his security services. There he stood in his beautifully embroidered robe that was braided with gold. They seemed to wear ancient robes with each their own designs. In addition, the women wore expensive jewels and golden head bands like tiaras with more jewels.

Jerry took them to meet Sarah and the others. Harry Lennox was also with them, but hidden at the rear. There were fifteen in all including some important Andromedans. Because of Twinning, Andromedans also considered Earth one of their worlds, so they were also concerned about Mallory's progress.

'You've both arrived in time for lunch, so let's have something to eat before we show you to your rooms. After you've settled in, we can show you around,' Sarah said. Their trolley had arrived by another route and was taken elsewhere.

'What a beautiful place you have here. It's even more ornate than Buckingham Palace. Is it all real gold?' Roseanne asked, overwhelmed by the golden statues and other items of art that appeared to have been sculptured or moulded from pure 24 carrot gold. The lustre of the place was extreme.

'Of course! Gold is very durable and on our world it's used for almost everything. To us it's just another metal, with no special significance. There are many planets of gold that are mined by our robots at little cost,' Sarah said.

'I understand. I see it but I don't want to believe it. I never thought it was possible to experience such delightful sights. This place is truly paradise,' Roseanne replied, numbed by it all.

'Would you like to live with us here on Eden?' Sarah asked.

'Yes, Madam Sarah, we would love to,' Roseanne said, with an element of humility in her voice. Despite initial fears, she was presently convince that the planet was a true Heaven.

'Well, you both have been assigned a small protectorate of several hundred thousand hectares. It is raw land, but you need only give the word and your palace will be built for you in your absence. However we would like you both to continue your programs on Earth for now. It's very important for the long-term survival of humanity and Earth.'

'I understand. But I suppose it will be possible for us to visit occasionally?' Roseanne replied.

'Yes! We shall advise you when the time is right, for security reasons.'

'Thank you, Mam!'

'How is my father? Did you see him before you left?' Sarah inquired.

'He came to our wedding yesterday and was very happy and full of fun. I think he is very pleased with the way things are going. All our current programs are progressing satisfactorily and in many ways ahead of schedule. But he is quite busy with his other programs,' Roseanne replied.

'That's good to hear. I think you and your husband have done a marvellous job. Therefore you are to relax and enjoy yourselves during your stay here with us. You will soon find that our world is free from most unwanted things, including crime, famine, starvation, poverty, perversions, sickness, death and natural disasters. We are just normal people,' Sarah said, while they entered the large dining room. Roseanne was surprised but wondered what price was paid for such perfection.

There were many in waiting and the large golden table had been set by several uniformed androids. They were very similar to those in Sol-Newtown. However there were several young guards wearing grey federation uniforms with insignias and hats throughout the palace. They were human and of both sexes. All had small weapons in metallic holsters. The different armbands, insignia and style of uniform were used to identify the different types of services.

'I hope you don't mind, but we are all vegetarians on Eden. However our preparations are indistinguishable from the real thing. Meats of every kind may be represented, thanks to our bio-engineers and nutritional experts. But never in the form of chicken legs or other animal parts, which remind us of a type of barbaric cannibalism. As you will see, most of our meals are based on standard Earth recipes that are quite enjoyable. Some are colour coded solely for the benefit of our Ancient friends who prefer it that way for cultural reasons.'

'I see! It's probably just as enjoyable, if not better!'

'You may both be seated here as my special guests,' she said. An android butler pulled the seats out for them. They were sitting at the bottom of the table, while Sarah and Lumak sat at the top with her other guests on either side. The table sat thirty-two in all. They included the young Andromedans like Jon and Lira, the Ancients like Meron, then Jerry and his wife, Sharon, Lennox and his girlfriend Joan, Plato, Princess Bawaki of Tarran and others of high standing in Solarian society. Today was also the eve of Lumak and Sarah's departure to Kalboron.

There was a generous choice of fruit juice and wine. Avocado pears could be observed in salads with cucumber, tomatoes and suchlike. It was their first real meal of the day and one on a strange world that was most enjoyable and satisfying.

After their meal they were shown to their room by two teenagers who had immediately taken a liking to the out-worlders and wanted to know more about Earth.

Later that day, after they had unpacked and had a refreshing bath, they tried the robes that were left for them and found the attire quite comfortable. Then the two young helpers took them to meet Sarah at one of the large verandas that surrounded the palace.

They were briefly shown around a local part of the palace. It was in what Sarah called the interior gardens. Most of the images in those areas were Virtual and created by computers to simulate any type of scene, from beautiful gardens to alien worlds. Even ancient Rome, Greece and others could be created as vividly as the real thing and were fully interactive with the human attendants.

'These are my Simulacron Chambers or V-rooms. Within these areas we can fight strategic battles, become queens, kings or emperors, in ancient Rome or such places; face dangers and live out our greatest fears, fantasies and desires. You will see the chambers alive tomorrow. We shall have a small party tonight,' Sarah said.

After she had shown them enough of the local rooms, she took them to see her little boy who was about two years old. Even at that age he was being educated by special androids in the presence of a trained nanny who kept a perpetual eye on him.

They immediately observed a resemblance between him and the Son of Destiny and knew that they were both Sarah's sons. Even so, they could not mention a word on that topic to anyone, least of all Sarah.

As they journeyed through the palace all the senior humans wore robes and Roseanne wondered why such an advanced civilization should have worn such basic attire.

'This place reminds me of ancient Greece or Rome, with their togas. Doesn't anyone of importance here wear ordinary fashionable clothes like jeans?' Roseanne inquired.

'I suppose it's a kind of uniform of authority. It's also quite comfortable. It doesn't cling to the skin as much as our clothes,'

Mallory replied.

At nighttime the guests began to arrive for the party. It was one of those occasions when they could wear informal dress. Many wore suits and casual wear as worn on Earth. Others like the Andromedans wore robes, which were their natural attire. Meron and those that had lived on Earth were in splendid suits and more fashionable attire. Mallory wondered whether it was done for their benefit, to make them feel more at home.

'Darling, these people are so socially inclined. They must have such parties almost every day of the week,' Roseanne said.

'Yes, I know! In a place like this, where most of the work is done by robots, the only thing left to do is learning, creating, socialising, games and parties. The real workers must be those in the cities and even they must be assisted by more robots. Anyway, I doubt whether they would do any work if they didn't like the idea, because they must all be multi millionaires by now,' he replied.

'Yea, but I just can't get over their incredible sea-blue eyes, six fingers and larger thumbs. Yet, they are so like us!' she said and he showed a happy smile.

After they had all arrived, champagne and other drinks were served with a variety of snacks. Sarah then called Mallory and Roseanne to join her and began to give one of her speeches.

'I brought us all here together for a twofold purpose; first of all, to greet our friends Roseanne and Mallory from Earth, and to mentioned to those of you, who haven't yet heard of our leave of this world for a short vacation on my husband's home world. That world is within the Globular Cluster of Kalboron. It's like a mini spherical galaxy in orbit about our main Osmaron Galaxy. It will be my first visit to my husband's world and we shall leave with the great ships tomorrow.'

'Bon voyage!' they shouted.

'Princess Bawaki also returns to her home world, Tarran, to begin the construction of the city of Ziona. Because of those reasons, both giant ships will be needed.'

'God speed, Princess Bawaki!' they shouted.

'Therefore may we raise our glasses to wish her and our close friends from Earth, success in all their future ventures, and happiness in their lives?' Then they lifted their glasses and drank.

'To success, love and happiness!' they shouted together.

Afterwards they moved to the main hall. Many soon took to dancing. The band was composed of android players. The android violinist was probably as good as the best human violinist at that time.

When they retired that evening, they hadn't had such fun for a very long time. As they entered their room the place was radiantly lit. Light was everywhere but not from any single source.

"You may choose one of several virtual scenes from the panel. Would you prefer a scene of tranquillity?" the computer said.

'Yes, please!' Mallory replied, out of curiosity.

The scene comprised a beautiful Japanese landscape with a stream and bridge, including the most beautiful butterflies slowly moving from flower to flower. It was all put together in such a manner as to make its participants restful.

They soon fell into a deep slumber from which there was no recourse, until another voice was heard in the early morning.

"Would you like me to run your baths before breakfast? Breakfast is in one hour," the computer reminded courteously, as Roseanne stirred.

'Yes, please!' she said.

As they observed their rooms in more detail, it seemed to them to look like one from a modern five star hotel on Earth. With the exception that most of the knobs and ornaments were of solid gold. They soon realised why money meant so little to Solarians. Every metal and jewel could be mined for next to nothing by robots. Crop growing, bio-farming and general labouring, were all carried out by robots and androids. Those automatons were made to last a very long time and seldom failed. The computers that drove them were even more clever than the humans they served. They didn't require a salary and hadn't families to feed and homes to keep.

One of their main concerns were in preventing their robotic culture from getting to Earth before the people there were suitably conditioned to handle it. Any excess gold, jewels and other rear metals could have destabilized the economies of certain countries on Earth with dire effects globally. From what they had observed, people lived on Eden because of a desire to do so. Such a culture could never have existed on Earth at the present time, which had always been predatory and capitalistic in nature.

Solarians were highly organized and peaceful, with a range of technologies, education and games that were engineered to relieve any type of boredom. Most of Earth's games like football and tennis had been adopted to their financial way of life. While on Eden androids had been meticulously trained to teach humans of all ages in those games freely.

All services within the Solarian society were absolutely free. Most of the non essential products were either credited minimally or inexpensive. No one ever went without food, shelter or clothing and many preferred one or more vocations or careers to fill their lives. Such lifestyles could be changed or tailored to their own way of life. However most of their time was spent visiting friends and socialising. There were also many temples and citadels where they would visit to freely follow their beliefs. Their main religion was based on Senoism, which was from the Ancient's profit Seno of Mond, who laid down rules for perfect cosmic survival. His followers were called Senots. Even so, there were many other Earthy religions and mixtures thereof. Religious freedom was a birthright, providing one didn't use such beliefs for selfish or negative reasons.

The seniors were mainly councillors, who democratically planned for the future and on certain days held sessions in chamber. During those meetings they would listen to the problems of their subjects, advise and make recommendations for treatment or a change in lifestyle.

Nevertheless the real controller of Eden was the Supreme Macron (Mac). She controlled all androids and systems and were of incredible intelligence. She was also considered a member of the Grand Council and could take the form of virtually any lifeform, but mostly human. On that world everyone including Macrons and androids were of equal status and governed by strict law.

Psychological and other illnesses were extremely rear on Eden. Any ailment could be quickly cured on a permanent basis. Unlike Earth with its many viruses, germs and disease, the planets atmosphere was charged with certain pollen which had a positive effect on both body and mind, with a tendency to heal.

They considered every child a member of their society and therefore belonging to every senior member of that society. Each child earned credits from birth that they could use later in their lives on the rear occasions when money was required. Such credits could be used to buy luxury items of holidays and trips outside of Eden. However not all worlds in the federation were free from such methods.

The human population of Eden were only twelve million. About six million remained within Eden City, while others were dispersed throughout the many protectorate states, small towns, farming communities and other occupations that could not be fully automated. A new city was being built over one hundred kilometres to the north. It was meant to relieve some of the congestion from Eden City which had persisted since the evacuation.

The following morning Sarah asked Mallory and Roseanne to accompany her to one of her private rooms for a chat.

'As you both know, Jeff and I are off for two weeks vacation, but we would like you both to enjoy yourselves in our absence. Therefore Jerry will be your advisor and guardian during this period. He will show you around Eden and explain our ways and customs to you. The children are here in the palace to assist, so if you need anything please ask them.

'I have assigned the boy Gregory and the girl Grace to you. They seem to have taken well to you both, but you must not spoil them. They will ensure your stay in the palace is quite comfortable. All teenagers on Eden have to undergo apprenticeship in order to appreciate values. However those two are not allowed outside of the palace confines without a guardian and only those with councillor status may be considered suitable guardians. It is all part of their apprenticeship, to learn obedience and responsibility.'

'I see!' Mallory interjected.

'Portals lead from the palace to all destinations throughout Eden, but for security reasons, the same sets cannot be used in both directions. Leaving is easy, but returning is infinitely more difficult. However Jerry knows the system well and may advise you both on its usage.'

'I understand!' Roseanne said.

'Is there any questions you would like to ask?' Sarah inquired.

'Madam Sarah, are the insects and other life in the fields dangerous to us?' Roseanne asked.

'No! The indigenous life on land masses of this world are in no way dangerous to us humans. As a matter of fact, this environment is infinitely safer than anywhere on Earth. However, a few people have been known to suffer from slight attacks of hay fever and others from extreme pollen intoxication. Nevertheless we have permanent cures for all such allergies.

'Intoxication?' Mallory was intrigued.

'There are also alien students, but they are like human adolescent children with about the same intelligence and can speak perfect English and sunolingua... the language of the Ancients... among other languages. On Eden English is our main language.'

'English speaking lions?' Roseanne was equally amused.

'Those you observed near the university were cat people from planet Tarran. Back to the topic of dangers faced on this world. Life within the domes and seas are a different matter, with many wild predators. Aquatic creatures here are extremely ferocious. Those within the domes are managed in natural habitats as would have been in their jungles or deserts on Earth and elsewhere. They are kept in sealed confines, with special observation platforms for visitors and observers. So as far as you are concerned, there are no real dangers on Eden.'

'I see!' Mallory said.

'I would have enjoyed showing you the great ships, but we leave at three p.m. today and I am afraid, it won't be possible now. Perhaps another time, and on that occasion we might visit another distant world together. In the mean time, please carry on your good work and enjoy yourselves in our absence,' Sarah said.

'Thank you very much, Mam, for having us!' Roseanne said, completely humbled.

Roseanne was now to decide whether to adapt the Solarian principles for her future existence or reject them in favour of a short-lived and decadent Earthly one that she had known all her life.

CHAPTER 57

Fertilate Separation

Since the public's knowledge of the Terminal Disease and relevant methods of the Antidote's distribution, it became essential for Fertilate resettlement well away from large city areas. Therefore most Fertilate young families were resettled in Environmental Domes and specially isolated Security Residential Blocks. All such structures and buildings were protected by specially trained security guards.

Under Mallory, many rehousing organizations had been formed for that purpose. Most were initially financed by Solarian Banking. That process was also essential for easy distribution of the Terminal Antidote. Further, such buildings could be frequently fumigated and sterilized with inbuilt systems.

All main cities now contained Infilates who were mainly neglected. Governments saw little need for such people, who were mainly elderly or criminal. Nevertheless Infilates lived with the false hope for a cure. However those cities were now the abode of all main criminal gangs.

Dr. Hal Seaton (Green Chameleon or Phantom) soon realized he was winning a losing battle against those street criminals. Further, since the relocation of Fertilate families, city streets had been cleared of young people and their children, so his job had been made redundant. Nevertheless his main desire was to kill all Infilates globally instead of waiting for 100 years for their deaths by old age. Therefore it was time to change his plans and use a quicker and more global method of termination.

'Hi, Powell!'

'Hello Boss!'

'Since Fertilate resettlement, we have the opportunity to clean this world of ours. I recently engineered a bug based on the Bubonic Plague, but it has to be rehoused in certain canisters. Particularly those used as Fire Extinguishers in Train Stations. Also, on the day of release we need some explosions as distraction. On the containers we can use a simple wireless operated valve and micro explosive. These will have to be placed in over 1000 cities throughout the globe. I don't care how much it costs. You will get 100 million dollars up front,' Hal said, and Powell was intrigued.

'Is there an antidote?'

'The Terminal Antidote!'

'The Terminal Antidote works also with that variant of the Bubonic Plague?'

'Yep! It terns off certain chromosomes within its reproductive cycle. Making this most deadly disease ineffective against Fertilates. All our guys can have extra doses of Antidote if worried.' Hal said.

'What a device! I can't imagine being selected for such an important task!'

'Well, you are! One more thing, you are now back with our Group of thirteen. We lost number 12 recently. You are the new number 12, so keep your nose clean and very respectable from now if you want to live forever!'

'What do you mean, "live for ever"?' Powell became over excited.

'Let's say we now have the technology. Just don't die on me before then!'

'When do you think?'

'Within ten years or so! I must go!'

'Thanks! I'll keep you up to date on progress,' Powell said.

Epilogue

Present time .... 2062 CE (2062 AD)

The Terminal Disease is now pandemic on Earth. Every member of the human race is being tested for infection. Only the young and those below the age of forty five will be selected. Out of those only a few of the correct genetic mix will be allowed to procreate. That process of refinement and selection will continue until just 500 million are chosen from a population close to 11 billion.

During this time no one on Earth realises the Solarian plans for Earth or the reasons why their populations are being culled. They think it's all due to a naturally occurring Terminal Virus. However the Terminal Disease and the chosen method of culling was created by the Solarians for the sole purpose of controlling Earth. As far as they were concerned everything was proceeding to schedule and plan before the Javols invasion.

Mallory had built a large base called Warland where his Specials were being trained. They will be given advanced weapons unknown to Earth's technologies. With the introduction of Brain Implants, his chosen Specials will have the ability to think and deploy many times faster. They can operate within a Virtual Space as opposed to the real world, making their reflexes and responses over ten times faster than normal humans. His new army with their Plasma Weapons will be virtually unbeatable and almost indestructible.

Mallory has decided to track down the main gang responsible for paedo smuggling and is slowly infiltrating their organization. There are many sacrifices to be made during his slow and relentless progress, but he is winning. During this time of extreme turbulence on Earth, he has to constantly watch his back. Many paid assassins are after his head and he has to constantly use disguises. The great struggle will continue until the Son of Destiny becomes of age to lead humanity in the final battle against the almost indestructible Javols.

To be continued with **Infilates**

The Chronicles of Galaxy Osmaron Series

The Chronicles of Osmaron series point a way to one of our possible futures. In this future, technology is more advanced. But our real problems come from another galaxy, where another human species have accidentally created the ideal nano-bot type soldier. They are truly unique in the sense that they are almost indestructible, can copy and replicate almost anything, can live for ever, can reproduce their own kind and require living organisms like us for food. At least that was the unintended nano-bot type demon that came out of the mould after their second and final experiment.

Those nano-bot Javols went on to destroy all major animal life, including their creators, within Andromeda and are presently on their way to our Osmaron (Milky Way galaxy). The most advanced in our galaxy, which are non-human, decide to fight back for the survival of all naturally evolving life, but have to first inform lesser civilizations like us of the impending danger.

Before we can confront the demon Javols, we must first advance our technologies to Class 5. This is about 100,000 years more advanced than Earth's present levels. During this period Earth undergoes many changes due to Global Warming and human overpopulation, but manages to survive the onslaught.

Wars will rage, but apparently ubiquitous humans will always find ways to survive and win the day.